ARIZONA Brides

Three New Loves Blossom in the Old West

CAROL COX

BARBOUR
PUBLISHING

Land of Promise © 2004 by Carol Cox
Refining Fire © 2004 by Carol Cox
Road to Forgiveness © 2005 by Carol Cox

ISBN 978-1-59789-841-6

Scripture quotations are taken from the King James Version of the Bible.

This book is a work of fiction. Names, characters, places, and incidents are either products of the author's imagination or used fictitiously. Any similarity to actual people, organizations, and/or events is purely coincidental.

Cover image © Tony Gervis/Getty Images

Published by Barbour Publishing, Inc., P.O. Box 719, Uhrichsville, Ohio 44683, www.barbourbooks.com

Our mission is to publish and distribute inspirational products offering exceptional value and biblical encouragement to the masses.

 Member of the
Evangelical Christian
Publishers Association

Printed in the United States of America.

Dear Reader,

As a native Arizonan, I'm part of the third generation of my family to live in the forty-eighth state. Growing up in Phoenix—back in the days before dairy farms and cotton fields gave way to asphalt and new construction—I knew people who had lived here far longer than my own family, and I have long been fascinated by stories of Arizona's early years.

A move to the northern part of the state put me within an hour of Prescott, Arizona's first territorial capital. I made numerous visits to Sharlot Hall Museum, learning about the beginnings of the territory and exploring the rambling log cabin that served as the original governor's mansion. I love the way Prescott's history has been preserved. The layout of the downtown area is much the same as it was in the earliest territorial days, certainly enough to spark a writer's imagination!

To do my own small part in keeping the past alive, I wanted to write a story—a series of them, as it turned out—depicting life in Arizona's territorial years. I knew that, due to political struggles, the capital had been moved several times—from Prescott to Tucson, back to Prescott, and finally to Phoenix. This gave me the framework for the four stories that emerged, each set in a different territorial capital during some of Arizona's most exciting days. The first three of those stories are found here, in *Arizona Brides*.

I hope you will enjoy reading these stories as much as I enjoyed telling them! To learn more about me and my books, please visit my Web site at www.CarolCoxBooks.com. I'd love to have you stop by!

Blessings,
Carol Cox

Dedication

To my parents,
James and Geneva Hussey

And to my aunts and uncle,
Marjorie Grenger, Mary Lois Hawkins, and George Hussey,
whose tales of the early years of statehood
stirred my imagination
and made me proud to be an Arizonan.

Land of Promise

Prologue

February 1867
Prescott, Arizona Territory

Richard Bartlett leaned into the biting wind as he walked along, hating the wind, hating the cold, and finding no beauty in the brilliant streaks of rose and gold that tinged the late afternoon sky. The letter tucked into his waistcoat pocket crackled with every step, reminding him of his dilemma. Should he tell his wife that fool of a girl had written again, proposing a visit? And if he did, how should he break it to her? Letitia was hard enough to please in the best of times, but with her laid up now, and after their recent trouble, she was more sharp-tongued than ever. With his head turned down, chin tucked into the woolen scarf around his neck, he paid little heed to the rugged beauty around him.

A stocky figure stepped out of the shadows, planting its solid bulk directly in the preoccupied man's path, not flinching when the inevitable collision came.

"Why don't you watch where you're. . ." Richard broke off, realizing who he had run into. His face flushed, then cooled. "Timothy! I'm sorry. I didn't see you." He tried a weak laugh that didn't quite come off.

The shorter man adjusted the bowler hat the impact had knocked askew and rolled his cigar from one corner of his mouth to the other. "No problem, my friend. No problem at all." He waved his hand in a magnanimous gesture. "You look like a man with a lot on his mind." Timothy's shrewd blue eyes had noted Richard's involuntary start, and the ends of his handlebar mustache twitched upward in a satisfied smile. He hooked his thumbs in the pockets of his waistcoat in a comfortable, habitual gesture. "And probably with good reason." His eyes narrowed appraisingly. "Things haven't been going well for you lately, have they, Richard?"

Richard eyed Timothy's florid face suspiciously. Did a hidden meaning lie beyond the sympathetic words? He drew his handkerchief from his coat pocket and patted his forehead, despising the way his hands shook. "You're speaking of my wife's accident, of course," he replied, willing his voice to remain steady. "It was a shock, naturally, but the doctor assures us she'll recover in time." He pressed his lips together in irritation. Did Timothy deliberately smoke those cigars to veil his face in the dense cloud of smoke? Richard wouldn't put it past him. Timothy seldom missed an opportunity to put others at a disadvantage.

"Ah, Richard, Richard." Timothy's sorrowful tone grated on Richard's nerves. "I can understand a man having to maintain his pride, even in a situation like this. But you should know you can confide in me." He patted Richard's shoulder solicitously. "Walk with me." He nodded toward the broad plaza across the street. "It will do you good to unburden yourself."

"Really, Timothy, I must get home. My wife will worry."

The blue eyes took on a glint of steely gray. "Then let us say that it would be to your advantage to talk to me, Richard. . .and to your disadvantage not to." The voice sounded no less menacing for its gentle tone. "Come walk with me." For all Richard's advantage in height, it was his shorter companion who radiated confidence and power as they strolled across the open area.

Richard felt his stomach tighten, as though preparing to ward off a blow. How much did Timothy know? How much more could he guess?

"A lovely place, this." Timothy nodded approvingly at the square set aside by the territorial capital's founders to provide a community gathering place. "A natural spot for two friends to cross going home in the evening, but with no place for listening ears to hide." He slowed and turned to face Richard. "How long do you think it will be before people find out you're destitute?"

The directness of the question took Richard's breath away. "I don't know what you—"

"Come, come." Timothy's voice registered impatience now. "If you think you can bluster your way through with everyone else, you can try that and see how far it gets you. But you're talking to me now, Richard, and I *know.*" He breathed the last word in an ominous whisper. "You invested everything you had in that mining stock Josh Wheeler was selling. Everything," he emphasized. "And the stock and the mine both turned out to be a sham. And instead of making a fortune, you're left penniless." He smiled at the shock on Richard's face and breathed out another wreath of cigar smoke.

"Not a pretty picture, is it? You're a political appointee out here, the same as me. The government has entrusted the running of this territory to the likes of us. How do you think they'll feel about your ability to manage a role in territorial government when you can't manage your own money?"

"I'm not the only one Wheeler took in." Richard made an effort to rise to his own defense. "There were plenty of others."

Timothy nodded slowly, as though weighing the statement. "True. But none of the others invested everything he had in the world. And none of the others had already lost one fortune before ever coming west." He chuckled at Richard's gaping mouth. "Did you think no one would ever learn of that?" he asked gently, then shook his head. "Knowledge is power, Richard. Remember that. I've made it my business to be a very knowledgeable man."

"Just what do you intend to do with that knowledge?" Richard's voice came out in a hoarse rasp, forced through a throat that had gone dry. Timothy's love of power was legendary, his use of it notorious. If word of Richard's folly spread through the frontier community, he would never be able to look people in the eye again, much less hold on to public office. And how many more fresh beginnings could a man in his fifties expect to have?

"That's entirely up to you," Timothy responded. "Personally, I would hate to see you humiliated and sent off in disgrace. We've worked well together in the past; I think we can do so in the future. Provided you're still here, of course," he added casually.

Richard fought to breathe, laboring against the tight band constricting his chest. "All right. What, exactly, do you want from me?"

"Ah, now we're getting down to business!" Timothy's face was wreathed in a genial smile, radiating goodwill. The sight turned Richard's stomach. "You've met my son, haven't you?" Timothy asked abruptly.

Richard nodded, wondering at the change of subject. "Several times. Why?"

"He's the pride of my life," Timothy answered, "a fitting heir for the legacy I'm building for him. Even if he doesn't care about it yet." He tossed the cigar stub down and ground it out with a vicious dig of his heel. "He's a stubborn lad. At the moment, he tells me he doesn't have an interest in politics, but that will change. And when it does, all the groundwork I've laid will be waiting for him. He'll be able to step right into a life of power, wealth, and influence." His voice trailed off, and he stood staring at the darkening sky as if watching his words become reality.

Richard shifted uncomfortably. "But what does that have to do with—"

"Up to now," Timothy continued as if Richard hadn't spoken, "he's shown no interest in marriage, but mark my word, it's only a matter of time until some woman realizes what a catch he is and sets her sights on him. When that happens, I don't want to see him as the target of one of these backwoods bumpkins. I won't have it!" Timothy's eyes glittered menacingly. "He needs a wife who will be an asset to him, who knows how to move in the right social circles, not one of the pathetic rubes you'll find around here."

"I still don't see—"

"I need a girl," Timothy stated. "And you're going to provide one for me." He threw back his head and bellowed with laughter at Richard's look of utter astonishment, his ample stomach shaking beneath the gaudy vest. "Think it through," he commanded. "You have connections back in Philadelphia, and at the moment, you still have a reputation worth upholding. Surely you know some girl of good family who would be a match for my boy. One of refinement, whose background would enhance his political career."

He watched the unbidden play of emotions on Richard's face and smiled serenely. "I thought so. Then here is the bargain: Get her out here to Arizona Territory. You could use your wife's injuries as an excuse. Arrange for her to meet my son. Tell her what a bright future he has."

Timothy's voice dropped to a murmur so low that Richard had to strain to hear him. "Help them get acquainted. Give them every opportunity to spend time together. She'll be such a contrast to the backward females he sees here, he'll be captivated by her. And if you do your job well, I expect her to be equally fascinated by the prospect of marriage to him.

"Make that marriage a reality, Richard, and not only will I hold my tongue about your disastrous financial blunder, but I will reward you handsomely." He leaned forward and named a sum large enough to make Richard's eyes bulge.

Timothy eyed his companion closely, then nodded. "That is our arrangement. I get what I want; you get what you want, and no one is the wiser. Are we agreed?"

Richard's mind reeled. To go from the threat of exposure to the promise of restored wealth! To be able to offer Letitia the means of recouping their loss and getting back on their feet without losing face! She would grasp the opportunity as eagerly as he.

"Agreed," he said and shook Timothy's hand in a firm grip. He turned away and started for home once more, wiping his palm on his pant leg as soon as he was sure Timothy's back was turned. Once again, he patted his vest pocket, feeling the reassuring crackle of the letter, and smiled for the first time in weeks.

Chapter 1

Elizabeth Simmons closed her bedroom door behind her and moved to the head of the curving staircase, casting a scornful glance at the glittering scene below. Brilliant ball gowns glowed like jewels on a black cloth against the men's dark evening dress, and the murmur of refined voices rose to Elizabeth's ears. The cream of Philadelphia society was present tonight, a coup that would further enhance her mother's already high social standing.

Mama must be delighted, she thought sourly. Elizabeth surveyed the spectacle from her vantage point, wanting to delay her descent as long as possible. *Empty words, empty minds, empty people. What a waste of an evening!*

A slender figure in emerald velvet hurried to the foot of the stairs. "Elizabeth, come quickly!" Her sister Carrie's urgent voice floated upward. Light from the chandeliers caught the reddish glints in the young girl's hair, turning them to threads of burnished copper. "Mama's been asking and asking where you are, and she's beginning to get very cross."

Elizabeth watched her sister swirl back into the eddy of activity and gave a sigh of resignation. Like it or not, her presence was demanded. She moved down the staircase, the rustle of her sapphire satin gown barely audible over the swell of voices and the strains of music drifting from the ballroom.

Elizabeth braced herself for the ordeal of taking part in the mindless chatter that was a standard feature of her mother's social affairs. Seeing one of her mother's closest friends hovering at the foot of the stairs, she forced a smile. "Good evening, Mrs. Stephens. How nice to see you here."

"How nice of *you* to make time to come down and join us," the older woman returned with a glacial stare. "Really, Elizabeth, it's too bad of you. You know how much tonight means to your mother. After all the preparations the poor woman has made to ensure the success of this evening, you might at least make an effort not to embarrass her by your tardiness. Come along," she ordered, gripping Elizabeth's elbow with a proprietary air and propelling her forward. "You must let her know at once that you've decided to grace the festivities. The poor woman is quite distraught."

"Oh, you've found her." Both women turned at the sound of the rich baritone voice, and Elizabeth brightened at the sight of her neighbor, James Reilly.

"I've come to make sure Elizabeth is mingling with the guests. Would you be kind enough to let Mrs. Simmons know she has come down while I escort her to her duties?" James bent over Mrs. Stephens's blue-veined hand in a courtly gesture. "And may I say just how stunning you look tonight?"

Elizabeth's lips twitched in amusement at the sight of her unwelcome chaperone simpering with delight at James's attention. The older woman sailed off to carry the message to her friend, and James steered Elizabeth through the crowd.

"However did you manage to appear on the scene at just the right moment?" she asked, weaving her way through the sea of frock coats and voluminous skirts. "I wouldn't have been able to hold my tongue one second longer."

James threw back his head and laughed, drawing an admiring glance from more than one of the young ladies they passed. "You've never held your tongue concerning any issue you felt strongly about in all your life." He tucked her hand more firmly into the crook of his arm and gave it a squeeze. "It's one of the things I value most about you."

"I suppose you expect me to be grateful for that insufferably condescending remark?" Elizabeth sniffed, attempting a show of indignation belied by the curve of her lips. "Never mind. You do deserve some gratitude for rescuing me."

"Rescuing Muriel Stephens, you mean," James countered with a chuckle. "She'll never know what a narrow escape she had. Besides, if you'll recall, you once promised to marry me. That gives me a vested interest in your welfare."

Elizabeth snorted. "If *you'll* recall, that promise was made when I was all of four years old, and you were six. You're hardly likely to hold me to it now. Besides, you know very well I'm much too strong-minded for you." She turned left, toward the ballroom, then frowned when James guided her in the opposite direction. "Where are we going?"

"I promised you'd be mingling dutifully with the guests. But I didn't say which guests, did I?" James smiled, opening the library door and ushering Elizabeth inside.

"Here she is," he announced. A fire crackled in the hearth, silhouetting the two men who rose to bow in greeting. "Elizabeth, may I introduce Thomas Brady and Elliot Carpenter? Gentlemen, this is Miss Simmons."

"So this is the woman who has more on her mind than her next visit to the dressmaker?" Thomas Brady took the hand Elizabeth offered and quirked an eyebrow in James's direction. "You neglected to tell us she is also a delight to the eye, James."

Elizabeth snatched her hand away. "Don't praise my mind in one sentence, then insult my intelligence in the next, Mr. Brady. I'm quite aware of my physical shortcomings. My eyes and hair are a dreary brown, and I'm far too short of stature to be considered attractive, let alone beautiful. Fortunately, my value as a woman and as a child of God rests in my character and not my physical attributes."

Thomas Brady stood speechless, and James hooted with laughter at his friend's discomfiture. "I did mention that she was outspoken, didn't I?"

"And as always, you are a man of your word," Thomas agreed when he found his voice again. "Miss Simmons, please accept my apology for what must have seemed gratuitous flattery. I would take issue with your assessment of yourself if I didn't fear offending you again, but I must say I am thoroughly intrigued, and I look forward to hearing the views of a woman of your perspicacity. And that," he said, raising his hand solemnly, "is the truth, the whole truth, and nothing but the truth."

Elizabeth searched his face, wondering if she were being made the butt of a masculine joke, but found no sign of duplicity. She smiled and extended her hand to his companion. "And you, Mr. Carpenter? Are you willing to exchange views with a mere woman?"

"I believe we shall meet on equal footing," he responded with a laugh. "Or if we do not meet as equals, it will be because your intelligence surpasses ours. I can see that I shall need to have all my wits about me so I am not totally outclassed."

"Shall we all sit down?" James asked as easily as if he were the master of the house. "Thomas, Elliot, and I have been discussing the issue of women's suffrage. I thought you could give us an articulate woman's view of the subject."

Elizabeth's pulse quickened. Maybe this evening wouldn't be a bore, after all. With a sense of anticipation, she settled herself in her father's favorite leather chair, prepared to hold forth on a cherished topic. The men drew up chairs in a semicircle facing hers, the two visitors placing theirs at a cautious distance. Elizabeth clasped her hands in her lap, back erect, and looked at her audience like a professor inspecting a new class of pupils.

"Giving women their due is hardly a new idea," she began. "Nearly thirty years ago, two American women went to the World Anti-slavery Convention in London. They were bona fide delegates, but because they were women, they were not allowed to participate. Imagine traveling all that way for such a worthy cause, only to be told you had to sit in a curtained-off area away from those taking an active part, merely because the people in charge didn't approve of your gender!"

She scrutinized each face, seeking their reactions. James nodded encouragingly, having heard this discourse before. Elliot Carpenter sat with his chair turned slightly away from her, propping his chin on one hand. His expression was carefully neutral, but Elizabeth thought she detected an amused glint in his eyes. Thomas Brady leaned forward, elbows on his knees, apparently weighing her words carefully. She focused her attention on him.

"I'm sure you've heard their names before, gentlemen. Lucretia Mott and Elizabeth Cady Stanton will long be remembered for the part they held." Elizabeth tried to stem her excitement at the thought of her heroines. "Eight long years passed before they convened the first women's rights convention in Seneca Falls. Even then, their success was measured more in the sense of accomplishment for taking this momentous step than in realizing any tangible gains.

"Explain to me, if you can, why so many northern men could recognize the iniquity of slavery but continue to hold their sisters, wives, and daughters in what is tantamount to a benevolent captivity?"

"Oh, I say! Don't you think that's a bit harsh?" Thomas expostulated. "Look at the ladies here tonight. I don't believe one of them would think of themselves as deprived. When do you think was the last time any of them were denied anything?"

"Exactly my point, Mr. Brady. They've been spoiled and cosseted, treated more like pampered pets than thinking human beings. That in itself denies them the ability to think for themselves. And women *are* thinking creatures." Out of the corner of her eye, she noted Elliot Carpenter straightening in his chair and suppressed a satisfied smile. He was listening now, really listening. And she had barely gotten started.

"Women have proven their worth over and over again. Elizabeth Blackwell won her medical degree in 1849. Was that a feat some 'frivolous woman' could have accomplished? And only a few years ago during the war, Elizabeth Cady Stanton helped organize the Women's Loyal National League. Those women managed to gather over three hundred thousand signatures on a petition demanding that the Senate abolish slavery by a constitutional amendment. Three hundred thousand! That was not the work of a group of tea-sipping females who had nothing but cotton wool between their ears.

"God gave us minds, gentlemen. I believe He did not equip us with intelligence and plenty of drive if He did not intend for us to use them."

"But you've just proven women do use their minds and in very profitable ways." Elliot Carpenter scooted his chair closer to Elizabeth's and faced her squarely. "Having the right to mark a ballot won't change any of these God-given attributes."

Elizabeth's temper flared at the sight of his self-satisfied smile. Making a deliberate effort to keep her indignation in check, she held his gaze with hers, measuring her words with care. "Less than a century ago, our forefathers were able to use their gifts and abilities, but they felt strongly about being allowed to govern themselves. I see no difference, Mr. Carpenter."

"I see a great difference!" Elliot sputtered, shaken from his easy calm. "That was about taxation and commerce and—"

"And self-respect," Elizabeth put in. "As thinking men, they wanted the opportunity to have a say in matters that concerned them. Thinking women want no less."

The debate continued in earnest, with Thomas and Elliot voicing their long-held beliefs as though talking to another man and Elizabeth fielding their questions and objections with ease.

The library door swung open abruptly. "I thought I heard voices," said a shrill female voice. "Who is in here?"

The four occupants of the room jumped as if caught in some misdeed. Elizabeth blinked, realizing for the first time how low the fire burned in the hearth. "It's just James and me, Mother," she called. "And two of his friends. We've been talking."

Cora Simmons stepped through the doorway, lips parted in disbelief. "Do you mean to tell me that this is where you've been all night? I was given to understand that you were fulfilling your responsibilities in attending to my guests. Have you been shut up in here the whole time? With three men?" Her piercing voice rose to a higher pitch with every syllable.

James and his visitors took their cue, rising with alacrity to bid their hostess good night. While James and Elliot Carpenter were thus occupied, Thomas Brady took advantage of the opportunity to bow over Elizabeth's hand.

"Thank you for a most informative evening," he said. "You have given me much to think about. And since I'm about to leave," he added, one corner of his mouth twitching upward, "I will repeat my former statement. Despite your own opinion, Miss Simmons, you are a lovely lady. Perhaps when you look in the mirror, you have never noticed the way your hair glistens with a chestnut sheen or watched your eyes flash green fire when your emotions are aroused. But I have, and I am utterly captivated." He gave a quick nod and turned away before Elizabeth could think of a suitable retort.

Thomas joined his companions in thanking Mrs. Simmons for an enjoyable evening. Elizabeth heard her mother acknowledge their speeches politely but noted her decidedly cool response. In the dim glow from the fireplace, with the only other light filtering in from the hall, the light gray streaks were no longer visible in hair that had once been a vibrant red. Nor could anyone see the lines of discontent etched on her face. Cora's slender build looked almost girlish, and in the waning light, Elizabeth could glimpse traces of her mother's former beauty.

"I'll see you gentlemen to the door," Cora said. "The other guests have already taken their leave." She herded the three subdued men through the open doorway, then turned to face her daughter. "Elizabeth, you will remain here until I return. . .with your father. This unseemly behavior of yours has gone too far."

Elizabeth watched the door close, knowing a storm was about to break. How many times had they played out a similar scene in the past? This time, though, the play would have an entirely different ending. She moved to the fireplace and checked behind the mantel clock, reassuring herself the papers were where she had left them that afternoon. Her original intention had been to show them to her family tomorrow, but it appeared her plan would have to be revised.

Even so, she would make sure tonight's confrontation would be as much to her advantage as possible. Elizabeth stirred the fire back to life with the poker and lit two lamps, placing them on low tables and arranging the seating to best suit her strategy. By the time she heard voices in the hallway outside, she stood ready, determined to take control of the confrontation to come.

Her mother entered the room first, eyes blazing. Elizabeth's father followed, an obviously unwilling participant. Before the door closed, Carrie slipped into the room with her usual quick grace, with Virginia, the middle sister, gliding in behind her. Carrie moved at once to a pocket of shadow near the bookcase, while Virginia positioned herself near their mother, her smirk indicating she planned to enjoy the fun.

Elizabeth acted quickly before she could lose her advantage. "Sit here, please, Mother," she said, pointing to the comfortable leather chair she had recently vacated. Cora gaped at the order but sank into the seat indicated. "Carrie, Virginia, you may sit in the wing chairs." Elizabeth smiled inwardly, watching her sisters' predictable placement, with Virginia taking the chair nearest their mother and Carrie scooting slightly closer to Elizabeth.

"Father—"

"I'll stand, thank you." His tone sounded gruff, but he smiled at his eldest daughter with genuine affection, tilting up the corners of his mustache and puffing his rounded cheeks. The smile faded when he turned to face his wife. "What's this all about, Cora? Can't it wait until morning?"

"No, Monroe, it cannot." Cora had recovered from her initial confusion. "We need to discuss the disgraceful behavior of your daughter."

"Which one?" The feigned ignorance in those hazel eyes so like her own made Elizabeth want to burst out laughing. As if he didn't know! Creamy-skinned Virginia, whose only interests in life consisted of social prominence and an ample supply of creature comforts, was very much the product of her mother's upbringing. Cora would never find fault with her. And Carrie, with her gentle spirit, might agree with most of Elizabeth's views but would never openly defy her mother. Tonight's culprit would be the same daughter who had always caused her mother distress, and well Monroe knew that.

Apparently, Cora thought so, too. Her nostrils flared as she drew a deep breath and pressed her lips together. Elizabeth, realizing she might soon lose her opportunity, hurried to seize the moment.

"I'm glad you're all here," she began, ignoring her mother's gasp of surprise and the appreciative twinkle in her father's eyes. "I had planned to discuss something with you tomorrow morning, but I believe this would be a better time." She stepped across to the fireplace and drew two envelopes from behind the mantel clock. "Both of these letters arrived in this afternoon's post. I've only opened the one addressed to me, but I believe I can tell you what you'll find in the other one."

"Whatever are you babbling about?" Cora stretched out her hand in a silent demand for the letters, but Elizabeth moved away from her. "*You* are the topic of discussion here, young lady, and those letters can be of no possible interest to us right now."

Monroe rocked back on his heels, eyeing Elizabeth shrewdly. "She's a sharp girl, Cora. Let her have her say." He nodded at Elizabeth. "All right, tell us what's in the letter."

"As I said, I haven't opened this one," she said, handing the envelope to him. "It's addressed to you and Mother, from Mr. and Mrs. Bartlett. I believe when you read it, you'll find an account of how Mrs. Bartlett suffered severe injuries in a fall."

"Letitia?" For once, her mother seemed concerned about someone other than herself. "What happened? Will she recover?"

"According to Mr. Bartlett's letter, she slipped on a patch of ice on the path outside their home and fractured her right arm when she tried to break her fall. She landed up against the porch steps, and the force of the blow cracked a rib and caused some deep bruising." Elizabeth watched her mother's face grow pale and took pity on her. "They are sure she will recover, but it will take time."

"Poor Letitia!" Cora pressed her hand to her heaving bosom. "However will she manage out in that forsaken wilderness? Why Richard insisted on dragging her out to such a horrid wasteland, I will never know."

"He didn't have much choice," Monroe answered drily. "Running a cotton mill during the war was not a money-making proposition. That political appointment came at an opportune time."

"But to take a refined woman like that to a place inhabited only by ruffians and savages!" Cora dabbed at her eyes with a lace handkerchief. "I've said it before and I'll say it again—it was a heartless thing to do."

"And how does this concern you, Elizabeth?" Monroe asked. "You said this had some bearing on your wanting to talk to us."

"It does." Elizabeth drew a deep breath, studying the faces of her family. "You're quite right, Mother. While Mrs. Bartlett is expected to recover, she requires a great deal of help. This letter," she said, holding up the remaining missive, "is a request for me to travel to Arizona Territory to give her the help she needs."

Chapter 2

Cora's shriek of dismay was the only sound in the room. Carrie and Virginia stared at Elizabeth wordlessly, and even Monroe seemed taken aback. "Why you?" he asked incredulously. "Granted, we've known the Bartletts for years, but you've never been particularly close to them. I wouldn't have guessed they were especially fond of you."

"Actually, this was more my doing than theirs." Elizabeth squared her shoulders, framing her answer carefully. She was painfully aware that a misstep now might prove to be her undoing. "Last December, I wrote to the Bartletts, asking if I might visit them for a time." Cora uttered a strangled cry. Elizabeth flinched but went on. "I received no response, and I didn't know whether my message had reached them or not. I wrote again a month ago, repeating my request. My letter arrived shortly after Mrs. Bartlett was injured. This time, Mr. Bartlett was quick to reply."

"You asked to go there?" Bewilderment flooded Carrie's features. "But why, Elizabeth?"

Blessing her sister for providing the very opening she needed, Elizabeth gathered her courage and plunged ahead. "I want to see what Arizona has to offer. The territory was created only four years ago. It's young, wide open, and waiting for people of initiative and drive. It's a perfect place to test a person's mettle and see if their dreams—if *my* dreams—can succeed."

Virginia brushed her auburn curls back in a languorous gesture. "And once you've thoroughly explored the possibilities, I suppose you'll come back and enlighten those of us without your spirit of adventure," she taunted.

"That's just it," Elizabeth stated. "I'm not coming back." This time even Monroe gasped. "My plans have been made for some time," she continued before anyone else could speak. "I only needed the opportunity to set them in motion. I'll be able to get acquainted with the area while I'm tending to Mrs. Bartlett. That will give me the chance I need to see what goods or services the territory needs. When I'm ready, I'll set up my own business and see what I can make of myself."

"And just how do you plan to support yourself?" Cora drew herself erect. "Do you think for one minute your father and I will finance this mad expedition?"

"I don't need your backing, Mother," Elizabeth said quietly. "Don't forget the money Grandmother Simmons left me. It's mine, free and clear, to do with as I wish. And since I'm a year past my twenty-first birthday, I don't have to ask anyone's permission to do this."

For a full minute, only the ticking of the mantel clock intruded on the stunned silence. Then Carrie spoke, her blue-green eyes wide with dismay. "Oh, Elizabeth, I can't imagine it! You, all alone out there in a savage country. However will you manage?" Her voice softened to a dreamy sigh. "But what a glorious adventure it will be!"

Elizabeth smiled her appreciation at Carrie and glanced toward her other sister. Virginia contented herself with lounging back in her chair and expressing her feelings with a disdainful smirk.

Monroe's face wore a faraway look. "It reminds me of the way I felt when I was young," he murmured. "Opportunities abounded for a person with grit and determination—those were exciting days."

"Have you all gone quite mad?" Cora screeched, digging her fingers into the damask upholstery. She turned to Monroe, directing the brunt of her fury at him. "You're to blame for this! You've treated her more like a son than a daughter since the day she was born. What kind of father lets his daughter accompany him to his factory from the time she could walk? I ask you, what possible interest could a decent young lady have in metalworks? Monroe, I have done my best and been thwarted at every turn. I have made every effort to bring Elizabeth up in a genteel fashion, yet you've continued to discuss business matters and current affairs with her as though she were one of your cronies.

"As if that weren't enough, your mother filled her head with all sorts of unfeminine notions she gleaned from her friendship with that Stanton woman. I told you no good would come of it when she left that sum of money to Elizabeth. I hold you completely accountable for this!" she fumed, red-faced, her bosom heaving.

Monroe's forbidding expression could have been chiseled out of granite. "If you're saying I'm responsible for honing Elizabeth's mind and developing her character, Cora, I'll take that as a compliment. She has a fine intellect and a keen wit, not to mention a good head for business. More than once, I've profited from her insight. And as far as my mother's influence is concerned, I can only say I'm sorry she didn't have a greater impact on all our daughters."

Ignoring Cora's gasp of outrage, he stared into the fire for a moment, then turned to Elizabeth, his features softening. "I'll miss you, my dear, but I wish you every success. You have my blessing."

With a rush of gratitude, Elizabeth flung herself into his open arms.

Three days later, Elizabeth stood before her open trunk, trying to wedge in one more dress. Carrie added her weight to the trunk lid and together they managed to close the latch.

"How I envy you, Elizabeth." Carrie settled herself on the edge of the bed with a little flounce, her aquamarine eyes alight with excitement. "If only I had the courage, I'd go with you."

Elizabeth whirled from the dressing table where she was placing the last of her personal effects into a reticule. "Would you, Carrie? I have plenty of money to pay your way. If the Bartletts don't have room for both of us, I'll find a place for you to live until we get our bearings."

Carrie shook her head ruefully. The red-gold tendrils framing her fine-boned face caught the shaft of morning sunlight streaming through the window. "I know myself too well. Though I admire you with all my heart, I don't have your strength of character. Much as I hate to admit it, I'm far too much a product of Mama's upbringing. I'd never have the gumption to give up the comforts of home and go off like that, with only myself to rely upon."

The young girl sighed and wrapped her arms around her knees. "I shall have to experience all my adventures through you, so you must be sure to write often and tell me absolutely everything that is going on. Promise?"

"I promise." Elizabeth bent to give her sister a warm hug.

"What a touching scene," Virginia said from the doorway, her lip curled in a contemptuous sneer. "But after that exhibition of yours the other night, I should have expected nothing less than high drama." She moved to a pile of dresses next to Elizabeth's trunk and fingered the rich fabrics. "You're leaving these behind? I'd try to feel sorry for you, but out where you're going you'll be more in need of homespun and buckskin, won't you?"

"Contrary to what you and Mother believe," Elizabeth retorted, "what lies within a person's heart is far more important than what clothes the surface. My wardrobe is perfectly adequate."

Virginia shrugged and moved to a vantage point from which she could look out the large window. "I believe I'll have my things moved into your room once you've gone. I always did envy your view, and this room is much larger than mine." She pivoted, tapping her finger against her lips while she considered the possibilities. "Yes, it will do nicely, even if I won't be here much longer myself."

Carrie's mouth dropped open, and Elizabeth felt her own curiosity rising. Curiosity and irritation, mixed. Virginia never could resist tantalizing others when she had news. "And just where are you going?" Elizabeth asked. "I haven't heard you mention any plans."

"You're not the only one who can have aspirations and keep secrets, dear sister." Virginia's expression reminded Elizabeth of a sleek, haughty cat. "Before the year is out, I have every intention of being the mistress of my own home."

Carrie gasped and bounced to her feet. "Are you engaged, Virginia? Who is it?"

Virginia leaned against the bedpost. "I don't know yet, but I expect to soon." She laughed at Carrie's consternation. "Sister dear, there are at least three highly eligible gentlemen vying for my hand at the moment. All I need to do is make up my mind which one has the most to offer me."

"You mean which one you truly love, don't you?" Carrie asked, a doubtful note in her voice.

Virginia tossed back her mane of russet hair and laughed. "You are such a child! Surely I knew more about life when I was sixteen. Love has little to do with it. All three of them adore me."

"And that's all that matters to you, isn't it?" Elizabeth planted her fists on her hips and glared at her sister. "Virginia, have you ever spent a moment considering anyone's happiness but your own? Do you honestly think these three suitors of yours have nothing better to do than dance attendance on you for the rest of their days?"

Virginia preened herself in front of Elizabeth's looking glass. "I have two very simple criteria for choosing a husband. One, I must be the most important thing in his life. Two, he must be able to maintain me in a lifestyle comparable or superior to what Papa has provided."

Elizabeth shook her head and snorted in disgust. "It's obvious you've placed your own importance before that of everyone else—including God. You'll never find happiness until He has first place in your life. You've heard Pastor Whitcomb say so often enough."

"And what about you?" Virginia flung back, for once shaken from her air of unruffled superiority. "You're going off to see 'what you can make of yourself.' How does that focus on anyone but you?"

Elizabeth stiffened. "It's not the same," she countered. "It's not the same at all."

❧

The stagecoach swayed along the uneven road, bouncing over a rut with a jolt that snapped Elizabeth's drooping head against the frame. The impact jarred her awake, and she brushed a hand across her eyes before looking out the window to take note of her surroundings.

It had been nearly two weeks since she'd left Philadelphia. Two weary, bone-rattling weeks. Elizabeth stretched as much as she could in the confined space, careful to avoid contact with the army captain who got on at Fort Wingate and the two hopeful miners bound for the gold fields. The train ride to Kansas City hadn't been too bad, although she'd grown heartily tired of her various garrulous seatmates long before it ended. The stage, though, had been a different story. Surely the contraption had been designed for the express purpose of shaking the passengers loose at every joint.

Elizabeth had occupied herself by watching the changing landscape, marveling as the gently rolling hills gave way to the vast plains, then to the majestically rugged western mountain country. The red cliffs near Santa Fe had delighted her, and she reveled in the many hues playing across the hills. Even the accounts she pored over in the eastern newspapers had not prepared her for the vivid purples, golds, and crimsons. The land opened wide before her, wild and untamed, with stunning vistas on every side, and her breath quickened in anticipation. Here was her land of promise. Would she be equal to its challenge?

She closed her eyes, reliving the scene before she boarded the train, with James and her father fussing over her like mother hens, anxious to see her baggage stowed away properly and that she had everything she needed for the journey. Elizabeth stifled a wry laugh, remembering how her mother had come down with an attack of the vapors shortly before her departure, conveniently assuring that Carrie and Virginia would have to stay home to care for her.

No matter. Elizabeth and Carrie had said their good-byes the night before. Not having to deal with Virginia's scorn and her mother's cold disapproval made the parting just that much easier.

She had been pleasantly surprised when Pastor Whitcomb came to bid her farewell. He'd pushed his way through the crowd at the last minute, the displaced strands of silver-gray hair marring his usually immaculate appearance. "My dear," he puffed, mopping his brow with a handkerchief, "I feared I had already missed you."

Elizabeth smiled at the man who had been her spiritual teacher since she was a toddler. "It was good of you to come."

"How could I miss the opportunity to say good-bye to one of my favorite parishioners?" His eyes held an affectionate gleam. "You have always shown courage and determination, Elizabeth. Independence, too. All very admirable qualities when exercised properly." His genial face then took on a more somber expression. "Just be certain you do not try to become independent of God."

"We're gettin' close, aren't we?" The cracked voice of one of the miners broke into her thoughts, and she opened her eyes again. They had entered the broad valley now. The crisp breeze swept through the open coach windows. Elizabeth declined the captain's offer to lower the window canvas. Even though patches of snow lay under the tall pines, the bright sun's warmth was invigorating.

"About two hours more, I figure," the miner's companion answered. "I'll be right glad to get down out of this vee-hicle and start finding those nuggets."

Elizabeth shifted position slightly, trying to ease her knotted muscles. Soon this interminable trip would be over and the real adventure would begin.

It was closer to three hours later by Elizabeth's estimation when the stage finally, blessedly pulled to a stop in Prescott. The captain immediately pushed the door open and sprang to the ground, then turned to hand Elizabeth down.

She tottered out on unsteady limbs and stepped away from the coach, surveying her new home. Clapboard storefronts lined the street before her, and across it was a broad, open square. The cross street to her right seemed to be a hub of activity, judging from the steady stream of men entering and leaving its buildings. Through their swinging doors came raucous laughter and the tinny sounds of pianos played by inexpert hands. A flicker of uncertainty assailed her. Where could Mr. Bartlett be?

"Just arrived, have you, dearie?"

Elizabeth turned to face the diminutive figure at her elbow. The woman's wrinkled face broadened in a kind smile. "Of course you have," she chuckled, "seeing as how I saw you step down off the stage. Isn't anyone here to meet you?"

"I was expecting someone, yes," Elizabeth admitted. Seeing the woman tilt her head in curiosity, she added, "I've come to help care for an acquaintance who's ill."

"Bless you, now! She must be grateful to have a faithful friend like you." Her eyes darkened, and her gaze fastened on a point beyond Elizabeth's shoulder. "And what is he up to, I wonder?" she muttered. "Supposed to be tending to government business, but more likely coming straight from a faro game, by the looks of him."

Elizabeth pivoted and followed her companion's gaze. Richard Bartlett hurried toward her from the direction of the saloons.

"Elizabeth!" he called. "You've arrived at last. Welcome to Arizona Territory." He cast a nervous look at the woman next to her. "Good afternoon, Mrs. Ehle."

The tiny woman narrowed her eyes and grasped Elizabeth's elbow. "Is it her you've come to take care of? His wife?"

Elizabeth nodded mutely.

Mrs. Ehle shook her head. "You seem like far too nice a girl to be abused by that old Tartar." She patted Elizabeth's arm. "I'll be praying for you, dearie. You'll need it!"

Chapter 3

With a shake of her head, the old woman walked on down the street. Elizabeth stared in bewilderment, then turned to face Richard Bartlett. A sour expression crossed his face, which was replaced by an ingratiating smile when he saw her looking at him.

"You'll find the people here more coarse than what you're used to," he said with a short laugh. "Which are your bags?" She pointed out her carpetbag, and he hefted it with a grunt. "I'll arrange for your trunk to be sent to the house. Let's get you settled in."

Elizabeth blinked, then broke into a smile. At home, she would have been met by a carriage and driven to their destination in fine style. She had never expected to walk to her new dwelling. But this was the West, her new home. She would learn to adapt to the way things were done here.

She studied her companion covertly while they walked along. More gray sprinkled his hair than when she last saw him. His face seemed thinner, more pinched, the beaklike nose even more prominent. Perhaps she should attribute it to the natural effects of aging.

Richard led her one block east, then turned north. "This seems odd to you, I know. So different from what you are accustomed to. But give it a chance, my dear. You'll come to appreciate the place and, someday, its people."

He leaned toward her, and she caught the sour smell of liquor on his breath, faint but unmistakable. Her nose wrinkled at the pungent odor, and she experienced a vague sense of unease. It couldn't be later than three in the afternoon. Had Richard drunk spirits in the middle of the day back in Philadelphia? She didn't think so, but as her father had pointed out, she had never been close to the Bartletts.

"I can't tell you how happy we are to have you here." Richard's lips parted in a grimace she supposed was meant to look like a welcoming smile. His geniality seemed at variance with what Elizabeth remembered of him. She tucked that impression away for future reference and forced a polite smile in return. She would only be with the Bartletts temporarily. She didn't have to understand them, just appreciate this means of getting to know Prescott.

Still, his jaunty tone struck a sour note. Perhaps it was due to relief at having the responsibility for his wife's care lifted from his shoulders. But Richard's tone sounded like a man ready to celebrate.

❦

Michael O'Roarke crossed the plaza with quick steps, making no attempt to

24

shield his face from the brisk April wind. He could have sent his clerk to run the errand for him, but spending hours bent over his desk checking freight manifests had made him long for a taste of the outdoors. Verifying Clifford Johnson's latest order might be a menial task, but the trek across town gave him the chance to stretch his legs and fill his lungs with the bracing air.

Hands in his pockets, he crossed the plaza. Strains of music wafted from one of the saloons that lined the opposite side of Montezuma Street, otherwise known as Whiskey Row.

"Each time I see the sun set
Beyond the distant hills. . ."

The clear soprano voice rang out against the tinny piano notes.

Without conscious volition, Michael's steps slowed, and he stopped to listen. The sadness in the singer's voice fit the haunting lyrics to a T. And well it should. Michael could imagine no more sordid existence for a young woman than to be caught up in the vice and degradation of saloon life.

The new Arizona Territory had been called a land of opportunity, and the name held true for many. For others, though, like this plaintive-voiced singer, it could only be a miserable end.

The song ended, but to Michael, the last few longing notes seemed to hang in the clear spring air. How could anyone connected with the saloons and what went on there possess so pure a voice? Maybe a better question would be: How could anyone so gifted sink to such depths?

Only God had the answers. Michael breathed a quick prayer for the unknown singer. He couldn't solve such philosophical questions this afternoon. He could, however, take care of his own responsibilities.

He waved to the driver of the departing stagecoach and crossed Gurley Street in its wake, wondering if the stage had brought yet more fortune seekers to the capital. Adventure and the quest for personal advancement seemed to draw politically ambitious men out of the woodwork. Michael ought to know; his father had been one of the first.

At the next corner, he stopped to get his bearings. He had only been to Johnson's place once before. Was it farther along this street, or did he need to go east one block farther?

Michael rubbed warmth back into his fingers and wished he hadn't left his gloves back in his desk drawer. Turning east, he took a few more steps, then noticed a man and woman walking toward him. He headed their way, planning to ask for directions.

On second glance, he recognized the man and took a quick turn down a side street instead. Richard Bartlett. In Michael's opinion, the man embodied all the worst qualities of those who came to Arizona seeking their fortunes. He'd rather spend extra time finding Cliff Johnson than exchange words with someone for whom he had so little respect.

Richard stopped in midstride and waved his free hand. Elizabeth followed his gaze but saw only a dark-haired man striding away from them. She cast a quizzical glance at Richard, who shrugged.

"I thought to introduce you to one of our local young men. He must not have seen us. Another time, perhaps. As I was saying, we're glad to have you here. In time, I'm sure you will come to appreciate Prescott's finer qualities." He grinned at her again.

Once more, Richard's buoyant tone seemed out of place and reminded Elizabeth of a patent remedy salesman she'd heard years before. Could she attribute his odd demeanor to his drinking and his drinking to worry about his wife's health? If so, that should settle down now that she was here to help. And what if it didn't?

No, she wouldn't borrow trouble. Right now she felt exhausted from her trip, very glad to be at journey's end, and eager to rest up a bit before taking over her duties with Letitia. Time enough later on to deal with Richard's drinking problem, if he did indeed have one.

Her thoughts were interrupted when Richard stopped before a white house with dark blue shutters. "We're home," he announced.

Elizabeth took in the neat frame building. If her acquaintances back home expected her to take up residence in a log cabin or primitive adobe shack, they would be sadly disappointed. The Bartlett home could have been transplanted straight from some Midwestern street, from the neat bay window to the rose that twined along the porch railing.

Inside, the front door opened onto the parlor, where Elizabeth recognized a few pieces from the Bartletts' home in Philadelphia. A sudden wave of weariness swept over her.

"This will be your room. I hope it's satisfactory." Richard turned down a short hallway and set her carpetbag down just inside the door on the right.

Tired as she was, Elizabeth would have been happy with the barest of essentials. The sunlit room with its white eyelet curtains and matching bed covers provided a balm to her travel-weary soul. The soft bed called to her to nestle within its depths.

"Letitia's room is this way. She'll be anxious to see you."

Of course. This was, after all, the reason she had come. She shook her head to clear it and accompanied Richard to the room opposite hers. Her own needs would have to wait.

It took a moment for her eyes to adjust to the dimness and make out Letitia, who was propped up against a stack of pillows. In contrast to her own room, awash with light, the sickroom drapes were closed, giving the room a suffocating quality. Elizabeth approached the bed.

"Look who's here," Richard boomed in a jovial voice. "Elizabeth has arrived at last."

Letitia turned her head and lifted her hand from her cocoon of blankets. She grasped Elizabeth's arm with fingers that clutched like a bird's claw. "Bless you for coming, my dear."

Elizabeth eased free of the woman's grip. "Wouldn't you like me to open the curtains? I'm sure you'd feel much better just for being able to see outside and having some light in here."

"That's a wonderful idea. You see, Richard, she's only just arrived and she already knows just what to do."

Elizabeth busied herself pulling back the heavy curtains and looping the ties over their hooks in the window frame. What was it about the Bartletts' manner that disturbed her so?

No question about her being welcome. They seemed happy enough to have her there. More than happy, almost giddy. Maybe that was what jarred. She remembered the Bartletts as somber, rather dour people. This exuberance seemed completely at odds with the people of her memory. She gave the curtains one last twitch and turned back to the bed.

"What an improvement! I feel better already. Come sit beside me, where I can look at you." Letitia's scrawny hand patted at the coverlet.

Elizabeth took a closer look at her patient, viewing the woman's sallow complexion with concern. She seated herself on the edge of the bed, trying not to flinch when Letitia's waxy hand grabbed at hers.

The afternoon light showed the injured woman's features in unforgiving detail. Limp, graying hair straggled along her cheeks and fell in a tangled mass around her shoulders. The deep vertical lines etched between her eyebrows revealed the woman Elizabeth remembered, confirmed by the fine lines radiating from her lips. This was a mouth more often pursed in disapproval than relaxed in good humor.

Letitia narrowed her pale blue eyes and studied Elizabeth for several moments. Then she patted Elizabeth's hand, and her thin lips stretched in a smile.

Elizabeth returned her scrutiny. The notion struck her that she had entered an animal's den and was about to be devoured.

What a foolish fancy! Elizabeth pressed her fingers to her temples. She must be even more tired than she thought to harbor such uncharitable thoughts about an unwell woman.

"You must be exhausted." Letitia's syrupy voice echoed her thoughts. "Why don't you go lie down for a while?"

"An excellent idea," Richard said. "Time enough to unpack and get settled after you've rested a bit."

"But. . .I'm here to take care of Mrs. Bartlett, not the other way around."

"Nonsense. We can't have you falling ill before you even get started. Now go along and get some rest. We insist, don't we, dear?"

"Absolutely. A lovely girl like you needs to take care to maintain her appearance. Once word of your arrival gets out, suitors will be lining up outside our door."

Elizabeth ignored the implied compliment and plumped up Letitia's pillows. "If you have any concerns about my motive for coming out here, let me assure you that finding a husband is the farthest thing from my mind. I have no intention of entertaining suitors."

She eased Letitia back onto the pillows and went to her room, where she found her trunk had already been delivered. She unpacked in short order. Her dresses would need ironing before they were fit to wear, but she could deal with that later.

The two leather bags in the bottom of her trunk, however, did require immediate attention. She lifted the sacks out one at a time, noting that the tie string on one of them was loose. She knotted it tight. She hadn't brought her inheritance money clear across the country to lose it now.

She found Richard in his study. "I need to set up a banking account," she told him. "Could you tell me where the nearest bank is?"

"I'm afraid we don't have one yet." He slid open the bottom drawer of his desk. "But I can keep your valuables in my strongbox, if you like."

"Thank you." She smiled. "It will be a great relief to know it's secure."

Bringing the bags from her room, she watched him put her money inside the strongbox, then lock it and return the key to his pocket. She heaved a sigh of relief and turned to go. Time now to return to Letitia and get on with the job she had come west to do.

"Back so soon?" Letitia's eyebrows arched high on her forehead. "Why, you've barely had enough time to close your eyes, let alone put your things in order."

"On the contrary, I've unpacked and found a place for everything. I'm ready to get to work. What would you like me to do first?"

Letitia gaped at her. "My dear, you must have traveled light. When is the rest of your luggage coming?"

Elizabeth straightened the clutter of tiny bottles on Letitia's vanity table. "There isn't anymore. I brought everything I thought I'd need with me." She swiped a dust cloth across the tabletop. The dust swirled and settled in time with her movements.

"It's so dry here, compared to Philadelphia. You'll have to dampen the cloth to catch the dust. But Richard said you had only a carpetbag and one small trunk. Do you mean to tell me that's all you brought? No party frocks? No ball gowns?"

Elizabeth smiled and shook her head. "Don't you worry a bit, Mrs. Bartlett. I'm here to take care of you. Being a part of the local fashionable society doesn't hold a bit of interest for me."

Lifting the pitcher from the washstand, she poured a small amount of water onto the dust rag and worked it through the cloth with her hand. Letitia was right; the dust clung to the cloth and the walnut surface began to gleam.

Chapter 4

C an I get you anything else?" Elizabeth lifted an empty serving bowl and scooped up a basket of leftover rolls with her free hand.

"I could use some more coffee," Richard said. "Bring a cup for yourself and join us."

"Yes," Letitia said. "You're not a servant, you know. You're a member of the household."

Elizabeth carried the coffeepot and an extra cup to the small table she had set up in Letitia's room. Having the couple share meals together in a more normal setting, she reasoned, might boost Letitia's spirits and hasten her recovery.

After a week, signs of improvement were evident. Already a faint bloom of color had appeared in Letitia's sallow cheeks, and her strength increased by the day. Dr. Warren had been most pleased with her progress on his last visit. The next step in Elizabeth's plan was to coax her charge to take a few steps across the room and perhaps spend some time sitting up in the platform rocker. Maybe this would be a good day to try.

She poured coffee for the three of them and continued to plan her strategy. Richard's voice interrupted her thoughts. "You're certainly quiet today."

"She's probably thinking about all the friends she left behind," Letitia said, giving Elizabeth a probing look.

"On the contrary. I'm enjoying my stay here immensely."

Letitia simpered. Again, Elizabeth wondered at the smile, so at odds with the lines time had imprinted on her face.

"Even so," Letitia pressed, "there must be someone you miss. A special young man, perhaps? Your coming out here must have left many of them brokenhearted."

Elizabeth stood and began gathering the cups and saucers. "Let me assure you, I am quite content to be here on my own. The men back home are more than capable of carrying on in my absence."

"That's their loss, then." Richard leaned back in his chair and loosened the bottom button on his waistcoat. "Our western men won't be so slow to appreciate your spirit and finer qualities."

"To be sure." Letitia bobbed her head in agreement. "There is any number of young men who would be most anxious to meet you. But you must let us introduce you to the right ones. With your looks and family background, you're sure to receive a worthy proposal in a matter of weeks." For the first time, Elizabeth saw a spark of excitement light her face.

Elizabeth lifted the armload of dirty dishes and turned toward the door. "You don't have to worry about finding suitable prospects for me. Marriage is the last thing on my mind."

A choking sound made her pivot back toward the bed. "You can't mean that." The color in Letitia's cheeks ebbed away, leaving them an ashen gray.

Elizabeth set the dishes down and hurried to the bedside. "Are you feeling unwell? Do I need to call the doctor?"

Letitia waved her away. "I was startled by what you said, that's all." She fixed Elizabeth with a piercing gaze. "You didn't mean that, of course. About having no interest in marriage."

Elizabeth studied the other woman's pasty complexion. If one offhand comment had that effect on her, what would hearing the whole truth do?

She shot a quick glance at Richard. He looked as discomfited as his wife. She wavered, then made her decision. Better to get it all out in the open as soon as possible.

She folded her hands in front of her and drew a deep breath. "My reason for choosing to come out here was not because I had limited prospects at home. I had no interest in attracting suitors then; I have none now. My focus lies in quite another direction."

"And what might that be?" Richard asked, his voice taut.

"To seek my own way as an individual rather than as an appendage attached to a successful man. I want to achieve success on my own. I have no need to divert my energies hunting for a husband."

"That's outrageous!" Richard's indignant sputter brought her explanation to an abrupt halt. "The very idea of a woman striking out on her own!"

"Indeed," Letitia put in. "God made woman to be man's helpmate. A woman isn't complete without a husband."

"Not at all. That may have been the case in years past, but look what women have accomplished just in this century. Why, only last year the American Equal Rights Association was founded for the express purpose of assuring the rights of all citizens regardless of their race, color, or sex."

Letitia stared, her face twisted into its more accustomed scowl. "Rights? What are you talking about? You're beginning to sound like one of those wicked suffragists. I can't believe I'm hearing such things from your lips, Elizabeth Simmons. I'm sure your mother never subscribed to a view like that."

"My mother and I have never seen eye to eye on the topic," Elizabeth admitted. "But that doesn't make my opinion any less—"

"That will be quite enough out of you, young lady." Richard's tone brooked no response. "I cannot control the thoughts you allow to infect your mind, but you had better remember you are here at our invitation. And while you are a guest in this house, I insist you refrain from expressing those sentiments aloud again. Is that clear?"

Letitia punctuated his statement with a firm nod.

Elizabeth stared at them both for a long moment. "Perfectly." She retrieved the coffee service and marched to the kitchen.

The seemingly endless stream of kitchen chores had been put to rest, at least for the moment. Elizabeth pulled her bedroom curtain to one side and took in the view that was becoming more familiar by the day: miners and muleskinners in their rough garb; the better-dressed members of the Territorial Legislature conferring earnestly as they passed along the street. An undercurrent of excitement seemed to pervade every aspect of the new capital. And behind it all, the bulk of Thumb Butte formed a backdrop against the western sky.

One day, as soon as Letitia recovered enough to manage on her own, Elizabeth, too, would be a part of it all.

Recalling Letitia and their heated exchange, Elizabeth tried to set aside her ruffled feelings. Pastor Whitcomb had cautioned her often enough about the dangers of speaking in anger.

Had she done it again? Without a doubt. "I'm sorry, Lord," she whispered, pressing her forehead against the windowpane. "Help me to remember what a wonderful opportunity I've been given. You've provided me with a place to stay and the chance to learn about the possibilities here. Help me to be appreciative and hold my tongue. . .and my temper."

The front door closed with a decisive click. Elizabeth watched Richard descend the porch steps and set off toward the center of town. She followed his progress, wondering if she should apologize for her earlier outburst. She had no intention of changing her opinions, of course, but perhaps she should tone down the way she expressed herself.

"Any mail for me?" Michael scanned the shelves of canned goods, while Nate Smith riffled through the envelopes behind the counter of the general store that doubled as the community post office. Nate separated one letter from the stack and held it up, giving Michael a gap-toothed grin.

Michael took the missive and smiled when he noted the return address. Amy had responded to his last letter even more quickly than usual. Regardless of their differing opinions on his being in Arizona, he could always count on his sister's steadfast devotion. Nice to know he had at least one family member he could rely on—and to be able to talk to regarding their father's behavior.

He stepped back from the counter and slit the envelope open with his pocketknife. The customer behind him jostled his arm, and he glanced up to see Richard Bartlett staring at him through his spectacles.

The older man's irritated expression turned to one of pleasure. "Ah, Michael. I've been hoping to run into you."

"Excuse me," Michael said. "I have some family business to attend to." He held up the envelope in silent explanation and moved outside into a shadowy corner behind a stack of shipping crates, hoping the maneuver would put him outside Richard's notice.

He slid the thin sheet of stationery out of the envelope and spread it open.

Dearest Brother,

I pray this letter finds you well. And to set your mind at ease, let me assure you right away of my abiding love and support. My questions as to the wisdom of your going to the new territory are due only to my concern for what is best for you. Your description of our father's latest peccadilloes saddens but does not surprise me, these being but one more entry in a long list of misdeeds.

While my love for you never changes, I continue to find myself at a loss to understand your insistence on throwing away your own prospects for a bright future for the sake of a man who not only robbed us of a normal family life but cut short our mother's life, as well.

The rattle of boots rumbled along the boardwalk, and Michael saw the object of his sister's scorn approaching. Thumbs hooked in his vest pockets, his father held the attention of a small group of men with practiced ease.

Not a group selected from Prescott's finest citizens, Michael noted. What could his father be up to now? He faded back into the shadows and waited. The group stopped just past his place of concealment.

"So you see my dilemma, O'Roarke." The speaker, a florid man with side whiskers, spread his hands wide. "I've submitted my bid to the legislature, but that sanctimonious clerk wouldn't tell me whether I've been undercut by Bauer's crew. I knew if anyone could make sure I get that contract, it would be you." He slid an envelope from his inner pocket into O'Roarke's waiting hand.

Michael's father glanced inside the envelope, smiled, and tucked it away. "That will take care of things nicely. A word in the right ears, and I'm sure I can clear this up for you. Always glad to be of service to a hard-working man like yourself."

"We could use more of your kind in public service," the man said. His companions nodded agreement.

"That's what I like about you, O'Roarke. You always know how to get things done. . .even if it isn't always quite within the confines of the law." The speaker elbowed Michael's father, while the others guffawed.

The knot of men moved on down the street. Michael eased out from behind the crates, swallowing against the taste of bile that rose in his throat. How long did his father think he could sow this kind of corruption before he reaped a harvest of retribution?

He clenched his fists and felt something crackle in his fingers. Amy's letter. He smoothed it out as best he could and tucked it inside the inner pocket of his sack coat. Amy would no doubt classify this as yet another example of their father's unsavory lifestyle. And she would be right. She would also question once again Michael's wisdom in following their father to Arizona.

For the first time, he wondered if Amy could be right on that account as well. Had he made a mistake in thinking his presence might put a damper on their father's shady activities and help bring him to faith in Christ?

Back in Albany, he would have been finishing up the college degree the war had interrupted. He'd be preparing for law school and mapping out his future—and worrying himself sick about his father.

There, he'd be losing sleep wondering what new scheme his father was about to launch. Here, he knew the schemes all too well, but at least he had the chance to be around when his father's misdeeds caught up with him and he finally hit bottom. No getting around it, he needed to be in Prescott.

Chapter 5

Won't Mr. Bartlett be surprised when he sees you sitting up on your own?" Elizabeth fluffed one of the bed pillows and slipped it between Letitia's back and the platform rocker. "Are you comfortable?"

"As much as I can be, considering the constant pain I'm in."

Elizabeth bit her tongue and slipped out to the kitchen before she said something she would regret. Letitia had been through an ordeal, no doubt about it. Still, Elizabeth couldn't shake the nagging feeling that Letitia's condition had improved more than she was willing to admit.

She ladled a thick bean soup into a flowered tureen and set it, along with bowls and spoons, on a serving tray. On the bright side, Letitia looked better, even if her attitude showed little improvement.

Elizabeth had spent the morning coaxing Letitia to allow her to wash and dress her hair and helped her change into a housecoat of a soft rose hue that brought a bloom of pink to her cheeks.

She had everything set in place by the time Richard's footsteps sounded on the front porch.

He entered Letitia's room and stopped short when he saw his wife in the chair. The smile that spread over his face gave Elizabeth all the reward she needed. "Wonderful to see you up, my dear." He dropped a kiss on Letitia's forehead and seated himself across from her. "Don't leave just yet, Elizabeth." He pulled a packet of letters from his pocket and handed three to her.

"Three letters!" Letitia gasped. "You must have a host of friends to keep up the steady stream of mail you've been getting."

Elizabeth responded with a brief smile and glanced through the missives. She recognized her mother's fine script on the first envelope and set it aside. The second was from Carrie.

Guess what event brought Philadelphia's elite to our home last Friday night? None other than Virginia's engagement party!

Elizabeth raised her eyebrows and scanned the letter for the name of her future brother-in-law.

Emerson Fairfield. That figured. Just like Virginia to pick the most solvent of her suitors rather than one with character.

"That's a solemn look," Richard said. "Nothing wrong, I hope."

"It seems my sister, Virginia, has just become engaged to Emerson Fairfield. You may remember him."

Richard sat up straight. "Of the Baltimore Fairfields? She's made a fine match indeed. Your parents must be very happy."

"I'm sure Mother will be thrilled," she replied. She glanced at the third letter. James again. It would be fun to read his take on Virginia's impending nuptials. She started to slit the envelope open, then remembered where she was and turned to go. She would read James's letter back in the kitchen.

"Wait. Why don't you bring another chair and eat with us?" Letitia suggested.

"Of course," Richard said. "No need for you to stay confined to the kitchen like a servant. We've benefited by your help, but we haven't taken time just to sit and chat."

"What a lot of mail you receive!" Letitia gushed when they had all filled their bowls. She cast a sidelong glance at Elizabeth. "You must miss your home very much."

Elizabeth confined herself to a noncommittal murmur.

Apparently misinterpreting this as a sign of agreement, Richard leaned forward, an anxious frown crinkling his forehead. "Perfectly understandable, of course, but you must understand that life out here isn't all drudgery. We're hoping you will extend your stay past the point when Letitia is well again in order for us to prove it to you."

Elizabeth drew a deep breath and patted her lips with her napkin. "I may as well tell you that once Mrs. Bartlett has recovered, I plan to make my home in Prescott permanently."

Richard and Letitia stared at one another, then looked at her with broad smiles.

"What a wonderful idea," Letitia said. "And there will be plenty of prospects for you to choose from, just you wait and see."

"That isn't exactly what I had in mind."

"Good for you." Richard regarded her with approval. "It's important to be cautious. This is, after all, an untamed territory. We do have our share of riffraff around here."

"Yes, indeed. You can't be too careful." Letitia looked at Richard, her face alight as though she had just come up with a brilliant idea. "And we can help, to repay you for your kindness in taking care of me."

"But I really don't—"

"Of course." Richard picked up on Letitia's thought and forged ahead. "After all, we do know the right people in the territory. We'll help you get acquainted. In fact, I already have an ideal candidate in mind."

Letitia wore a look that reminded Elizabeth of a cat with cream on its whiskers. "We'll have a party—"

"Or perhaps a more intimate dinner—"

"With candlelight and soft music. Maude Avery's son plays the violin—"

"Wait!" Elizabeth planted her palms on the table and pushed herself to her feet, finally bringing the juggernaut to a halt.

"You don't understand." She stared from one of the Bartletts to the other, appalled. "I do plan to stay, but I have no intention of using my time here in pursuit of a husband."

Their looks of astonishment would have been ludicrous if not for the crackle of tension building up in the room. She pushed her chair forward and gripped its back, readying herself to launch into an explanation.

"I want to use my time during Mrs. Bartlett's convalescence to get to know the area and learn its needs. When the time is right, I plan to launch my own business. At the moment, I'm thinking about dealing in mining supplies. There's certainly a need for them at present and will be for some time to come. Once I'm established, I can expand my inventory as needed."

A long silence followed, broken only by the ticking of the clock on the mantel. Finally, Richard cleared his throat.

"I will speak to you as I would to my own daughter. The business world is no place for a young woman, especially one who comes from such a fine family as yours. I'm certain your parents would never countenance such a thing. Your father is sure to refuse any request for funds to finance such a mad venture."

Elizabeth squeezed the chair back more tightly. "Any number of women have run their own businesses—and quite successfully." She looked out the window and waved her hand at the activity outside. "One reason for my coming to Arizona is that it's new and open and holds such opportunity. And as for needing my father's support, rest assured that I have my own money *and* my father's good wishes. The money I asked you to keep for me is more than enough to open my own business. Its success or failure is up to me."

Letitia pushed herself forward in the rocker. Her eyes held an angry glint. "You're certainly a young woman of strong viewpoints. Unfortunately, propriety dictates—"

"We'll discuss it later," Richard interrupted. "Alone."

The Bartletts continued their meal in stony silence. Elizabeth crumbled a biscuit into her bowl, but the meal she had prepared no longer held any appeal. She set down her spoon, ready to leave.

No. She would not allow them to chase her away from the table as though she were a petulant child. She had done nothing more than express her opinion and outline her plans to them. True, she was a guest in their home, but that didn't mean they could control her thoughts or dictate her future.

She settled back in her chair and pulled Carrie's letter from her pocket. Typically, Carrie had filled it with news of dinners, balls, and plans for Virginia's wedding. And one wistful comment: *And while all this activity fills my days, I wonder how much of it is of any lasting value. How I wish I could be with you!*

So do I, Carrie dear, so do I. She tucked the letter back in its envelope. The Bartletts maintained their silence, Richard steadfastly ignoring her, Letitia casting quick glances her way from time to time.

James's ebullient personality flowed from his written words as though she could actually hear him speak:

I had a lively discussion with some of the men in my club in regard to women's rights. They thought they had me, until I presented them with some of your arguments. You should have seen how it stopped them cold!

Elizabeth chuckled at the picture his words painted.

"Pleasant news, I trust?" Letitia's voice rasped in the otherwise still room.

Elizabeth grimaced, then forced a smile. "Yes. An amusing story from a dear friend back home." She started to add more but decided to let it go at that.

"Sending letters across the country is not an inexpensive proposition. You must be loved very much to receive such a quantity of mail." The statement came out sounding more like a question, one Elizabeth chose not to answer.

What business was it of the Bartletts how much mail she received?

Chapter 6

As a counterpoint to the steadily warming trend in the weather during the days that followed, Letitia's attitude grew increasingly frosty.

"Be more careful with my hair this time. If you keep yanking through it like you did yesterday, I won't have any left."

Elizabeth reached for the porcelain-backed hairbrush and gripped it so tightly the handle bit into her palm. "Such a lovely morning. Would you like me to move your chair so you can see the robins outside?"

"It's no good trying to distract me. Just watch the way you handle that brush."

Elizabeth drew the brush through Letitia's graying locks with gentle strokes and searched through her memory for verses on forbearance. Paul spoke of charity in his first letter to the Corinthians, she remembered. What were some of the characteristics he listed? Oh yes. According to Paul, charity suffers long and is kind. It bears all things and is not easily provoked.

Paul never met Letitia Bartlett. Elizabeth rebuked herself for the unworthy thought. She would hold her tongue and not respond in kind, however tempting that might be.

Smoothing Letitia's hair into a soft bun, Elizabeth pulled a few strands of hair from the brush and tucked them into the hair receiver on the vanity table.

"Don't think I didn't see that," Letitia snapped. "The way you pull and tug, my poor hair is coming out by the handful."

Teeth clamped together, Elizabeth let herself out of the room and leaned against the wall, fighting for control.

"Difficult morning?"

She whirled to see Richard outlined in the sunlight coming through the kitchen window.

Richard grimaced, and Elizabeth knew she must have failed to keep her irritation from showing.

"You aren't thinking of leaving, are you?"

"Of course not." She tried to ignore her longing to do just that.

Richard took a step toward her, fidgeting with his tie. He glanced at the closed bedroom door and lowered his voice. "I know Letitia is not always an easy person to get along with."

A bear with a toothache might have a sweeter disposition. "Please don't worry. I can manage." She had to. If she let herself be bested by one woman's sour attitude, how could she find the fortitude it would take to make it in the business world out on the frontier?

"I want you to know how much we appreciate everything you're doing."

If he pulls that tie much tighter, he'll choke himself.

Richard took a handkerchief from his coat pocket and mopped his forehead. "Letitia has always been high-strung and tends to have a rather sharp tongue." He paused, seeming to gauge the reaction his words brought. "I'm afraid the accident has only made that worse."

He shook his head, the picture of despair. "I know she hasn't made life pleasant for you lately, and I'm sorry."

You'd better make up your mind whose side you're on. Elizabeth bit back the tart remark. Richard alternated between taking Letitia's part and apologizing for her with a speed that left Elizabeth dizzy.

He went on, his brow creasing. "You've been working too hard. I'm afraid we've taken advantage of your generous nature."

Elizabeth blinked. What could he be leading up to?

"We can't afford to lose you. You need some time off. Starting today, in fact. Why don't I relieve you after lunch, and you can call the rest of the day your own?"

If his wavering attitude kept her off balance, this offer threatened to bowl her over. "That would be. . .very nice. Thank you."

Tension seemed to ebb from Richard's frame. "And if there is anything else that will make your stay more pleasant, you must let me know at once. We couldn't bear the thought of your leaving us." He opened his mouth, then pressed his thin lips together and gave a brief nod. "It's settled, then. I'll be home promptly at lunchtime."

※

Elizabeth drew in a breath of pine-scented air and reveled in the freedom of this glorious spring day. Although she'd occasionally run a few quick errands for Letitia, she had chafed at not being able to explore the town on her own. This unexpected time off had proved to be more of a boon than Richard could have known.

He returned as promised and shooed Elizabeth out the door without waiting for his lunch to be served. "I'll see to everything," he promised. "Just enjoy yourself."

What got into him, Lord? The more time she spent around Richard and Letitia, the less she understood them.

No matter. The afternoon was hers to do with as she wished, and she intended to make the most of it.

Freedom beckoned. Elizabeth made her way past the scattered houses until the plaza came into view. She stopped for a moment to take in the scene. Wagons loaded with freight lined up along Gurley Street, awaiting the order to depart. Self-important politicos hurried along the boardwalk, rubbing elbows with dusty miners in town to replenish their supplies. The bustle of a new city trying to discover its identity—much like Elizabeth herself.

A light breeze drifted from the northwest, carrying the scent of fresh-cut lumber from the sawmill. . .a pungent raw smell, full of promise.

If you could capture the excitement and hope of this new land in a fragrance, it would smell like that. Elizabeth filled her lungs with the heady aroma. *This is what God made me for. He brought me out here to be a part of this.* The seed of thought took root and sprang up as a certainty in her heart. "I could stay here forever," she whispered.

She walked to the center of the plaza and pivoted in a slow circle, surveying her surroundings. Where to start? If Richard kept his word and gave her at least one half day a week off, she could make a systematic reconnaissance of the businesses already in place.

Knowing how changeable both Bartletts could be, that might be a pretty big "if." She'd better accomplish as much as possible today.

The saloons of Whiskey Row lined Montezuma Street on the plaza's west side. That eliminated one fourth of the area she needed to investigate. She turned her attention to the buildings on the north side of Gurley Street.

Prescott Market. Blake & Co., Assayers. The Hadley House. The Bowen Mercantile caught her notice. A steady stream of customers entered the clapboard building. Elizabeth saw few women among them, but it didn't matter. What she sought was information. She crossed Gurley Street and pushed open the door.

Inside, a mustachioed man wearing a white apron looked her way.

"Can I help you, Miss?"

Perhaps it would be well to play the part of an ordinary customer rather than a potential competitor. "A packet of pins, please." Elizabeth scanned the shelves for other likely purchases. "And a penny's worth of those horehound drops."

With her reason for being there established, she scanned the faces of the men clustered near the pickle barrel.

"Good afternoon," she ventured. Several of the men nodded; others watched her with guarded expressions.

All right. In for a penny, in for a pound. "I'm thinking of starting a business here. What do you think of Prescott's future prospects?"

The group stared at her as though she had sprouted an extra head. One bearded fellow worked his jaws slowly, then sent a stream of tobacco juice into the sawdust around the cuspidor.

"We've already got a dressmaker," he said, eyeing the pins the proprietor held out to her. "I'm afraid me and the boys won't give you much business that way." His sally brought chuckles from the group.

"You mistake my meaning," Elizabeth retorted. "I'm talking about something more substantial—selling dry goods, perhaps, or mining supplies."

The chuckles grew to outright laughter.

Michael checked off the last item on his freight manifest and pulled the tarpaulin down tight across the wagon box. He turned to the lead driver. "Looks like you're ready, Ben. Keep a sharp eye out for Indians. I want all you boys to make it back safely."

The weathered driver leaned out from the wagon seat and spat in the dust. "I aim to do just that. This trip down to Big Bug may not be a Sunday stroll, but it sure beats that drive in from the river." He wagged his head. "A hundred and eighty miles from La Paz, and only six water holes between there and Date Creek. Dries out a man's bones, just remembering it."

"Well, make this one as quick as you can. I'll see you when you get back." Michael stepped back and lifted his hand to Ben and the drivers of the two wagons behind him. Leather harnesses slapped against mule hides, and the heavy wagons set off.

A small whirlwind spun a column of dust along the street and sent Michael's hat tumbling along the boardwalk. He caught it just past the market and slapped it against his leg to beat out the dust.

The creak of the wagon wheels receded in the distance. His wagons. His business. A business that gave every appearance of growing into a thriving concern. Hard work and fair prices had built a name for the O'Roarke Freight Company, a reputation based on reliability and trust.

Michael knew just how precious that reputation was. He had worked as hard to live down the stigma his father had given to the name O'Roarke as he had to build up the business itself.

A sarsaparilla would go well right now to cut the dust in his throat, he decided. He scanned the length of Gurley Street.

Farther along the block, the door to Bowen Mercantile opened and a woman emerged. Her chestnut curls glinted in the afternoon light as she stood for a moment, then set off in the opposite direction with quick, decisive steps.

For a moment, Michael thought he recognized her, but his memory couldn't supply a name. He squinted against the sun's glare. No, she was no one he knew. But she'd just come out of the mercantile. Someone there might know her.

A wave of laughter trailed off when he pushed through the door. "A bottle of sarsaparilla, please," he said, then turned to the chuckling men.

"Everett been telling more of his stories?"

"Not this time." Roy Guthrie wiped tears of mirth from the corners of his eyes with a frayed bandanna. "He didn't have to. That eastern gal gave us plenty to laugh about without any help from him."

"Eastern gal?" Michael took the sarsaparilla, tossed a coin on the counter, and took a long pull from the bottle.

"The one who skedaddled out of here like Jael getting in the mood to smite Sisera. You must have just missed her."

"She sure didn't miss Everett," put in Harry Goldberg.

"What do you mean?" For the first time, Michael realized Everett was busy mopping himself dry with an empty burlap sack.

Roy grinned broadly. "She came waltzing in here telling us she 'planned to go in business for herself.'" His voice rose to a falsetto pitch, mimicking her tone. "When we tried to guess what kind of business she was after, she said she wanted to sell mining supplies. Can you beat that?"

"So where does Everett come in?"

Roy raised his hand to quell the rumble of laughter. "We thought that was pretty funny, but Everett's the one who told her how to make her fortune."

Michael fixed Everett with a dubious gaze. "Which was?"

Everett gave his face a final scrub with the coarse sack and looked up with a wounded expression. "All I said was, 'If you were sellin' kisses, we'd each buy a hundred.'"

"That's when she grabbed a tin cup from the counter and doused him with pickle juice," Roy explained. He let out a whoop that set the tails of his mustache dancing.

Michael grinned as he hunkered down and rubbed the bottom of the bottle back and forth across his knee. "Any idea who she is?"

Roy shot a keen glance his way. "You wouldn't be fixin' to make yourself a target, too, would you?"

"Just curious," Michael said. "I didn't even get a good look at her, remember?"

"Don't know what her name is," Roy told him. "But I seen her before. She's staying over at Bartletts'."

Michael's blooming interest wilted like a fragile flower in the Arizona sun. Richard Bartlett seemed to pop up everywhere he turned lately.

What was it about that couple that set his teeth on edge? He couldn't pin his feelings on anything specific, but he'd sooner trust a rattlesnake than either of those two. They were on a par with his father, the type who hurried out to the new territory, not to build it into something fine, but to get whatever they could out of it for themselves.

If this chestnut-haired woman was part of that simpering, self-centered crowd with its pompous ways, she held no interest for him at all.

Chapter 7

W here have you been? I can't imagine what you could have found to do that kept you out so long."

"Now, Letitia, I told you she would be gone for the afternoon." Richard gave his wife a consoling pat and shot a furtive glance at Elizabeth. "Remember, we want her to be happy here."

Elizabeth clamped her tongue between her teeth. What a contrast to the sense of freedom she had felt during the past few hours. Already she felt like she'd stepped back into a cage.

Charity suffereth long. It couldn't be easy for Letitia, bound to her bed and chair for weeks on end. Small wonder her temper flared.

"I'm back now. I'll get a fresh nightgown ready and start heating water for your bath."

"Just a moment." Richard's voice stopped her. "I picked up the mail on my way home at noon. This letter is yours. I forgot to give it to you earlier."

Elizabeth accepted it gladly. Spying Carrie's handwriting, she tore the envelope open, eager for news from home. Her sister's girlish chatter about Virginia's wedding preparations would be just the thing to counteract the sour taste left in her mouth by Letitia's greeting.

Are you sitting down, Elizabeth? Papa would have written himself, but he's spending every minute down at his office, and Mama is busy having yet another attack of the vapors. I don't understand all the ins and outs of the situation, but it seems some of Papa's business investments have gone sour, and we find ourselves on the brink of financial disaster. "In serious straits," Papa calls it, although Mama claims we are on the verge of poverty. You should be here to see the uproar!

Virginia storms through the house bemoaning our state in the most dramatic fashion. Not out of concern for Mama and Papa, I'm afraid, but for fear this will hinder her plans for the wedding of the century. Or—horror of horrors!—cause Emerson to reconsider his proposal entirely.

As for me, dear Elizabeth, I am sure my attitude disappoints Mama very much. Instead of feeling we're going through a great tragedy, I have a tremendous sense of anticipation about what lies ahead. All my life, I've heard Pastor Whitcomb assure us that God is able to supply our needs, no matter what the circumstance. And now I shall experience the truth of that

*statement firsthand. I no longer have to sit and moon about the excitement
I've missed by not being with you. I'm having my very own adventure,
right here at home! Papa sends his warmest regards. He is so glad you have
money of your own so you don't have to worry.*

With all my love,
Carrie

*P.S. Papa has said I may come to work for him as a secretary. It will save
him some money, and I may need those skills to help provide some income
if things don't turn around soon. Needless to say, I am delighted, and poor
Mama is utterly scandalized.*

The letter slipped from Elizabeth's fingers. The room receded and instead
she saw the image of Carrie's laughing face. Papa's business in ruins? Impossible!
And yet, she knew Carrie wouldn't exaggerate. How could this have happened?
More to the point, what should she do?

"Are you going to stand there staring into space or take care of me?" The
harsh voice snapped her back to the present.

"Letitia." Richard's voice held a pleading note.

"She's quite right." Elizabeth picked up and pocketed the letter. "I've had my
free afternoon. It's time I got back to work."

She set her mind on straightening the bed sheets and fluffing the pillows.
All the while, her mind whirled with the question of what she ought to do.

She could take the next stagecoach and return to Philadelphia. The thought
curdled her stomach, but it had to be faced. Her family needed her.

She smoothed a wrinkle from Letitia's blanket, turning the possibilities over
in her mind. If she did go back, would she be a help or a liability? Perhaps it made
it easier on them to have one less mouth to feed.

Then there was Emerson. She cringed at the thought of the effect the news
of his future bride's impending poverty would have on the Fairfield family. They
cared about their money and prestige almost as much as Virginia did.

No doubt he would be too embarrassed to break things off with Virginia now
that their engagement had been formally announced. But he'd also be mortified
for his fiancée to come from an impoverished family.

She nodded, satisfied that Emerson would do everything in his power to see
that the Simmons family's fortunes were restored as quickly as possible.

She poured fresh water into Letitia's tumbler, a little guilty at the relief she
felt at knowing she didn't have to leave. But this, too, could be of benefit to her
family.

Once her business started making a profit, she would be in the delightful
position of being able to send money back to help out. Then both Mother and
Virginia would have to admit her initiative was something to be appreciated.

And you'll have to ask forgiveness for your insufferable pride.

That thought tempered her elation somewhat. A woman had an obligation to use the gifts God gave her. She remained convinced of that. How did one do that and still not be prideful about it? There must be a balance; how could she find it?

❦

"Back again, are you, Miss Simmons?" Jake Bowen, proprietor of Bowen Mercantile, shoved his glasses farther up the bridge of his nose and scratched his bald pate.

"I'm afraid so. Are you getting tired of my visits?"

"Not in the least. I enjoy a lady who's as much a pleasure to look at as she is to argue with." His cherubic smile took away any offense his words might have caused. "You've got one of the best minds in the territory, I reckon. Even if everyone else around here doesn't see it that way."

Elizabeth stopped in the act of examining a bolt of printed muslin and forced herself to take a calming breath. Mr. Bowen couldn't be blamed for the opinions of the unenlightened. And she shouldn't be surprised that some people objected to her outspoken views. On the other hand, she didn't have to like it.

"So what do you think of my plan to supply equipment to the miners?"

"Appears to me your idea is a good one. Mining's the magnet that draws people to Prescott, but it's the merchants selling to 'em that makes the real money."

"That's my reasoning exactly." Elizabeth basked in a warm glow of gratification. "There's a lot of call for mining supplies right now. I can start out stocking those and expand my inventory as I become more established. I don't have any plans to encroach on your territory of handling general merchandise, though," she added with a grin.

Bowen chuckled. "You've got a good head on your shoulders, all right." He peered at her over his eyeglasses. "I didn't say it."

"Say what?"

"For a woman. That was what you were expectin', wasn't it? For a minute there, you got all fluffed up like a hen ready to protect her chicks."

Elizabeth drew herself up and lifted her chin. "Surely not." She caught sight of her reflection in the window and laughed. "Well, perhaps you have a point. But have no fear, Mr. Bowen. In my mind, you are definitely on the side of the angels."

She turned at the sound of the door opening and groaned when Harry Goldberg and Everett Watson walked in. Two who were most definitely not on the angelic side of the ledger. Another man entered behind them and stood off to one side.

"Look who's here." Everett sauntered toward her. "That pickle-juice-slinging female who thinks she's going to be a businessman."

Elizabeth narrowed her eyes. She would not be intimidated by the likes of

Everett Watson. "God gave women minds, just as surely as He gave them to men. In contrast to you, however, I intend to use the one He blessed me with."

She held her skirts aside and swept past the dumbfounded man as his companion burst into laughter.

"She got you good," Harry sputtered. "She didn't even need any pickle juice this time."

Too incensed to make any further reply, Elizabeth pushed her way toward the door. The third man stood nearby, regarding her with a broad smile.

Elizabeth jerked to a halt in front of him. "And I suppose you're another one who thinks a woman's place is confined to the cookstove?"

The dark-haired man shook his head. "If I had presumed to hold such an opinion before, I would certainly change it now. You most definitely have a quick mind."

Elizabeth waited for him to add "and a lively tongue." When he didn't, she eyed him closely to see if he was making fun of her. Every line of his face showed sincerity—and could that be a hint of admiration?

Her face flamed with embarrassment at her impulsive speech. "My apologies, sir. It seems I leaped to a totally unfounded conclusion." She looked back at the other two men. "I've seen so much of a different attitude lately, I'm afraid I assumed the worst."

The heat in her cheeks told her she must be as red-faced as Everett. She extended her hand. "I am Elizabeth Simmons. It's a pleasure to make the acquaintance of one of the few men out here who is able to see a woman as a person of worth in her own right."

❦

She had a firm, confident grip. Not surprising, after the scene he'd just witnessed. Michael caught himself before the smile that threatened to spread across his face could surface. He had a feeling she'd never believe he was laughing at her victims and not her.

"I'm Michael O'Roarke." He released her fingers reluctantly, missing the contact with her soft skin as soon as she withdrew her hand.

So this was the woman who had bested Everett once before. Michael took his first close look at the mass of chestnut curls framing her oval face. The top of her head didn't come any higher than his nose. He'd seen children taller than that.

But that fiery spirit didn't belong in a child's body. She had dressed Everett down in no uncertain manner. He wouldn't have believed it, had he not seen it with his own eyes. How could so much explosive power be packed into such a small package? Being around Elizabeth Simmons could prove as dangerous as juggling a twenty-pound keg of black powder.

But Michael had a feeling it would be a lot more fun.

Chapter 8

Richard poked his head into Letitia's room, where Elizabeth sat reading to her. "I've brought some friends home. Make some coffee and bring it to the parlor. And some of those sweet rolls you made last night."

Elizabeth started at his peremptory tone and glanced at Letitia, who took the interruption with surprising grace. "Go along," she said. "It's some of his political cronies. You'll find that more business is often done in gatherings like this than in official meetings.

"Go on," she urged when Elizabeth hesitated. "It's a fine opportunity to meet some of the right people. Connections like this will be important to you, since you plan to stay on."

Elizabeth moved to the kitchen, pausing in the parlor doorway long enough to count the guests. Five men besides Richard filed in through the front door.

He could have given me some warning. She filled the coffeepot and stirred up the fire in the cookstove, then searched through the cupboards for something suitable to serve as refreshments.

Only a few of the rolls remained. She cut them into halves to make it look like more. Hardly a lavish repast, but it would have to do.

It could have been worse. At least he didn't show up and demand supper for all those men. She carried in the tray of rolls, then went back for the coffee service.

"Pour for us, would you, Elizabeth?" Richard tossed the request out with a casual air.

"Of course." She filled six cups with the dark, steaming liquid, using the time to inspect Richard's guests more closely.

Opposites might attract in some circumstances, but Richard's cronies looked to be men of his own type. Their physical attributes differed, but each one had the appearance of a man totally focused on himself.

"If they'd just listen to me, we could solve this issue in two minutes."

"McCormick's still shaken by his wife's death. He isn't in a mood to listen to anyone right now."

"Maybe we need a new governor, have you thought about that?"

Elizabeth handed out five cups of coffee and looked at the one left over on her tray. Surely she had seen six men enter the room?

Movement from the far corner caught her attention. The sixth man stood in the shadows, observing the goings-on with casual interest, but taking no part in them himself.

With one of his thumbs hooked in a pocket of his vest, he used the fingers of his other hand to preen his enormous handlebar mustache with slow, deliberate strokes.

His gaze fastened on Elizabeth. She picked up the last cup to carry it to him, then set it back on the tray. Something about the way he watched her brought gooseflesh up on her arms. He could come get his own coffee, if he were so inclined.

"I have something here, if you'd care to touch up your coffee a bit." Richard produced a bottle half filled with amber liquid.

Elizabeth wrinkled her nose. With her duties as hostess completed, there was no reason for her to remain. She turned to go back to Letitia.

"Stay here, Elizabeth. We may need you for/something."

She shot a startled glance at Richard. Stay in the room with five strange men? Feeling like a fly in a spider's web, she moved to the farthest corner of the room and stood quietly, hands clasped in front of her.

The low murmur of conversation resumed, although several of the men glanced her way from time to time. Elizabeth began to feel like an exhibit on display and disliked the sensation heartily.

A narrow-faced man set his cup down in its saucer with a clank that made her wince. "Where's that bottle, Richard?" he slurred. "I hate wasting good bourbon like that. Get me a glass, and I'll drink it straight."

"Elizabeth! Mr. Matthews needs a shot glass." The slur in Richard's own voice alerted her to the likelihood that he'd started drinking well before coming home.

"They're in the sideboard," she stated, making no move to fetch one. She might have to stay in the room as a courtesy to her host; she did not have to contribute to his guests' debauchery.

Richard sent a furious look her way but relaxed when the other men laughed. "Over here," he told them, pulling out a glass for each one. "Let's wet our whistles with something that hasn't been diluted by coffee."

Elizabeth shrank back against the wall, wishing she had chosen a station closer to the door. To leave now, she would have to cross the room, right past the drinking men.

What about the door to Richard's study? She quickly gave up that idea when she remembered the lone man standing in front of it. Elizabeth darted a glance at him in spite of herself and stifled a cry when she found him staring straight at her.

He didn't flinch at her scrutiny but continued to study her with an intensity that made her skin crawl.

"Sure a pretty one you've got helping out," called Matthews.

"I'll say." A tall, thin-faced man favored her with a loose-lipped leer. "We need more like that around this town."

Richard only tipped a glass of bourbon down his throat. "I'll have to agree that there's a shortage of eligible young ladies in the capital." He looked at the man in the corner and raised his eyebrows questioningly.

The man in the shadows met Richard's gaze, then turned his attention to Elizabeth. Once more she had the feeling of being under inspection. Without making eye contact with her again, the man looked back at Richard and gave him a slow nod that chilled her.

Someone brushed her elbow, and she jumped. Matthews stood only inches from her.

"A real looker, that's what you are." He bobbed his head up and down, a move that threatened to upset his already precarious balance.

Elizabeth moved away, wishing she could disappear.

"Yessir, once the word gets out, every young buck in the territory will be lining up to meet you. Better get all the work out of her you can now," he called across the room to Richard. "This one'll be married off before you know it."

"Enough!"

Her outburst shocked the gathering into silence. Elizabeth felt as stunned as the rest looked. Still, she had their attention; she might as well speak her mind before she lost her nerve.

"Since my future seems to be of such great interest to all of you, let me make one thing perfectly clear. I have no intention of marrying just to assure myself of security. I plan to make my own future."

The two men closest to her chuckled indulgently. Another laughed out loud.

Richard's expression held all the friendliness of a thundercloud. "That will be all from you."

Elizabeth raked him with a scathing look. "I'll be with Mrs. Bartlett if you need me."

❧

"Richard told me of your behavior this afternoon." Letitia pushed away her pie plate and set her fork down with fingers that trembled. "You owe an apology to him, not to mention all the other gentlemen you offended with your rudeness."

Elizabeth felt her back grow rigid. "Not a one of them deserves to be called a gentleman, much less merits an apology."

"We've heard quite enough out of you today, young lady." Two helpings of venison stew plus a large slice of dried apple pie had toned down Richard's tipsiness somewhat.

He hadn't begun to hear all she had on her mind. "I don't intend to allow a crowd of half-drunken boors to discuss my life."

"Yes, you made your opinions quite clear. And managed to offend some of the territory's most influential men in the process."

"I'm sorry you feel I've been rude to guests in your home. At the same time, their remarks were inappropriate. It is certainly none of their business what my plans for marriage—or lack of them—might be."

The Bartletts exchanged startled looks. "You spoke in haste," Richard said in an appeasing tone. "I can understand that some of their comments might have caused you to say things you didn't mean."

"On the contrary. I meant every word."

"Nonsense," Letitia snapped. "No young woman in her right mind chooses to be a spinster. It isn't respectable."

"Quite right. You have plenty of drive and resourcefulness, and those are fine qualities, in their place. But it's time you started thinking about settling down. You don't want to focus all your energies on a daydream, only to wake up one day and find out it's too late to have a normal life."

"And we can help." Letitia had dropped her waspish mood and now seemed positively eager. "We'd be happy to introduce you to a young acquaintance of ours."

Elizabeth hesitated, bewildered by the abrupt change in Letitia's demeanor. "Please try to understand. I believe a woman ought to be more than mere decoration. I don't discount the idea of marriage, but I know I possess intelligence and abilities. If I do marry someday, I want to be more to my husband than someone to cook his meals, wash his clothes, and warm his bed."

Letitia's gasp cut off the rest of her intended statement. Richard's face darkened. "I will not sit here and listen to this," he thundered. "You have much to learn about propriety." He tossed his napkin on the table and stalked out of the room.

Elizabeth cleared away the supper dishes in silence and returned to help Letitia prepare for bed. Letitia raised her arms and waited for Elizabeth to slide the cotton nightgown over her head.

"You've upset Mr. Bartlett quite badly."

What about the way he and his guests treated me? "That wasn't my intention. But I do hold strong opinions about what women are capable of and feel I have the right to express them."

"You might want to think less of your rights and more of your obligations." Letitia scooted back on her bed and settled against the pillows. "Remember whom you have to thank for bringing you out here." She didn't wait until Elizabeth had exited the room before blowing out her light.

Elizabeth pulled the bedroom door closed with a soft click instead of the slam she longed to give it.

Chapter 9

Michael whistled as he strode beneath a row of piñon pines along Granite Creek. A freshly signed freighting contract crackled in his pocket. If business continued to pick up at this pace, everyone in Prescott would soon know the O'Roarke Freight Company was the best freight line around. Assuming he could control his drivers long enough to keep his wagons moving.

His happy mood faded at the memory of Walt Logan's disappearance. . . and where he had finally located him. He understood the loneliness men experienced on the frontier, where they outnumbered the women twenty to one. But he could never comprehend the need to seek comfort in the arms of fallen women.

Ben, his lead driver, shared his opinion. But they parted company over Ben's opinion that the women were to blame for the situation. Michael agreed that what they did was wrong, but his heart ached at the idea that many saw that kind of life as their only means of survival. More than one woman left on her own had felt reduced to selling herself to stay alive. He'd like to kick the stuffing out of the men who trafficked in such trade.

He stopped in the shade of a large pine and mopped his brow. The weather had turned warm again after a brief cold snap, but that was typical of weather in this mountain capital. It could just as easily snow again before summer settled in to stay.

From his vantage point on the high bank, he watched the water trickle along the creek bed. He scooped up a handful of pebbles and tossed them into the water one by one. A lovely spot, this, if one could forget what went on in some of the buildings only a stone's throw away.

A woman's high-pitched shriek shattered the idyllic silence. Michael spun around, trying to pinpoint its location.

Another piercing cry. He sprinted toward the source of the sound.

Voices rose on the far side of a row of small buildings. Michael rounded the corner at a dead run and saw a couple entwined at the end of the row. He put on a burst of speed.

In the moment before he reached them, he realized two things: The woman's screams were punctuated by giggles. And the man who held her in his arms was his father.

Dust and gravel sprayed from under his boot heels when he skidded to a halt.

"Indians chasing you?" His father regarded him with a look of cool amusement.

Michael stared from his father to the painted woman at his side, unable to speak a word.

"Cat got your tongue? Allow me to introduce you to Ruby, one of Prescott's most delightful young women. Ruby, my son, Michael."

The woman wrapped one arm around his father's ample waist and gave Michael a broad wink. "I see the resemblance."

"Don't go getting your hopes up, honey. Michael doesn't indulge."

"That's a pity." Ruby's rouge-coated lower lip protruded in a pout.

Michael looked at his father in disbelief. "I thought you had at least enough decency not to carry on your affairs in public."

"Not so very public." His father looked around at the deserted alley and the creek beyond. "Not until you came charging up, anyway. Speaking of that, what brings you back this way? A sudden decline in your scruples, perhaps? Or maybe you're more like me than you've let on."

Ruby giggled and gave Michael a speculative grin.

Michael ignored her and looked straight at his incorrigible parent. "We need to talk. Now."

His father gave an exaggerated sigh. "I can see things aren't going to work out today, Ruby dear. Run along for now. I'll see you soon."

Ruby trailed her hand along his cheek and turned to go. His father stared after her, then turned to face Michael.

"All right, what do you have to say that can't wait?"

Righteous anger exploded in Michael's brain. "I can't believe you've sunk so low." Couldn't he? His father hadn't earned his reputation as a womanizer from idle gossip. But seeing it firsthand made him sick.

"Nothing to get all excited about, my boy. Just letting off a little steam. You wouldn't want to begrudge me that, would you?"

What Michael wanted most at that moment was to grab his father by his jacket collar and fling him down the steep bank of Granite Creek. A good dousing in the icy water might be just what he needed.

"And wipe that sour look off your face. It isn't as if I'm planning to make her your stepmother. She's good for a bit of fun, that's all."

"Good? You don't even know the meaning of the word."

"Where's that Christian charity I hear you harping about so much?" His father roared with laughter at Michael's shocked silence, then moved toward him and draped his arm over Michael's shoulder.

"Come walk with me, son. I've been meaning to speak to you. This is as good a time as any. I won't mince words, Michael. You need a wife. You've put it off long enough, but it's time you got married. Past time."

Michael twisted to one side and flung his father's arm off his shoulder. "How can you speak to me of marriage when I've just found you behaving like that in broad daylight?"

"Another matter entirely, my boy. You're going to be somebody someday. And I don't mean the owner of a piddling freight business. I haven't spent my life setting the stage for your future to see you throw yourself away on some insignificant enterprise."

"No." Bitterness laced Michael's tone. "You've spent your life focusing on one thing and one thing only: getting whatever you wanted for yourself."

His father pulled a cigar from an inner pocket and took his time trimming and lighting it. He closed his eyes and puffed contentedly before he responded. "I'll grant you it may seem that I've promoted my own interest at times. And I'll admit diversions like little Ruby have been strictly a matter of pleasure. But my political aspirations haven't been only for my benefit. The country is expanding. We're on the edge of the frontier now, but this place won't live in isolation much longer.

"We're building this territory, seeing it start from nothing and shaping it into what it will become. But I'm building something beyond that, Michael. Something for you and me." He blew smoke into the air in a series of quick puffs. "I've sought one thing for years: power. And it's just about within my grasp. I'm talking about a dynasty, son. A legacy we can share."

Michael stared into his father's keen blue eyes. Eyes so like his own, as was the dark, curly hair. He might be looking at a picture of himself twenty-five years in the future. He prayed the resemblance would only be external.

His anger evaporated, leaving sorrow in its place. "I wish I could make you understand. Your goals are not mine. We're both interested in building this territory, but in vastly different ways. I'm not interested in your brand of wheeling and dealing. I know there's a place in politics for men of God—and heaven knows we need them there—but it isn't the place He's called me to be."

"You fool!" His father spat the half-smoked cigar onto the ground. With one quick thrust of his foot, he sent it flying down the slope and into the creek below. "I didn't raise a man, I raised a simpering fool! Or, rather, your mother did. It's all the same in the long run." He glared at Michael. "One day, you'll see the truth. I just hope it won't be too late."

❧

"Dear God, how can he believe that web of lies he's spun?" Michael leaned his elbows on his desk and cradled his head in his hands. He didn't remember the walk back to his office, couldn't have told which route he'd taken. He'd returned by pure instinct and holed up like a wounded animal in its den.

Wounded. That's exactly how he felt. His father hadn't dealt him a physical blow, but the result was just as painful. Perhaps more so.

"How have I failed him? Where did I go wrong?" To think that after trying his best to live out the truth of the Gospel before his father, the man could still think he'd be willing to drop it all and join him in his power-hungry quest.

His reason for coming to Arizona Territory hadn't been to found a business or make a name for himself. It had been for the sole purpose of shining the light of Christ into the dark corners of his father's life.

And he'd failed. Failed miserably.

Amy had warned him. Before he left Albany and in every letter since, she continued to point out the hopelessness of trying to convince someone who didn't want to be swayed.

When his father ignored all his efforts at first, Michael only dug in and tried harder. Every setback had fueled both Amy's conviction that their father was a lost cause and Michael's determination to prove he wasn't.

Up to now.

What was it Amy had said in her last letter? That their father had robbed them of a normal life? Michael couldn't argue with her there. What about the charge that he'd cut short their mother's life?

A picture of Ruby in his father's arms sprang unbidden to his mind. Michael gasped as though the wind had been knocked out of him.

Could Amy be right? As if a dam had burst, scenes from the past flooded his memory. His gentle, godly mother reading her Bible alone while his father gallivanted off somewhere. Coming across his mother in her sitting room and asking why her cheeks were damp. Seeing her square her shoulders and putting on a brave smile before capturing his attention with some childish diversion.

And once, listening to a conversation between his mother and her best friend. A conversation he wasn't meant to overhear.

"It's happening again, Grace." He remembered the sound of his mother's voice, choked and tight. "I confronted him about it last night. He didn't even bother to deny it, just told me I needn't think he'd let my objections stand in his way. What am I to do?"

Her words had puzzled him at the time. Today, the pieces fell together, revealing the whole ugly picture. How she must have suffered over the years!

Michael clenched his fists. Could Amy be right? Had their father's philandering cost them precious years of their mother's presence?

He had always defended his decision to join their father in Arizona by telling Amy he knew it was the right thing to do. Their mother had prayed faithfully for her husband's salvation. He only wanted to finish the job that meant so much to her.

Now he wondered. Maybe Amy had been right all along. Maybe their father had truly reached a point beyond repentance.

And if that were the case, did he have a reason to stay on here?

Chapter 10

*G*old pans. Shovels. Blasting caps.
Elizabeth nibbled on the end of her pen. Had she missed anything? She went over the list again, trying to think of other items a miner might need.

Picks. Candles.

She put down her pen and surveyed the list once more. A thrill shivered up and down her spine. One day soon, her store would carry the best selection of mining equipment this side of Denver.

Elizabeth wished her father could be with her to share her joy. Years of watching him work had taught her the value of advance planning. He would be as excited as she to watch her dreams take shape.

More questions remained to be answered. Where would be the best location for her new venture? And what would she need in a building? Elizabeth pulled out another sheet of paper and sank into thought.

A knock on the front door roused her. She left her papers spread out across the table and went through the parlor to admit Dr. Warren.

"How is our patient today?" asked the genial man.

"Quite well, in my opinion." Elizabeth swung the door closed and lowered her voice. "Although she still complains of pain and feeling weak."

The doctor snorted. "Letitia Bartlett complains of everything that could possibly be wrong and a great deal that couldn't. I'll just go have a look, shall I?"

"Of course. You don't need me, do you?" He shook his head, and she returned to her planning. Once Letitia no longer needed her help, she could start setting her plans into motion. She picked up her pen and started sketching ideas for a floor plan. It seemed no time at all before Dr. Warren stopped by to take his leave.

"How is she, Doctor?"

"She'll always have a bit of trouble with that arm, but for all that, she's as fit as can be expected."

"When can she start getting up and around?"

"She could have been up for some time now. Don't let her get away with languishing in her bed all day. She needs to be moving. See that she does." He paused in the doorway. "You've done a fine job, Elizabeth. Just don't let her bully you. I can't stand malingerers."

Elizabeth rushed to the sickroom, expecting to find Letitia as elated as she felt. "Dr. Warren told me the news. Isn't it wonderful?"

"The old fool." The corners of Letitia's mouth curved downward, accentuating the deep lines in her cheeks. "He can say anything he likes. He doesn't have to live with my pain." She let out a piteous moan and sank back against the pillows.

"Straighten my blanket, Elizabeth. That quack couldn't be bothered."

Elizabeth hesitated. Surely the doctor knew what he was talking about. And the sooner Letitia could manage on her own, the sooner Elizabeth could make her dreams a reality.

She grasped a corner of the blankets and threw them to the end of the bed. Ignoring Letitia's indignant yelp, she helped the older woman into a sitting position and draped her robe around her bony shoulders.

"Let's get you out into the parlor. You'll feel much better once you're sitting up among all your lovely things. Come on, now."

"Have you taken leave of your senses? I need my rest."

"You can rest in the wing chair. I'll bring some pillows to make you more comfortable."

She put her words into action over Letitia's protests and soon had her seated in the parlor.

"Now, isn't that nicer than staring at the same four walls day in and day out?"

With a colorful quilt draped across her knees and a pink flush tingeing her cheeks, Letitia already looked more robust, although Elizabeth thought the flush might be due more to anger than health.

"What am I supposed to do, just sit here all alone?"

"Why don't I bring my papers from the kitchen and work on them here to keep you company?"

"Why ask for my permission? You'll do as you wish, anyway."

Ignoring the jibe, Elizabeth brought out her papers and spread them next to her on the settee. She bent over the rough map she had drawn of the town. Would it be best to locate her store facing the plaza or on one of the outlying roads? She touched different spots with her finger, trying to envision her business in each place.

"You mean you're still bent on pursuing this foolish notion? You'll wake up one day and realize all the good husbands have been taken, mark my words."

"I'm not worried about it." She returned her attention to her map. Perhaps she could find a suitable building already in place. That would save her a good deal of time.

"And think of children. They'll be a comfort in your old age."

"Really, Mrs. Bartlett—"

"Richard and I always wanted a large family, but it was not meant to be, more's the pity."

The front door opened, saving Elizabeth from another onslaught.

"You're up, my dear!" Richard burst into the room.

"Only because she forced me here. That idiot doctor is trying to say I'm fully recovered. You must make him understand that I still have a long way to go."

"Good, good," Richard murmured.

"Good? Richard, do you hear a word I'm saying? I still need Elizabeth's help. You must make him see reason." She glanced at the mantel clock. "What are you doing home so early? It's only the middle of the afternoon."

"Ah yes." Richard darted a quick glance from his wife to Elizabeth, then back to Letitia again. "Everything's in a bit of a muddle. Mr. Fleury is all stirred up. Some flap about missing money."

Letitia's hands knotted in the folds of her quilt. "And they sent you home?"

"They sent everyone home while he and Alsap go over the books. I'm sure it will come to nothing. More than likely, a clerical error. It's sure to turn up before long."

He beamed and rubbed his hands together. "In the meantime, let's celebrate your progress. With you on the mend, Elizabeth will have time to pursue a social life," he said, emphasizing the last two words.

Letitia's mouth formed an O. "You're right. We were just discussing that, weren't we, Elizabeth? Now we'll be able to pay you back for your kindness and help you meet a fine young man. Doesn't that sound like a good plan, Richard?"

"Yes, and the sooner the better. We've imposed upon her good nature for far too long." He pulled two letters from his coat pocket and glanced at the envelopes. He handed the top one to Letitia. "And this one's for you, Elizabeth."

"Thank you." She accepted the letter without looking at it, not wanting to be sidetracked. "But please don't feel you owe me anything. It was my choice to come out here, and that was to seek out business opportunities, not to enlist you as matchmakers."

She waved her hands as she spoke, and the envelope flew from her fingers, landing on the floor near Letitia's feet. Letitia bent forward and stared down at it, then gave Elizabeth a sharp glance.

"Who spends so much time writing to you? That's the same handwriting I've seen on several other letters, and I know it isn't your mother's."

It is none of your business who does or doesn't write to me. As Elizabeth scooped up the envelope bearing James's bold scrawl, an idea dawned in her mind. Maybe she could convince them she didn't need to find a beau.

"It's from a dear friend at home," she said brightly. "A gentleman friend."

Their reaction couldn't have been more satisfactory. Letitia gaped; Richard sputtered.

The Bartletts exchanged a long glance. "Is it—"

Richard cleared his throat, interrupting Letitia. "Is it a serious relationship?" he asked. "As your protector while you are away from your father's care, I feel a responsibility for you. What are this man's intentions?"

Elizabeth suppressed a smile. Here was her chance to lay their plans to rest once and for all. "You remember James Reilly, don't you? I can assure you his intentions are entirely honorable." The memory of their childhood pledge popped into her mind. "As a matter of fact," she added with a playful laugh, "he asked me to marry him some time ago."

Letitia's anguished cry echoed through the parlor. Richard's jaw hung slack.

Elizabeth stared at them, mystified. Why should her marriage plans—or lack of them—matter to the Bartletts one way or another? She hadn't expected to shock them so. Still, if that tidbit of information put an end to their scheming, so be it.

"Why didn't you tell us?" Letitia demanded. "You should have let us know you had an understanding with this man, instead of coming to us under false pretenses."

Elizabeth blinked at her. She turned to Richard, hoping for some explanation, but he stood as if frozen, staring across the room. He clutched one hand to his chest, and his face took on a grayish hue.

He looks like he's about to collapse. Dear Lord, what have I done? Elizabeth took a tentative step toward him, but he waved her away and staggered toward the door.

"I must let Timothy know," he called to Letitia, just before the door closed.

Time seemed to stop, while Elizabeth's mind whirled, trying to make some sense of what had just happened. Richard looked terrible, and somehow she felt responsible.

"Do you think he'll be all right? Should I go after him?"

Letitia directed such a malevolent glare at Elizabeth that she held up her hands, as if warding off a physical blow. "Leave him alone. You've done enough."

"But all I said was—"

"You said more than enough. If something does happen to him, it will be your fault. Now take me to my bedroom. I need to lie down."

Elizabeth complied without a word.

~≈~

Pale gray light seeped into Elizabeth's room. She had struggled throughout the night to comprehend what she had done to stir up such a hornet's nest, but she was no closer to understanding Richard's strange behavior than before. Her memory of the previous evening remained a blur of catering to Letitia's every whim, then turning out the lights and settling in for the night. Later, the click of the front door marked Richard's return, followed by urgent whispers coming from Letitia's room.

She hadn't even had the energy to light a candle at bedtime, let alone undress. She lowered her feet to the floor and pushed herself upright, feeling as frowsy and rumpled as her clothing.

She had hoped for enlightenment during the long night hours, for clarity of thought that would show her what she'd done. Instead, she only felt confused and resentful at the treatment she had received.

The light grew stronger. Elizabeth reached for her Bible as though grasping a lifeline. Somewhere in its pages, she ought to find some answers. Pastor Whitcomb had been particularly fond of Ephesians. She turned to the spot, her gaze settling on the fourth chapter.

" 'And be ye kind one to another. . .' " *Ha! The Bartletts have shown me anything but kindness.* " '. . .tenderhearted, forgiving one another. . .' " Another area where they fell short. A less tender heart than Letitia Bartlett's would be hard to find.

"Forgiving one another. . ." Wait a minute, Lord. Am I supposed to hold them blameless for the outrageous way they've treated me?

Maybe one of the Gospels would have the comfort she sought. Matthew, perhaps.

" 'And why beholdest thou the mote that is in thy brother's eye, but considerest not the beam that is in thine own eye?' "

Elizabeth read the passage through twice, then read it again. "No, Lord. It's the other way around. They have the beam; I have the mote."

She flipped through the pages hurriedly. Surely there would be a verse that would shed light on how wrong the Bartletts were.

" 'Obey them that have the rule over you. . . .' " She slammed her Bible shut. The Bartletts didn't rule her life. *No, but they invited you here and let you stay in their home without charge.* But that didn't put them in authority over her, did it?

Didn't it?

"All right, Lord, I wouldn't be here if it weren't for their generosity. This is their home, and I'm only a guest here. I'll try to be more kind, but I'm going to need Your help."

She picked out a clean dress and prepared to fix breakfast.

Chapter 11

*W*herefore take unto you the whole armour of God, that ye may be able to withstand in the evil day, and having done all, to stand."

Michael stared at Paul's words to the Ephesians, then slowly closed the leather cover and sat with his hands folded atop his Bible.

He wished the full meaning of the words could somehow seep from the printed page through his fingers, then into his mind. No, his mind understood them all right. He needed to have them imprinted on his heart. He pressed the heels of his hands against his eyes. Hadn't he done everything possible to show his father the value of putting God first in his life? Hadn't he given up prospects for a bright future in Albany for his sake?

And for what? To watch his father pawing a woman of ill repute right out in public? The memory of the scene he'd witnessed sickened him.

No son could have done more than he had. Few would have done as much. He couldn't think of one thing more he could do.

"And having done all, to stand."

Michael spread his arms wide and turned his face toward heaven. "Stand, Lord? Just stand by and watch while he brings more shame to our family?"

His words seemed to bounce back off the ceiling. Silence settled around him like a blanket.

"Why is it so difficult just to stand and watch You work, Lord? I know my limits, know them all too well. It seems a simple enough thing to step back and get out of Your way, but it's harder than it sounds. I guess I never thought of standing firm for my beliefs as being such a passive job."

The memory of Elizabeth Simmons lecturing the men in the mercantile came to mind. Michael chuckled, despite his frustration. Elizabeth's brand of feistiness was far more in line with what he'd always thought of as standing up for one's convictions.

Now there was a woman who knew what she believed and stood ready to defend it. Just the thought of those flashing hazel eyes and all that energy wrapped up in such a petite frame lightened his mood. Under other circumstances, he'd think seriously about paying Miss Elizabeth Simmons a call.

That pleasant image dissolved when he pictured himself climbing the porch steps of the Bartlett house. For the hundredth time, he wondered how such a vibrant woman could be associated with that couple. It didn't make sense.

Michael returned his Bible to its place on the corner of his desk and straightened a stack of invoices. He probably ought to declare Elizabeth strictly out-of-bounds. But he had the uneasy feeling she had already staked a claim in his heart.

❧

"Good morning."

Richard and Letitia looked up when Elizabeth entered the kitchen.

She made her way to the stove, determined to follow the scriptures and show them kindness. She glanced at her charge while she cracked eggs into a large bowl. Either Richard had helped Letitia with her clothing or she had managed to dress on her own. A quick look at Richard revealed he had regained his normal color, a welcome sight after last night's scare.

Richard slid an unopened envelope across the table to his wife. "It's from Muriel Stephens, back home. I found it on the parlor floor. You never did read it yesterday after. . ."

"After that spectacle Elizabeth put on," Letitia finished for him. She opened the letter without further comment.

Elizabeth opened her mouth to make a retort, then clenched her teeth and concentrated on whipping the eggs into a frothy mass. While they cooked, she sliced off thick slabs of bread and set out bowls of jelly along with the place settings.

"Be ye kind one to another, tenderhearted." She slid the eggs onto a serving platter and reached for the coffeepot.

Letitia gasped. "Oh, Richard!"

Elizabeth pivoted so quickly that several scalding droplets splashed on her hand. "What is it? Are you ill?" She set the coffeepot on the table and dabbed at her hand with a dish towel.

Letitia waved her hand as if shooing away a fly and shoved the letter at her husband. "Richard, read this." She indicated a point halfway down the page.

Richard's features sharpened as he skimmed the letter, then spread the sheet of paper out and went over the message a second time. He raised his gaze to meet Letitia's.

Elizabeth blew on the spot where the hot drops had spattered on her skin and tried to decipher the unspoken messages that flashed between the couple.

"Is everything all right? Have you had bad news?"

A delighted smile lit Richard's face, to be swiftly replaced by a concerned frown. "Not at all. Not us, that is." He motioned to her chair. "Maybe you'd better sit down."

Letitia reached over and patted her arm. "You poor dear. You'd better tell her, Richard."

Elizabeth gaped at Letitia and felt her knees buckle, dropping her to the chair seat. Had something happened to her family?

Richard held up the letter. "Mrs. Stephens has shared some surprising news.

I'm afraid you may find this upsetting." His somber tone didn't match the exultant gleam in his eyes.

"She sends news of several mutual acquaintances," he went on. "Your James Reilly is one of them." He looked her straight in the eye and cleared his throat. "It seems Mr. Reilly has just announced his engagement to Josephine Brown."

Elizabeth waited for stunning news, then realized she had just heard it. She smiled at the Bartletts, both watching her intently.

"That's wonderful news. Josephine has a mind sharp enough to match wits with James, but a gentle spirit. She'll be a perfect match."

"There, now." Letitia leaned close and put her hand on Elizabeth's. "There's no need for you to put on a brave front."

"Brave front? But—"

"Certainly not," Richard said. "A cad like that doesn't deserve defending."

"I'm not defending him. I—"

"It's all right, dear. We know you must be heartbroken."

"Heartbroken? Over James?" Elizabeth laughed aloud.

"She's becoming hysterical, Richard. What should we do?"

Still sputtering with laughter, Elizabeth put up her hands to fend off their ministrations. "I'm neither heartbroken nor hysterical. The very idea! Whatever gave you such a notion?" Her mirth faded as she watched their expressions change from sympathy to suspicion.

Richard's eyes narrowed. "It's very odd that you take this so lightly, since he's the one you promised to marry."

"Marry James? Oh!" She remembered her lighthearted comment of the night before and chuckled. "That happened when we were children." She stared with growing concern at their hostile expressions. "What's the matter?"

"What do you mean, when you were children?" Letitia's breath came in ragged gasps.

"It's no great mystery," Elizabeth said with a return of her former spirit. "We grew up next door to each other, as I'm sure you remember."

Richard's face hardened. "But you told us you were engaged to him."

"You may have taken it that way," Elizabeth countered. Her conscience prodded her. Of course they had. Wasn't that exactly what she'd intended?

She sat straighter in her chair and looked squarely at them. While she felt they had brought this on themselves, she knew they deserved an explanation.

"It's all because you were pressing so hard to attach me to someone out here. I thought perhaps I could put a stop to it if you thought I was unavailable. I only said that to—"

"You lied!" Richard slammed his fist on the table, rattling the untouched breakfast dishes.

"Lied!" Letitia echoed. She covered her face with her hands and sank into her chair, loud sobs racking her body. "What are we to do, Richard? Is it too late to talk to Timothy?"

"I don't understand." Elizabeth raised her voice to be heard over Letitia's wails. "I apologize for any misunderstanding, but I fail to see—"

"That's just it." Richard's harsh tone cut across her words. "You don't see at all."

He loomed over her and planted his hands on either side of her against the chair back. Elizabeth shrank back against the unyielding wood. His hot breath puffed against her face. For a moment the world existed only of Letitia's keening and Richard's contorted features.

"We're ruined." Elizabeth could see the veins on his forehead pulse as he ground out the words. "Do you understand? Ruined!"

Chapter 12

Letitia raised her head and looked daggers at Elizabeth. Her hair had escaped from its pins and stringy gray strands dangled on either side of her tear-streaked face. "You haven't been honest with us from the moment you arrived, have you? You wanted a way out here and you used us as a reason to come. We'd planned such a wonderful future for you, but you wanted nothing to do with it. All you've been interested in is following your own desires."

"That isn't true."

"Do you deny that you misled us about your relationship with James Reilly?"

"Misled, yes. Maliciously, no. I only meant to deflect your interest in finding me a beau. I never intended to cause you any harm." Elizabeth stared from one of the distraught pair to the other.

"But just how could my statement about James bring you to ruin? I don't understand."

Richard opened his mouth, then closed it again as he shoved himself away from her chair. Letitia swiped a clump of hair back away from her face and pushed herself to her feet.

"I'll tell you how." Ignoring Richard's cautioning gesture, she declared, "Our money is gone. All of it."

"Financial reversals," Richard put in.

"We had one chance to recoup our losses. Just one."

"An offer from an old and trusted friend."

"His son needs a wife," Letitia said. "All we had to do was produce a suitable candidate—"

"And let nature take its course, so to speak."

"All you had to do was let us introduce you to this young man. You're attractive enough when you aren't spouting off those idiotic ideas about women's rights. You could have caught his attention if you'd only tried."

"Things move quickly out here," Richard said. "You could have been married before Christmas."

"Married!" Elizabeth heard her voice come out in a squeak.

"All you had to do was agree to meet him. We could have kept things going from there." Letitia's voice rose to a piercing level. "But, no. You couldn't be bothered to show us the least amount of gratitude for bringing you out here, for giving you our protection and a roof over your head. Not the least bit of cooperation. And now it's too late!" The shrill scream echoed through the house, leaving a bitter silence in its wake.

"Too late? Too late for what?"

"For giving us the help we needed, you foolish girl! After you led us to believe you were engaged to James Reilly, Richard went to tell Timothy the deal was off. And now, after you've shattered any hope we had of restoring our fortune, you tell us it was all a lie."

Elizabeth remembered Richard's parting words the night before. She leaned forward in her chair. "Let me get this straight. My meeting this person was going to help you regain your wealth?" A horrible notion struck her. "Do you mean to sit there and tell me you were going to provide me as a wife to this man's son. . . for a price?" She sprang to her feet, quivering with rage.

"All you had to do was—"

"All I had to do was sell myself—no, allow myself to be sold. Isn't that right?" She searched their faces and found confirmation. "My mother worried about my living in the midst of ruffians and cutthroats. When she said that, she had no idea I'd be living under their very roof. This is barbaric!"

"That will do, young lady!" Richard thundered. He pointed a trembling finger straight at Elizabeth's face. "I will not have you speak to either my wife or me with disrespect."

Elizabeth pushed his hand aside. "How dare you speak of disrespect! This country just endured years of war to *end* the abominable practice of people being bought and sold like commodities."

"You can talk, can't you?" Letitia stood and joined Richard. "You've never experienced want a day in your life. You have no idea what it means to have everything stripped away from you, then have one chance to turn it all around again. And then see it snatched away by an arrogant chit of a girl." Her face darkened, then twisted with anger. "Get out! I won't have you in my home another day!"

Elizabeth held her gaze, chest heaving. "Very well. I'll be only too happy to leave this place." Without another word, she swept out of the kitchen.

It took little time to jam her belongings back into her trunk and carpetbag. She set the carpetbag on the front porch, then returned for the trunk. With clenched teeth, she tugged at the handle, dragging it across the floor with a screech she knew would set Letitia's teeth on edge.

Out on the porch, she closed the front door with a bang. After a pause to catch her breath, she picked up her carpetbag and prepared to set out. . .and realized she hadn't the least idea where she should go.

Wagons creaked along the dusty roads. Children called back and forth from neighboring yards. The pound of hammers resounded from building sites. The town teemed with activity, but none of it related to her.

The carpetbag weighed heavy at the end of her arm. She had dreamed of one day leaving this house to venture out on her own, but she'd planned to have a destination in mind when that day arrived.

Perhaps a boardinghouse. Of course. One that accepted ladies. And she had spotted just such a place on one of her jaunts around town. Mrs. Keller's establishment would fit the bill nicely.

She set off toward Cortez Street, the carpetbag bumping against her leg with every step. Surely Mrs. Keller would know someone she could send after the trunk. If not, she would come back and drag it every inch of the way there herself.

Elizabeth strode south on Cortez, revising her carefully laid plans. Her agenda had been to order stock and locate a site before moving out, but she could adjust her plans to compensate.

She would get settled in her new lodgings this morning. If she could inspect the properties she had in mind in the afternoon, she might be able to finalize the purchase of her new property within the week.

She came to an abrupt halt in the middle of the street, bringing a squawk of protest from the driver of a freight wagon.

Her money still rested in Richard's strongbox. The little she carried in her reticule might pay for a few nights' lodging but would hardly serve to strike a business deal.

She had no desire to return to the Bartletts' home. But she had no choice. Turning around, she retraced her steps. She started up the front porch steps, then paused. It would be all too easy for the Bartletts to ignore her knock. Very well, she wouldn't give them the opportunity.

She set the carpetbag down at the foot of the steps and hurried around the house to the kitchen door. Turning the knob, she stepped inside.

Letitia's eyes bulged. "How dare you enter this house without knocking!"

Elizabeth held her ground. "I'm only here to collect the last of my things." She turned to Richard. "The money I gave you for safekeeping. If you'll just get it for me, I'll be on my way."

Both the Bartletts froze. Richard's face darkened, while Letitia turned pale. *Now what?* Whatever response she'd anticipated, she hadn't foreseen anything like this.

Richard's high color faded to a pasty gray. Elizabeth reached out to him, fearing he was about to collapse.

"Pull a chair up behind him, quickly," Letitia ordered. She fluttered next to her husband and helped him into the chair Elizabeth brought.

"Is there anything I can get for him?" Elizabeth asked.

Letitia stood with her hand on Richard's shoulder and faced Elizabeth. "The best thing you can do for either of us is to leave. Right now."

"But my money. If you could just get that for me first—"

"Gone," Richard said in a hollow voice. "All gone. I lost it in a faro game."

"You. . .you lost my money? You gambled it away?"

"Only part of it at first." He stared at a point on the wall across the room. "Thought I could win it back and return it all before you ever knew it was gone. But I hit an unlucky streak. The cards took it all. Every bit of it."

"That money was mine! You stole it. I'm going straight to the sheriff's office."

"It won't do you any good." Richard's eyes had lost their glassy look. "You don't have a receipt for it. It'll be your word against mine."

"But. . .you stole it."

"Don't talk to us about stealing after what you've done." Letitia's voice shook. "You've cost us far more than that. Now get out of this house, and don't come back."

In a daze, Elizabeth returned to the porch for her carpetbag and headed back to Cortez Street.

❧

"Here I am, Lord, on my own. No one to rely on but myself. And You, of course. That's just what I asked for, isn't it?"

Elizabeth perched gingerly on the narrow bed's thin mattress and surveyed her new domain. The trunk, delivered by Mrs. Keller's handyman, took up most of the floor space. At the foot of the bed, a rickety table held a chipped basin and pitcher. A plain wooden chair sat against the opposite wall under a row of pegs to hold whatever clothing wouldn't fit in the narrow dresser. She would have to leave most of her belongings folded in her trunk.

Elizabeth edged between the bed and the trunk toward the tiny window. Her weight on the floorboards sent the basin and pitcher to vibrating.

"Somehow this isn't quite the way I'd envisioned it, Father. I'm supposed to be conquering new worlds, not hiding out in a cramped little room wondering how I'll manage once my money's gone."

Amazing, the difference twenty-four hours could make. Yesterday she had been happily planning her future. Today she had gone from that to learning she'd been brought out here as merchandise to being cast out, alone and penniless.

Feeling sorry for herself wouldn't do a bit of good. There had to be something she could do, a job of some sort to help her get back on her feet. But what? She thought of the saloons lining Whiskey Row, the last resort of more than one woman left on her own.

No. Never that. She'd starve first.

In better times, she could have written to her father. He wouldn't hesitate to send her money to tide her over. If he had it himself. Which he didn't.

She could appeal to Virginia and her fiancé. The very thought twisted her stomach.

Stop it! There had to be a way, something she wasn't seeing yet. Even Carrie had shown more spirit, looking forward to God's provision like a child who fully expected her Father to live up to His promise.

All right, then. Did she think God's arm was too short to extend to Arizona Territory? She had to shake off this panic and get a grip on her emotions.

She could start by arranging her room. Once she put that small space in order, she'd be in a better frame of mind to plan her next move.

The dresser filled quickly. Elizabeth hung most of her dresses from the pegs on the wall. She reached into the trunk for her heavy flannel nightgown, then put it back. The nights had been growing warmer, and this room promised to be downright stuffy. Where had she packed her lighter gown?

She found it squashed flat in the bottom of the trunk. No matter. No one would see her wearing it. Something clinked when she pulled it out.

Elizabeth bent to investigate. A gold double eagle nestled against the lining. She remembered having to retie the strings when she pulled the second bag of money out to give to Richard. This piece must have fallen out then. But one wouldn't clink by itself. She pushed aside her clothes and found two more.

The three coins lay in the palm of her hand. Sixty dollars, the remnant of her fortune. Each coin carried the new motto: In God We Trust.

A slow smile spread across Elizabeth's face. "Okay, Lord, it's a start. Let's find out what You're going to do next." She placed the coins in her reticule and descended the narrow stairs.

"I'm going out for a bit, Mrs. Keller."

"Really, dear, you don't need to check in with me every time you leave." Her landlady's cheerful countenance added to the resurgence of Elizabeth's confidence.

Elizabeth set her face to the north and walked up Cortez, feeling a shiver of anticipation run up her arms. God had promised to provide. He owned the cattle on a thousand hills; the wealth of the universe was His. Surely He could meet the needs of one young woman.

She paused at the corner and waited for a buggy to pass before she crossed Goodwin Street. "We walk by faith and not by sight, Lord," she murmured. "Guide my steps and show me the way."

Hurrying across in the buggy's wake, she stopped again on the opposite corner. A pair of miners hovered nearby, leaning against a loaded wagon.

"If you're sure we've got everything, we can head back to the claim," one said, climbing to the wagon seat.

A spasm of frustration clenched at Elizabeth's stomach. If all had gone according to plan, those same miners would have been her customers, purchasing their goods from her store.

"Guess we've got everything on the list," the second miner replied. He scratched his stomach with a grimy hand. "Only one thing I'd like to have and can't, and that's a cherry pie.

"Or peach pie, or apple pie. Or even an applesauce cake. Old George Bernard makes a mean venison chili, but I haven't had decent baked goods since I left St.

Louis." The bearded man shook his head mournfully and climbed up beside his partner. With a shake of the reins, he started their wagon down the street.

Elizabeth stared after them. Baked goods? She'd never considered the need for those before, but she could turn out as fine a pie crust as any baker. Her only domestic accomplishment, her mother called it.

If those miners wanted baked goods, then baked goods she could give them. All she needed were equipment, ingredients, and a place to do her baking.

"I don't have any of those, Lord. What are we going to do about that? Oh, and a place to sell them would be helpful, too."

She proceeded north on Cortez, skirting around a cluster of men standing on the edge of an empty lot.

"You're really pulling out for good, Bill?"

A barrel-chested man nodded. "I came with all these grand ideas of making enough to get a new start, but they've all come to nothing. Guess I'm just not cut out to be a miner. It's time for me to go back to farming and making harnesses."

"Sorry to see that happen," his friend replied. "This would have been a nice place for a saddle shop."

Elizabeth's steps slowed, and she stopped, eavesdropping shamelessly.

"It's yours, if you want it," Bill said. "I just want what I paid for it. That'll get me the rest of what I need to head out."

"Excuse me." The group parted as Elizabeth marched up to the one called Bill. "Did I understand you to say you're selling a piece of property here?"

"This very lot we're standing in front of," he said. "I'm bound for Kansas as soon as I get rid of it."

"How much do you want for it?" She ignored the snickers behind her.

The brawny man grinned. "Lady, I paid forty dollars for this piece when they auctioned the first lots in '64. If I can get that back, I'll be on my way."

Forty dollars. Two-thirds the sum total of her worldly goods.

"Would you accept half now and half later? I'd be happy to have papers drawn up to that effect."

"Twenty dollars now and twenty more by the end of the week, and the place will be yours. Let's go find one of the lawyers here to write up a quitclaim deed."

Two hours later, Elizabeth burst into the boardinghouse. "Mrs. Keller, may I use your oven? And some of your pie pans?"

Mrs. Keller looked up from setting lunch on the table. "I don't see any reason why not." She smiled at Elizabeth's exuberance.

"Bless you! The delivery boy is bringing flour, lard, and dried fruit from the market. I'll get started making pies as soon as I change my dress. I'm going to open a bakery, Mrs. Keller. If I hurry, I just might make my first sale today!"

※

PIES FOR SALE

The hastily lettered sign hung from a plank stretched across two empty wooden crates. Steam rose from the six apple pies set out on the crude counter.

Elizabeth pulled her handkerchief from her sleeve and dabbed at her forehead. After the breakneck pace of the last few hours, she felt drained. Drained, and yet energized.

She squinted into the late afternoon sun. People strolled around the plaza. A number of miners were headed for Whiskey Row. In another hour or two, she would know whether she had made a solid business decision or thrown her money away.

"At least this lot is mine. Even if nothing comes of the bakery, I still have enough to pay what I owe on it. I'll have an investment in the property, if nothing else."

"Talking to yourself?"

Elizabeth looked up into a pair of merry blue eyes. "Mr. O'Roarke. Would you like to buy a pie?"

"I was drawn in equal parts by the delectable aroma and the opportunity to talk to the best conversationalist in Arizona Territory. Even if she's already talking to herself." The skin crinkled at the corners of his eyes when he smiled. Elizabeth found herself smiling back.

"As I live and breathe, I did smell apple pie." A man appeared at the edge of Elizabeth's lot and hurried to the makeshift counter. "I'll take this one. No, make it two." He reached in his pocket.

"This one is already taken." Michael scooped up the nearest one. "It looks like business is booming." He gave her a wink that shot a surge of delight right through her.

"Thank you. And you, sir." Elizabeth beamed at her other customer.

"Is this a onetime sale, or will you be back again?" he asked.

Elizabeth looked at her three remaining pies, then at the group of men heading her way from the plaza. "The Capital Bakery will be open for business tomorrow." She grinned at Michael and squared her shoulders. "And for a long time after that."

Chapter 13

Elizabeth put up her hand to shield her eyes from the bright noontime sun shining down on the plaza area. Soon, she would have to put up an awning to protect her from its heat. Today, though, the dazzling rays reflected her own sunny mood.

After selling out her entire inventory her first day in business, she had invested her proceeds in more ingredients and some pie tins. She sold out again the following day. And the next, and the next. Capital Bakery had become an overnight success. She had enough to pay Bill Wilson the remainder of what she owed on the lot and some left over besides.

Elizabeth breathed a prayer of thanks and smiled at the customers heading her way. The miners had turned out to be her biggest advertisers, spreading the news about her wares throughout the community.

Elizabeth chuckled. Miners had been her intended customers from the beginning. Only her wares had changed. "You knew it all the time, didn't You, Lord?"

She watched a group of three miners who had just bought a pie together split it into chunks and begin eating. Maybe she could add a few tables and chairs, give them a place to sit, and sell it by the slice. It would make good advertising, as well as more profit.

"A penny for your thoughts."

"Add some more and you can buy a pie. I'm sure it would be tastier than my thoughts."

Michael shook his head. "I'm equally sure it wouldn't. Your thinking is very fresh and just as delightful to the senses." Michael leaned over to savor the aroma of each pie. "But the conversation would be even better accompanied by some of that peach pie."

Elizabeth grinned and handed it to him. "And what would you like to discuss today? The Indian problem, perhaps, or the suffrage issue?"

"I was thinking more along the lines of whether a certain bakery proprietor would like to go with me to C. C. Bean's Bible study."

"It sounds wonderful." Her shoulders drooped. "But I don't see how I can."

"Oh?"

"Mrs. Keller has been wonderful about letting me use her oven, but I can't be in the way when she's cooking for her boarders. The only way I've been able to produce pies in this quantity is to work in the kitchen at night."

Michael let out a low whistle. "I never thought about what you had to do to make this many." His brow wrinkled. "But you're here from late morning on. When do you sleep?"

She gave him a tired smile. "I catch a nap while the last pies are baking, and I rest a little more before I come down here, then try not to think about it the rest of the time." She laced her fingers together and stretched her arms in front of her, then rolled her head from side to side to work the kinks out of her neck.

An evening discussing the Bible with Michael did sound good. But as long as she had to stay up baking all night and selling pies all day, it was a luxury she couldn't afford.

Michael's forehead puckered. "What would it take to put up a building here so you could bake at your convenience?"

Elizabeth stared. "I've been so focused on getting started, I haven't thought much further than just the moment at hand." She stepped out to the street and turned back to survey her property.

Could she do it? The thought of putting up her own building made her giddy.

"I wouldn't need to set out makeshift seating. I could make it large enough to have a dining area inside."

Michael stepped closer. "And a kitchen where you could bake while you're open for business. The smells will drive people wild."

"And a place to sleep," she said, envisioning her own quarters in the rear of the building. The benefits of the idea convinced her. She turned to Michael. "Would you be willing to escort me to the sawmill this afternoon? I need to get some prices."

❧

Elizabeth stared up at the rough wood building. Fresh paint glistened on the lettering over the door: CAPITAL RESTAURANT & BAKERY.

"What do you think?"

Michael beamed. "I like the name. It may not be the fanciest place in the town, but it serves the best pies around."

"I never thought I'd be able to keep working while this was going up, but we did it."

"*You* did it. This never would have happened without your grit and determination. And Prescott would have lost out on a fine new business."

Elizabeth smoothed her apron and smiled. "I can't believe I'll be able to work during the day and sleep all night. What luxury!"

"For awhile, maybe." Michael studied her, his eyes shadowed by concern. "When business picks up, you'll be just as busy as before. You need to hire someone, Elizabeth. You're strong, but you can't do it all on your own."

"I might, but I need to be sure I'm making enough to pay for the building before I take on another expense."

"If you don't spend a little more to give yourself some rest, you'll wind up losing the business anyway."

"I'll have you know I slept for five hours straight last night. I felt positively slothful." She chuckled at Michael's worried expression, then sobered. "All right, I'll consider hiring someone. I know I can't keep up this pace much longer."

The relief in his eyes warmed her more than the morning sun. *Thank You, Lord, for sending me a friend like Michael, someone who accepts me as I am and likes me that way. Being able to talk to him is almost as good as having James around.*

No, better. The thought shook her to the soles of her shoes. She had left James behind in Philadelphia without a second thought, sure of his undying friendship but knowing they would keep in touch through the mail.

Could she do without Michael's presence so easily? Elizabeth tried to imagine spending her days without a glimpse of his dark, curly hair and ready smile. Without his stimulating conversation. Without his strength and support.

The thought painted a thoroughly dismal picture. And a frightening one.

When had she started relying on someone other than herself? If she intended to make her way on her own, could she afford this strong attachment she felt for him? Was it too late to back away?

And did she want to?

"I need to check on my pies. It wouldn't do to let them burn while I'm getting used to the new oven."

Michael followed her through the dining room and into the kitchen. He leaned on the counter and scooped up a glob of leftover dough with one finger.

"You never did tell me why you decided to start a bakery instead of selling mining supplies." He popped the dough into his mouth and smacked his lips.

Elizabeth opened the oven door and peeked at the pies inside. They still needed a few more minutes. "I needed something I could open right away and operate on a shoestring." Prompted by Michael's puzzled look, she recounted the way Richard had squandered her money.

"That's outrageous! The man ought to be horsewhipped."

"I would have been glad to volunteer, but it wouldn't have gotten my money back." Michael's outrage cut through her assumed nonchalance. It felt good to have someone care. What would he say if she told him about the Bartletts' purpose in bringing her out to the territory? No, she could never do that. Even now, the memory made her blush. She could only imagine Michael's reaction. He'd probably offer to string Richard up from the nearest cottonwood.

And when did you start relying on a man to fight your battles for you, Elizabeth Simmons?

"I'm thinking about adding more to my menu. Serving full meals instead of just baked goods and coffee."

"Sounds good, if you can find the time. I still say you need to hire some help." He used another blob of dough to scrape a large drop of filling from the bottom of a bowl. "Mmm." He closed his eyes blissfully. "Do you cook as well as you bake?"

Elizabeth slid the pies from the oven to the counter. "That's just it. I don't. Soup is about the extent of my abilities. But I ought to be able to put together something simple, don't you think? Venison stew and biscuits, perhaps?"

"Sure, that's about all they serve over at the Juniper House, and I know I'd rather look at you while I'm eating than stare at Mr. Bernard's scruffy beard."

Michael walked across the open plaza, enjoying the late afternoon sun. With this contract to deliver freight for the new mercantile, he was set for a profitable summer. Now, if he could keep his drivers on the road and the Indians from stealing his teams, he could begin to expand.

Glancing toward Elizabeth's bakery, he thought of heading over there to sample one of the new pastries she had added. No, better not. If he kept on eating her wares, more than his business would expand.

The tinny sounds of a saloon piano jarred his thoughts and filled the air with a crude melody. Knots of well-dressed men and women clustered along the west side of the plaza, looking across toward Whiskey Row. Michael shook his head. He would never cease to be amazed by the way Prescott's upstanding citizens felt comfortable standing and listening to the songs that emanated from the saloons, places they would never be seen entering.

The rapt expressions on the faces of a group opposite the Nugget caught his attention. Drawn by the haunting voice that floated across the way, he walked over to join them.

"Beautiful, isn't it?" the woman nearest him murmured.

Michael nodded, so captivated by the sweet tones he couldn't bring himself to speak. The clear notes drifted outside on the early summer breeze. The same voice singing the same song that had captured his interest once before.

"Each time I see the sun set
Beyond the distant hills,
My heart remembers how far you have gone.
So think of me each evening,
And until you come again,
I'll dream of you in our dear mountain home."

The song ended to raucous cheers from the saloon's patrons. The listeners on the plaza let out a collective sigh.

"What a lovely voice!" a woman exclaimed.

"Yes, it's a shame she chose to waste it in a barroom." Her male companion led her away, and the rest of the group dispersed.

Michael bristled at the comments. Did they really believe any woman would go into that life if she had any choice? And one with as sweet and pure a voice as that?

He turned to go back to his office, but his feet refused to carry him there. He looked back over his shoulder at the saloon. Someone rattled the piano keys in a noisy rendition of a Stephen Foster melody. Apparently, the singer was taking a break.

Michael started to leave again and, once more, found he couldn't. *What is it, Lord? Are You trying to tell me something?*

The Nugget pulled at him like a magnet, drawing him across the street. Michael followed the compulsion, wondering with every step what he was getting himself into.

When he reached the boardwalk, the jangling piano tune ceased, and the plaintive soprano voice started in again.

"Brennan came riding across the broad moor,
His beautiful maiden to find.
'Oh, where have they hidden that comely young lass,
That raven-haired sweetheart of mine?' "

Michael reached the entrance of the Nugget. He gripped the top of the rough swinging door, clenching his hand until he could feel slivers of wood dig into his palm. *Lord, if this is You, You're leading me into some awfully strange places.*

Hoping he hadn't lost his mind, he pushed open the door and stepped into the saloon.

Michael blinked, adjusting his eyes to the dimness after the bright sunlight outside. No one paid the slightest attention to his entrance, which suited him fine. The saloons of Prescott were hardly his usual haunts, although his father spent plenty of time in them.

He sidled along the back wall to a pocket of shadow and stood riveted, his gaze focused on the girl on the stage.

The noisy hubbub ceased, and the men turned their attention to the singer, to all appearances as entranced as Michael.

The girl sang on, her eyes fixed on a point high above Michael's head, paying no heed to her audience. The lamplight created a halo effect around her blond hair and brought out its reddish glints. She was small, Michael noted, though taller than Elizabeth. Her frame seemed much too small to house such a glorious voice.

Lord, this is no hardened saloon girl. Look at that sweet face. What is she doing here? Michael watched, fascinated by the contrast between her and the painted women hanging on the customers near the bar.

She wore a plain, pale blue dress and no makeup, hardly the garb one would expect in such a place. The dim lighting of the shadowy interior accentuated the deep wells of sadness in her eyes. The more he watched, the more Michael's confusion grew. Who could this girl be? And what was the purpose of his coming here?

The wistful song ended, and once again, the listening men offered loud applause. The young girl stepped off the low stage and made her way through the boisterous crowd, ignoring the crude comments and invitations as she shouldered past the leering patrons.

She started for the staircase at the back of the saloon. A burly, flat-eyed man near the bar shook his head and gestured toward the tables up front. The girl's face pinched in a look of pain.

Holding her head high despite her defeated expression, she walked toward a table where a rowdy group of miners greeted her with loose-lipped smiles.

"Come for a little visit, darlin'? Here, you sweet thing, sit right down beside me."

"There's no room for another chair," another said. "She can sit on my lap." Bawdy laughter erupted as the speaker grabbed the girl's arm and pulled her toward him.

She shook free of his grip and edged away from the group. The man at the bar scowled and started toward her.

Without a second thought, Michael stepped forward and took the girl by the arm. She flinched and whirled to face him, wide-eyed.

He made an effort to control his anger and keep his voice even. "Would you join me over there?" He pointed to an empty table some distance from the pawing drunks.

She stared up at him like a frightened animal, jerking her head back and forth as she looked first at him, then the man by the bar, then at Michael again. He could feel her tremble beneath his touch.

"I only want to talk to you."

Something in his tone seemed to steady her. She nodded briefly and sat down in the chair he held out for her. Michael saw the heavy man at the bar nod smugly.

"My name is Michael O'Roarke." He stared into eyes the color of turquoise. "Do you mind telling me who you are?"

After a long pause, she lowered her gaze to the table and answered. "I'm Jenny. Jenny Davis. And you're the first man who's spoken decently to me since I came here." She raised her head and studied him. "I don't remember seeing you before."

"I'm not exactly a regular. And if you'll forgive me for saying so, you don't look like you belong here, yourself."

Jenny's chin quivered. "I don't, mister. I don't belong here at all."

"Then why. . . ?" Michael held up his hands, then dropped them on the table. "I shouldn't have asked. I'm sorry."

"No, it's all right. It just seems like a long time since anyone cared."

"Do you want to tell me about it?"

She hesitated, then nodded. "I've only been here a month or so. Up until then, I lived with my family on our farm out toward Chino Valley."

"Your family lives nearby, and they don't mind you being part of this?"

"That's just it. They aren't here anymore. They aren't anywhere." Her features grew taut, and she clenched her hands. "The Apaches raided our place a couple of months ago. They killed my ma and pa and my little brother, too. I was out in the root cellar the whole time, so they never knew I was there." She pressed the heels of her hands against her eyes. "But I saw the whole thing. And I heard it." A shudder ran through her body.

Michael reached out and laid his hand on her arm. This time she didn't flinch. "And you came here because you had nowhere else to go?"

She shook her head violently. "I would have died before I came to a place like this on my own. Martin Lester—he was a friend of my pa's—came by the day of the funeral. He showed me some papers where Pa had made him guardian for us kids if anything happened to our folks. Only I was the only one left." She squeezed her eyelids shut. Tiny crystal droplets appeared on her lashes.

"He took me home with him, said he was going to be a father to me. But he. . .he wanted to act more like a husband than a father."

Michael squeezed her hand. "You mean he forced himself on you?"

"No!" Jenny looked around nervously and lowered her voice. "He tried, but I fended him off time after time until he got tired of it. He said he'd spent plenty of money on my room and board and had to get some kind of return on it. So he brought me here. He knows the owner real well." She nodded toward the man at the bar. "That's Burleigh Ames. They're good friends. Martin traded me to Burleigh for a supply of whiskey."

"Traded you?" This time Michael was the one who had to lower his voice. "You mean he thinks he owns you?"

"He doesn't think so, mister. He knows so."

"What does he have you do here?" Michael asked slowly, not sure he wanted to know the answer.

"He makes me sing for my room and board. So far, I've kept from having to go further, but he's pushing me in that direction all the time."

She laid her fingers on Michael's forearm, her touch as light as a butterfly's wing. "And it's wearing me down. I'm terrified I'll turn out to be like one of them." She flicked a glance toward the rear of the building, where two laughing women helped a drunken miner stagger up the back stairs.

She turned back to Michael and shook her head. "I don't know why I'm telling you this. Maybe it's because you're the first person who's been willing to listen."

"I think I know why." He'd been led here for a purpose; he felt sure of it.

"How about if I help you get away from here?"

"You mean escape? Are you crazy? He'd kill me if I tried that."

"Where do you sleep?" At Jenny's startled look, Michael held up his hand. "I only need to know so I can plan the best way to get you out of here. What time do things settle down around here?"

"Everyone's pretty well gone by midnight. And my room's upstairs, right at the back."

"Can you stay awake until then? Be ready to meet me in the back alley at, say, one o'clock?"

Jenny's eyes were blue-green pools of wonder. "I can do that. But I still think you're crazy. Where am I supposed to go?"

Where indeed? He hadn't considered anything beyond actually getting Jenny off the premises. She would need a place to stay, someone strong to protect and guide her. A broad grin stretched across his face.

"I know just the place. You'll be safe there, I promise."

Jenny gave him a long, measuring look. He could understand her hesitation. After what she'd been through, why should she trust him. . .or any man, for that matter?

Finally, she nodded. "I don't know a thing about you, Michael O'Roarke, except your name and that you're a good listener. Whatever you have in mind, it can't be worse than what I've already gone through. I may be as crazy as you are, but I'll trust you."

"Good. I'll meet you out back, then. One o'clock."

Michael shouldered his way through the crowd. He caught Burleigh Ames glaring at him when he neared the door. *No, I didn't buy a drink, did I? And I'm going to cost you a lot more than that if my plan works out.*

Chapter 14

A heavy blanket of clouds massed overhead, shrouding the town and blocking out the moon's light. Michael crept along the alleyway behind the row of saloons.

His foot sent an empty bottle rattling across the gravel and he froze, listening. The darkness worked to his advantage in keeping him unseen, but he would have given a lot for just a bit of light right now.

A soft breeze stirred the treetops. From farther down the street, he heard a woman's shrill laugh. No one seemed to be aware of his presence, or if they were, they didn't care. He advanced a few yards farther and checked his position. The Nugget should be the next building down.

He picked his way along the alley and pressed against the wall. Now what? He should have arranged some sort of signal, but the thought hadn't occurred to him. Was Jenny still in her room or outside waiting for him?

He didn't want to risk making a sound, but he didn't have much choice. "Jenny?" The low whisper wasn't much louder than the breeze.

A dark figure detached itself from the blackness and moved toward him. "I'm here."

She wore a hooded cloak of a dark material that blended into the night. When she raised her head, he could just make out the pale oval of her face.

Michael put his arm around her shoulders and felt her muscles tense. "Don't be afraid. I just need to know where you are so I can guide us out of here."

They moved through the darkness step by cautious step. Michael's pulse raced in direct contrast to their slow pace. Every instinct screamed at him to run, but to do so would be to invite discovery.

The hair on the back of his neck stood on end. At any moment, he expected the rear door of the Nugget to fly open to reveal Burleigh Ames in pursuit.

They reached Gurley Street without incident, and Michael allowed himself to believe they might actually make good their escape.

"Do you know where we are?"

Jenny shook her head. "I hardly ever came into town when we lived on the farm. And I haven't been outside once since Burleigh had me."

"We're going to follow this street for a ways, then cross the plaza. Come on." He took her hand and led the way.

Near the middle of the plaza, Jenny pulled back. "Where are you taking me?"

"To the Capital Bakery, just ahead. It belongs to a friend of mine. A woman friend." Jenny hesitated only a moment, then allowed him to guide her the rest of the way.

At Elizabeth's back door, she gripped his arm. "She didn't mind the idea of taking me in, once she knew where I've been?"

I knew I forgot something. "I'm sure she'll be happy to help." Michael raised his hand and tapped on the door.

"You mean you haven't told her about me?" Jenny's voice rose in panic. "She doesn't know I'm coming?"

"Don't worry. It'll be fine." *Lord, please let it be all right.*

Elizabeth stood outside her home in Philadelphia. All the lights were on, as though a party was in progress. She reached for the ornate knocker and let it fall.

Tap. Tap. Tap.

Why didn't they let her in? Why didn't someone answer the door?

Tap. Tap.

Elizabeth rolled over and sat up in her bed. Her hair draped over her shoulder in a loose braid. She wiped the sleep from her eyes, amazed at how real her dream had seemed.

Tap. Tap.

The low murmur of voices carried into her sleeping quarters. Elizabeth scrubbed her face with her hands and got up, pulling a blanket around her shoulders.

Padding across the plank floor in her bare feet, she pressed her lips close to the back door. "Who is it?"

"It's Michael. I need your help."

She glanced down at her thin nightgown. She really ought to go get dressed first, but he sounded desperate. She wrapped the blanket more closely around her and swung the door open.

"Michael, what time is it? What. . . ?" She scrabbled for a match.

"Don't light the lamp until the door's closed. We need to get inside without being seen."

We? For the first time she noticed the dark figure behind him. The strain in his voice told her something was seriously wrong. "Come inside, then. Hurry." She bolted the door and lit the lamp.

Michael, dressed in dark pants and shirt, looked at her with an anxious gaze and turned his hat in his hands. Beside him stood a wary-eyed young girl in a deep blue cloak.

Elizabeth glanced down at her nightgown, bare toes, and makeshift wrap, then back at Michael. "Would you mind telling me what's going on?"

"This is Jenny Davis." Michael urged the girl forward. "She needs a place to stay."

You bring a total stranger—and a lovely one at that—to my door in the dead of night and expect me to make her welcome? What is going on, Michael O'Roarke?

The silence grew while she hesitated. Jenny stared at Elizabeth as if expecting her to order her back outside. Her chin lifted defiantly, a gesture that reminded Elizabeth of herself.

"You don't have to let me stay if you don't want to," she said. "I'll understand."

Elizabeth's gaze met Michael's over the girl's head. He sent her a pleading glance and silently mouthed, "Please."

Whatever was happening here, it was plain Michael needed her help. "Of course you may stay," she said.

Michael's shoulders sagged in obvious relief, and he gave the girl's shoulder a squeeze. "You're in good hands for tonight, Jenny. I'll come back in the morning, and we'll figure out what to do next."

"You're leaving?" Jenny's tone bordered on panic.

"Just for a few hours. You'll be safe here, I promise."

"He can stay a few minutes longer while I fix a place for you to sleep." Elizabeth gave Michael a look that dared him to do otherwise. She hurried to the storeroom, where she piled folded blankets on the floor to make a pallet. Another blanket, rolled tight and stuffed into a pillowcase, would serve as a pillow. Not fancy lodgings, by any means, but adequate for one night. Or what was left of it.

She returned to find Michael watching Jenny, who sagged in a chair. "Your room is just around the corner," Elizabeth told her. "You might as well get settled in for the night." Jenny took the candle Elizabeth handed her and left without a word.

Michael opened the door and stepped outside. "I'll see you in the morning."

"Not so fast." Elizabeth followed him and closed the door behind her. "I'll never get a wink of sleep until I have some answers. Who is your friend, and why is she here?"

"I don't know much about her. I just met her today."

Elizabeth folded her arms. "You certainly build up acquaintances quickly." She felt great satisfaction when he squirmed under her scrutiny.

"I heard her singing at the Nugget—"

"Wait a minute. You're leaving a saloon girl on my doorstep?"

"So I went inside—"

"Now you frequent saloons?"

"And she told me her story."

"I'll bet it was a good one."

"It'll melt your heart." Michael gave a quick overview of Jenny's situation. "She needs a place to stay and someone to protect her. I'll admit I should have asked you first—"

"I won't argue with that."

"But you were the only person I could think of. I couldn't very well take her home with me, could I?"

Not and live to tell about it. "You're right. She needs a place to stay, and I'll keep her for the night. But I'd better not find some gun-toting saloon keeper banging on my door in the middle of the night."

Michael's grin lit up in the moonlight. "Heaven help him if he does."

Elizabeth bolted the door and pushed a chair in front of it for good measure, then carried the lamp to the storeroom. "Do you have everything you need?"

Jenny perched on a sack of flour, still wrapped in her hooded cloak. With her arms folded tightly across her chest and the sullen expression she wore, she reminded Elizabeth of a sulky twelve year old.

"You don't want me here, do you?" The bald statement caught Elizabeth off guard.

"You took me by surprise, that's all. I'm not in the habit of having callers in the wee hours. Do you need to borrow a nightgown?"

"I'll sleep in my dress. I don't want to put you out any more than I already have. Don't worry, I'll be out of your way tomorrow." She loosened the tie at her throat and let the cloak slide off her shoulders.

It took all the restraint Elizabeth could muster to keep from reaching out to touch the golden hair. Gold, with hints of burnished copper, just like Carrie's. "You have beautiful hair," she managed to say.

Jenny looked directly at her for the first time. Blue-green eyes. Carrie's eyes. Elizabeth felt swept away on a wave of homesickness. She remembered the story Michael had whispered to her on the doorstep. "How old are you?"

Jenny's chin jutted forward. "Eighteen."

Only two years older than Carrie. An image of her sister, bereft of family and forced into an intolerable situation, crossed Elizabeth's mind, melting away her suspicion and doubt.

"Jenny, you're welcome here. You can stay with me as long as you like."

Elizabeth lay awake long after she blew out the lamp. She wanted to help Jenny, but. . .how did Michael just happen to come across her, and exactly what did Jenny mean to him?

She's lovely; there's no denying it.

She sighed and punched the pillow, longing for sleep that wouldn't come.

❧

"Is there something I can do to help?"

Elizabeth turned from the counter. Jenny stood diffidently in the doorway, a shy expression replacing the sullen stare of the night before.

"I'm surprised you're up so early. Did you sleep at all?" The dark circles under Jenny's eyes gave her the answer.

Jenny moved two steps closer and peered into the pot Elizabeth was stirring. "What are you doing?"

"Trying to salvage what's left of these mashed potatoes. I'd planned to offer them as part of today's lunch, but they're too runny."

"You ruined mashed potatoes? How could you do that?"

"I managed." Elizabeth wiped her forehead with her sleeve. "I'm afraid cooking is not my strong point."

Jenny moved right up next to her. "It looks like you forgot to drain them."

"You drain them first?" Elizabeth stared at the pot. "Is there any way to fix them?"

Jenny offered her a smile. "You can chop some onion into it and call it potato soup."

Elizabeth laughed ruefully. "So you know how to cook?"

"My ma taught me. I've been doing it for years."

"And you enjoy it?"

"Sure, doesn't everyone?" She grinned. "I don't bake very well, but I can fix a pot roast that'll make your mouth water."

Elizabeth tapped her fingers on the counter. "How would you like a job?"

"Where? You mean here? With you?"

"If you're willing to fix the main meals and teach me to cook, I'll pay you plus give you room and board. What do you think?"

"You'll pay me just to cook?"

"For a large crowd of very hungry men."

"And I can stay here?"

"We'll fix up a more suitable place for you this evening. What do you think, Jenny? You'll be safe here. I won't let anybody hurt you. Do we have a deal?"

Jenny's turquoise eyes misted. "When do I start?"

"Right now. Go out front and add potato soup to the menu."

Chapter 15

Y ou've done wonders with Jenny." Michael cupped his hand under Elizabeth's elbow when she stepped down off the boardwalk.

"She's done wonders for me, you mean. I can't believe I actually have time to stroll outdoors like this. I'm not hurrying out for supplies, just taking a little time to relax. Jenny's doing a wonderful job of handling things, although I only leave her on her own when I know she won't have to deal with a crowd of customers." They walked across Cortez Street and circled the perimeter of the plaza. A dusty haze softened the glare of the westering sun and gave the scene a gentle glow.

Elizabeth sauntered alongside Michael, content just to enjoy the pleasure of his company. When they turned back in the direction of the restaurant, she felt her steps dragging. It would be nice to shake off responsibility for just one day, to leave the demands of her business behind and go for a picnic under the pines with Michael.

Across the street, a figure strode toward them. Elizabeth stiffened when she recognized Letitia Bartlett. Letitia noticed Elizabeth at the same moment. She stood stock-still and stared directly at her. Even at that distance, Elizabeth could see the malevolent gleam in her eyes. Letitia's lips curled back in a snarl. She stretched her arm out like a prophetess pronouncing judgment and pointed straight at Elizabeth, her thin hand trembling wildly.

Suddenly, the restaurant seemed like the perfect place to be. Before she could say a word, Michael took her arm and veered between two buildings, safely out of the reach of Letitia Bartlett.

Elizabeth cast one last glance over her shoulder. Letitia stood in the same position, like a statue, still staring, still pointing.

"Thank you," she said, hurrying to keep pace with Michael's long strides.

He patted her hand where she clutched at his elbow. "I had a feeling she was the last person in the world you wanted to see right now."

"I'm ashamed to admit it, but you're right." She hadn't seen Letitia since that explosive morning in the Bartletts' kitchen and didn't care to renew her acquaintance. Her breath came in quick gasps. "I think we can slow down now."

"Sure, we're almost there anyway." He reached for the knob to open the door.

Elizabeth entered eagerly. Never before had it seemed such a place of refuge. She looked around the empty dining room with a sense of coming home.

Home. Despite her near miss with Letitia, excitement rippled inside her. She walked to the window and planted her hands on the sill.

Outside, the laughter of early evening strollers gave an air of peace to this place. It was a good place.

Her place.

Elizabeth's heart swelled. Out here in this raw land, she had found the focus for her life, the place where she could truly be herself. This restaurant would be a place of shelter, a haven for both herself and Jenny.

"Thank you for that wonderful break, Michael. It was just what I needed." She turned back to him, stood on her toes, and kissed his cheek. "Good night."

❦

"Where is she?" The rasping voice carried all the way back to the kitchen.

Jenny hurried in from the dining room, round-eyed. "Someone's asking for you."

"So I heard." Elizabeth covered a mound of pie crust dough with a damp dish towel and wiped the flour from her hands before going to see who the belligerent visitor might be. She pushed open the swinging door and stopped as though she'd walked into a tree.

The walls of her sanctuary had been breached.

Letitia Bartlett stood in the center of the dining room, her mouth set in a grim line, body rigid, face contorted. "So here you are!"

Not here, not in front of her customers. "Let's go into the back, shall we?" Elizabeth gripped the woman's bony arm and propelled her past Jenny and the gaping patrons.

Letitia shook off Elizabeth's hand as soon as they reached the kitchen. "Was this your plan all along?"

Elizabeth looked around at the restaurant she had built. "My plan?" She edged away, wishing she hadn't positioned Letitia between her and the door. The woman's manner seemed positively demented.

"Don't play the innocent with me!" An ugly red color suffused Letitia's face. She moved closer to Elizabeth. "You played us for fools from the beginning, didn't you?"

What could she use to defend herself? Elizabeth took a quick inventory of the items within her reach: spoons, bowls, a pastry cloth—those wouldn't be of any use. The maple rolling pin might come in handy, though.

She tried to inject a soothing note into her voice. "I'm not sure what you mean."

Letitia swept her arm along the counter, knocking three freshly baked pies to the floor. "Did you imagine we wouldn't find out?"

Lord, help me! She's gone crazy.

Letitia continued to advance. Elizabeth took a step back and bumped against the counter. Without taking her gaze off Letitia, she stretched out her hand along the wooden surface. Her fingers closed around the rolling pin and gripped it tight.

"I saw you yesterday. Don't try to deny it. I know you saw me, too, even though you tried to pretend you didn't."

Was that what this tirade was all about?

"How long have the two of you been walking out together?"

Elizabeth shook her head slowly. "What does this have to do with Michael?"

"Which one of you came up with the idea to cheat us out of our money, you or him?"

"Cheat you? Whatever are you talking about?"

"As if you didn't know! I'm talking about the money we were promised for bringing you together."

Elizabeth pressed her free hand against her throbbing temple. "Does this have something to do with your arrangement to sell me off as someone's wife?" The memory of that nightmare made her temper flare anew.

"Spare me your theatrics. I'll admit you had us fooled, standing there in our kitchen and acting so horrified at the idea of us making you a fine match. And here you've been seeing him behind our backs all the time!"

Letitia's accusation sliced through the confusing fog like a lighthouse beacon. From the dining room, Elizabeth could hear low voices and the faint clink of silverware. Out there, life went on as usual. In the kitchen, time stood still.

She let go of the rolling pin and clasped her hands against her middle. When she was five, a visiting relative's son had punched her in the stomach. She felt the same sense of shock, the same inability to breathe now.

Only back then, James had been around to come to her aid, giving the boy a taste of his own medicine before sending him howling back to his parents.

James wasn't here now.

Michael was.

Michael.

Closing her eyes against the pain, she focused all her efforts on drawing one long, deep breath. "Are you saying that Michael O'Roarke is the man you were supposed to find a wife for?"

"He's Timothy O'Roarke's son, isn't he?"

Elizabeth wrapped one arm around her roiling stomach and used the other to pull herself up.

"Get out." She lifted her head and stared straight at Letitia.

"Don't think you've heard the last of this."

"I said, get out of my restaurant. Now."

Letitia started to speak, then took another look at Elizabeth's face. She snapped her mouth closed and left without another word.

Elizabeth let herself sink down to the floor. The hard surface bit into her knees but couldn't hold a candle to the pain that twisted through her heart.

Michael, a party to the Bartletts' sordid scheme?

She couldn't believe it—didn't want to believe it.

But Letitia's anger had been all too real.

She wrapped both arms around her middle and rocked forward until her head rested on her knees. Hadn't Michael supported her, encouraged her, shown her friendship? But he'd never mentioned his father, not once. Because he and his father didn't get along or because he didn't want to admit to being in on a devious plot?

She remembered his outrage on learning how Richard had squandered her money. Had his indignation been real or feigned?

Just yesterday, he had seemed to pick up on her unwillingness to face Letitia and helped her hurry away. A chivalrous gesture or an attempt to keep her from learning the truth?

Her Michael, a deceiver?

And when, she wondered, had she started thinking of him as "her" Michael?

No more. She wiped her tear-soaked cheeks with her palms and pulled herself to her feet. She would have to deal with Michael's perfidy another time.

Right now, there were customers to attend to and pies to bake.

⁂

"Are you all right?" Jenny asked, coming into the kitchen.

Elizabeth slapped a ball of pie crust dough onto the counter. "Why do you ask?"

Jenny watched her pound it into a flat, round disk with the side of her fist. "Didn't you tell me light pastry required a light touch? You look like you'd rather be punching someone in the face."

The idea didn't sound half bad. At the moment, she had no lack of ideas for potential targets. Still, her customers didn't need to suffer for her inner turmoil. She stepped back from the counter and took a series of slow, calming breaths.

"It was that woman, wasn't it?" Jenny went on. "The one who came in here this morning. You've barely spoken since she left."

Elizabeth rolled the dough out with smooth, even strokes and settled the crust into a waiting pie tin. "She said some things that upset me, but I shouldn't be taking it out on you. You had nothing to do with it." *Unless Michael O'Roarke planned to deceive you, too. In which case, I will most definitely punch him in the nose!*

Jenny brightened. "I'm glad. I was afraid I might have done something wrong."

"No, I just found out I was wrong about someone, and that's never pleasant. But I'll get over it. No harm's been done." *Except to my pride. And my heart.*

She rolled out the rest of the dough and lined the other pie tins. Cutting vents into the top crusts for the steam to escape and crimping the edges together kept her hands moving, soothing her with the practiced motions of a familiar task. She slid the four pies into the oven.

"There. While those are baking, how about that lesson in making gravy?"

Jenny dipped a spoon into the gravy and brought it to her lips. "Perfect," she proclaimed.

"It can't be," Elizabeth stated. "I've never made perfect gravy in my life or any that was remotely close to perfect." She sampled her own spoonful, and her eyes widened. "It isn't bad, is it? I can't believe it. Why didn't anyone ever tell me cooking could be this much fun?"

"Wait until I teach you to make fried chicken. Then we'll try baked ham."

"And roast turkey?"

"That, too." A knock at the back door interrupted their laughter.

"I'll get it." Jenny pulled off her apron and started toward the door.

"No, let me." Elizabeth hurried past her. The thought that Burleigh Ames could be searching for Jenny kept Elizabeth vigilant.

She pulled the door open a crack and looked out.

"It's a beautiful evening," Michael said, smiling. "How about a walk in the moonlight?"

Angry tears stung her eyes, and she blinked them back. She would not show him how he'd hurt her.

"I can't, Michael, I'm much too busy tonight."

His smile dimmed only a fraction. "Then why don't I come in, and we can talk while you work?"

"No, Jenny and I have a lot to do. Girl things." She started to close the door. Michael reached up and blocked it with his palm. Concern creased his forehead.

"Tomorrow, then? I can come by right after you close."

Elizabeth felt her throat closing. A deep heartache compressed her chest. "I'm afraid I'm going to be unavailable then, too. It's a really busy time." Michael stared at her a moment, then withdrew his hand and walked away.

She bolted the door before he could say anything more. Tears threatened, and she turned to hurry to her room before they spilled over. Jenny stood behind her, leaning against the wall with her arms folded.

"It's him, isn't it? I thought it was just that awful old woman, but it has something to do with Michael, too, doesn't it?"

Elizabeth held her head high and tried to draw a deep breath. Instead, she heard a ragged gasp. She squeezed her eyelids shut. She would not cry. She would not lose control.

The tears slid past her closed lids and down her cheeks. She felt Jenny's arm slip around her shoulders.

"Even a white knight gets knocked off his horse sometimes. Now, what are those girl things we're going to be doing this evening?"

Chapter 16

Elizabeth stood by the counter watching Jenny work, but her thoughts kept going back over the last week. She truly had kept busy, but mostly to prevent herself from thinking too much.

"Like this?" Jenny lapped one side of the thin circle of dough over the other and lifted it cautiously. The tip of her tongue protruded from one corner of her mouth.

"That's right." Elizabeth fought back the urge to reach out and help. Jenny had to learn on her own—was determined to, in fact. Elizabeth had come to realize that Jenny had a streak of independence that rivaled her own.

Jenny settled the folded dough in place atop a peach pie, then spread it open again and let out a pent-up breath. "I always have a problem with the next part." She pressed the tip of her thumb and the knuckle of her first finger at the rim of the pie plate, then used her other thumb to push the overlapping dough into the vee they formed.

She looked at her work and beamed. "That looks pretty good, though, doesn't it?"

"Just right," Elizabeth affirmed.

Jenny continued to work around the rim of the pie, methodically crimping the edges. Elizabeth dampened a cloth and began wiping down the counter.

"You're getting better every day, Jenny. Pretty soon, I'll be able to turn all the cooking over to you."

Jenny laughed. "Not anytime soon. I still don't quite have the hang of this." Her hands moved in rhythm now, pinching and pushing the dough into sharp peaks.

"You'll see." Elizabeth scooped the loose flour into a pile and swept it off the counter into her cupped hand. "Before long, I'll be able to sit back and become a lady of leisure. I thank God every day that He brought you here. But I'm sure you've already thanked Him plenty of times for getting you out of the hands of men like your guardian and that saloon keeper."

Jenny's hands stilled. Elizabeth could see the girl's shoulders tense beneath her light blue dress. "No, and that won't happen anytime soon, either," Jenny murmured. She shoved the dough into a lopsided mound. "I don't think God is all that interested in hearing what I have to say."

Elizabeth paused in the act of dusting the flour off her hands. "You aren't serious, are you? Of course He is. God loves you, Jenny."

"Really? He sure has a funny way of showing it." Her hands moved like uncoordinated pistons.

"He brought you here. He got you out of that horrid place."

"I wound up there because I wouldn't put up with Martin Lester's advances. And that wouldn't have happened if my parents hadn't died." Jenny's voice choked off.

"But surely you can see—"

"Do you have any idea what it's like to hide in the darkness of a root cellar and know your family's being massacred? To hear your ma plead for mercy and find none?"

"Jenny, I—"

"To peek out long enough to see your little brother run away and try to get back to the cabin, then hear him scream and know he didn't make it?" She picked up a lump of dough and squeezed it until it oozed through her fingers.

Elizabeth kneaded the damp cloth in her hands, praying for the right words. But how could any words make sense of Jenny's loss? "I can't answer that. I have no idea why He would allow that to happen. All I can say is that He must have something planned for you, some reason you were spared."

"Spared?" Jenny slammed her hand on the counter, flattening the dough under her palm. "You call it being spared when I live with those images every day of my life? When I wake up at night thinking I hear my mama screaming?"

"But the Bible says—"

"I know. I remember the stories. He's supposed to love everyone. I thought He loved me. Maybe He did, once. But He didn't love me when that was happening. And He can't love me anymore. Not after the saloon."

"That wasn't your doing, any of it. You didn't choose to be in that place."

Jenny picked up the dough again and rolled it into a ball. "Being pawed like that was enough to make me feel like I'd already become like those other girls. But I never did go upstairs with any man. Not once. And it wasn't all the men who came in there who were bad. Some of them just ignored me. It was the other ones, the ones who'd had too much to drink. They'd grab me when I walked by, grab me and. . ." She threw down the dough and covered her face with her hands. Her shoulders heaved.

Elizabeth wrapped her arms around the sobbing girl and pulled her close. "It's over, Jenny. Over for good. No one is going to treat you like that again." She stroked the soft golden hair. "And Jenny? You can trust God. He does love you."

Jenny straightened and backed away, mopping her blotchy face with her hands. "What about Michael? I think he loves you, but you don't trust him." She turned on her heel and ran to her room.

Elizabeth stared after her. "Oh Lord, how do I get through to her? It's not the same at all. Michael couldn't love me and be a party to that vile scheme. I don't *want* him to love me. Do I?"

Michael's horse brought him through the trees to the edge of town. His mule herd was grazing about three miles from Fort Whipple, and the herders hadn't had any trouble from Indians. His competition had all lost animals to raids, but so far, God continued to protect his business.

His stomach growled on the way down the hill into town. He could go home and make do with whatever he could find on his shelves. *But I want a real meal.* He reached the plaza. The Pine Cone Eatery would have chili, if his stomach could handle all the chili powder they used to cover up the taste of spoiled meat.

He glanced across the plaza, and his gaze locked on the Capital Restaurant. The pain of being ignored warred with his longing for a good meal.

Hunger won out. As soon as he put his horse away, he'd wash off the trail dust and head straight for the restaurant and a decent supper.

If Elizabeth didn't throw him out.

Michael pondered the situation all the while he brushed and fed his horse and sluiced water over his head and arms. Elizabeth's first refusal to go walking had puzzled him, but he'd put it down to pressures of the business. That he could accept. But her subsequent rejections didn't seem to have any logical explanation. He put on a clean shirt and headed out the door. Maybe the extra hours spent training Jenny were taking their toll.

Jenny. Michael snapped his fingers. Could Jenny have done something to cause Elizabeth's sudden change in attitude?

But that didn't explain why she'd taken such a sudden aversion to him. Unless she blamed him for Jenny's presence in her life. Michael nodded his head. *It's my fault.*

Looking back, he knew he'd made a mistake in not telling Elizabeth about his plans to rescue Jenny ahead of time. He thought she'd taken their surprise midnight visit rather well, but obviously, that wasn't the case. That must be it. He grinned, pleased at having discovered the source of the trouble.

He crossed the plaza with a lighter step. A man couldn't fix a problem if he didn't know what was wrong. Now that he did, he would talk to Elizabeth, apologize, and get back in her good graces.

He could spend time at the restaurant again without feeling like a pariah. She'd even go out walking with him again. That would be nice. He really missed her company.

He missed her spunk, her wit. Missed her smile and that green fire in her eyes when she got riled.

"Face it," he told himself, "you miss *her*, pure and simple. This is more than friendship."

He felt the truth of his words. Without him noticing, Elizabeth had captured his heart. . .had become so much a part of the fabric of his life that he couldn't imagine having any kind of happiness without her.

With a prayer for God to work it all out, he walked into the restaurant. Jenny stood taking an order from a table of miners. He smiled and gave her a brief wave, then sat down near the window. When she came to take his order, he could ask to see Elizabeth.

He would offer his apology, she would accept, and things would smooth out just fine. Heartened by the knowledge that they'd soon be laughing over their little misunderstanding, he scanned the menu tacked to a board on the wall. His stomach rumbled as he perused the list: venison steak, roast beef, venison pie. . . . The roast beef, he decided. Just the thing for a hungry man who wanted something tasty under his belt before he had to dine on crow.

Jenny headed his way, a smile of welcome lighting her face as she threaded her way between the tables.

"Well, hello, little darlin'." A grimy, middle-aged man scooted his chair back, barring her way. Jenny halted abruptly, then gave him a tight smile and circled to her left.

The man stood quickly and blocked her path. "Don't you recognize me, sweet thing?"

Other customers interrupted their conversations and turned to watch. Jenny's eyes darted back and forth like a hunted animal seeking a way to escape.

A pulse throbbed in Michael's throat. He jumped to his feet and waded through a sea of empty chairs, shoving them aside like Moses parting the waters.

"Aw, come on. I know you remember. When you were singing over at the Nugget, I used to think your songs were meant just for me." The man made a lunge for Jenny's wrist. Michael redoubled his speed.

Before he could reach Jenny, the door to the kitchen flew open and a whirlwind erupted.

"What do you think you're doing?" Elizabeth, all five foot two of her, glared up at the man, a diminutive David ready to take on Goliath.

"No need to get upset, little lady. I'm just renewing an old acquaintance. This little gal and I are friends from the Nugget, aren't we?" He gave Jenny a suggestive wink. She pivoted on her heel and escaped through the swinging door to the kitchen.

Elizabeth pointed to the door. "Get out of my restaurant before I have you arrested."

"This doesn't concern you." His meaty hand reached out as if to brush Elizabeth aside.

Michael blocked the movement by grabbing a handful of the man's shirt and swinging him around in one motion. "You heard the lady. It's time to leave."

Jenny's tormentor started to swing, then took a second look at Michael and reconsidered. He stepped back, loosening the wad of fabric at his throat.

"Sure, mister. There's no problem here. Just a little misunderstanding, that's all." He picked up his hat and backed toward the door, giving Michael a wide berth.

Not until the door swung shut behind the retreating form did Michael turn back to Elizabeth. "Are you all right?"

She nodded, her eyes still focused on the doorway. "Thank you for stepping in." Her gaze met his for a brief moment, then skittered away. "Jenny needs me," she muttered and disappeared into the kitchen.

The other customers, deprived of any better entertainment, focused their attention on him. Michael looked once more at the list of delectable offerings, then headed for the front door and home.

His appetite had disappeared.

❧

"Jenny?" Elizabeth tapped again on the girl's door and huffed out a frustrated sigh when she got no answer. That Jenny needed to be with someone was obvious. That she had every intention of keeping the rest of the world—Elizabeth included—at arm's length was equally clear.

Elizabeth pressed her forehead against the door frame. She needed to see Jenny, talk to her, and make sure she was all right. Together, they could pray and lay the whole ugly incident in the hands of the only One who could take the pain out of Jenny's past.

She needed to get back to her customers, especially now that it appeared she would be waiting tables and manning the kitchen on her own for the time being. She needed to decide what to say to Michael back in the dining room.

I can't go that many directions at once, Lord! The wood bit into her forehead. She pushed away from the door frame and rubbed the tender spot, hoping the pressure hadn't left a mark. The last thing she needed right now was one more reason for her customers to gawk at her.

That odious man! The memory of his effrontery and Jenny's white face brought the moment back all over again. What right did he have, coming into her place of business and casting aspersions on Jenny's character, right in front of a roomful of people?

If Michael hadn't stepped in when he did. . .

If Michael hadn't stepped in, she'd have thrown the lout out herself. His willingness to help had been appreciated, though surprising, but she would have been perfectly capable of handling the situation on her own.

Just like she'd be capable of going on with the rest of her life without Michael's assistance. The knowledge left a raw wound, but she reminded herself of the need to be strong. How could she ever trust someone who would stoop to scheming with the Bartletts?

She couldn't. Life had seemed for a moment to hold such promise. But the lovely dream had turned out to be a nightmare instead. She would have to wake up to reality and go on.

Bracing herself for the encounter, she pushed through the door to the dining room. A dozen faces, still alive with curiosity, turned to greet her.

None of them belonged to Michael.

Her shoulders sagged, and she felt as though the wind had been let out of her sails. Relief, she assured herself.

Really? That empty sensation felt a lot like disappointment.

Disappointment? At not seeing Michael O'Roarke? Ridiculous! She had no patience with the man and not the slightest desire to talk to him again, not after what he had done.

Chapter 17

"*Pssst!*" From his vantage point behind a bush across the alley in back of the restaurant, Michael watched Jenny jump as if shot and fall back against the building's rough wooden exterior. Maybe he should have made his presence known a little more openly.

"It's me," he said, standing and stepping out into the alley behind the restaurant.

"Michael!" Jenny fanned herself with her hand and looked down at the old flour sack filled with loose garbage she'd dropped in her fright. Bones, peels, and egg shells lay strewn in the dust. "I thought it was—well, never mind." She stooped and started gathering the trash.

She thought it was Martin Lester, come to take her back, you idiot! "Let me do that." He knelt beside her and picked up a handful of garbage.

"Have at it." Jenny stood and left him to deal with the smelly mess. "I think you scared me out of a year's growth."

Remorse warred with his reason for lurking in the bushes like a thief. "I needed to talk to you."

"Most people would come inside the restaurant to do that."

"No, I need to talk to you. Just you, without Elizabeth around." He picked up the reeking mass of garbage and held it out in front of him. Whatever was dripping found its way down his arm and soaked into his sleeve.

"You won't be able to sneak up on anyone now." Jenny wrinkled her nose and took two steps away from him.

He dropped the sack into the barrel and wiped his hands off. The smell still lingered. He moved downwind from Jenny, wishing he could move upwind of himself. "It's about Elizabeth," he began. "What's going on? I thought she enjoyed spending time with me, but now she won't give me the time of day."

Jenny's eyes grew round. "You mean you don't know?" She shook her head. "The way she's been acting, I was certain the two of you had some kind of argument."

"Nope. One day we're the best of friends, and the next she's refusing to walk out with me and treating me like a leper. I was hoping you'd know."

Jenny's brow furrowed. "She hasn't been the same since that horrid woman came to the restaurant. Something was said that upset Elizabeth, I'm sure of it, but I have no idea what it was. . .or what connection you have with it all."

"Connection? Me?" Michael's mind whirled as he tried—and failed—to make some sense of what he heard. What woman? What had she said? And how could it possibly involve him?

"I'd better get back inside." Jenny's voice interrupted his thoughts. "Elizabeth worries if I'm outside on my own. And for a moment there, I thought she was right!" She gave a shaky laugh.

Michael put out his hand to stop her. "If you hear anything about what I'm supposed to have done, will you let me know?" He gave Jenny a quick hug. "And I'm sorry I scared you."

Jenny's half smile spoke of her pity for his plight. "I'll do what I can to find out," she promised. "But don't get your hopes up too high."

"What if I wait out here every night and try to catch Elizabeth?"

"I'm the one who takes the trash out." Jenny smiled. "You might do better not to scare her like you did me."

❦

"Excuse me, we'd like to place our order." The plump matron waved Elizabeth toward her table in the manner of a queen summoning an underling.

Elizabeth shifted the tray of dirty dishes to one hip and tried to smile. "I'll let Jenny know you're ready," she told the woman and her two companions. "She'll be right out."

"Just a moment." The spokeswoman held up her hand in an imperious gesture, halting Elizabeth's escape. "We would prefer you did it. I have heard that the food is good here, but I have no desire to have any dealings with. . ." She lowered her voice. "She *is* the one who used to work at that awful saloon, is she not?" Her lower chin wobbled indignantly as her companions nodded their agreement.

Elizabeth set the tray down on a neighboring table with a crash, unmindful of the rattle of crockery. Her anger erupted in a rush. "Jenny Davis is a fine young woman, with more decency than the three of you put together!"

All three ladies squawked in protest. "How dare you speak to us like that!" their leader demanded. "We will not be treated this way!"

"Then maybe you would prefer eating elsewhere." Elizabeth fixed the trio with a gimlet stare while they gathered their things and trooped out. She swept up the tray and made her way back to the kitchen, ignoring the stares that followed her. Would this kind of thing keep happening? *How does a person restore a damaged reputation?*

At least Jenny hadn't heard the disparaging comments. . .this time. But what about the next time? And the next?

It would be so much easier for Jenny if she let God be a part of her life. Then she could let Him help her carry her burdens. And Jenny had plenty of those. *I don't know what to say to her. I don't know why You let all those things happen or why this is happening now. Maybe You can even use something like this to draw Jenny to*

You, although it's hard for me to see how.

Despite her anger at her three former customers, she felt a small thrill of victory. She'd dealt with today's confrontation—without the help of Michael O'Roarke. The knowledge brought mingled pleasure and pain.

"I'll take this trash out, Jenny."

Jenny scrambled for a dish towel and wiped her hands free of soapsuds. "I can do it. I don't mind."

"No, you go on washing those dishes. You've taken care of the trash every night for a week now. I'm surprised you haven't complained about having to handle the smelly stuff."

"You may be surprised about more than just that."

Elizabeth had to strain to hear Jenny's cryptic remark. With a quizzical glance, she gathered up the rubbish and went out. Outside, she savored a long, slow breath of the evening air. Look at that sunset! Thumb Butte wore its display of vivid violets and crimsons like a royal robe. It would be wonderful just to walk among the pines and enjoy all this beauty as she used to with Michael. Before. She dumped the lard tin into the garbage barrel and turned to go back inside.

Michael stood waiting on the doorstep.

Elizabeth eyed him warily. Arms folded across his chest, feet planted well apart, he looked like a man ready to withstand an army.

Shock surged into anger. The nerve of the man, thinking he could intimidate her by blocking the way to her own door! She could go right through him if she needed to.

She crossed her arms and prepared for battle. "What do you think you're doing here?"

"I've come for an explanation."

Elizabeth felt the heat rise from her neck to her hairline. She took one step forward, and Michael raised his hands, turning them palm out in a gesture of surrender.

"Please," he said.

The appeal brought her up short, and she looked at him more closely. The same curly, dark hair, the same vivid blue eyes. The same smile that always set her heart dancing. The same features that always made her think of him as her Michael.

How could he look just as before yet cause her heart so much pain? Her Michael? Not anymore.

He seemed to take her hesitation as a sign of a truce and took an eager step forward. "It seems I've done something to upset you, but I don't know what. I'd like nothing more than to have things like they were before, but you'll have to tell me what's wrong."

His feigned innocence took away any softer feelings she was beginning to have. "Wrong?" She planted her fists on her hips. "Did you really think you could keep it from me?"

His puzzled look would have been convincing if she hadn't learned the sorry truth from Letitia. The act sent her anger over the edge.

"What kind of man buys a wife?"

Michael's head snapped back. "What?"

"You heard me. How low does a man have to sink to send off for a wife like he'd place an order for seeds from a catalog?"

The fire of her anger mounted. "At least a mail-order bride answers an advertisement and enters the bargain of her own accord. Not like your despicable scheme." Her words battered Michael back a step. "How could you possibly believe I wouldn't get wind of this? Did you and the Bartletts believe you could pull the wool over my eyes forever, or was it enough to think you could fool me until after the wedding?"

She could feel her arms shaking and knew that tears weren't far away. She grasped the door handle. "I've been played for a fool, and I don't like it a bit. That's what is wrong!"

The door slammed behind her with a most satisfying crash.

※

Michael didn't know how long he stared at the closed door. The echo of Elizabeth's words swirled through his brain like a swarm of angry hornets. He tried to make some sense of the flurry of accusations she had flung at him. What was all that about mail-order brides and buying a wife? Had she been talking about herself when she referred to being sent for like some kind of merchandise?

A smile tugged at his lips in spite of his confusion. Merchandise implied something passive, unable to speak for itself. Elizabeth Simmons would never fit that description.

His mood sobered again. From what he could gather, Elizabeth felt she had been the victim of some kind of scheme and, for some reason, had decided he was part of it. And she obviously had no intention of giving him a chance to defend himself.

And where did the Bartletts fit into this? How could she have gotten the notion that he was in league with them? The very idea of being put in the same category as those two made him feel degraded. The last thing he would ever want to do would be to link his lot with the likes of Richard and Letitia Bartlett.

But he knew someone who would.

Chapter 18

What do you mean, you hired them to find me a wife?" Michael's bellow reverberated off the walls, but the stocky man facing him seemed unmoved.

"I care about my son and his future. There's no crime in that." Timothy O'Roarke rocked back on his heels and puffed on his half-finished cigar, sending a cloud of gray smoke floating toward the ceiling.

Michael stared at the man he called his father, wondering if it was possible for a person to stray so far that they put themselves beyond God's mercy.

"You don't deny it, then? You admit you offered the Bartletts money to lure some unsuspecting woman out here so I could marry her?"

" 'Lure' has such an unpleasant ring to it. I prefer to think of it as bringing out a likely prospect and allowing nature to take its course." Timothy stroked his mustache with the back of his forefinger. "As it did, you must admit." He hooked his thumbs in his waistcoat pockets and stared at Michael with a benevolent smile.

Michael pulled his collar open. "Did you ever once stop to think how Miss Simmons—how *I*—might feel about being pawns in your little game?"

Timothy swung his hand through the air, waving Michael's objection away with the haze of smoke that wreathed his head. "That's why you weren't meant to know about it," he said in a tone of sweet reason. "I thought you might overreact like this. But all's well that ends well, my boy. I've seen the young lady, and I approve. You do, too, apparently." He lowered his eyelid in a suggestive wink.

Michael gritted his teeth. "Unfortunately, the young lady doesn't approve of your methods any more than I do. Especially since she thinks I was a party to the whole thing. That's why you're going to explain it to her."

The cigar drooped in the corner of Timothy's mouth. "I'm going to. . . No, no. I'm sure she'd rather hear it from you, my boy."

"Unfortunately, she doesn't want to hear anything I have to say at the moment." Michael gripped his father's arm above the elbow and steered him toward the door. "But with your cooperation, I'm hoping that's about to change."

※

"Any more orders, Jenny?" Elizabeth set two bowls of venison stew on a serving tray and wiped her brow with her forearm.

"That's the lot, for now at least. It looks like things are slowing down for a bit."

"After that rush at lunchtime, I won't complain."

Jenny laughed. "Why don't you sit down for a while? You look like you could use a break." She picked up the tray and backed through the swinging door. Elizabeth heard her soft gasp and looked up to see Jenny staring into the dining room like one transfixed.

"What's wrong? Another rush?"

Jenny cast a wide-eyed glance over her shoulder. "You could say that." She stepped into the dining room, letting the door swing shut behind her.

A large hand pushed it open on the next swing, and Michael stepped into the room, pushing another man in front of him.

Elizabeth bristled. How dare he enter her restaurant! And straight into her private domain, no less. She opened her mouth to tell him what she thought of his behavior when something about his companion caught her attention.

She took a second look at the man, then a third. What was it about him that triggered that sense of recognition?

A series of scenes came flooding into her mind. Keen eyes studying her from the corner of the Bartletts' parlor. Eyes that probed and judged her.

His eyes. Her skin crawled, just as it had the first time she'd seen him. Who was this man, and why was he standing in her kitchen? She glared at Michael, her lips pressed together and her chin jutting forward, wordlessly demanding an explanation.

Michael's face wore a grim expression. "There's something you need to know, Elizabeth. Something you need to hear. From him." He indicated his companion with a jerk of his head. "Allow me to introduce you to my father, Timothy O'Roarke."

Timothy? Snippets of remembered comments Richard had made flashed through her mind. So this was the man he'd had to report to when he thought she was unavailable. The same Timothy who refused to pay them off once he found out they had no goods to offer him. The reason for Letitia's abusive diatribe.

And Michael's father? The floor tilted beneath her, and she grasped the edge of the counter to keep from falling.

Michael, his brow wrinkled in concern, hurried to support her, but she dashed his arm aside and forced herself to stand upright. "I don't need your assistance."

Timothy O'Roarke. It made sense, now that all the pieces had been put in place. He had struck the deal with the Bartletts. Only natural that he would come by to check out the merchandise.

Elizabeth could see the physical resemblance, the eyes and hair so like Michael's and yet so different. Her breath quickened, and she felt her strength return as her body responded to her anger. How had they managed to contrive her first meetings with Michael? Timothy must be a master puppeteer. . .and she had been his puppet.

"You need to leave. Both of you." Her voice barely quavered. Good.

"Not until you hear what he has to say." Michael's voice held a ring of authority. He prodded his father's shoulder. "Go on, tell her."

Timothy tugged the gaudy waistcoat down over his ample stomach and cleared his throat. "It's really not as big a thing as the boy makes out," he began. "Just a father trying to do what's best for his son."

He flashed a confident grin at Elizabeth, who glowered at him in return. He shifted his gaze and went on.

"You see, I care about my son here. I've worked hard all my life to carve a niche he could step into. He has what it takes to rise to the top. With a little effort on his part, he could be a part of the legislature, even become a senator once this territory becomes a state.

"Only one thing does he lack, and that's a proper wife. One befitting the status he will attain. One who knows the ways of polite society and will be an asset to him when he has to move in the right circles back in Washington.

"In a word, someone like you." He paused and looked straight at her now, narrowing his gaze as if waiting for her reaction.

"And so the two of you and the Bartletts cooked up this conspiracy to bring me out here?"

"Well, not exactly." For the first time, Timothy's confidence seemed to waver. "Michael tends to be a bit stubborn about some things. Takes after his mother that way. I had a feeling—just an inkling, you understand—that he might not see the wisdom of what we were about. I thought it would be better if he learned about it later."

"How much later?"

Timothy shrugged as if his coat had suddenly become too small for his thickset frame. "I would have told him when the banns were announced. By the wedding, at the latest."

Elizabeth stared into Michael's blue gaze. "You mean you didn't know? You weren't a party to this?"

His head moved from side to side. "I had no idea. Not until you lit into me about plotting with the Bartletts."

The icy fingers around Elizabeth's heart began to thaw. He hadn't betrayed her trust. He was still the same Michael. Her Michael? The glimmer of hope sent a rush of warmth throughout her being, melting the ice around her heart and washing away the pain.

Timothy's voice broke the silence. "Well, now that it's settled, I'll be on my way." He twirled one end of his mustache and winked at Elizabeth. "All's well that ends well, I always say. And this looks like a fine ending, although I still don't know what Michael was so wrought up about." With a smug look, he strolled out.

Elizabeth watched him go, then turned to Michael. "However can you put up with him?" Her eyes grew wide, and she pressed her hand against her lips, too late to stop the sharp words. Michael didn't seem put off, though, so she took courage and continued. "I'm sorry. I know that's a horrid thing to say about your father, but—"

"You can't possibly say anything about him I haven't said or thought myself." He passed his hand across his face and leaned back against the counter as if welcoming its support.

"My father. . .well, you've seen for yourself. He doesn't play by anyone's rules but his own. And the object of the game is the advancement of Timothy O'Roarke, no matter who or what gets in the way."

"What about this plot he concocted with the Bartletts? Was that for him or for you?"

Michael raked his fingers through his hair. "I'm still trying to figure out how the man's mind works. He has some idea of building a political legacy, and he refuses to believe I'm not willing to become his successor. In his mind, he may honestly believe he's looking out for my best interests. I'm sure he sees me as obstinate and unappreciative, since I don't see things the same way he does."

"Did he follow you out here?"

"No, it was the other way around. When he heard how a new city was being built to serve as the territorial capital, all his political machinations geared up. He pulled every string he could think of to secure an appointment out here. He'd already tasted the beginnings of power back home. He planned to build on that out here for a few years, then head back east trailing streams of glory. He really thinks he's going to build a dynasty. I'm the one who followed him here."

Elizabeth rubbed her arms as though chilled. "But why?" An unsettling thought struck her. "You didn't have political aspirations, too, did you?"

Michael burst out laughing. "Perish the thought! I've seen enough greed and corruption to last me a lifetime. My motives were much simpler—to keep an eye on my father."

"You've taken on quite a burden. It must weigh heavily on you."

"Call it an obligation, if you will. An obligation to my mother's memory." His face lit up at her mention. "She's the one who held our family together. She made sure my sister and I knew we were loved and taught us about a heavenly Father who loved us, too, and would never leave us. All the qualities our earthly father lacked." Michael straightened and stood.

"She's the one who introduced us to Jesus and told us how He could become our Savior. And even after all the years of neglect from our father, she spent hours on her knees, praying for him to come to know the Lord, as well. His behavior sickens me. Sometimes I think I'd like nothing better than to live in a place where no one's ever heard of Timothy O'Roarke and will never know I'm his son." He shoved his hands into his pants pockets.

"But if I did that, I would feel like I'd be turning my back on all my mother's efforts. I can't do that," he stated simply. "If I'm out here, I can reason with him, try to make him see what he's missing. And in the meantime, maybe I can at least keep him from going too far." He shrugged. "Obviously, I haven't done a very good job of that."

Elizabeth moved across the floor to stand directly in front of him. "I think you've done a fine job." She reached up to smooth a dark curl off his forehead.

"You can't make choices for someone else. All you can do is point the way and try to warn them about pitfalls ahead. The rest is up to them." Her voice softened to a whisper. "I think you're a very special man, Michael O'Roarke."

Michael probed her gaze and raised his hand to capture hers where it still lingered near his hairline. Unable to tear her gaze from his, she felt his other hand slide around her shoulders and pull her close.

She rested her cheek against the smooth surface of his shirt. His heartbeat drummed in her ear, keeping time with her own quickening pulse.

The nearest she had come to a man's embrace had been James's brotherly hugs. She didn't want suitors. . .had avoided them, in fact. She was a person in her own right—with no need to diminish her own individuality by merging into the identity of another.

But being wrapped in Michael's arms didn't make her feel diminished. Rather, like two separated parts finally finding each other and becoming a whole.

His fingers cupped her chin and tilted it upward so that she looked into his blue eyes. "And you're a very remarkable woman, Elizabeth Simmons." His gaze seemed to search her heart, questioning, then he lowered his head, and his lips sought hers.

Elizabeth's arms found their way around Michael's broad shoulders, twining around his neck and pulling him closer, finding the other half that made her feel complete. Michael knew her strong will, yet accepted her as she was.

And loved her? The thought sent joy careening through her whole body. She leaned into his embrace. She would sort out her feelings later. For now, it was enough to rest in Michael's arms.

"Is everything all right back here?" Jenny's voice sounded from the doorway. "I thought I smelled something scorching on the stove." Footsteps clattered to a halt. "Oh! Um. . .it looks like the stew has burned. I'll just move it off the stove, shall I?" A pot rattled. "Then I'll. . .I'll just go tidy up the dining room and wait. For customers. Or something." The door swung open, then shut, cutting off the sound of her retreating footsteps.

Michael brushed his lips along her cheek, her ear, her neck. . . . He nestled his head in the hollow of her shoulder. "I suppose we owe her an explanation," he murmured.

Elizabeth nodded. Jenny deserved that.

But it could wait.

Chapter 19

Michael pushed open the door to the kitchen, where he found Elizabeth wiping down the counters. "Are you about ready to go? I'm eager to hear C. C. Bean's thoughts on the Resurrection. It should be an interesting evening."

"Just let me get a shawl from my room. We can leave as soon as Jenny comes back in from taking the garbage out. We're a little late getting things finished up tonight." She hurried to her room, where she pulled her shawl from its peg, then paused in front of the mirror. She cringed. A day spent over a hot stove had left her hair hanging in limp strands. Michael hadn't mentioned her disheveled appearance, but she wasn't about to go to a Bible study looking like that.

Pulling the pins from her hair, she brushed through it quickly, trying to coax some life back into her chestnut curls. She ran the comb down the center of her head to make a neat part, pulled her hair back on the sides, then secured it in place with two tortoiseshell combs.

She turned her head from side to side to study the effect. Not perfect, but certainly an improvement.

Back in the kitchen, she found Michael scooping a wedge of apple pie from a pan. He looked up with a sheepish grin. "I didn't have much supper. Just thought I'd help with the leftovers."

Elizabeth chuckled and watched him wolf down the slice. It felt good to laugh, good to see Michael at home in her kitchen again, and good to have him back as a part of her life. Life itself was good.

Michael wiped the crumbs from his face and replaced the cloth that covered the pie pan. Elizabeth reached for her reticule. "Ready to go?" she asked.

"I thought we were waiting for Jenny."

"Didn't she come back in yet? I'll go see what's keeping her, while you check the lock on the front door."

She stepped outside into a perfect summer evening. A light breeze from the north caressed her cheek, bringing with it the scent of lilacs. A dove perched in a nearby juniper tree called to another in a piñon pine. It would be a beautiful night for strolling to the Bible study.

"Jenny?" She was probably savoring the lovely evening on her own and had forgotten they were waiting for her.

No answer.

Elizabeth scanned the alleyway, trying to think where Jenny might have gone. She usually stayed well within the shelter of the restaurant's walls, keeping her safe from both snide remarks and the possibility of contact with Martin Lester or Burleigh Ames.

"Jenny?" She called louder this time. Surely Jenny wouldn't have ventured too far afield. Where could she be?

A vague sense of unease settled in the pit of her stomach. She moved past the doorstep to the garbage barrel.

Scraps of food lay scattered across the ground. Her unease blossomed into fear.

"Jenny!" The word floated out into the night but brought no response.

❧

"Michael, she's gone!" Elizabeth stormed into the kitchen, her face flushed and her features taut. The back door banged shut behind her, punctuating her words.

"Gone where?"

"I don't know. She isn't outside. I've looked everywhere. Where can she be?"

"Take it easy. Have you checked her room? Maybe she came in while I was locking the front door and I didn't notice." He followed her to the former storeroom.

Elizabeth tapped on the door, then pushed it open. Michael peered over her shoulder. A cot, neatly made, took up most of the floor space. Jenny's dresses hung from pegs on the walls. A tidy room awaited its occupant's return.

But no sign of Jenny.

Michael caught sight of Elizabeth's trembling lips and laid his hands on her shoulders. "Calm down. There's surely an explanation. Where else could she have gone?"

Elizabeth whirled and clutched his arms. "That's just it. There isn't anyplace else. She worried about Ames showing up to bother her. We both did. Throwing out the garbage gave her a chance to get outdoors, but it was close enough to be safe. Or so we thought." Her fingers dug into his arms. "Oh, Michael, where is she? What are we going to do?"

He stared down at her hazel eyes, puddled with unshed tears. He'd never seen Elizabeth at a loss before, but now this independent woman was asking for his help, and he knew he had to rise to the occasion.

"Bring that lamp, and let's look outside again. I want to check for tracks, signs. . .anything that might give us a clue." Elizabeth flashed him a grateful smile, picked up the lamp, and followed him outside.

"See?" She pointed at the pile of debris on the ground. "Jenny would never have gone off and left this mess."

Michael nodded, remembering the time she had dropped the garbage. She had made sure every scrap had been picked up before she left. He stood still, letting his gaze roam around the pool of lamplight, trying to get a sense of what must have happened.

"Over here." He strode farther out into the alleyway, where two parallel lines marked the dust. He squatted to examine them more closely.

"Wagon tracks," he stated. "And fresh ones. See how sharp the edges are? Someone came along here not too long ago." He motioned for Elizabeth to wait there and carried the lamp down the alley, following the wagon's progress, careful not to mar any possible signs with his own tracks.

Returning, he noted the print Elizabeth's shoes made and compared them to the other tracks nearby. Those, then, must be Jenny's. And up ahead. . . He drew back, startled.

"What's the matter?" Elizabeth asked.

"It doesn't make sense. I expected to see signs of a struggle. But look at this." He led her a few steps ahead.

"The wagon stopped here." He pointed as he spoke, inviting her to read the story written in the dust. "A man stepped down, but he didn't approach the spot where Jenny stood. Those are her prints, passing behind you and ending up by the wagon."

Elizabeth studied the ground. "That still doesn't tell me where she is."

"Look at this. See that slight shuffling there? That's where they stood and talked. And since her tracks don't lead away. . ." His voice trailed off, and he glanced up at Elizabeth, wondering how to break it to her.

"From everything I see here, it looks like she got into the wagon and rode away of her own free will."

"But that doesn't make sense!" Elizabeth scanned the area, trying to find something that would refute Michael's conclusion. "She wouldn't have gone off like that of her own accord without a word to either one of us."

"I wouldn't have thought so, either. But the evidence shows—"

"I don't care what it shows! Jenny's been living with me, remember? I know her, Michael! She hated having to stay cooped up indoors, but she was terrified her guardian might try to catch her unawares and take her back. The only time she ever came outside was to throw out the garbage or use the privy."

She cast a hopeful glance at the small wooden structure beyond. "Do you think. . . ?"

Michael gave her a look of sympathy but shook his head. "There aren't any fresh prints heading in that direction. The only places she went are the garbage barrel and here."

※

Elizabeth stared at the footprints in the dust, the final connection Jenny had with this place. She took the lamp from Michael and followed the marks the wagon had left until she reached the end of the alley. No more tracks. No more Jenny.

It was totally unlike Jenny to jump into a wagon and just take off.

As far as you know.

The only people in Prescott Jenny trusted were Elizabeth and Michael.

As far as you know.

"No, I won't believe it." Elizabeth silenced the insidious little voice of doubt. "Something is wrong, Michael. I know what the signs show, but I know Jenny, too." *I do,* she assured herself. "It would be completely out of character for her to up and leave like that. She knew we were waiting for her and that we were just inside the building."

A shiver of apprehension threaded up her spine. It was easy to hear through the restaurant walls. Jenny had only to call out, and they would have rushed to help her. What had happened to keep her from doing just that?

"Get the sheriff, Michael."

He shook his head sorrowfully, and her voice sharpened. "Something is wrong. Go get him."

Michael heaved a sigh. "He's gone. I heard this afternoon. He's off dealing with a dispute over some claim jumpers down around Big Bug."

No. What was he doing, trying to sort out some foolish mining problem when Jenny needed help? Chest heaving, Elizabeth fought for control. "When will he be back?"

"Maybe by morning. Maybe not for days. It all depends on how things go out there."

"We can't wait for days!"

"I know that." He stroked her cheek with the backs of his fingers. "But we're going to have to wait until morning. There's no way we can follow them tonight. I'll check around town, find out if anyone has seen her."

Elizabeth's body stiffened in denial all the while her mind accepted the hard truth of Michael's reasoning.

"We can't trail them until daylight," Michael continued. "But I promise you, I'll be here as soon as the sun comes up."

"Before," Elizabeth demanded. "We need to be ready to leave the moment it's light." She raised her hands, then let them fall to her sides. "I can't just sit around this evening doing nothing, as if she'd gone off to spend the night with a friend."

"Pray that she has." Michael cupped the back of her head in his hand and pulled her close, cradling her against his body as if she were a child. "For that matter, just pray."

※

By the time Michael tapped on the door the next morning, Elizabeth was dressed and waiting.

"Come inside. The coffee's on." She ushered him in and cast a glance at the overcast sky. Pale gray fingers of light pushed their way through the cloud bank. It wouldn't be long now.

She poured two cups of coffee and sat across the table from Michael, drawing comfort from the warmth of the steaming brew. Even in the summer months, nights grew cold here in the mountains. She shuddered, wondering how Jenny had passed the night.

And where.

Michael cradled his cup in his hands. "Did you come up with any ideas during the night?"

She shook her head slowly. "I have no idea who she would have gone with willingly. Or why."

Only the glimmer of a thought had kept her awake all through the long night hours.

Could Jenny's disappearance have anything to do with seeing the kiss she had shared with Michael the day before?

That Jenny had seen them, she knew without a doubt. Her gasp of surprise and quick departure confirmed that. She hadn't said a word about it later, though, and Elizabeth hadn't found time to explain it to her. Had something about their embrace upset her to the point she would run away without a word?

And if so, what could it be? Elizabeth couldn't think of any reason, save one: What if Jenny cared for Michael herself?

It would be natural enough. After the treatment she had received, first at the hands of Martin Lester, then Burleigh Ames and his customers, any kindness shown by a man would make him seem like her knight in shining armor. Could that account for Jenny's abrupt departure?

"I wonder. . ."

Michael looked up eagerly. "Yes?"

"Never mind." Elizabeth gathered their cups and set them in the basin. She couldn't tell him. Not yet. It was enough to shoulder the burden of guilt at the possibility that her actions might have driven Jenny away. She couldn't bear the shame of admitting it to Michael.

Especially if her suspicions turned out to be true.

"Let's go." She blew out the lamp and stepped outside into the first light of dawn.

On any other morning, she would have gloried in the promise of a new day. Now she felt weighed down by the responsibility of finding Jenny—and the realization that she had no idea what to do first.

"I didn't find anybody who had seen her last night. Let's take a better look at those tracks now that it's daylight." Michael strode to the end of the alley, radiating confidence. She followed, grateful to have a starting point.

"Do they tell you anything?"

"Not much," he admitted. "Only that the wagon turned west from here. The tracks are so mixed in with the other traffic, I won't be able to follow them."

Elizabeth stared westward, willing herself to spot some sign, some scrap of information that would give them a clue. Except for a few other early risers, the street was empty.

"We'll go that way, then." She walked briskly, putting action to her words. "Someone must have seen them. We just have to find out who."

They queried everyone they met without success until they came upon an old man sweeping his front porch.

"Yesterday evening?" He fingered the tuft of white hair over his right ear. "Sure, I saw a wagon down this way just before sunset. Surprised me some. I thought Lester lived out toward Chino Valley. Don't know what he'd be doing, heading off down the south road."

"Lester?" Misgiving spread through Elizabeth and wrapped itself around her heart. "Martin Lester?"

"That's him. Never did think much of him, to tell you the truth, but that gal with him seemed a nice enough sort."

"A girl?" Dread gripped her heart. Hard. She felt Michael's supporting hand on her back.

"Mm-hm. Pretty little thing, too. Not the type I would have expected to take up with him, if you know what I mean."

Michael saved her from having to respond. "Thanks for the information," he said. He laced his fingers through Elizabeth's and gave them a reassuring squeeze. "At least we know which direction they went."

Chapter 20

I t's wrong, Michael. It doesn't make a bit of sense." Elizabeth shifted on the seat of the wagon Michael had provided and studied the empty landscape in front of them. The early morning clouds had built into thunderheads that covered the afternoon sky.

"If Jenny went off with someone willingly, the last person she'd pick would be Martin Lester. She was terrified of the man." At least she could put to rest her fears that the sight of their embrace had sent Jenny on the run. She clung to that knowledge as her only shred of comfort.

"Whether it makes sense or not, it's the only lead we have." Michael urged the horses forward over the rough terrain. "They were seen together. There's a reason for it; we just don't know what it is yet." He slapped the reins against the horses' rumps and pressed his lips together in a tight line. "But we will."

They pressed on, following the faint trail that had turned off the south road some miles back. Up ahead they spotted a prospector plodding toward them. He stopped and rested his arm on his mule's neck, waiting for them to approach.

"Afternoon," Michael said, pulling the team to a halt.

"Howdy." The grizzled man gazed at them with undisguised interest. "If more folks start coming out this way, I may have to move on to someplace less crowded. Appears this spot is becoming right popular."

"Oh?" Elizabeth could feel Michael's quiver of excitement as he leaned forward. "How's that?"

"You're the second wagon I've seen come through here since morning. Two in one day! This is turning into a regular highway."

Michael's fingers tightened on the reins. "Another wagon, you say? Where was it headed?"

"Same place you are, I reckon." The man tilted his head and regarded them quizzically. "The only thing farther out this way is that old claim Zeb Andrews abandoned six months back. Funny, those other two fellows asked the same question." He slapped his hat against his thigh, sending a cloud of dust into the air. "You'd think if a passel of folks were headed to the same place, they'd have some idea of where they were all going, wouldn't you?"

Elizabeth focused on the only part of his commentary that mattered. "Two fellows? You mean there were two men in the wagon?"

"Yes, ma'am. Two men and a pile of gear in the back. That and a gunnysack that was squirming to beat the band."

110

He grinned. "I told them if they were planning to drown a cat, they were looking in the wrong place. There isn't a drop of water in that creek bed that runs through Zeb's old place except when there's a downpour. That's why he up and left." He pushed his tattered hat back on his head and scanned the leaden sky. "This just might be the day it'll catch some rain."

Michael shot a quick glance at Elizabeth. "What did they say about the cat?"

The prospector chuckled. "The driver wasn't real sociable, didn't say much of anything. The fellow with him just laughed and said they had a cat in there, all right. A wildcat that needed taming." He cackled. "Whatever it was, he turned around and cuffed it once, and it settled right back down again."

He wiped his brow, leaving a grimy trail across his forehead. "I don't know, maybe they had a dog they were going to train. Seems funny they'd have it all tied up in a sack like that, but you never can tell about some folks."

"They sound strange, all right," Michael agreed. "The one who did all the talking, what did he look like?"

"Big fellow, broader than you. Looked like a brawler. Kind of a sour type, except for the one time he laughed. Friend of yours?"

"No," Michael said. "I wouldn't say that."

The man peered into the back of their wagon, empty save for canteens of water and some food Elizabeth had hastily packed. "You ain't planning to train no dogs, I see. You out hunting or something?"

"We might be." Michael's tone was ominous. "We just might be." He shook the reins, and the horses started off, then Michael turned around and called back over his shoulder, "How far ahead is that claim you mentioned?"

"Couple of miles or so. Not much there, just a dried-up creek and Zeb's old shack."

"Much obliged." Michael settled back in the seat and clucked at the horses.

"Are we on the right track?" Elizabeth asked. "He said two men."

Michael nodded with a grim expression. "Did you recognize the description of the second man?"

Elizabeth shook her head.

"I did. It fits Burleigh Ames like a glove."

"From the Nugget?" She looked at Michael with a growing sense of horror. "Then the bag in the back of their wagon. . ."

"Was Jenny."

A wave of numbness shrouded Elizabeth's brain. Maybe it would have been better if Jenny had run away. She could feel anger then, hurt and disappointment, instead of this feeling of being caught in a nightmare that wouldn't end.

"How much farther?"

"Less than a mile now. Just before we reach the top of that rise, we'll leave the wagon and walk the rest of the way."

A thought struck her. "You did leave word for the sheriff, didn't you?"

Michael hesitated a moment. "No."

Elizabeth jerked back as if she'd been slapped. "What? If he gets back from Big Bug anytime soon, he can head out here to help us."

Michael guided the horses away from the track and headed them into a clump of manzanita. "Not much cover," he said, "but it's the best we're going to get."

He took his time setting the brake, then faced her squarely. "There's something you need to understand. Martin Lester is Jenny's legal guardian, duly appointed by her father. And she's only eighteen, still a minor. In the eyes of the law, he has every right to take her back."

Elizabeth gaped. "After the things he's done? Surely—"

Michael laid his fingers across her lips. "But he never actually did anything prosecutable. The law won't hang a man for what he threatens to do, only for what he succeeds in doing. Even if the sheriff were here right now, his hands would be tied."

Thunder rumbled in the distance. "Then that means. . ."

Michael nodded. "We're on our own."

⤙⤚

"That's the place?" Elizabeth stared at the sorry excuse for a cabin in the hollow below them.

"It has to be," Michael answered. "I can see the tail of their wagon sticking out past the corner."

Elizabeth rubbed her ankles, tender after their hike, and took stock of their position.

On the far side of the ramshackle structure, a dry creek bed meandered off into the distance. Between the rolling hilltops and the basin where the cabin lay, the slopes held only grass, the sole exception being the cluster of small juniper trees where she and Michael had concealed themselves.

"How are we going to cross that open ground without them seeing us?"

"We can't," he said. "We'll have to wait for nightfall."

"That's hours away yet! Think about what could be happening to Jenny in the meantime. They may not even be expecting anyone to be tailing them."

"I'm not about to take that chance." Michael held up his hand to still Elizabeth's protest. "Let's say I leave you here and make it to the cabin without being seen. That still leaves them with a two-to-one advantage. And they have Jenny."

He leaned back against a juniper trunk and stretched his legs out in front of him. "And that's assuming I make it. Let's say they spot me before I reach the shack. Not only can they pick me off at their leisure, but that leaves both you and Jenny alone out here, at their mercy, and with no hope of rescue. I'm not going to risk either one of you like that."

"So if you wait until dark and get down there safely, then what?"

Michael smiled. "Then the odds will be different. I'll have you with me."

"You didn't really expect I'd stay behind, did you?"

"Chivalry says I ought to leave you here or even take you back to town and return here myself, maybe with more men. But there's no guarantee Ames and Lester wouldn't be gone by the time I got back. And to tell the truth, Elizabeth, there's no one I'd rather have backing me up than you."

That declaration sustained her all through the long hours of waiting, with the two of them sheltered beneath the junipers. Elizabeth impatiently traced the course of the sun across the sky, passing the time by making plans with Michael.

And praying. Prayers for Jenny, that somehow she would be protected during their enforced wait. For her and Michael, that the rescue they had worked out would go without a hitch, bringing Jenny back to safety and keeping the three of them safe.

Prayers for the two men inside the cabin came harder. *I know You love them, Lord, no matter what they've done. You died for them, just like You did for me. But I just can't find it in myself to feel much compassion for them right now.*

The sun set with agonizing slowness. Elizabeth watched its descent toward the horizon, willing it to hurry up and drop behind the mountaintops.

Shadows lengthened and stretched across the barren ground from the distant hills, finally reaching the hollow where their objective lay.

The time had come. Finally! Elizabeth sat up under the sheltering branches and stretched. She welcomed the chance to do something tangible. She dreaded it just as much.

Beside her, Michael checked the loads in his pistol and shoved two brass shells into the shotgun at his side. "Ready?"

Even with the cover of darkness, their movement across the open ground felt all too exposed. Elizabeth watched the cabin window, now glowing with lamplight, for signs of anyone keeping watch. An occasional shadow crossed the opening, but no one stopped or looked out.

At the edge of the grass, Michael reached for her arm and pulled her to a stop. "This is where we separate," he whispered, drawing her close. "Do you remember everything?"

She nodded. They had gone over their plan often enough during the weary hours of waiting.

He placed the shotgun in her hands. "Remember, it's going to take me awhile to lead their horses a distance away. While I'm gone, I want you just to sit tight. Don't try anything on your own." He gathered her in his arms and held her tight. "Promise me you'll be careful. It ought to work, but there's always the possibility of something going wrong. Whatever happens, take care of yourself. If anything happened to you. . ." He seized her shoulders and pressed his lips to hers in a brief, hard kiss. Then he was gone.

Elizabeth waited a moment, listening to the faint rustle as his boots swept through the grass. The hint of a breeze grazed her cheek. Over near the creek bed, a lone cricket set up a steady chirping.

And in the cabin, Jenny waited. The thought spurred Elizabeth into action. Making no more noise than Michael had, she slipped through the shadows until she reached the end of the shack. The cricket ceased its chirping; otherwise, nothing else seemed to take note of her nocturnal prowling.

She flattened herself against the weathered wall and edged toward the open window. Her foot caught on an object, and she reached down to probe the obstruction with her fingers. A half-buried tin can stuck up out of the ground. She stepped around it, careful to make no sound. Evidently, Zeb hadn't been too careful about keeping the place picked up. She knelt down and crept ahead on her hands and knees, the shotgun making her progress awkward.

Voices murmured through the window. Elizabeth reached her goal and sat beneath it, trying to control the trembling in her limbs. Michael should have reached the horses by now.

The windowsill lay just inches above her head. Did she dare rise up and look inside? She balanced on the balls of her feet and inched upward, then jerked to a stop. Elizabeth yanked impatiently at the hem of her skirt, where it had gotten caught under the toes of her shoes.

She tried again, feeling the sharpness of the rough-cut wood as her fingers crept up the wall. Her head had just reached the level of the windowsill when a man's back appeared in the opening. She ducked back down out of sight, panting, and strained to hear what was going on inside.

Boots scraped across the floor. She heard the clatter of dishes, and the scent of bacon drifted out into the night.

"About time we got fed."

Elizabeth froze, focusing her attention on the deep voice.

"Right about that," the second man responded in a higher-pitched tone. "I was about to starve. It's hard to think straight when your belly's empty. She can cook, anyway. At least she's good for something."

Elizabeth let out a sigh. At least Jenny was still alive, from the sounds of it.

"She better be good for more than that. I traded you that whiskey in good faith, and I need to get something back on my investment. And I don't mean singing."

So the deeper voice belonged to Burleigh Ames. That meant Martin Lester possessed the high, whiny tone.

"You will, you will," Lester assured him. "Just give her time to warm up to the notion. I found this place and got her out here for you, didn't I?"

"For all the good it's done us so far. She hasn't even said a word."

"We just needed a place out away from people and a little time to convince her that life will be a whole lot easier if she gets over her highfalutin' ways and decides to cooperate."

Ames grunted. "She'd better get around to cooperating pretty soon. I've got a business to run."

"Don't worry. She gets hungry enough, and she'll come around. Fixing all that food for us when she hasn't had a bite to eat since I picked her up last night should persuade her soon enough." Lester snickered.

Ames responded with a rumbling chuckle that made Elizabeth's blood run cold. How much longer would it take Michael to lead the horses far enough away?

"Just like breaking a horse, I reckon," Ames said. "With some, you've gotta use more persuasion. Hey!" His voice sharpened. "Get away from the door!" Footsteps pounded on the wooden floor.

"You get back there and clean up the supper dishes," Lester snarled. "If you decide to sweeten up and change your tune, we might let you eat breakfast with us in the morning. You're fixing flapjacks, did I tell you? And I brought some eggs along, too. Or you can be stubborn and wait until lunch. Or dinner. Or the middle of next week, for all I care." His voice took on a more threatening note. "Or we can stake you out somewhere and leave you for the Apaches to find. What do you think about that?"

His menacing tone changed to a yelp of alarm. Elizabeth heard a loud, clanging noise, followed by a series of scrambling sounds and angry yells. Only her fear of getting ahead of the plan and spoiling their chances kept her from jumping up to peer through the window.

"I told you to stay away from that door!" Ames's bellow cut through the room. "Tie her in that chair again. We can't take a chance on her getting away."

"I'll teach you to sling a pan of hot grease at me," Lester shouted. "Get over here and sit down. I'll snug these ropes up so tight you won't get another chance to run, you little wildcat."

"Watch her teeth!" Ames called.

Lester cursed. Elizabeth heard the sound of a hand striking flesh, followed by a cry from Jenny.

"Maybe now you'll keep still."

Elizabeth clamped her lower lip between her teeth. If Michael didn't come back soon, she would be sorely tempted to take action on her own.

"Here," Ames said. "Have something to settle your nerves."

Glasses clinked, and Elizabeth could hear liquid gurgling. Liquor on top of their already violent mood?

Hurry, Michael!

Chapter 21

Michael slid out of the darkness as if in answer to her silent call and pressed his mouth close to her ear. "Have you been able to look inside?" he asked in a barely audible whisper.

"No." She kept her voice as low as his. "But I've heard more than enough." She quickly recounted what had transpired and could tell Michael's anger equaled her own.

"If they've started drinking, we can't afford to waste any time. Are you ready?"

Elizabeth nodded. After what she had just listened to, she was more than eager to see their plan through.

She gripped the stock of the shotgun in both hands and crouched beneath the window. Michael should just about have had enough time to reach the door. Any moment, he would kick it open.

There! She heard the sound of splintering wood and the crash as the door slammed back against the wall. She sprang to her feet in time to see both men leap back in surprise and reach for their guns.

"I wouldn't," she called.

Their heads swiveled toward the sound of her voice, any temptation to discount a mere woman's order nullified by the twin barrels she aimed at them.

"What do you think you're doing, busting in here like that?" the scrawny one yelled. Elizabeth pegged him for Martin Lester. She recognized the other from the description the prospector had given them: Burleigh Ames. Even from across the room, the man emanated a sense of malice.

But where was Jenny? She hadn't made a sound since her cry of pain, and Elizabeth couldn't see her from where she stood.

"Just keep your hands in the air," Michael ordered. To Elizabeth, he called, "You can come inside now."

She ran to the front of the cabin and joined him in the single room. The men stood next to their overturned chairs behind a rickety table where a lamp flickered. To her left was a rusty cookstove.

And over near the far wall sat Jenny, bound hand and foot to a chair. Even in the dim glow of the lamp, the bright red imprint of a hand showed clearly on her cheek. Her head drooped listlessly. Was she unconscious or merely dazed from the blow she'd received?

Elizabeth edged toward her, keeping her shotgun aimed toward Lester and Ames.

"Both of you, throw down your guns and get over there against the wall," Michael said.

Two pistols thudded to the floor, and the men stepped back slowly. "Ain't no call for you to be interfering," Lester whined. "We're just trying to reclaim what's rightfully ours."

Michael's expression could have been carved out of stone. "Guardianship doesn't give you the right to abuse a woman. We aren't about to stand by and let that happen."

"Ames!" Michael hollered at the big man. "Move away from the window. Elizabeth, keep them covered while I find something to tie them with." He rummaged through the goods Jenny's abductors had piled in a corner.

Burleigh Ames lifted his left hand, which still held the bottle of whiskey. "You won't begrudge me a last drink before you truss me up, will you?" He raised his arm slowly, then drew it back and flung the bottle straight at Michael.

Elizabeth shouted a warning. Michael jumped to one side. The bottle hit the lamp, then both rolled off the table and across the floor in a spray of whiskey, flame, and shattered glass.

In the near darkness, Elizabeth saw Ames dive for his gun. Michael kicked it out of the way. Ames then reached for Michael, and the two grappled and rolled across the floor.

Flames licked up the wall, catching the tattered tarp that hung near the window and spreading into a blaze.

"Michael!" she screamed. "We've got to get out of here!" The place was a tinderbox. It wouldn't take more than a few minutes for the whole shack to be consumed. Fighting desperately to keep his gun hand out of Burleigh's reach, he didn't answer.

Martin Lester started toward the door. "Hold it right there," she told him. "You don't move until I tell you to."

"Elizabeth?"

She glanced over her shoulder. Jenny stared at the floor, unable to move away from the flames that crept dangerously close to the hem of her skirt. Elizabeth saw movement at the edge of her vision and swung back around. Lester had taken advantage of her momentary distraction and was on the floor scrabbling for his gun.

No time for orders or threats. In one fluid movement, she brought the barrel of the shotgun down on his head, producing a dull thud. He dropped flat and lay still.

"Elizabeth!" Jenny, fully alert now, was straining away from the flames with terror-filled eyes.

Elizabeth wrapped her arms around Jenny's body and dragged her backward, chair and all. She dropped to her knees and pulled frantically at the ropes.

"Knife. By the stove." Jenny's voice came in staccato bursts.

By the stove. . . There it was! Elizabeth seized it and raced back to Jenny. She sawed through the ropes with relative ease, giving thanks for the sharp blade.

When the last strand had been cut, she pulled Jenny out of the chair. Jenny sagged against her, and she braced herself to support the girl's weight.

"Get her out!" Michael yelled.

She had no problem finding her way to the door. The flames that now covered two walls and threatened a third bathed the cabin in a bright yellow light.

She half-carried, half-dragged Jenny to a spot a safe distance from the burning shack. She sat Jenny down and set the shotgun beside her, then turned back to the blazing building—Michael was still inside.

She raced back to the doorway, pushing forward despite the heat of the flames. Burleigh Ames had both hands wrapped around Michael's throat, slowly choking the life out of him.

Elizabeth grabbed the chair Jenny had occupied and raised it high above her head. With every ounce of strength she possessed, she brought it down on Burleigh Ames's shoulders.

He reared back with a loud bellow, loosening his hold on Michael, who pulled his fist back and flattened Ames with a crushing blow to the temple. Elizabeth backed out the door as Michael seized the unconscious man's collar and dragged him outside. Martin Lester roused and stumbled out the door behind them seconds before the roof collapsed, sending a shower of sparks skyward.

Michael returned with the wagon just as Burleigh Ames sat up and moaned. Elizabeth sat guard with the shotgun, covering both him and Martin Lester.

Michael scooped Jenny up as if she weighed no more than a sack of feathers and laid her in the back of the wagon. He turned to Elizabeth and lifted her to the seat. "Time to go home," he said.

"Wait a minute," Lester called. "What about us?"

Michael stepped up to the wagon seat and gave him a look of contempt. "Consider yourselves lucky to be alive."

"You don't mean you're going to leave us here? Where's our horses?"

"Halfway to Prescott," Michael said. He pulled a canteen from the wagon bed behind him and tossed it onto the ground near Lester's feet.

"You can't take her from me! I know my rights."

"You'd better ration that water," Michael told him. "It's a long walk home. It should give both of you plenty of time to think about those rights of yours." A rumble of thunder rolled across the sky. "And I'd get started soon, if I were you. It looks like it's going to rain any time now."

The moon shone in the eastern sky, still free of the clouds that were blowing in from the west. Elizabeth blessed the fact that it gave them light to retrace their path back to the south road. She looked at Jenny's slender form, huddled in the wagon bed.

"Are you all right?" A stupid thing to ask, considering all the girl had gone through, but she needed to hear something from Jenny's lips.

She stared up at Elizabeth. "How did you get away to come find me?"

"Get away? What do you mean?"

"Martin Lester drove around back when I was taking out the trash last night. It nearly scared me to death when I saw who it was. He told me Burleigh had gone in the front door and had you tied up inside. He said Burleigh would kill you if I didn't go with him."

"Oh, honey! So that's why you went off with him without a fight." She leaned over to stroke Jenny's hair. "That didn't happen. It was all a lie."

Jenny's countenance crumpled. "I should have known. He never told me the truth about anything before. . .except when he said he was trading me to Burleigh." She reached up for Elizabeth's hand and squeezed it. "I was so scared."

"So were we, honey. So were we."

Jenny's fingers relaxed their grip. "She's asleep," Elizabeth told Michael.

"She has to be exhausted after what she's been through." He put his arm around Elizabeth and pulled her head to his shoulder. "You probably are, too. Why don't you try to sleep on the way back?"

"I couldn't possibly. I'm still too stirred up."

The next thing she knew, Michael was shaking her gently. "We're home," he said. She let him help her down, then held the door open while he carried Jenny to her room.

After he left the room, she helped Jenny undress and put her to bed. When she came back into the kitchen, Michael had coffee ready.

"How is she?"

Elizabeth rested her elbow on the table and propped her head on her hand. "Physically, I'd say she's all right. A little banged up from being bounced around in the back of Martin Lester's wagon, but nothing a good night's sleep and a few days of rest won't cure. As far as her thinking, though. . ." Her voice trailed off.

"It's only natural for her to be scared. She's been through quite an ordeal."

"She isn't scared, Michael. She's angry."

"At Lester and Ames? That may be a good thing. Anger's more of a tonic than fear any day."

"Not at them. At God. According to her, this is just one more time He let her down."

Michael leaned back in his chair. "Wait a minute. What about Him leading us right to her and keeping her protected all that time? Doesn't He get any credit for that?"

Elizabeth shook her head wearily. "The way she sees it, He could have kept them from nabbing her in the first place, but He didn't. Further proof in her mind that while He may love everybody else, He doesn't love Jenny Davis." She laced her fingers together so tightly her knuckles turned white. "What should I do? I don't know how to reach her."

Michael reached across the table and covered both her hands with his. "You once told me you can't force a person to believe. You can only point the way for them. I think that applies here as well."

"Maybe. But I'm not giving up on her."

A glimmer of laughter sparked in his eyes. "I never for a moment thought that you would."

Without moving the hand covering hers, Michael scooted his chair closer and leaned toward her. "Jenny isn't the only one who was scared tonight."

Her hand tightened under his. "What do you mean?"

"When I was on the floor, wrestling with Burleigh Ames, I looked up and saw you standing in the middle of that inferno. It occurred to me that maybe neither one of us would make it out of there." He stroked the back of her hand with his thumb.

She searched his eyes. "And that scared you?"

"More than you can imagine. You know what else scares me? The idea of living the rest of my life without you." He pushed back his chair and stood, pulling her up with him.

"I know you treasure your independence. Your strength is one of the things I admire most about you. God placed us both here and brought us together. It seems to me He must have had a reason."

He lifted both her hands in his and pressed them against his heart. "I know this isn't the setting we would have had back home. I would have asked for your father's consent and come to you with a ring in my pocket. And I'm sure your mother would be shocked at the idea of me proposing to you in your kitchen. Although," he added with a smile that sent a glow flowing through her like warm honey, "I can't think of a more pleasant place to be."

Raising her hands to his lips, he kissed each fingertip. "I guess there's another thing that scares me, and that's the possibility that you may say no. But what scares me even more is the thought I should have asked you and didn't." Keeping his gaze locked on hers, he bent down on one knee.

"I love you, Elizabeth. Love you and admire you for your courage and your spirit. I can't imagine life without you. Will you marry me?"

When had the tears started flowing down her cheeks? She looked down at her dear Michael's face. Here was a man who accepted her as she was. The man God had put in her life. The man she wanted in her life forever. "I'd be honored to," she whispered.

Michael bounded to his feet and wrapped his arms around her in a crushing embrace. "Thank You, Lord," she heard him whisper. Then he lowered his head to hers and kissed her with an intensity that drove all other thoughts from her mind.

Dear Carrie,

You've complained that I haven't included enough adventure in my letters of late. Settle back in a comfortable chair, dear sister, for what I am about to relate will satisfy even your romantic soul. . . .

Chapter 22

S he just arrived." The minister took his stand behind the pulpit and winked at Michael. "I guess you missed your chance to slip out the back, if you were so inclined."

Michael stood his ground at the front of the church and grinned in response.

"No second thoughts?" the parson teased.

"Not a one." Michael felt the truth of his words ring in his statement. He was ready—more than ready—for this moment. He had never felt so sure about anything in his life.

A year ago, who would have foreseen him standing before this crowd of witnesses, ready to take a wife? But then, a year ago, he hadn't met Elizabeth Simmons. He wished his mother could be here to see this day, knowing she would have approved his choice of a helpmeet without reservation. Elizabeth would never be one to hover in the shadow of her husband. She would be a partner in the truest sense of the word, standing beside him, ready to face life and whatever it might bring.

And he wouldn't have it any other way.

He scanned the crowd, noting one familiar face after another, but not finding the one he sought. Michael squared his shoulders and fought down his sense of disappointment. He should have known his father would find something more important requiring his attention on this day.

A chord from the organ brought Michael back to the moment, and he fixed his gaze on the heavy door at the rear. His breath caught in his throat when it swung open. Not yet, he reminded himself. Elizabeth would make her entrance last. Jenny entered and started down the aisle toward him.

And then Elizabeth appeared, and everything else in the room seemed to fade away. In only a few brief moments, they would be joined together for a lifetime. A dozen steps more, and she reached his side and placed her hand in his.

The minister beamed at them both and opened his Bible. "Dearly beloved, we are gathered here today in the sight of God and of these witnesses. . . ."

Michael repeated the vows in his turn, but never took his gaze away from Elizabeth's dear face. The sense of wonder in her expression matched his own.

Finally he heard the words, "I now pronounce you man and wife. You may kiss the bride."

Michael had never known such pleasure in complying with a request. With

Elizabeth's lips pressed against his, the crowd of guests faded away again. Only the two of them remained, lost in the miracle of their love.

"Ladies and gentlemen, I present to you Mr. and Mrs. Michael O'Roarke."

Cheers erupted from the assembled well-wishers.

Moisture clouded Elizabeth's vision and she ducked her head to wipe it away. Goodness, it seemed she had shed more tears today than in the past few months combined!

Most of them, she knew, came from the sheer joy of becoming Michael's wife. But a few were due to the sorrow of not having any of her family present. How she would have loved it if Carrie could have stood up with her at her wedding!

Elizabeth shook off the regret and lifted her chin. What was wrong with her? She had a wonderful husband, and a dear friend in Jenny, whom she loved like a sister. Why, if she wanted to, she could almost pretend it was Carrie standing there beside her. The same eyes, the same hair. . .hadn't the resemblance amazed her all along?

She caught sight of the loneliness in Jenny's face, and all similarity between the two vanished. Her sister's whole being radiated optimism and the joy of living, whereas Jenny's. . .

The emptiness she saw there twisted at Elizabeth's heart. Even after her rescue and seeing God's provision firsthand, Jenny remained angry and bitter beyond anything Carrie had ever been. But then, Jenny bore more hurt than Carrie had ever experienced.

Lord, somehow let her look past all the people who have hurt her so she can find You.

It seemed an impossible request, yet she knew He could do it. Look at what He had done already! She came to Arizona Territory with hopes of building a new life and had found one beyond her wildest imaginings. He had blessed her with a place to belong, a renewed walk with Him, and a husband who. . .

Michael's arm encircled her waist and pulled her close against his side. His breath brushed against her ear when he whispered, "Are you happy. . .Mrs. O'Roarke?"

Elizabeth's joyful laugh rang through the church.

Without a doubt, she had found her land of promise.

Refining
Fire

Dedication

*To Dave,
now and always*

Chapter 1

Two bowls of venison stew, one order of roast beef, and one of fried chicken. And some of whatever the couple at the next table are having for dessert."

"That's dried peach cobbler." Jenny Davis smiled at the man seated with his young family at the front table of the Capital Restaurant & Bakery.

"Mmm. Can I just skip the stew and start with that, Pa?" the older of two freckle-faced boys asked.

Jenny laughed along with the boy's parents. Heading back to the kitchen, she repeated their order to Elizabeth O'Roarke, the restaurant's owner and Jenny's dearest friend.

"I'm going to set aside four pieces of this cobbler," she told Elizabeth. "That little boy's eyes lit up like he hadn't had a sweet in months!" She didn't mention the pleasure she felt at knowing one of her own baked creations had produced such a craving.

Elizabeth grinned at Jenny, her hazel eyes glowing with pride. "If he thinks it looks good, just wait until he tries a bite. You've developed a real knack for improving the recipes we started out with."

Jenny basked in Elizabeth's praise while she served the family their supper and tended to the other patrons in the crowded dining room. In the two years she'd worked at the restaurant, Elizabeth had taught her a great deal—not only the finer points of turning out mouthwatering pies, cakes, and pastries, but the meaning of friendship and loyalty as well.

She owed a lot to Elizabeth and her husband, Michael. Far more than she would ever be able to repay by waiting tables and helping in the kitchen. Being rescued carried a high price.

And the O'Roarkes had come to her rescue more than once. First from the local saloon keeper her unscrupulous guardian had traded her to for a supply of whiskey. Then again after her former guardian and the saloon keeper kidnapped her in an effort to regain their lost "property."

It had taken many months for Jenny to make the transformation from the frightened girl Elizabeth and Michael had taken under their wing to the more confident young woman she had become. During those months, she had learned what it was like to belong again, to feel like part of a family—a person of worth. Despite her initial sullenness and mistrust, both the O'Roarkes believed in her. And that belief had made all the difference.

She smiled at Elizabeth when she pushed through the swinging door to the kitchen. "If it wasn't almost closing time, you could probably keep on serving for hours yet. Business is going well."

Elizabeth beamed. "Isn't it wonderful how God has continued to bless us?"

They believed in God, too, something Jenny didn't begrudge them in the least. She just wished they wouldn't try to keep pushing their perception of Jenny's need for Him down her throat. Faith was a wonderful thing, as long as the object of your faith lived up to His obligation to take care of His people. When He allowed awful things to happen to them, as He'd done with Jenny and her family, it was hard to muster up the unquestioning trust that seemed to come so easily to Elizabeth and Michael.

That topic had been the only real point of disagreement Jenny and Elizabeth ever had, a point on which Jenny adamantly dug in her heels and refused to budge.

"But everyone has faith in something," Elizabeth had argued more than once. "What do you have faith in?"

That was easy: herself. She didn't tell Elizabeth that, though. She knew all too well the look of sadness that would fill her friend's eyes. Instead, she always shrugged and said she was still trying to figure that out.

The truth was, she had settled the issue in her mind a long time ago—back when she cowered in a root cellar, listening to the screams of her dying parents and little brother at the hands of Apache warriors.

Back when Martin Lester, her guardian, decided he wanted to treat her more as a wife than a foster daughter. . . back when he tired of her fending him off and traded her to Burleigh Ames, the owner of the Nugget Saloon. . .back when she knew beyond a doubt that if God had loved Jenny Davis once, He didn't any longer. How could a God of love allow all the things that had happened to her?

She wet a rag and carried it to the dining room, where she proceeded to wipe down the empty tables. The family at the front finished their meal and got ready to take their leave.

"That was sure good cobbler," called the little boy. "I hope Pa brings us in again soon."

Jenny smiled at the departing family. The door opened again just after they left, and Michael O'Roarke strolled in.

"Is Elizabeth ready to go? We can enjoy a twilight stroll and still get to the Bible study on time for once if we leave now."

Jenny laughed and nodded toward the rear of the room. "She's in the kitchen. She should just about be finished now. If she isn't, I'll take care of anything that's left so you can be on your way."

Michael grinned at her offer. "Thanks. I appreciate it. You're sure you don't want to go with us?"

"Not this time." It had been her standard answer for the past two years. She was thankful that neither one of them seemed to take offense.

Elizabeth hurried in from the kitchen, wiping her hands on a towel. "I think I have everything put to rights back there. The dough is rising for tomorrow morning." She patted her hair into place and turned to Jenny. "You're sure—"

"I already asked her," Michael put in with a smile. "Not this time."

Elizabeth nodded, and Michael pulled down the shades covering the front windows while the two women began to blow out the lamps.

"We'll probably head straight home after the Bible study," Elizabeth told Jenny. "Make sure the front door is locked securely after we leave."

"I will." Jenny waited until the two of them set off down Cortez Street, then dropped the bar across the front door. She hadn't needed the reminder. Even when she and Elizabeth both made their home in the rear of the restaurant, securing the place for the night had always been a high priority. Now that she lived there alone, she took even more precautions.

After blowing out the last lamp in the dusky dining room, she pushed through the swinging door into the kitchen, lit the lamp on the counter, then made her way through the kitchen to her room, which had once been Elizabeth's. She set the lamp on the dresser, dropped onto her bed, and reached for her hairbrush. Pulling the brush slowly through her long curls, she thought about her friends and what a nice couple they made. Maybe God really did have a hand in bringing the two of them together. Wouldn't it be nice if He would bring someone as wonderful as Michael into her own life? But she knew she couldn't count on His intervention for that. . .or anything else.

No, she couldn't expect any help from the Almighty. He'd proven that more than once. Michael and Elizabeth would argue the point, of course, but they'd never faced the things Jenny had. Never seen their whole world ripped asunder so that they despaired of ever piecing the fragments back together again.

And they had never been forced to work in a place like the Nugget, singing to the customers, praying her voice would draw in enough extra business to satisfy Burleigh Ames so he wouldn't make good on his threats to force her to do more.

Two years later, the memory of the short time she'd spent in the saloon made Jenny shudder. Shame, raw fear, and her naïveté about the rights of her new guardian had kept her from running away. But unlike the other girls in Burleigh's employ, she had never taken one of the customers upstairs to her room. Even so, having to endure the leers, the comments, and the pawing hands of the customers downstairs left her feeling soiled.

No, God couldn't love her anymore. Not after that. His people were pure, like Elizabeth and Michael. People who went to church and to Bible studies, who prayed expecting answers, and got them. She'd given up on God's love. She knew she wasn't worthy of it. The past had tainted her beyond redemption, and she accepted that fact. All she wanted to do now was forget.

If only other people would let her.

Jenny changed into her nightgown, then slipped barefoot through the darkened kitchen and dining room to check the locks on the doors one last time. Moonlight filtered through a crack in the shades, giving her enough light to accomplish her purpose. She gripped the bar and shook it. Yes, it rested solidly in place.

Jenny turned to go, and her foot struck something, sending the object skittering across the floor like a dry leaf. With a sense of dread, she located it in the dim light and bent to pick it up. She held the thin, folded sheet of paper between her fingers, knowing before she ever opened it what she would find.

No, please. Not again.

❧

Andrew Garrett gazed across the broad valley below him. On the other side of that valley, the ground rose up again, the last in the series of low hills he had crossed that day. Beyond that, according to the directions he'd been given, would be the town of Prescott. *A nice place to build a town,* he reflected. Plenty of piñon pines, and juniper trees and rolling slopes dotted with manzanita. Nothing like Denver, but a pretty spot all the same.

He urged his horse forward and continued across the valley's level floor, crossing a creek before he came to the last hill. When he reached the top, he pulled his horse to a halt and surveyed the scene before him.

Prescott. A town on the rise, to all appearances. In the neighborhood of a couple of thousand inhabitants, he'd guess. That wouldn't include the others outside the town proper who toiled away at their sluice boxes or knelt in the cold streams, endlessly swirling their gold pans in the hope of finding a nugget.

The gold rush that hit Prescott five years before hadn't been as big as the rush to California in '49. Still, a considerable amount of ore had already been shipped to San Francisco. The question was, how much was still left for the taking?

Which was the question that brought Andrew to Arizona Territory. Flush with the proceeds from their investments in local mines, the Denver Consolidated Mining Company had decided to investigate other likely regions and hired Andrew to use his expertise as a mining engineer to scout out the prospects in Arizona. If the underground ore proved to be as rich as rumor had it, he had been authorized to purchase claims in the name of the group of investors.

Andrew studied the bustling town below him, lying in a basin edged by large pine trees. Mountains rose in the distance to the south, and a large, thumb-shaped butte dominated the landscape in the west. Most of the activity seemed to be centered on the area surrounding a broad, open square that reminded him of Santa Fe's town plaza.

Nothing like Denver's more polished atmosphere, but the same brash spirit, the same feeling of heady optimism he'd experienced in other locales in the midst of a mining boom. The same certainty that the next big strike was just about to happen. But hope alone wouldn't carry the day. Sound investments required a solid foundation, and that was just what Andrew's training had equipped him to look for.

Andrew touched his heels to his horse's flanks and set off down the hill. The men who flocked to the gold fields were the same everywhere, sure the next big strike would be on the claim they owned. Andrew's job was to see if he could make that dream a certainty for the Denver investors.

❧

"Are you going to tell me what's wrong?"

Jenny spun around at the sound of Elizabeth's voice. Managing a shaky laugh at her nervous reaction, she attempted a casual smile. "These raisin tarts. I can't seem to get the dough right."

Elizabeth stepped across the kitchen and squeezed a pinch of the dough between her fingers. "It's a little dry, don't you think? Try adding just a bit more water."

She turned back to Jenny, holding her with a steady gaze that made Jenny wish she could disappear. "What's going on? You don't make mistakes like that."

"Except for when I forgot the baking powder and the biscuits were like rocks. And don't forget the time I put the salt in those piecrusts twice. Remember how that poor man's eyes watered when he bit into it?"

"Months ago, on both counts. Don't try to distract me. This has nothing to do with pastry making. Own up, now. What's wrong?"

Jenny opened her mouth to make a light comment but thought better of it. Trying to sidetrack Elizabeth once she had her mind set on something was like trying to persuade a terrier to part with a cherished bone. She wiped the crumbly dough from her hands with a tea towel and fished a piece of paper from her apron pocket. She handed it over without a word and turned back to add drops of water to her dough.

Behind her, Elizabeth gasped. "Where did this come from?"

"Someone slipped it under the front door last night. I found it after you left."

"I can't believe anyone would write these things." Elizabeth shook the paper under Jenny's nose.

Jenny turned away again. She didn't need to be reminded. The words were forever etched in her memory. *Harlot. Fallen woman. Go back to Whiskey Row.*

Elizabeth studied the wrinkled paper and glanced up at Jenny. "You crumpled this up, then smoothed it out and kept it. Why?"

Jenny shrugged. How could she explain an action she didn't understand herself? Her first thought had been to wad the ugly note into a ball, light a match, and send it into oblivion. Instead, she'd picked the wrinkled folds apart, spread the hateful message open, and folded it neatly in her pocket. Why, indeed? She looked up to find Elizabeth still watching her.

"Do you have any idea who did this?" Elizabeth's voice was sharp.

"No." Jenny gave a short laugh. "And believe me, I spent most of the night trying to figure that out."

Elizabeth's brow furrowed, and she grasped Jenny's arm. "You don't suppose Martin Lester is still around?"

"I don't think so." Even the mention of her erstwhile guardian brought a tightening in her chest. "Last I heard, he'd pulled out and left the territory. He can stay gone forever, for all I care."

"Then who?" Elizabeth waved the note. "This didn't get here all by itself." When Jenny didn't reply, she lifted a burner from the cookstove and dropped the note into the glowing coals. "There. It's gone."

Jenny watched the paper blacken at the edges, then fold in upon itself before it burst into flames and turned to ash. All well and good, and perhaps it would let Elizabeth think she'd put the hateful words to rest.

As for her, it would take more than mere flames to erase the message from her heart.

Jenny carried a tray laden with flapjacks and bacon to a table near the front window. After an unexpectedly large breakfast rush, the steady stream of customers had dwindled to a trickle, letting Elizabeth leave the kitchen long enough to help clear the empty tables. Maybe the two of them could catch their breath if the lunch crowd held off for a bit.

Jenny removed the last plate of flapjacks from her tray and set it on the table. "That ought to satisfy even a hungry man's appetite." She smiled at the four robust miners, then scanned the room. Two women had just seated themselves at a corner table. She wove her way across the room to greet them.

"Good morning, ladies. Are you ready to order?"

The woman sitting nearest her looked up with a pleasant smile. "I believe I'll have the eggs and biscuits," she began.

The woman on the other side of her tapped the speaker on the shoulder. She leaned over and whispered to her companion, shielding their faces with her spread fingers.

The first woman stared up at Jenny. "That's the one? Oh!" Her smile faded and her gaze darted around the room. "Excuse me," she called to Elizabeth, who was hurrying past with a load of dirty dishes. "Could you take our order, please?"

Elizabeth halted beside Jenny with a puzzled frown. "Didn't you. . ." Her voice trailed off as comprehension spread across her face. Her mouth set in a grim line.

"It's all right," Jenny told her through stiff lips. "I'll take these things back to the kitchen." She lifted the dishes out of Elizabeth's arms and pushed through the swinging door.

Setting the dishes on the counter with a clatter, she knotted her hands into fists and pressed them against her flaming cheeks. Would it never end?

Probably not. News spread all too quickly in a close-knit community like Prescott. News and gossip both—hateful, hurtful words, spreading like a deadly plague from one person to the next.

Her stomach roiled and she clapped one hand over her mouth until the acid taste went away. At least Elizabeth hadn't ordered the women out of the restaurant, as she'd been known to do to customers who had impugned Jenny's reputation in the past. While Jenny appreciated her friend's loyalty, the uproar involved and the stares and whispers from the remaining customers were as hard to bear as the insults themselves.

The swinging door burst open, admitting Elizabeth, her eyes blazing. Her expression softened when she saw Jenny's distress.

"I'm sorry," she said, hurrying to wrap her arm around Jenny's shoulders. "So sorry."

The show of sympathy proved to be Jenny's undoing. "Look at me," she whispered through her tears, not wanting her words to carry to the patrons in the dining room. "What do you see? Is there something about me that screams, 'This woman once worked in a saloon. Avoid her, lest you be tainted, too'?"

"Of course not. It isn't—"

"Then why does it keep on happening? You know working in the Nugget wasn't something I chose to do. I never would have entered the doors of that place if I hadn't been taken there by force. Doesn't that count for something?" She slapped her hand against the counter. "I've done everything I can think of to show people I'm a decent person. All I want to do is leave the past behind me. Why won't they let me do that?"

"I don't know," Elizabeth said, wiping away her own tears. "I truly don't. But no matter how horrible other people may be, always remember I'm your friend." She pulled Jenny close. "And I'll be praying for you."

Don't bother. Jenny nodded her thanks and moved back to the counter to chop vegetables to put in the stew that would be on the evening's menu. Not for the world would she intentionally hurt Elizabeth's feelings, but her friend might as well save her breath. Jenny knew all too well the futility of calling out to a God who didn't care about her.

If anything were going to turn her life around, she would have to be the one to make it happen.

Chapter 2

Andrew Garrett strolled across the plaza, enjoying the scent of pines and the odor of fresh-cut lumber emanating from the sawmill. He scanned the signs on the various businesses facing the open square until he found the one he sought: the Capital Restaurant & Bakery. A simple enough edifice, but surface looks, as he had discovered long ago in his line of work, didn't necessarily reflect what lay within. Earl Waggoner had told him the place served the best food in town.

The corner of his mouth quirked up into a half smile. Apparently, the owner hadn't seen fit to change the name, even though Prescott had lost its status of territorial capital to Tucson two years previously. Maybe they saw it as a statement of the quality of the food. He grinned at the thought.

Inside the modest dining room, he looked around for Waggoner but didn't spot him. No matter. When he and Lute Bledsoe discussed the purchase of Bledsoe's mining claim the day before, Waggoner had stepped up and introduced himself as the miner's agent. Waggoner's slick attitude had struck Andrew wrong at the time, but knowing Bledsoe couldn't read the contract he was offering, he could understand the miner's need for someone to look after his interests. He had to admit, though, that a few moments to enjoy his meal before he had to share table space with Waggoner would help him keep his appetite.

A petite, dark-haired woman stopped to take his order of roast beef and new potatoes, then left Andrew free to study the faces of the other patrons, a pastime he thoroughly enjoyed. The table he'd chosen near the kitchen gave him a good view of the whole room.

If he didn't miss his guess, the young family near the front window had come into town from their farm for supplies. Their simple, threadbare clothing spoke of people who had to pinch their pennies. Enjoying a meal she hadn't cooked herself was probably a rare luxury for the thin-faced wife. Her husband beamed throughout the meal, obviously proud of being able to provide her with this treat.

What about the lone diner in the far corner? Andrew summed up the man's slicked-back, dark hair and flashy clothing in one word: gambler. He'd seen plenty of those around Denver. This fellow would fit right in with them.

He smiled his thanks when the waitress set his order before him. *Mmm.* If the fragrant aroma gave any indication of the taste, Waggoner hadn't exaggerated his claims about the quality of the restaurant's food a bit. Andrew lifted a bite of the roast to his lips and closed his eyes, the better to savor the home-cooked flavor.

Just the way roast beef ought to taste. Not at all the bland fare he might have expected from a small-town restaurant. He'd eaten in the finest dining establishments from St. Louis to San Francisco. This food would hold its own with any of them.

A bright shaft of light beamed across the floor when the front door opened. Earl Waggoner paused in the doorway until he caught sight of Andrew, then hurried over to join him.

"Sorry to be late." Waggoner took off his hat and set it on the corner of the empty chair next to him. "I was unavoidably detained."

"Don't mention it," Andrew said. "As you can see, I've already started eating. Why don't you order, and we can talk business after we've finished?"

"No need to wait on my account. I'd just as soon get down to business right now." Waggoner flagged down the waitress and ordered beef stew and biscuits, then pulled out a folded paper and pushed it across the table to Andrew.

"Here is my authorization to act as agent for Lute Bledsoe. As he told you yesterday, he can't even sign his own name, let alone read a sales contract. That's why he's asked me to take care of all this on his behalf. You've already made the verbal agreement with him." He paused as the waitress set down his food, then continued, "I'm just here to finalize the legal end of things."

Andrew chewed another bite of beef and took his time studying the paper. He couldn't put his finger on just what it was about Waggoner that gave him pause, but something about the man set off warning bells in Andrew's brain. "Where is Bledsoe?" he asked casually.

Waggoner chuckled. "He left early this morning. Said he was going out to find another claim that would bring in even more money than this one."

Andrew set down the sheet and gave it a last looking over before handing it back to Waggoner. "Everything appears to be in order." *Unfortunately.*

"Good." Waggoner wolfed down his last bite of stew and rubbed his napkin across his mouth, then carefully wiped each end of his mustache. "Let's get down to it, then."

He wadded his napkin and dropped it onto his plate. Shoving the plate aside, he planted his elbows on the table and leaned toward Andrew. "My understanding is that you offered to purchase Bledsoe's claim for the sum of five hundred dollars. Is that correct?"

"That's what we agreed on." Andrew pulled a sheaf of papers from his coat pocket and handed them to Waggoner. "You can read the contract for yourself. It's a fair price."

"Bledsoe is more than satisfied with that amount. And I'm sure your Colorado group would feel they've made a good bargain." Waggoner's thin lips spread and lifted his mustache in a wolfish grin. "But what about you?"

"Me?" The question startled Andrew. "I'm hired to acquire properties at the best price possible. My own concern in this is to be sure the agreement is fair to both parties. I believe I've done that."

"But are you getting enough out of the deal?"

"I told you, I'm in the employ of the Denver Consolidated Mining Company. I don't have a financial interest in the deal."

"Then you're missing out on some easy money." Waggoner's eyes held an eager light. "I have a proposition for you. Write out a new agreement, but make the selling price on this one seven hundred dollars. That's still low enough that it won't raise any concern from your investors."

The faint warning bells grew into clanging gongs. Andrew tried to keep his voice calm. "Are you telling me Bledsoe has changed his mind and wants to raise his price?"

Waggoner snorted. "Bledsoe won't know anything about it. He'll get the money he's expecting and that will be all, as far as he's concerned."

"Then the additional money. . ." Andrew let his voice trail off, waiting for Waggoner to finish the thought.

"Will be split between you and me, fifty-fifty." Waggoner leaned back and laced his fingers across his stomach. "A nice little profit for both of us, don't you agree?"

"No. I don't agree." Andrew shoved his chair back and stood, towering over the other man. "Have you ever done any mining? Ever squatted for hours in an icy stream on a placer claim, scooping up pan after pan of gravel and swirling it back and forth, waiting to spot just one bit of gold dust? Ever spent days on end shaking a rocker until you thought your arms were ready to fall off?"

He planted his fists on the table and leaned over, just inches from Waggoner's face. "Well, I have, and I'm here to tell you it's brutally hard work. Bledsoe located that claim through his own sweat and determination. He didn't try to make a killing on this deal. He just wanted a fair price in return for his labor. I don't hold with covert transactions. If you can't let your business dealings be known in public, there's something wrong with them."

He tucked the contract back inside his inner coat pocket. "I'll hand Bledsoe his money directly. And I'll make sure he knows exactly how you planned to repay his trust."

"If you can find him." Waggoner sneered. "He's out in the Bradshaws by now."

"No, he isn't." A gray-haired man at a neighboring table turned toward them. "I saw him just this morning, over at Bowen Mercantile. Said he was waiting for some money so he could stock up on supplies before he headed out." He fixed Waggoner with a level gaze. "This young fellow won't be the only one spreading the word about how you do business. No one will trust you to so much as hold his horse for him by the time this day is out."

Waggoner's expression now reminded Andrew more of a slinking coyote than a hungry wolf. "I'll get to Bledsoe first and block the sale. No one's going to make a profit out of this." He stormed out, leaving a relieved silence behind him.

Jenny drew away from the swinging door and turned her attention back to dishing up the next order. Altercations like that weren't commonplace in the restaurant, unless she counted Elizabeth springing to Jenny's defense whenever some unwise customer made a disparaging remark about her background. The raised voices had caught her notice; the words that carried through the door riveted her attention.

She hadn't recognized either of the voices, although she felt an immediate distrust for Waggoner, just by hearing his oily tone.

The other man, though—that rich baritone inspired confidence, even without a glimpse of his face.

Jenny sliced another serving of roast and set it on a plate, her curiosity piqued by the argument she had heard. Most of their customers wouldn't be so scrupulous about turning down an easy profit.

Good thing this one had. Jenny knew Bledsoe as one of the miners who frequented the restaurant. Knew him and liked him. He'd worked hard to find that claim. He didn't deserve to be cheated by some unscrupulous would-be agent.

Apparently, the mellow-voiced man felt the same way. Jenny's mind raced while she ladled out a helping of carrots. What manner of man would behave that way? And for someone he didn't even know?

His actions didn't mesh with what she'd seen in the majority of the men she'd known. After her experiences with Martin Lester, Burleigh Ames, and the customers at the Nugget, Jenny had pretty much given up on men altogether. If she were ever going to be interested in a man, he would have to be one with the mellow-voiced stranger's brand of integrity.

"Jenny?" Elizabeth came through the swinging door, her face alight with curiosity. "There's a customer out there who wants to talk to you."

"With me?" Jenny threw a wary glance toward the dining room. "Who is it?"

Elizabeth shook her head. "I've never seen him before. And he didn't mention you by name, just asked if he could speak with the cook."

Jenny smoothed her apron and patted her hair into place, pondering the strange request. A sudden thought struck her. Could it be the man she'd just heard? The one who put another man's welfare ahead of his own gain? Her heart quickened at the idea of meeting him face-to-face.

Hoping her face wasn't too flushed from the heat of the kitchen, she pushed open the door and stepped into the dining room.

Chapter 3

After Waggoner stomped out, Andrew realized every gaze in the restaurant was turned his way. Let them look. He knew he'd raised his voice and lost his temper, but he didn't see how he could have done otherwise. The idea of Waggoner fleecing both Bledsoe and the group of investors galled him. The agent's casual assumption that Andrew would be willing to go along with the plan sickened him.

The dark-haired man Andrew had taken for a gambler raised his hand and called the waitress over. She spoke to him, then hurried off to the kitchen, and the customers turned back to their meals.

Andrew fished in his pocket. He'd pay his bill and get out of there while he was no longer the center of attention. It looked like he'd be paying Waggoner's bill, too, he noted grimly. One more black mark against the man's name.

The kitchen door swung open again, and a slender young woman stepped into the dining room. Andrew's breath caught in his throat. Her face could have come straight out of a Gainsborough portrait. Curly blond bangs hung loosely over her high forehead. The rest of her hair, pulled up to the crown of her head in the back, descended in ringlets to just below her shoulders.

She glanced around the room, her blond curls reflecting glints of copper in the light that streamed in through the front window. Then her blue-green gaze met Andrew's, and for a moment his heart felt like it had frozen in his chest.

Who was she? What was she like? Everything within him yearned to find the answers to those questions. But that would take time. Time he didn't have. The Denver Consolidated Mining Company trusted him to carry out the job they'd hired him to do. As soon as he paid Bledsoe, he had to head down to Tucson to investigate the rumors of gold, silver, and copper in the southern part of the territory.

Once he'd finished his business there, though, he might just come back and make the acquaintance of the girl with the coppery highlights in her hair. It would give him a reason to complete his business in Tucson as quickly as possible.

For now, though. . . He tore his gaze away, left his money on the table, and stepped through the door to find the Bowen Mercantile and talk to Lute Bledsoe.

❦

Jenny caught sight of a tall, sandy-haired man staring at her. Her heart sped up even more. Could this be the one who had asked to speak with her? Then he looked away, set some money on the table, and walked out.

138

With a sense of loss, she watched him go, then scanned the rest of the room. A man in the far corner beckoned to her. He rose to greet her as she made her way to his table.

"Are you the one responsible for the delicious meal I've just enjoyed?" He favored her with a slight bow. "Allow me to introduce myself. My name is Evan Townsend."

Jenny took in his frock coat and embroidered vest. Coupled with his confident air, they reminded her of some of the habitués of the Nugget's gaming tables. "How do you do? I'm Jenny Davis." She offered her hand, wondering why he had summoned her.

His soft fingers enveloped hers in a warm grip. "And you truly are the one who did the cooking today? The ham, the crumb cake?"

Jenny nodded. "Elizabeth and I share the cooking duties, but I did fix those."

His eyes glowed. "Beauty and talent in the same package. A rare find."

Jenny withdrew her hand and clasped her fingers behind her. "I need to get back to the kitchen, Mr. Townsend. If that's all you wanted. . . ?"

"No, wait. Forgive me for not coming straight to the point. I'd like to discuss a business proposition with you. Sit down." He pulled out a chair and flashed a brilliant smile. "Please."

Every instinct told Jenny to turn on her heel and march back to the kitchen. She'd had enough experience with bold men and their business schemes to last a lifetime. She studied Evan Townsend and his assured smile. At least he'd asked her to stay, not ordered her to. Still, everything about him spoke of a man used to getting his own way. If she had any sense, she ought to get out of his reach before he spoke another word.

To her amazement, she sat.

Evan's smile lit up the dim corner where they sat. "Thank you." He pushed in her chair and seated himself directly across from her. "Miss Davis, I'm a businessman. I have various holdings throughout the territory: part ownership in a freighting company in La Paz; a lumber mill not far from here; a store near Camp Verde. Right now, I'm focusing on starting some new ventures in Tucson."

Jenny nodded distractedly, her mind back on the tasks going undone in the kitchen. With Elizabeth back there at the moment, she knew nothing would be left to scorch on the stove. But there were still carrots to slice and potatoes to put on to boil. And that last batch of rolls should be finished rising.

Evan Townsend went on. "I'll admit Tucson hasn't been much of a showplace, but things have been changing since the territorial capital moved there two years ago. There are opportunities for a man who knows how to make things happen." He settled back in his chair and looked straight at her. "A man like me, Miss Davis."

"That's very interesting, Mr. Townsend. Now I really must—"

"I've purchased a building in a favorable location. Granted, it's small, but space can be added as needed. It's an ideal spot, close to the center of the action. There's plenty of profit to be made, and I'm just the man to do it."

Those rolls would be ready to overflow their pan if she didn't get back to them. Jenny pushed back her chair and stood, eager to escape this flow of information. "It was nice meeting you, Mr. Townsend."

He scrambled to his feet, a crestfallen expression twisting his features. "Then you're not interested?"

"Interested?" His astonishment made it apparent she'd missed something. But what?

"I thought I'd made it clear. I intend to open a restaurant in Tucson. I'll provide the building and the start-up capital, but I need someone with excellent cooking skills to make it a profitable investment. As soon as I tasted that meal, I knew I'd found one cook in a million." His face lightened again as he looked at her. "And once I met you, that sealed my decision. What do you say? Will you come in with me as my partner? Your culinary skills and my business acumen. We'll split the profits right down the middle."

Jenny's mind reeled. That was the second business proposal she'd heard in less than an hour. Both promised substantial earnings. Only one of them sounded honorable. And that one had been directed at her.

But leave Prescott? Part company with Elizabeth and Michael? She shook her head. "No, thank you, Mr. Townsend. Your opinion of my cooking is flattering, but my home is here. I couldn't think of leaving."

Disappointment shadowed his handsome features, then he gave a quick shrug. "You win some, you lose some." He reached into his vest pocket and dropped several coins on the table. "I'll be in town for two more days. I'm staying at the Prescott House. Let me know if you change your mind."

Jenny watched him stride away, then retreated to the safe familiarity of the kitchen. It would take more—much more—than a stranger's pretty promises to make her decide to uproot and leave.

<hr />

"Talk some sense into her, Michael. I've tried everything." Elizabeth leaned against a cupboard and folded her arms across her chest as though distancing herself from the conversation.

Her husband gave Jenny an apologetic smile. "We only want what's best for you." He spread his hands wide. "You know how much we both care about you."

Jenny's throat tightened. Of course she knew they cared. Without Elizabeth and Michael putting their very lives on the line to come to her rescue, she'd be living a life of degradation in the Nugget now.

"I can never repay what you've done for me," she began. "Without your help, I know only too well the kind of life I would have been forced into. Being freed of that was the best thing that ever happened to me." Her throat tightened. "But I'm not completely free, even now."

Michael's brow wrinkled in consternation. In answer to his unspoken question, Jenny reached into her pocket and held up a folded slip of paper. "Some people haven't forgotten where I've been, and they won't let me forget, either." She pressed the paper into Michael's hand and watched his eyebrows soar halfway to his hairline as he read.

"That's abominable!" He crumpled the sheet and tossed it from him. "But you can't let one incident push you into a hasty decision."

"It isn't just this once," Elizabeth interjected reluctantly. "This is the second one she's gotten."

"The fifth," Jenny corrected.

Elizabeth whirled and stared at her. "There've been more? All slipped under the door like these two? Why didn't you tell me?"

Jenny shrugged and picked at a loose thread on her cuff. "I tried to ignore them. I don't know, maybe I thought if I didn't mention them, they'd quit coming. It didn't work, though, did it?" The laugh she attempted caught in her throat.

"You mean to tell me someone's been sneaking around here at night and shoving these under the door?" Michael's voice rose to a near bellow.

"Not all of them. I found others out at the woodpile and stuck to the top of the barrel where I take out the trash. Whoever is doing this wants to make sure their messages reach me."

"But Michael's right," Elizabeth put in. "You can't make choices based on the action of one hateful individual."

"You don't understand." Jenny stared at her two dearest friends. How could they possibly comprehend the pain of being reminded about her unsavory past? "It isn't just whoever is writing these notes. Think about it, Elizabeth. How many times over the past two years have you gone to my defense when some customer mentioned my time at the Nugget?"

Elizabeth focused on a spot on the floor and didn't answer.

"It doesn't matter how hard I try to shake off the memories. There are people here who will never stop bringing it up." Jenny looked around the kitchen that had become so familiar, her heart aching at the thought of leaving it behind. "I thought I could keep ignoring these, but I can't. Even if we found out who's been leaving the notes and made them stop, it wouldn't change what's in people's minds. To some, I'll always be nothing more than a saloon girl. The only way I can get away from that is to leave."

Elizabeth's eyes glistened with unshed tears. She moved next to Michael, as if drawing comfort from his nearness. "Then there's nothing we can do to change your mind?"

Jenny blinked back tears of her own and gazed at her friends intently, imprinting their images on her memory so she could carry them with her in her heart. "It's something I have to do. I'll go over to the Prescott House first thing in the morning and tell Evan Townsend I've decided to take him up on his offer."

Chapter 4

*H*ot. Jenny stood in the minute bit of shade provided by the doorway of the adobe building Evan had named the Pueblo Restaurant. Heat rose in shimmering waves along the dusty street.

She pulled a handkerchief from her sleeve and used it to mop the perspiration from her face and neck. Her fingers twiddled with her top button. Did she dare loosen it? Modesty said no; comfort said yes. Comfort won out.

Ahh. Even that slight difference gave some relief. Jenny raised her hand to shield her eyes from the blazing afternoon sun. When she first arrived in Tucson, she found it hard to believe this could be the same sun that had illuminated the Prescott sky. Back home, it was a welcome friend, urging the chilly spring mornings toward the promise of summer warmth. This sun was relentless in its oppressive heat, searing the desert landscape.

The fiery orb hovered a little past its zenith. In Prescott, the day's activity would continue unabated. Here, the streets lay deserted, the population having retired indoors for their afternoon siesta. Later, when the scorching temperatures lessened, the town would come back to life.

Jenny picked up a damp rag and waved it back and forth, fanning a cooling breeze across her face. It was a harsh land, an arid land. And yet, unlikely as it seemed, it had become *her* land.

Looking along the Calle del Arroyo, she could see the Tucson Mountains in the distance, their barren peaks devoid of the forest that covered the slopes in the northern part of the territory. A desolate wasteland at first glance, until one looked beyond the bleak landscape and saw beauty in the spreading arms of the saguaro, the scarlet blooms atop the spindly ocotillo branches. The wide vistas invited her to lose herself in their vast expanse, and Jenny welcomed the opportunity. Here, an anonymous speck in a broad universe, she finally felt free of her past.

She had come here looking for sanctuary, a place where she could start anew. She had found all that and more.

And now I'd better find a place to get out of the sun. Jenny laughed softly. The custom of resting during the hottest part of the day had seemed peculiar at first.

After only a few days of pushing herself to keep working throughout the afternoon hours, she had embraced the local wisdom without question.

"You're still here?"

Jenny turned at the sound of a voice behind her. Evan leaned against the adobe wall, a friendly smile playing across his face. *About time he showed up.* Jenny hadn't seen him around the restaurant at all that day. He must have slipped in through the office door.

"I was just getting ready to leave." Jenny stepped past him to retrieve her bonnet from its peg on the wall of the small corner office.

"May I accompany you? There are a couple of things I'd like to discuss."

Jenny locked the front door and tucked her hand into the crook of Evan's arm. They strolled along the deserted street at an easy pace, their feet sending up tiny puffs of dust with every step.

She ducked her head against the bright glare that even the bonnet's wide brim couldn't block. Perhaps she should carry a parasol. At this rate, her fair skin would soon be a mass of blisters and freckles. And that might not be a bad thing. Her looks had caused her nothing but trouble and heartache thus far.

Evan broke into her thoughts. "I'm concerned about you. You've been working too hard. I wanted a business partner for this venture, not a slave."

Jenny chuckled and gave his arm a reassuring pat. "It's freedom I've found here, Evan, not slavery. For the first time, I'm building up something substantial for my future, something I can be proud of. You have no idea what that means to me."

Evan halted abruptly. Placing his fingers beneath her chin, he tilted her head up to face him. "Still, I'm worried about you. When I asked you to come here, I hadn't counted on problems arising with my other business interests. I didn't plan on being called away almost as soon as the restaurant got underway, and I never expected you to take on the business responsibilities in addition to doing all the cooking. You're spending far more time here than I ever intended."

"But don't you see, Evan? I've found out I'm able to do more than just cook. The menu planning, ordering supplies, keeping the books—having the responsibility for all those details is new to me, but I'm good at it." She gave him a brilliant smile. "I feel like I've finally found my place in life, and I'm loving every minute of it."

"Even in this blast furnace of a place? You aren't inclined to go rushing back to those cool mountain summers at the first opportunity?"

If you only knew. Jenny contented herself with a shake of her head. She hadn't told Evan her reasons for leaving Prescott and didn't plan to now. Or ever. That part of her life belonged to the past. This was a place of new beginnings.

"Let's talk about the future," she said. "If what we've brought in so far and our steady increase in customers are anything to go by, we could double our profits by next month."

Evan gave her a look of rueful admiration. "Is there ever a time you aren't thinking about profits?"

She grinned. "Face it, Evan. You have joined forces with a hardheaded businesswoman."

"But a lovely one." His smile grew tender.

Jenny looked away and set off down the street on her own. *Don't spoil it.*

After a moment, she heard Evan's footsteps catching up to her. "I'm not sure what I did to upset you," he said. "But would this hardheaded business-woman be willing to let me make it up to her by taking her to the playhouse this evening?"

"I don't think so, Evan. There are things I need to do."

"Like what?" Exasperation and amusement mingled in his tone. "Come up with new additions for the menu? You've already done that a dozen times."

"Actually, I was thinking of drawing up plans for a larger dining room. If things keep going as well as they have, we'll need some extra space before long."

For the second time, Evan stopped her, but this time his lips were twitching with suppressed mirth. "Jenny, Jenny. Only a few weeks in Tucson, and already you're planning to expand the business." He threw back his head and laughed. "I didn't hire a cook; I took on the most ambitious business partner in the territory!"

His laughter subsided, but the twinkle in his gray eyes lingered. "Even a tycoon has to take a night off now and then. Think of it as an opportunity to meet new people, potential customers you can lure to the restaurant. Better yet, think of it as a favor to me. I'm ready for a night out, and I need someone to keep an eye on me to make sure I don't spend all our hard-earned money."

Jenny studied his face for a long moment. "All right," she said and resumed walking. "Just this once."

"Wonderful! I'll pick you up at seven." He paused at the door of the house where she rented her small room. "And I'll tell you one thing: As hard a bargain as you drive, I'm glad you're on the same side of our business dealings as I am." He winked and gave her a brief wave as he turned away.

※

Jenny peered into her mirror and twisted the last ringlet into place. There. The coppery-blond curl draped over the shoulder of her sapphire-blue princess-cut dress. She smiled, enjoying the novelty of seeing herself dressed for an evening out rather than her usual wilted appearance after a day spent in a hot kitchen or laboring over the restaurant accounts.

Despite the disinterest she'd expressed to Evan, she felt a rising surge of anticipation. She had overheard her customers talk of the playhouses in Tucson, but she had never been to one herself. She'd never expected to, either.

But going out for an evening of entertainment went along with the lifestyle of a respectable woman making her mark in the community. Such a difference from the existence of the past few years, when her foremost goal had been to keep a low profile and hope others would forget her dismal past!

She lifted her new hat from its box. Purchased on impulse along with the blue gown with some of her first earnings from the Pueblo, it had lain untouched until now. With a sense of embarking on an adventure, she set it in place and tilted her head from side to side, studying the effect. Was the froth of ribbons and bows too much?

No, it suited the evening and her buoyant mood. She adjusted it once more, letting the front dip over her forehead.

There. She nodded approvingly at the image in the glass, no longer the solemn-faced girl she usually saw, but the picture of a respectable lady.

A shiver of excitement swept up and down her arms. An evening at the theater, her goal of making herself into the person she longed to be within reach—what other surprises did her new life hold?

Evan knocked at the door of the house promptly at seven. His black frock coat and gleaming white shirt took Jenny's breath away. An attractive man, no doubt about it. And in his evening attire, he looked downright handsome.

From the gleam in his eyes, he approved of her appearance in equal measure, but he forbore to comment. *Good.* Maybe he had learned from her reaction earlier. Whatever the reason, she appreciated his restraint.

The show proved even more wonderful than Jenny had imagined. The glow of the footlights, the cheers from the audience, and the lively music all combined to make it an evening of pure enjoyment.

During the intermission, Jenny strolled to the back of the seating area with Evan. Moving through the crowd, she couldn't miss the admiring glances he drew from the women they passed or the jealous looks they cast at her.

"Having a good time?" Evan bent close, his lips nearly brushing her ear so she could hear him over the noisy throng.

She smiled and nodded, not bothering to try to make herself heard. So this was what it felt like to spend time in the company of a man with no purpose but to enjoy herself, to be the object of envy and not scorn. She could find it easy to get used to this way of life. Very easy, indeed.

Evan placed a cup of punch in Jenny's hands, then led her over to a quiet corner of the room. "May I leave you here for just a moment? I need to discuss a bit of business with some of the gentlemen here." His eyelid dropped in a wink. "Nothing to do with the restaurant, I assure you. I wouldn't dare leave you out of that."

At her nod, he withdrew a few steps to where a small group of men waited.

Jenny sipped the fruity drink and contented herself with watching the milling crowd. One or two of the ladies who glanced her way bowed their heads and smiled a greeting. Jenny returned their nods with pleasure.

Respectability. Acceptance. Everything she had longed for and hadn't been able to achieve in Prescott appeared to be hers for the taking here. Elizabeth would have said a prayer of thanks; Jenny knew she had done it on her own.

Evan returned when the music signaled the end of intermission, trailed by two of his business associates. Just before he reached Jenny, she saw one of them pull him aside and shout to be heard over the crowd.

"I don't blame you for wanting to keep her to yourself," he said with a grin. "My compliments on escorting the most beautiful woman here."

Evan rejoined her and darted a glance over his shoulder at his departing companion. "I hope that didn't bother you," he murmured. "He meant it only as a compliment, I assure you."

"It didn't bother me," Jenny replied, filled with a sense of wonder when she realized it was true. For the first time in years, she didn't mind being admired for her looks. Truly, this place had worked its magic on her.

❧

Bright stars glittered across the desert sky. Jenny nestled into her pillow and watched the grand procession through the small window of her room.

A night like this should last forever. How long had it been since she'd been around people without bracing herself for the next scathing comment?

The Pleiades edged past the corner of her window. Jenny grinned at the familiar grouping and stretched her arms wide, then laced her fingers behind her head. She might have made some mistakes along the way, but moving to Tucson hadn't been one of them.

Snatches of one of the tunes she heard that night drifted into her mind. She closed her eyes and sang the words softly.

Her eyes snapped open again. She hadn't sung since performing for the crowd of half-drunk customers her last night at the Nugget, just a few hours before Michael O'Roarke rescued her from the dreadful place and spirited her away to safety. Singing always brought back memories of that dark time in her life, and she'd avoided it diligently.

Until now. She whispered a few more of the lyrics and felt something break loose within her. Like a dam weakened by a tiny fissure that grew until it could hold back its wall of water no longer, the protective wall Jenny had built up began to crumble. If it hadn't been the middle of the night, she would have flung off the bed covers and burst forth in full voice.

Tears of joy stung her eyes. Back when her family was laboring to make a living on their Chino Valley farm, singing had been one of the delights of her life. Back then, life meant love, safety, and security. She had thought she'd lost all those forever. Beginning her new life in Tucson had restored her joy in living again.

Her heart swelled in her chest until she thought she'd burst with gladness. After all that had happened, all the years of pain and humiliation, she was finally free.

She hummed a few more bars, reveling in her newfound liberty. Scenes from the evening floated through her memory, the bright lights, the music, the ladies and gentlemen of Tucson dressed in their finest.

Responding to bows and smiles and nods of greeting, and not one of them laced with a sneer of contempt. . . Jenny wanted to soar right out the window and join the stars in their celestial dance.

What was it Evan's friend had called her? The most beautiful woman there? And later, after the evening's entertainment had ended, Evan had introduced her to others of his acquaintance, each of them trying to outdo the flattery of the others.

For once, the praise hadn't bothered her. They had spoken in a friendly manner, with no innuendos or disreputable overtones, and their words acted as a refreshing rain on the parched ground of Jenny's soul.

Would she ever see any of those men again? It would be interesting to see if any of them lived up to their promises to dine at the Pueblo. Would she recognize them if they did? She had been introduced to such a number of new people, they all seemed to meld into a faceless blur.

Weariness overcame her at last. She rolled onto her side and folded her hands beneath her cheek. One face stood out in her mind, superseding all the others. Who could it be? Her sleepy mind puzzled over the mystery, sorting through the men she'd met that night.

Just before sleep claimed her, the answer came. She hadn't seen him that night at all. The tanned face, sandy hair, and clear blue eyes belonged to the man from Prescott, whose face seemed to be permanently etched in her memory.

❦

"How are you feeling today?" Evan lounged against the kitchen doorway, watching Jenny run a tea towel across a newly washed plate.

"I'm fine," Jenny replied. With the last of the lunch customers gone, she needed only to stack the dishes and wipe down the counters before she closed the doors for the afternoon. "Better than that, actually. I feel absolutely invigorated today."

Evan lifted one eyebrow. "You are aware, aren't you, that it's even hotter today than yesterday?"

"I'm fine," Jenny repeated. "Truly." She scrubbed the last section of the counter and rolled her sleeves back down, buttoning the cuffs in place.

Evan lifted his hands in surrender. "I won't argue with you. I don't have the energy. But I do have an idea how we can relieve you of some of your workload."

"But I don't—"

Evan cleared his throat, cutting off her protest. "You're doing a wonderful job of running the place, and I realize you're enjoying yourself, and that's fine—for now. But I'm looking at it from a larger perspective. What happens if you wear yourself out to the point you get sick? I'd have no trouble taking over the books, but I could never step in and manage the cooking. We'd have to shut the doors, Jenny. Do you want that?"

She stared at him, sobered by the picture his words painted.

He went on. "I want you to consider hiring a helper, someone you can train to cook your way. Think of it as an investment. You can still oversee the kitchen, but with another pair of hands to help, you'll be able to concentrate more on the management end of things. It looks like I'm going to have to spend more time away from here than I thought. I need to be able to count on you to run the whole place, and you can't do it alone."

Jenny squeezed the cleaning rag between her fingers. Evan had a point, especially when it came to giving her more time to do the office work. The discovery that she possessed a keen business mind and enjoyed using it buoyed her spirits. Much as she hated to admit it, though, she did feel tired at the end of the day. So tired, she often had to force herself to stay awake long enough to make the ledger entries and draw up supply orders every evening.

What if she followed Evan's suggestion? She wouldn't want just anyone working in her kitchen. She and Elizabeth had gotten along famously, but that surely wouldn't be the norm.

But the thought of spending more time ensconced in her little office tantalized her. If Evan was right, if she could find someone willing to learn to cook the way she did. . .

"I'll do it." She raised her gaze to his and chuckled at his look of surprise. "I'm a businesswoman, remember? And this will be the best choice for our business. But," she admonished, "you have to promise me one thing."

"What's that?"

Jenny folded her arms and lifted her chin. "Don't go looking for someone to fill the position. This is something I want to do myself."

A slow smile lit Evan's face. "I'm beginning to realize there are a lot of things you want to do for yourself. Have at it, then. You're the lady in charge."

Chapter 5

Jenny scooted a shipping crate across the floor of her new dwelling and set it in place next to a straight-backed chair, where it would serve as a small table. She draped a colorful serape over the crate and stood back to observe the effect. What a change this sun-drenched space was from her stuffy little rented room!

She twitched a corner of the serape into place, marveling at the transformation that had taken place in her life. Jenny Davis, businesswoman. Jenny Davis, part owner of the Pueblo Restaurant. And now, Jenny Davis, homeowner.

The concept still seemed foreign to her. Who would have thought the girl whose life had been shattered by tragedy would one day become the proud owner of this small but neat adobe home?

She reached for a jar to use as a vase on her makeshift table, then realized the time. The rest would have to wait until after supper. She yawned and stretched, already feeling the effects of missing her afternoon siesta. In just a few hours, she promised herself, she would be back to finish moving in and enjoy a well-earned night's sleep in her new home.

Outside, the late afternoon sun glinted off the little adobe's whitewashed walls. Jenny paused for a moment to cast a lingering glance at the rosebush blooming beside the front door. It looked like—no, it *was*—a real home. Her home.

Meyer Street had started coming back to life. Jenny passed a donkey-drawn *carreta* and smiled at a group of dust-covered children kicking an empty can along the way. When one of her regular customers called out her name and waved a greeting, she smiled and waved back.

Home. The word meant more than a roof over her head. More, even, than her whitewashed adobe dwelling. It signified a place where she was accepted, a place to belong. For the first time, Jenny felt she'd found that place. A place of contentment, or as near to contentment as a person could expect to come.

Jenny sidestepped a man carrying a load of firewood on his back, then continued her musings. Perfect peace wasn't an attainable goal for people like herself. She knew that and accepted it, even though the knowledge left an aching void she didn't often acknowledge.

Still, life here was good. Better than she had any reason to expect a few short months ago.

Her steps quickened when the Pueblo Restaurant came into view. Here she had a place to call her own and a business where she could indulge in doing the cooking she loved and improve on her newfound business skills. She had no cause for complaint.

She unlocked the front door and gazed around the dining room. In her mind's eye, she could already see the benefits an addition to the building would create. A bigger dining area, first of all. And certainly more kitchen space.

She hung her wide-brimmed bonnet on a peg in her office and hurried to the kitchen to don her apron and prepare the evening meal. Once the pork pie was in the oven, she scrubbed and peeled the potatoes methodically, smiling when she thought of Elizabeth's last letter where her friend had mentioned the possibility of building an addition to the Capital Restaurant & Bakery. Wouldn't she be surprised to hear about Jenny's own plans?

Thoughts of those plans kept her mind occupied while her hands were busy scraping carrots and making biscuits.

The afternoon passed quickly, and, before long, the scrape of the front door followed by the shuffle of feet announced the arrival of the evening's first diner. Jenny did a hasty check to make sure all was in order, then put on a welcoming smile and went to greet her guest.

"Red!" Her smile broadened in genuine pleasure when she recognized her favorite customer. Red Dwyer might not be as dapper and elegant as the men Evan had introduced her to the night before, but his presence never failed to lighten Jenny's spirits.

"And how are you this fine evening, Miss Jenny?" The wiry Irishman removed his floppy felt hat and brushed a light coating of dust off his miner's garb before seating himself at the table he preferred, nearest the kitchen.

"Ready to hear more of your stories about lost mines and buried treasure," Jenny teased. "But first, let me take your order. What would you like tonight?"

"Would you be having any of that pork pie you do so well? All the time I've been out in the Dragoon Mountains, my mouth's been watering for it."

Jenny laughed at the blatant flattery. "And since you're sitting where the aroma floats right out the kitchen door, you know perfectly well that it's on the menu."

Red's eyes glinted with good humor. "Ah, lass, you've too quick a mind for the likes of me. Bring me a portion of your pork pie, then, and fill the plate to overflowing."

Jenny complied, bringing herself a smaller serving as well. "It looks like a slow night," she said, glancing around at the otherwise empty room. "Mind if I sit with you? You can fill me in on your latest adventures while we eat."

"A succulent meal and the company of a charming lady to go with it?" Red gave a contented sigh. "What more could a man ask for?"

Jenny felt a faint blush rise to her cheeks. Red's constant Irish blarney had made her uncomfortable at first. It had taken her some time before she realized he meant it in a good-natured way and not with the unpleasant familiarity of many of the miners she'd known at the Nugget. Now she treated him with the easy camaraderie of someone she'd known for years rather than a stranger who'd only come into her life a few weeks before.

It's a little like the way Pa and I used to talk, she reflected. Red was older than her pa would have been, though. Probably in his mid to late fifties, although his sunbaked face made it hard to judge. And the gray strands that threaded through his dark red hair attested to his advancing years.

But his cheery disposition and sparkling sense of humor showed no signs of age. He took a bite of the pork pie and closed his eyes as if in transports of bliss. "This is it. The very flavor I've been dreaming of these past days." He dug into the rest of his meal with gusto, not speaking again until he had finished and blotted his lips with his napkin. "Jenny, you've saved a desperate man."

Jenny swallowed a bite of her own meal and shook her head. "Enough of the flattery, Red. Let's hear some more of your stories."

"Ah, well. Where shall I begin?" He slurped his coffee and settled back in his chair. "You've heard about me childhood in Clonlara, the fairest spot on the Emerald Isle, correct?"

"Mm-hm. And how you sailed to America to escape the terrible famine in Ireland."

"And my time in Boston up until I decided to follow the lure of riches and headed to the gold-encrusted hills of California to make me fortune?"

Jenny pushed her plate aside and leaned forward, enjoying the banter involved in recounting Red's history. "And instead of finding the mother lode, you barely made enough to keep yourself alive. And so. . ."

"And so I came to search for El Dorado here in Arizona Territory for one last try at making a strike before I get too old to pack up my burro and head off into those tempting hills."

Jenny laughed. Only Red would call the rocky hills surrounding Tucson tempting. She'd heard plenty of other terms for the area: bleak and barren, for starters.

"It must be so different here than where you grew up."

Red ran his hand through his hair and scratched the back of his head. "You're right about that. This heat-blasted country is a far cry from the Emerald Isle, to be sure. On the other hand, there's always that hint of treasure to be found, the promise of fortune lying just ahead. It's drawn me for years. I couldn't turn my back on it now if I wanted to."

Jenny tapped her fingers on the table. "I'm still waiting for my story."

"But, lass." Red spread his hands wide. "It sounds like you know my life history as well as I do. What more could I be telling?"

"It doesn't matter what you tell; it's the way you tell it. You could spin a grocery list into one of Scheherazade's tales. You've been gone five days. Surely you've had some adventures during that time. Things just don't stay quiet for long when you're around."

"Ah." Red tipped his chair back on two legs and drained the last of his coffee, seeming to ponder Jenny's accolade. "Well, if it's news of my latest wanderings you're wanting, you shall have it."

He rocked his chair forward, setting the front legs back on the clay floor with a thud. He cleared a space in front of him, planted his hands flat on the table, and looked straight into Jenny's eyes. "I've found it, lass."

"Found what?" she started to ask, but the dancing excitement in his eyes set a certainty growing in her mind.

"Red!" She glanced over her shoulder to make sure the place was still empty, then continued in hushed tones. "You mean you struck it rich out there?"

The wiry man rubbed his palms together and grinned. "The next thing to it, anyway. I've located a vein of silver out there. A big one, by the looks of her. The biggest this old rock pounder has ever seen. I saw a streak of white quartz on the side of a gully and went to check it out. And there she was, just sitting there as if she'd been waiting all these years for me to come along." His eyes gleamed with anticipation. "She's the strike I've dreamed of through all my days of wandering, lass. I know she is." His pale blue eyes glistened and seemed to focus on a scene far beyond the confines of the restaurant's walls.

Jenny stared in openmouthed wonder, then burst out laughing. "You old scoundrel! How long were you going to keep that to yourself if I hadn't dragged it out of you?"

"I had no fear about that." Red's mouth tweaked up in an impish grin. "Knowing how fond you are of stories, and all."

"So why are you sitting here talking to me instead of heading back out there to bring it out and come back a wealthy man?"

"Ah, there's the problem." Red rubbed his hand along his jawline. "It's a simple enough answer, though. I'm broke." He chuckled at her gasp of dismay. "I have enough to pay for my supper, never fear. And I'm able to pay for my lodging and otherwise keep body and soul together for the time being. But enough to finance the equipment I'll need for a venture like that. . .alas, no."

"But you can't just walk away from it. Not after you've worked so hard all these years."

"I won't walk away forever, lass. Just until I pull together the funds I need to see me through. Get some investors, perhaps. That vein of silver has waited for me this long. It won't be so bad for either of us to wait a little longer."

Jenny stared at him, turning the information over in her mind. "What do you plan to do?"

"Drive a wagon, haul adobe bricks, whatever happens to come along. I'm not too proud to do any honest work. If the good Lord intends for me to see this thing through, He'll provide a way; of that I'm sure. And in the meantime, I've heard of a young man who's worked with the mines up Colorado way. I may just strike up an acquaintance with him and see what advice he might have for me."

Jenny's long-ingrained suspicions kicked in. "Don't you go telling a total stranger about this, Red Dwyer. Do you hear me? You're a kind, honorable man and you think everyone else is the same way. But I'm here to tell you, people are capable of putting on a good front when they're after something. It isn't safe to give your trust to just anyone."

Red listened to her tirade, then fixed her with a shrewd glance mingled with a look of compassion. "I have the feeling you're speaking from experience, Jenny dear. Someday, maybe you'd like to turn the tables and be telling me your story for a change."

Jenny forced a tight smile. "Some things are better left forgotten, Red." She heard the sharpness in her voice and softened her tone. "But thank you for caring."

"I have no daughter of my own. It's easy to care about you. And anytime that burden from your past gets too heavy to bear, remember you can always share it with your old friend Red, will you?"

Jenny gave a brief nod, her mind already on other matters. "You mentioned getting investors. How much money do you think you'd need?"

Red pulled a slip of paper and a stub of pencil from his pocket and began jotting down figures. When he'd tallied them, he pushed the paper across to her.

Jenny drummed a light tattoo on the table with her fingertips. Her earnings from the restaurant had surpassed her fondest expectations, but after the purchase of her house, she couldn't come up with the full amount Red needed.

Still, what she could manage might be enough to make a difference. She'd seen Elizabeth take a similar chance on some of the miners around Prescott and knew the potential for profit existed. Perhaps investing in Red would be a way of helping both him and herself. If Evan could be involved in more than one moneymaking enterprise, so could she.

"What if I grubstaked you half of that?" The look of surprise in his eyes made her glad she'd asked.

"Girl, I'm not asking you to part with your hard-earned money. That wasn't my intention at all."

"I know." Jenny grinned. "If I'd thought you were asking, I might not have offered." She stood and brushed the wrinkles out of her apron. "There aren't many people in this world that I trust, Red. You're one of them." She extended her hand across the table. "If you're willing to take it, the money is yours."

Red hesitated only a moment, then scraped his chair back and stood facing her. "I've traveled halfway around the world, and I've met precious few people willing to take that kind of chance on me." His hand enveloped hers in a tight grip. "You won't lose out on this, lass. I promise. This strike will bring in enough to set us up for the rest of our days, wait and see."

Chapter 6

A flicker of doubt smote Jenny. Had she just made the blunder of a lifetime? She searched Red's eyes and found reassurance there. He was older and his appearance more grizzled, but in many ways he reminded her of Elizabeth's husband, Michael. She knew her trust hadn't been misplaced.

And if the promised wealth of the mine didn't materialize? It didn't matter. The Pueblo would continue to bring in money, and if she lost every cent of this investment, so be it. Some things were worth more than money. Friendship was one of them.

The door swung open behind her, and she turned to see Evan step inside. She shot a quick glance at Red, hoping he would understand her unspoken plea to keep their agreement just between the two of them.

"It's a quiet evening," she said, waving at the empty tables. "Any idea where all our customers have gone?"

"I do indeed." Evan let out a sharp bark of laughter. "A fistfight broke out between a couple of freighters, Maddox and Stewart. Half the men in town are standing on the sidelines, waiting to see how it turns out."

He grinned at Jenny's obvious concern. "Don't worry. The way Stewart is looking, the whole thing will be over in a matter of moments and you'll be deluged with hungry customers. And I haven't done so badly for myself, either."

"What do you mean?" Jenny had started for the kitchen to prepare for the onslaught, but Evan's last words brought her to a halt.

He slicked back his hair with both hands. "Anytime a match is even enough that the outcome is in doubt, men will be willing to bet their last dollar on the result. My job is to make sure as much of that loose cash as possible flows from their pockets into mine."

"Meaning?"

"Meaning that I covered a good many of the bets that were placed this afternoon." Evan wore a self-satisfied expression. "But I backed Maddox, not Stewart. I once saw him hit a stubborn ox and bring it to its knees."

He lifted one eyebrow at Jenny. "And what's behind that disapproving schoolmarm expression that's just settled on your face?" he asked, his voice tinged with amusement.

Jenny pressed her lips together and chose not to answer.

"Don't look so glum," Evan said. "I'm going back now to collect the profits of an afternoon well spent. Give me a little time to console the losers and send them this way. You'll have enough trade come through the door to make the cash box ring."

Jenny watched him stroll back outside, trying to control her temper.

"Are you all right, lass?"

She spun around at the sound of Red's quiet voice. "I'm fine," she told him, hoping the smile she pasted on her lips looked sincere. Not for the world would she admit she'd been so distraught by Evan's revelation she had forgotten her friend's presence.

Red stepped toward her, sharp lines of concern etched on his forehead. "You wouldn't be giving me a little blarney of your own, would you now? A few minutes ago, I saw trust and confidence in your eyes." He shook his head slowly. "It isn't there now."

"I'm just thinking ahead, trying to plan how to meet the demands of a herd of hungry customers arriving all at once." Her laugh didn't ring true, even to her own ears.

She hurried toward the kitchen, but Red held up his hand to stop her.

"I know you're busy, and I'll only be taking a moment more of your time." He paused and wet his lips. "I don't know what's happened to put such doubt about people in that sweet head of yours, but I want you to know there's someone else you can trust and talk to when I'm not around."

Jenny gave him a puzzled look. "Who are you talking about?"

"God."

Oh, no. Not you, too. She forced a bright smile to her lips and headed toward the kitchen door. "Trying to figure out how I'm going to cook, clean, and take orders from this mob all at the same time, I just wish I had someone I could trust enough to come in and do some odd jobs for me." The door swung shut behind her, cutting off Red's reply.

Jenny leaned her elbows on the counter and pressed her knuckles against her forehead. First Elizabeth, now Red. She cared for both of them and counted them as friends, something that didn't come easily for her. In every way, she had found them worthy of her trust.

If only they could be content to be her friends without having to bring God into it! She had already endured enough of Elizabeth's heartfelt pleading and assurances of God's love. Now Red had gotten into the act.

Who would have dreamed the feisty miner was of the same bent as Elizabeth and Michael? Maybe she shouldn't be surprised, though. He had the same steady look, the same calm assurance.

An assurance that could never be hers. She cupped her face in her palms, surprised to find her cheeks damp with unbidden tears. She dashed them away with the backs of her hands. Why couldn't her friends enjoy the benefits of their faith without having to emphasize the difference between them and her? Bad enough that her life had been torn apart by forces beyond her control. She didn't need to be reminded of the existence of a love she could never hope to share.

She slid a pan of biscuits into the oven, glad she had made an extra large batch that afternoon. From what Evan said, business ought to be booming in just a few minutes.

Evan. She heard his rumbling chuckle again, as though he stood beside her in the kitchen. So he found her distaste for gambling amusing? The unwanted tears stung her eyes again and she blinked them back. Let him laugh! She had seen enough of that vice in the dim cavern of the Nugget Saloon to last her a lifetime.

Faro, monte, poker—she'd watched grim-faced men playing all of them, seen the way the lure of unearned riches drew them farther and farther into its web. She checked the biscuits, trying to shake off her black mood. How had only a month at the Nugget made such a deep impression on her?

Was it there the seeds of distrust planted by her disreputable guardian took root? She didn't know and didn't care to ponder the matter. As she had told Red, some memories were better left alone.

But the question kept niggling at her. Had she become so hardened she was now incapable of giving her trust to anyone? Surely not. Look at Michael and Elizabeth. They had won her unqualified devotion two years before, and she considered them her dearest friends.

And then there was Red. Although she'd known him only a short time, something about him inspired the same kind of confidence.

And whom do you trust besides those three, Jenny Davis? She brushed the bothersome thought aside. Getting the restaurant set up and running had consumed her every waking moment. She hadn't gotten to know many people in Tucson yet. When the time was right, she would make more friends.

What about Evan? Surely their business partnership counted for something. She wouldn't have pulled up stakes and come to an unknown part of the territory with someone undependable, would she? His penchant for gambling aside, Evan had proven himself an astute businessman. She had made a good choice with him, as well.

There. Four people on her list of those she trusted didn't seem quite so bleak. Maybe she was making more progress than she'd thought.

And maybe someday she'd find someone she could believe in as wholeheartedly as Elizabeth trusted Michael. Red's company helped fill the void she felt without the O'Roarkes close at hand, and Jenny felt grateful for that.

Still, it would be nice to have a special someone in her life. Someone she could share her dreams and innermost thoughts with. Someone who could make her feel protected and safe.

She checked the biscuits one more time and pulled them from the oven. Could Evan possibly be the one? Jenny closed her eyes and tried to picture him in that role. The face that swam before her eyes, though, didn't belong to Evan Townsend.

Instead, she saw a rugged face, a firm jaw. Sandy hair she longed to smooth back with her fingertips. . .keen blue eyes that stared at her with an intensity that left her breathless. . .

The face she saw all too often in her dreams. The face of a man she'd never even spoken to: the stranger from Prescott.

Even though she had caught only a fleeting glimpse of him before he strode out of Elizabeth's restaurant, his features had been imprinted on her memory. She traced her finger along the countertop. Could he possibly be as wonderful as he had seemed from that one fleeting glance?

Her finger bumped the hot pan of biscuits, jolting her out of her reverie. She popped the wounded digit into her mouth, glad to have something to distract her attention from her daydream. Her finger throbbed, but she didn't mind the pain.

She deserved to be caught up short. It wasn't like her to allow her guard to drop like that. The stinging reminder served her right.

Of course he wouldn't be as wonderful as her imagination had played him up to be. She had built him up into some kind of fanciful hero based on nothing but fragments of an overheard conversation. Men like that didn't really exist. Not for her, at least.

The front door banged back against the wall, and footsteps clattered into the dining room. Jenny cast a practiced glance around the kitchen to make sure everything was ready and went out to greet her guests. It sounded like Evan's predicted crowd of diners had arrived at last.

〜※〜

Another morning, another day's worth of chores. Jenny carried the last of the breakfast dishes back to the kitchen and added them to the stack on the counter. She pressed her hands against the small of her back and twisted this way and that, trying to loosen the kinks in her muscles.

Evan was right. She couldn't keep on doing everything on her own much longer.

"Where are you, lass?" The familiar voice echoed in the dining room.

"I'll be right with you, Red." She wiped a stray smear of gravy off her fingers and hurried out, smiling at the surge of pleasure she felt at the prospect of her friend's company.

She pushed open the swinging door and stopped short when she saw Red standing with his arm draped across the shoulders of a small boy.

"What's this? Or, rather, who is this?" She softened the abrupt question with a smile and leaned down to extend her hand to the lad.

"Meet Manuel, Jenny. Manuel Ochoa, to be exact. He's the answer to your problems."

The dark-haired boy bowed over her hand with grave solemnity. "*Buenos dias, señorita.*" Then he looked up and a bright grin lit his face. "Good morning.

You see? I speak English. I learn from some of the American storekeepers."

Jenny's own smile widened in response. "Good morning, Manuel. I'm pleased to meet you." She straightened and looked at Red, puzzled. "Now what's this about Manuel being the answer to my problems?"

Red's grin matched Manuel's for brilliance. "You said last night you needed someone to do odd jobs. Well, I found him for you."

Jenny felt her forehead pucker and tried to keep her smile from fading. "Red, could I talk to you for a moment?" She gestured to a spot across the room. "Excuse us, Manuel."

She led the way to a corner of the dining room and turned so her back was toward the boy. "What's going on?" she asked in a low tone. "I meant someone who could clean the tables and floors and maybe help take orders. He's just a little boy."

Red's left eyelid lowered in a conspiratorial wink. "Don't you be worrying about that now. I've known Manuel since he was just a wee tyke. He's a fine lad and a hardworking one. He'll do a grand job for you."

"But he can't be more than eight or nine," Jenny protested.

"Why don't you ask him?" Red gestured toward the middle of the room, where Manuel stood.

"I don't believe I'm letting you talk me into this," Jenny muttered.

"You trust me, lass, remember?"

"I did up to now," she retorted, then strode back to the boy. "Manuel, how old are you? I must have someone who'll be able to do hard work."

"I am eleven." The youngster puffed out his chest and stood tall. "My cousin Rafael is bigger than me, and he is only ten. But he is *perezoso*, Señorita Davis. Lazy," he translated. "I will work hard for you."

"But I'll need someone to be here most of the day," Jenny said in a gentle tone. "What about school?"

The light in Manuel's eyes dimmed, but he kept the smile determinedly in place. "I do not go to school. My mother needs me to help bring in more money to care for the rest of my family."

"What about your father?"

The boy lifted his chin. "He is *muerto*. Dead. I am the man of the family now."

"He was helping to put up a building," Red whispered behind her. "The wall collapsed and landed on top of him."

Jenny looked down at the stoic little face and felt tears pool along her lower lids. She knew all too well the havoc wrought in a life when death tore a family asunder.

She knelt down to put herself on the boy's level. "Very well, Manuel. You're hired."

Chapter 7

I think the dining room is ready for this evening, Señorita Davis. Would you like to come and check before you leave for the afternoon?" Manuel stood straight and proud in the soft white shirt and dark trousers Jenny had given him to replace his cast-off clothing.

"I'll be right with you." Jenny spread a cloth over the pies she just had pulled out of the oven and followed her hired helper.

A quick survey of the room assured her all was in order. Every inch of the floor had been swept clean. Cups and silverware sat neatly at each place, ready to welcome their evening guests.

And she hadn't had to lift a finger. Jenny grinned at the thought that she would be able to leave for her siesta a good hour earlier than usual.

"Hiring you was one of the best business decisions I've made so far," she said as she walked back to check her dinner preparations once more.

"I told you I would be a hard worker." Manuel followed her into the kitchen and pinched off a bit of piecrust with an impudent grin. "Like you. You work very hard. Too hard, I think."

Jenny leaned against the counter and sighed. Did all the men in her life have to be obsessed with her workload? Even the little ones?

"I'm not working nearly as hard since you came," she reminded him.

"But still very hard." Manuel focused his gaze on a spot on the ceiling and went on in a voice oozing innocence. "I heard Señor Townsend talking to you about getting someone else to do the cooking."

Jenny thought back to her talk with Evan. They had been speaking in low voices in the kitchen at the time, with Manuel puttering about on the other side of the swinging door. *So much for a private conversation.* She shouldn't be surprised, though. She had already learned that Manuel had the ears of a cat. Nothing escaped his notice. "Not necessarily to take over all the cooking," she hedged. "Just to help me out a bit."

"My mother is a fine cook. She could be a great help." The boy looked directly at Jenny now, his face glowing with pride.

"Uh, Manuel, I don't know if that's such a good idea." At the sight of his crestfallen expression, she hastened to add, "I'm sure she's a very fine cook. But I'm looking for someone I can teach to cook the way I do. Your mother probably wouldn't want to change the way she does things."

The glow returned. "Oh no. She would be very happy to have you teach her. She says you must be a good woman to give me a job like this. She will be honored to learn from you, just like me."

How did we go from "she would" to "she will" in just a sentence? Manuel had been a pleasure to work with, a joy to have around. But sharing the kitchen with a grown woman who already had years of cooking experience?

"I will bring her with me in the morning so you can meet her. You will like her very much."

"But then who will care for the rest of your family?"

"My sister, Angelita, she helps with the younger ones."

Jenny sighed again, accepting the inevitable. "All right, Manuel. In the morning."

"Bueno!" He scampered to the door, ready to dash home and share his good news. He paused for a moment to call back over his shoulder, "And you can teach her English, too!"

Jenny stared at the boy's retreating back. She hadn't even thought about having to surmount a difference in language. Could she instruct someone in meal preparation using only hand gestures?

Another consideration came to mind: From what she'd learned from Manuel in the short time he'd been there, she had pieced together the story of the Ochoa family's meager existence after Mr. Ochoa's death. Manuel's mother needed all the help anyone could give her.

Elizabeth had helped Jenny when she was in dire straits. This could be Jenny's opportunity to rescue someone else, to be the one helping rather than the one in need for a change.

At any rate, thanks to Manuel, it seemed she had already committed herself.

Jenny Davis, what have you gotten yourself into?

❧

"This is my mother. Her name is Jacinta Ochoa. She is very glad to be here." Manuel wore a formal expression as he made the introductions and indicated the quiet woman at his side.

His mother gave Jenny a shy smile.

Jenny took in the woman's smooth complexion and slender figure. Too slender. Manuel had been eating some of his meals at the restaurant. She made a mental note to be sure Jacinta got her share of food, too. And she could send extra food home with the two of them at the end of each day. Tell them it was part of their pay, perhaps.

She smiled and tried not to let her misgivings show. "I'm happy to meet you, Jacinta. Would you like to see the kitchen now?"

The dark-eyed woman continued to smile but didn't move an inch. Manuel spoke a few words in Spanish, and his mother bobbed her head eagerly.

Jenny swallowed hard and led the way to the back of the restaurant.

"Manuel," she said out of the corner of her mouth, "doesn't your mother speak *any* English?"

Manuel fairly skipped along in his excitement. "Only a word or two. But you and I, we will teach her."

Jenny almost envied Elizabeth her ability to meet all her problems with prayer. If she thought God would listen to her, surely this would qualify as a time to call upon the Almighty.

"Today we're making biscuits to go with the stew." She waited while Manuel relayed her meaning to his mother in a flurry of Spanish words. Jacinta nodded and smiled. Jenny groaned inwardly. At this rate, it would take all day just to explain one simple recipe.

Jenny mixed the ingredients, keeping up a running commentary while Jacinta watched, hoping her pupil would remember items and amounts. She stirred the mixture together and turned the dough out on a floured board.

"Next, we knead the dough." She pressed the heels of her hands against the ball of dough, turned the mass a quarter turn, folded it over, and pressed again.

Jacinta reached for the doughy ball, then copied her actions. "Así?"

"Like that?" the ever-helpful Manuel translated.

"Exactly like that." Jenny watched the way Jacinta continued the process with her capable hands. Maybe lack of a common language wouldn't be such a problem after all.

Jacinta looked up, awaiting her next instructions.

"Now we pinch off the biscuits and pat them into circles." Jenny did the first one, then stepped back and motioned for the other woman to try her hand at it.

Jacinta pulled off a large glob of dough.

"A little smaller, perhaps," Jenny said, demonstrating again.

"Ah." A smile of comprehension lit Jacinta's face and she formed the next biscuit perfectly.

"That's right," Jenny told her. When Jacinta only looked puzzled, she added, "Good. Bueno."

Jacinta spoke rapidly to Manuel. "She wants to know if you want her to go ahead and finish the biscuits on her own," he told Jenny.

She hesitated only a moment. Jacinta seemed to have the hang of it. Maybe the best thing she could do was show trust in her new employee. If disaster struck, she would only be a few yards away. "That will be fine," she said. "I'll be in the office if you need me."

※

Before the week was out, any misgivings Jenny had about adding a second member of the Ochoa family to the payroll had vanished like early morning dew in the Tucson sun.

Jacinta had shown a marked ability to assimilate Jenny's cooking methods and work on her own with little supervision. With only minimal help from Jenny, she had taken over the breakfast preparations and much of the lunch duties, as well.

Her cooking and Manuel's work in the dining room left Jenny free to spend several hours a day in her office, time she spent going over the books, drawing up supply orders, and making plans.

Above all, making plans. She set her pen down on the desk and propped her chin on one hand, staring dreamily through the sheer muslin curtains.

Only months before, she'd been working at Elizabeth's restaurant for little more than her room and board. Just a couple of months ago, she had to brace herself every time she ventured out into the streets of Prescott, steeling herself for a possible onslaught of cutting remarks.

In that short time, she had gone from feeling like an outcast to enjoying life as a respected member of the community and earning her own living, a good one at that. What a difference the choice to relocate to Tucson had made!

She stood and walked to the window, staring out at the scene of burgeoning growth. Two years after replacing Prescott as the territorial capital, Tucson was shedding its image as a sleepy Mexican village where travelers dreaded traversing the crooked, filthy streets, and emerging as a city worthy of its new status.

Jenny folded her arms and leaned against the window frame. She and Tucson had a lot in common. Both had rough beginnings and times they'd prefer to forget. But both had been given a second chance, an opportunity to shake off the dust of the past and move ahead into a bright new future.

Speaking of the future. . . Jenny returned to her chair and picked up her pen again. If she could finish the sketches showing her plans for expansion, she could show them to Evan, along with her new ideas for the menus. Jacinta had shown her gratitude for her job and Jenny's cooking lessons by teaching Jenny to prepare some of her own favorite foods. If Evan agreed, Jenny planned to add several Mexican dishes to their menu, starting next week.

She rolled the pen between her fingers, delighting in the way things had come together. She had a home of her own, the restaurant was thriving, and even now Red was out on his new claim setting things in motion to further secure their futures. Jenny smiled. What would Red think of the changes that had come about since he brought Manuel to the Pueblo?

Voices rumbled in the outer room, signaling the arrival of the first lunch customers. Gathering up paper, pen, and ink, she carried the lot to a table in the far corner of the dining room. Seldom occupied unless they had an overabundance of diners, it made an ideal place to do work on her ledger and still interact with her patrons.

"There is mail for you, Señorita Davis." Manuel appeared at her elbow, a wrinkled envelope in his hand. "Señor Townsend left it here a little while ago."

"Evan was in here and didn't stop by the office?" Her initial pang of disappointment was quickly replaced by irritation. If Evan had time to visit with Manuel, he could have given her at least a few moments. She could have outlined her plans to him and gotten his initial reaction.

No, maybe it was better to complete the plans before showing them to him at all. He would probably be more likely to agree to them if he could see the whole picture at once.

Swallowing her frustration, she squared the stack of papers and got ready to get back to work. The envelope Manuel had left on the corner of the table caught her attention, and she picked it up, smiling when she saw the return address. She could always make time for one of Elizabeth's chatty letters.

She tore the envelope open, eager to read her friend's news.

Dear Jenny,

I hope this finds you well and your business thriving. What a wonderful success you've made of it! To all the excitement of your accomplishments, I'll add one caution, and I'm sure you can guess what it is: Give God a place in your life. Despite what you think, He does love you and longs for you to be His child. You know how often I've prayed for this, how much I desire to see it happen, so I won't belabor the point. But as much contentment as you think your life holds now, it does not begin to compare with the joy and peace that can be yours when you make God your partner in life.

Enough of my sermonizing for now. There is excitement aplenty in the O'Roarke household these days. Can you guess? After nearly two years, Michael and I have learned we are going to be parents. I am thrilled and terrified, all at once! The responsibility of rearing a child makes the day-to-day responsibilities of running a restaurant seem trivial in comparison.

I have one more exciting bit of news to impart. You know that my sister Carrie keeps me informed of the happenings back East. Her last letter was full of welcome news. It seems that just a few weeks ago, Susan B. Anthony and Elizabeth Cady Stanton organized the National Woman Suffrage Association with the goal of seeking an amendment to the U.S. Constitution. Imagine, Jenny. It may not be much longer before American women get the vote!

How I wish you could be here with me during these thrilling days, my dear friend. But I know you have made a new home for yourself in Tucson and I would not begrudge you that for anything. And we have already shared a number of exciting times together. As always, I will continue to keep you in my prayers.

With love,
Elizabeth

A shadow fell across the table, and Jenny looked up to see a thin, hatchet-faced man standing beside her. "Afternoon, Miss." He dipped his head and gave her a friendly smile. "I needed to speak to Townsend, but I don't see him anywhere around."

"He was here earlier," Jenny replied. "I'm not sure whether he'll be back later today or not. May I give him a message?"

"You can give him this, if you don't mind." He reached inside his broadcloth coat and drew out an envelope. Placing it on the table, he gave another nod and turned to leave.

"Whom shall I say it's from?" Jenny called after him.

He stopped in the doorway and gave her a slow wink. "Don't worry. He'll know."

Jenny slid the missive under her pile of sketches and scanned Elizabeth's letter once more before folding it and replacing it in its envelope.

A smile curved her lips. How like Elizabeth to be as excited about the new strides being made toward women's suffrage as she was about the prospect of motherhood.

They'll make wonderful parents. Jenny could easily picture her friends in their new roles. Elizabeth would provide firm but loving guidance and the assurance her children could do whatever they set their minds to. And Michael, with his quick sense of humor and protective spirit, would be sure his family was well cared for. Their children would grow up in a loving home, full of warmth and happiness.

The thought brought memories of her own childhood to Jenny's mind, and a leaden feeling filled her chest.

She took a deep breath, trying to sweep the sensation away, remembering that Elizabeth's letters always brought mingled joy and pain. Joy at hearing from someone she loved like a sister; pain at the reminder of the dark time in her life—the reason she'd fled Prescott in the first place.

She made a few tentative marks on her sketches, then swept the papers into a heap and carried them back to her office. Right now, she should go help Jacinta with lunch. Anything requiring concentration would have to wait until later.

Chapter 8

I f the new wing is added over here," Jenny extended the lines indicating the north and south walls of the dining room, "and we brought the kitchen out this far," she sketched in the larger area, "then we could make an archway in the existing east wall and have room for at least six more tables." She scribbled a line where the prospective archway would be and made a few quick slashes to indicate the new exterior walls.

She looked at her drawing with a critical eye, trying to spot any weak points Evan might notice. There might be some, she decided, but she couldn't begin to spot them tonight, tired as she was.

She stretched her arms wide and rolled her head from side to side. The lamp sputtered, almost out of oil. Jenny glanced at the clock, surprised at the lateness of the hour. She had worked on the details of her plan instead of taking her usual siesta, then worked on them further after the restaurant closed for the night.

Jenny hurried to undress and get into bed before the lamp gave out completely. The late hours and extra work would be worth it, though, when she convinced Evan it would be in their best interests to spend the money to enlarge their building.

She curled on her side and watched the edge of the curtain dance in the light breeze. Her eyelids drifted closed, and she forced them open again. She needed to stay awake long enough to plan for tomorrow.

In the morning, she would make a final copy of her plan, free of scribbles and extraneous lines. When Evan came in, she would present the idea to him. If he took to it right away, they could begin construction immediately, maybe even as early as next week.

She snuggled deeper into her pillow, allowing her muscles to relax. Her lids drooped shut again, and this time they didn't open.

The nightmare began as it always did. Jenny recognized it for what it was, even as it pulled her into its own distorted reality.

Harsh voices grated in her ears. Rough hands grabbed her and dragged her off, away from the shelter of Elizabeth's restaurant, no matter how she pleaded and struggled.

Someone lifted her, then dropped her onto the bed of a wagon. Her body slammed against the unyielding wood. A coarse burlap sack was forced over her head, past her shoulders, then tied shut beneath her feet. She lay alone in the darkness, with only the hated voices to keep her company.

More unpleasant sensations: bouncing, jostling, feeling new bruises form every time the wagon wheels lurched in and out of another deep rut.

It's the dream, nothing more. It isn't real. Jenny called on every bit of willpower she possessed to shake off the terror. Experience had taught her that if she could jolt herself awake, she could escape at this point while the images remained hazy. Some nights she managed to evade the dream before it recreated memories that were all too real.

Tonight would not be one of them. She felt herself sinking deeper into the nightmare, reliving the memories she tried to avoid in the daylight.

The wagon finally ceased its relentless jarring. Relief at that bit of respite ended with her burlap prison being dragged across the wagon bed, then lifted like a sack of meal. Footsteps plodded across the ground, then thudded across a plank floor. The sack, with Jenny in it, was dumped none too gently on the boards. She waited for what would come next.

"So what'll you do with her, now that you have her back?"

That high-pitched voice always started the conversation in her dream, just as it had the night she had been abducted by Martin Lester, the guardian who had betrayed her father's trust and traded her to the owner of the Nugget Saloon.

Liquid sloshed, and she heard a series of noisy gulps before the other voice replied, "I don't know. I can't take her back into town. That nosy biddy she's staying with will have everyone all stirred up, looking for her."

Even in her sleep, Jenny flinched at the sound of Burleigh Ames's voice. Singing for his customers at the Nugget had kept her from a worse fate, but Burleigh had plans to force her into a life she wanted no part of. Plans that had seemed all too likely to succeed until Michael O'Roarke helped her escape and find safety with Elizabeth.

And now the two men she feared most had her in their power again.

Boots scraped across the floor. One prodded her shoulder through the sacking. "She thinks she's too almighty good for the fellows in the saloon." It was Ames, then. "They want a girl who's willing, not one who'll spit in their eye. Some bill of goods you sold me, Lester. At least you got a load of whiskey out of the deal. I need a way to get my investment back."

The bottom of the bag jerked upward, and her feet lifted off the floor. In a moment, the cord holding the sack shut had been loosened.

"What are you doing?" Lester queried.

Ames dropped the end of the bag. Jenny's feet fell back to the hard floor. "Getting her out where I can look at her." His hand seized the upper end of the bag and yanked, tumbling her out onto the floor in a heap.

Jenny sat blinking in the sudden light, staring up at the menacing figures. Two of them, one of her. She could never overpower them on her own. But she'd die trying.

"Not much to look at right now, is she?" Burleigh Ames sneered.

"Oh, I don't know." Martin Lester circled her as though evaluating livestock. "Once you clean her up and get some of the dirt from the wagon off her, she wouldn't be so bad. She's got a fine, full figure, if you ask me." He cackled and took another swig from the bottle. "Maybe I'll just buy her back and keep her for myself."

Derisive laughter rumbled from Ames's barrel chest. "You had your chance with her before, and she was too much for you, remember? You'd never dare turn your back or go to sleep with her around." His face turned serious once more. "I'm the one who's losing out here. You already drank up the whiskey I traded you for her. I've got to get some kind of return for all my time and trouble."

Lester pursed his lips and eyed Jenny from head to toe with a look that made her skin crawl. "What about selling her again?"

"Who to?" Ames scoffed. "The whole town will be out looking for her."

"I'm not talking about anyone around town." Lester's voice held a crafty note. "What about selling her down in Mexico? Or trading her to the Indians?"

"Yeah." Ames drew the word out. He pondered the idea a moment longer. "Yeah, that'd work."

Jenny felt the blood drain from her face. She sat rigid, too paralyzed by fear to jump up and make a run for the door. She was done for. There would be no escape from the awful fate Lester outlined. They had won, and their victory would be her utter ruin.

"God, are You there?" She barely breathed the words aloud. "Why don't You help me?"

She jerked awake and lay in the half state between dream and reality, still whispering the words: "Are You there, God? Are You there?"

Then full awareness came, and she shuddered with sobs, using her light sheet to mop the tears from her face. She knew the answer to her questions all too well: Yes, God was there. . .for people good enough to merit His help.

But Jenny Davis wasn't one of them.

She turned her sodden pillow over and settled her cheek against the dry side. Loneliness washed over her in a wave. It would have been better if she'd been massacred along with the rest of her family. She wouldn't have to face this overwhelming sense of isolation, something she managed to ignore during her busy days but that came back to haunt her during the night hours.

If Elizabeth and Michael hadn't appeared like avenging angels, setting her free from her captors, where would she be now? She remembered sobbing in Elizabeth's arms after her rescue. "You came! I was all alone, but you came for me!" The wonder of being sought after, of being loved so much still hadn't left her, even after all this time.

Elizabeth had held her close and whispered, "But you weren't alone, dear. God was with you and kept you safe."

Jenny shook her head violently against the pillowcase, just as she had in Elizabeth's arms back then. If God had been with her, she would never have been taken captive in the first place, never have had to hear Martin Lester's derisive cackle or read the evil intent in Burleigh Ames's eyes.

Maybe God indeed led Michael and Elizabeth to the isolated cabin where she had been held prisoner. But if that were the case, it was because He cared about their distress, not hers.

She curled into a ball and pulled the sheet up tight around her shoulders. Rescue. Michael and Elizabeth had saved her that night, protected her from who knows what unspeakable end. But they were back in Prescott, and neither they nor anyone else could protect her now from the memories that threatened to undo her.

She drew her knees up tight against her chest. If only another strong protector would come into her life. Someone who would care for her and shield her from whatever dangers might come her way. Someone like her imaginary hero, who guarded the rights of others.

Her wistful laugh floated out into the darkness. That wasn't going to happen, and well she knew it. She would have to find another way to fill the empty longing deep inside her.

Wrapping her arms around her knees, she rocked back and forth, hoping sleep would claim her soon, sleep without dreams this time. The nightmare would come again, but please, not tonight.

If there was any mercy, not tonight.

Chapter 9

"Set it against that wall, please. And the desk goes over there, near the window." Jenny stepped back to give the struggling workmen space to maneuver the heavy pieces of furniture around in her small living room.

When they had placed the pieces to her satisfaction, Jenny closed the door behind them and looked around with delight. The serpentine-back sofa might look somewhat out of place against the rough adobe walls, but a few strategically placed wall hangings would soften the contrast.

And the desk! Jenny ran her fingers along the gleaming walnut surface and marveled at its satiny feel. She rolled the cylinder top back into its compartment to expose the writing surface, then slid it closed again.

It seemed a shame for Ambrose Long's belongings to be sold off when he died, but his widow needed money to live on once she returned to the States. She had obviously hated parting with her treasured furnishings, but she'd been happy enough to see Jenny as the new owner. "It comforts me to know they'll be appreciated," she put it.

Jenny lowered herself gently onto the sofa's delicate upholstery. To think that such elegance could be hers. And that she'd been able to afford it! The heavy furniture took up most of the space in the room. Jenny didn't mind; it gave the place a sense of solidity.

She went into her bedroom and stripped off the comforter, sheets, and pillow. The workmen would have to take care of moving the bed itself when they brought the Longs' maple spool bed later that afternoon.

Jenny eyed the dimensions of the room, hoping she hadn't misjudged the size of her new bed. It would be a tight fit, but surely they could squeeze it in. She wouldn't have much space left to move around, but it wouldn't matter when that wonderful bed would be hers. These new furnishings filled her house, making it more of a home, and gave her much pleasure. If only she could find something that would fill the void in her heart as easily.

❧

"Good morning, Jenny. Miss me?" Evan tossed his hat toward the corner of the office, where it settled neatly onto a peg.

"Morning? More like early afternoon." Jenny rose from her work with the ledger and faced him, her hands planted on her hips. "How can you stroll in here after being gone for five days straight with nothing more than a casual 'Morning, did you miss me'?"

A bright smile played across Evan's face. "You did miss me, then."

"I was worried, Evan. Worried sick! You were supposed to be back days ago. Where have you been all this time?"

He took off his jacket and draped it casually across the corner of the desk. "Working, my dear. And I've pulled in a good profit for my efforts."

Jenny narrowed her eyes. "Gambling, you mean. What town have you left poorer this time?"

"Ah, Jenny. You're beginning to sound more like a disapproving wife than a business partner." Evan chuckled and lifted her chin with his forefinger, a gesture that never failed to make her feel like a backward child. "When you agreed to come down here, I warned you I might not be around all the time."

"All the time?" She pulled away from him and folded her arms across her chest. "You're gone more than you're here. And it's what you're doing when you're gone that concerns me. You know how I feel about gambling."

He perched on the edge of the desk and grinned at her, unabashed. "I told you the day we met that I'm first and foremost a businessman, and it's true. Gambling is my business. It's the way I finance my other ventures, and I'm good at it. Very, very good. Now what is it you've been waiting to talk to me about these five long days?"

Jenny let out a huff of disgust but turned to pull her sketches of the proposed expansion from the desk drawer. It was impossible to pin Evan down about his behavior when he was in one of these playful moods. Better to swallow her irritation and get his approval of her plans while he seemed in a frame of mind to listen.

"I wanted to show you a few of my ideas and see what you think." She spread the papers out on the desk, and Evan stood to look at them.

"What's that?" Evan asked, pointing at the corner of an envelope that protruded from under one of the sheets.

"I have no idea." Jenny picked it up and recognition came to her. "Oh, I nearly forgot. A man left it with me to give to you a few days ago. Five days ago, to be exact," she added, unable to resist driving the point home once more. "The day you took off without a word." She wagged the envelope underneath Evan's nose.

He snatched it out of her hand, tapped her on the head with it, and tucked it inside his coat pocket without a second glance. "All right, consider it delivered. Your duty is done, Jenny dear. Your hardworking, Puritan soul can relax." He laughed outright at her look of distaste. "Now tell me about these plans of yours before you burst."

A half hour later, Evan still remained bent over the drawings. Jenny tiptoed past the office door for the tenth time in as many minutes and peered inside, trying to gauge his reaction.

"He is still there?"

She whirled at the unexpected voice. "Manuel!" she scolded. "You shouldn't sneak up on me like that."

"I did not sneak, Señorita Davis. You just did not hear me coming." His teeth flashed when he smiled. "There is a difference."

Jenny felt the corners of her lips tug upward. "I suppose you have a point," she said. "And the answer to your question is yes. He's still looking at the plans."

"Actually, he's finished looking." Evan's voice made them both jump, then laugh sheepishly. "Jenny, would you come inside? I'd like to discuss these with you. And you. . ." He pointed to Manuel. "You will find something to do besides listening at the door, understood?"

"Sí." Manuel showed no offense at the mild rebuke. "It is time to help my mother clean the kitchen before siesta."

"That boy's an incorrigible eavesdropper," he said, his crooked grin belying the stern words.

"He's an absolute delight," Jenny retorted, mirroring his smile. "And I don't know how I got along without him. Or Jacinta, either. He's bright, hardworking, and always here when I need him. Unlike some other person I could mention."

Evan raised his hands in surrender. "I give up. Point taken, message noted. I shall keep you apprised of my whereabouts from here on out. Will that satisfy you?"

"It will do for a start." Jenny tossed her head back, trying to cover the sudden nervousness that swept over her. What did he think about her plans?

"I've gone over your drawings and the lists you've come up with," he began. He stirred through the stack of papers with his forefinger, then looked straight at her. "And I must say I'm tremendously impressed."

Jenny let out a whoosh of air and he chuckled. "Nervous, were you? You needn't have been. You've done a very thorough job here. There's plenty of room on the property to make the changes you've suggested, and these lists you've made. . ." He lined up three sheets of paper along the desktop and shook his head admiringly.

"These are what decided me," he said, pointing to each sheet in turn. "You've given me a list of materials and their cost, the number of meals we can expect to serve in the new setup, and the overall profit we'll realize by carrying this out. If you needed a loan and I were a banker, I'd give you the money without a qualm."

"Then you agree we should do it?" Jenny's feet wanted to dance a jig across the floor. "When can we start?"

"How does next week sound?" Evan asked. "Assuming I can get the materials and workers lined up by then, of course."

"Wonderful!" Jenny clapped her hands. "And we'll be able to keep right on serving meals during most of the construction, too. Look, I've made some notes here." She riffled through the stack and pulled out another sheet.

Evan waved the paper away. "I'll take your word for it. I am thoroughly convinced you could have designed the Great Pyramids and drawn up the plans to do them. If you say it's feasible, that's good enough for me."

"Good-bye, Jacinta, Manuel. I'll see you this evening." Jenny ushered her employees out and locked the door behind them. She meant to take part of her afternoon break time to measure and mark the east wall for the archway, and she didn't want any interruptions.

Staccato taps sounded at the door even before she turned away. Hoping it was Jacinta coming back after some forgotten item and not a customer hoping for a late lunch, she drew the bolt and opened the door a crack.

"Red!" she cried in delight. She pulled the door wide open, then paused and gave him a second look. "At least I think it's you."

The wiry miner removed his obviously brand-new hat, his clean-shaven cheeks creasing when he smiled. "Aye, it's me, lass. All cleaned up and looking my finest. No wonder you thought it might be someone else."

Jenny shut the door when he stepped inside and turned to inspect her friend. "Look at you! I've never seen you looking so dapper."

"That's me," Red said with a proud grin. "A regular clothes-horse. I know you're closed for business now, but I wanted to talk to you without a passel of people around. Do you have time to talk to an old miner?"

"For you, Red, I always have time."

He sauntered to his favorite table and fixed her with a mischievous gaze. "Would you be having any pie taking up space in your kitchen that you need for other things?"

Jenny laughed aloud. "How about some dried apple pie? That's your favorite, as I recall."

Red rubbed his hands together. "Excellent! That will make it seem like a party, and Jenny girl, we have cause for celebrating."

"What—"

"No, you're not going to make me get ahead of myself. I've waited long enough to spring this news on you, and I'm going to do it my own way. Go ahead and get the pie, and bring a piece for yourself, too."

Thoroughly intrigued by his tantalizing remarks, Jenny hurried to comply. "All right," she said, setting the pie plates on the table and pulling up a chair. "What's all the mystery about? You come in here looking like a fine gentleman and hinting at some great revelation. What's going on?"

Red stood and spoke in an oratorical tone. "Miss Jenny Davis, I am pleased to report that your faith in me was not in vain. You are now not only a restaurateur, but part owner of the Silver Crown silver mine."

It took a moment for the impact of his news to sink in. Jenny leaped to her feet. "You mean it's done? The claim is filed, legal and everything? The mine is yours?"

"Not mine, lass. Ours." Red's eyes misted and he gave her a tender glance. "You gave me the help I needed to get back out there and stake the claim, and I'm not about to leave you out of the picture. You'll get back every penny of the money you invested in an old man's dream and a packet more besides."

"But I didn't mean to—"

"I know you didn't," Red cut in. "You only meant to help me out of the goodness of your heart, and that's why I want to return the favor."

Jenny's head felt light, as though she were soaring up through the clouds into the rosy dawn of a bright new day. Could this be happening to her? On top of her joy at Evan's lavish approval, the euphoria she felt was almost too much to bear.

"Are you all right?" Red's light touch on her shoulder and the lines of concern on his forehead brought her back to the moment.

"I'm fine. Just a little overwhelmed, I think. Let me get us some coffee, and you can tell me more about it."

Chapter 10

S o what's the next step?" Jenny asked after her heartbeat had returned to a more normal pace.

Red rubbed his chin. "I've been pondering that very question. Twenty years ago, I would have looked forward to conquering the rock with my own two hands. Just me and my own strength, pitted against that vein of silver." He took a long swallow of his coffee. "But now I'm that much older. Older and a wee bit wiser, I hope. Wise enough to know that I don't have the vigor to wrest the silver out of the ground myself, nor do I have the knowledge of the best way to do it."

He picked up a crumb from his plate and popped it into his mouth. "Most of the prospecting I did in California was for gold, and all I ever had there was a placer claim. Swirling a pan through the water hoping to find a nugget or two or some gold dust in the bottom is a far cry from putting together a major silver operation." He shook his head. "I was able to find the lode, lass, but I don't know the proper way to get at it."

Jenny furrowed her brow. "If we can't get the silver out, what good is the mine to us?"

"That's where we're going to need a third partner. Someone we can trust. Someone who understands the ins and outs of hard rock mining and can recognize the potential in what we have."

A hollow feeling settled in the region of Jenny's stomach. She should have known Red's big strike sounded too good to be true. Not wanting to burst his bubble too quickly, she asked gently, "And just where do you suppose you're going to find someone like that?"

Red slapped his palm on the table and grinned. "It's already done. Remember that fellow from Colorado I mentioned? He sounded like just the kind of man we need, so I looked him up as soon as I cleaned up a bit after I got back to town."

"Red, you didn't!" Jenny gaped at her friend. "You offered a perfect stranger a share in our mine without knowing a thing about him?"

"We spent a good bit of time visiting first. He had no idea he was talking to anything more than a fine-looking Irish gentleman." He gave her a saucy wink. "I learned all I needed to know before I said a word to him about the mine."

A feeling of despair welled up inside Jenny. "You're incorrigible, do you know that? You've only just met the man, and you're willing to trust him with the treasure you've been searching for your whole life?"

Her outburst didn't appear to have the least effect on Red's good humor. He leaned back in his chair and stretched his legs in front of him. "I've lived a good while, lass. Not as long as some, but far longer than others. You, for instance. How is it that an old codger like me, who's traveled far and wide and seen a good bit of the sorry side of human nature, can find it in his heart to take most people on faith while a lovely young thing like yourself doles out her trust like a starving man sharing his last crumb of bread?"

The accusation hit its mark. Jenny pushed herself to her feet. "I'll just clear these dishes," she said. "I'm late getting home."

"Wait." Red's fingertips barely touched the back of her hand but had the effect of pinning it to the table. "I may be overstepping my bounds, Jenny, but let me say this anyway. You've let it slip once or twice that you've no family left. I don't know what happened to them or to you, that you're so wary of life. But it might help to unburden yourself to a friend. Let me help you carry the load, so to speak."

Jenny grew rigid, feeling as if the blood in her veins had turned to ice. No one in Tucson knew of her past. She had planned to keep it that way, let her dark secrets stay dead and buried.

She darted a quick glance at Red's face and saw only compassion in his expression. She did trust Red and counted him as her friend. Did she have enough confidence in him to share the events that altered her life forever?

The moment hung suspended in time. Red seemed in no hurry, just waited patiently for her answer. When she didn't speak, he said, "I don't mean to be treading where I shouldn't. I have no daughter of my own. If you need someone to talk to about whatever it is that's weighting your heart so, I'd consider it a privilege if you'd let me stand in for your father."

Slowly, Jenny's knees unlocked and lowered her back into her chair. A father. How she missed her own! Maybe she could let Red stand in his place, just for a bit.

"You know my family's gone," she began, surprised to find the words flowed freely now that she had decided to unloose them. "But I don't think I ever told you how it happened." She drew a deep breath. Even Elizabeth hadn't heard everything. The wounds then had been too recent, too painful.

"We had a farm several miles north of Prescott, my parents, my little brother, and me. Pa raised beans and potatoes and corn. Ma had a kitchen garden I helped her with, and we kept a couple of cows. Nothing fancy, but it was ours." Her voice softened with the memory.

"Johnny—that's my brother—wanted so much to be like our pa. He was just getting old enough to help a lot with the outdoor work, and he followed Pa everywhere." While she spoke, the scene before her shifted and she saw, not Red and the restaurant, but images of that terrible day on the farm.

"That last day, Johnny had gone out to help Pa bring in the cows. It was cold that day, and Ma was fixing a stew. She sent me out to the root cellar to dig out some potatoes.

"It wasn't really a cellar, more like a pit we'd dug out of the side of the hill near our house. We kept it covered with brush so it didn't stand out. Pa always told us if any trouble came, we were to go straight to the root cellar and stay there." Her voice caught. "It was our safe place. Except I was the only one who stayed safe."

She closed her eyes but couldn't shut out the scenes of what happened next. "They showed up without any warning: six Apaches. We knew there had been depredations to the south of us, but we hadn't been bothered. Pa said he didn't expect any trouble, but it came anyway." She wadded the fabric of her skirt in one hand and brushed the tears from her cheeks with the other.

"I was pulling potatoes out of the straw when I heard shouting outside. I peeked past the brush and saw Pa standing near the barn, facing north. Johnny was behind him, flattened up against the side of the barn like a scared rabbit. They yelled something at Pa, then arrows started flying and he went down. I couldn't think, couldn't move. Then two of them got down and ran over to the house. The next thing I knew, Ma was screaming. She kept begging them to let her go, to take whatever they wanted and leave us alone. Then the screams got louder. Then they just. . .stopped." She lifted one hand and let it drop helplessly in her lap.

"All I could see of Pa were his legs stretched out past the corner of the barn. He wasn't moving." She drew a shuddering sigh. "And then I saw Johnny take off like a cottontail, heading for the cabin. He got out of my line of vision, but I saw one of the Indians take off after him. A moment later, I heard Johnny cry out, and I knew he hadn't made it."

Red wiped a knuckle across his eyes and cleared his throat. "What happened next, lass?"

"I wanted to run out there and help them, but I couldn't make myself move. I watched the Indians drive the cows and horses off and set fire to our house and the barn. And then they rode away. The next thing I remember, neighbors who'd seen the smoke came riding up and were calling my name."

Red reached across the table and tightened his fingers around hers. "I'm sorry. So sorry. You went through a horrible time." He pulled a handkerchief from his pocket and handed it to her.

She crumpled the soft cloth in her fist. "There's more." Now that she'd started, she found she wanted to unburden herself of the whole sordid story. "My father appointed a guardian for Johnny and me in case anything happened to him and our mother. I'd lost everyone I loved that day, but at least I knew I'd have a roof over my head." She dabbed at her nose with Red's handkerchief. "What I didn't know—and what Pa didn't, either—was the kind of man Martin Lester really was. He seemed happy enough to take me in. I had no idea he had other than kindly motives until he. . .started making advances."

"The blackguard!" Red's face grew dark. "Did anyone come to your aid?"

Jenny shook her head. "He had a farm a ways from ours. There weren't any near neighbors, nobody I could run to. And I didn't have the courage to take off across country on my own. Not after what happened to my family." Her voice quavered again and she cleared her throat before she went on.

"He kept me around for two months—giving me time to get adjusted to the idea, as he put it. Then he got tired of me fighting him off, and he. . ."

"What is it, lass?" Red urged. "What did he do?"

"He bartered me," Jenny said, her voice barely above a whisper. "Traded me to a saloon keeper for a load of whiskey. He traded me, Red! Just like a horse or a piece of property." The emotional dam she had guarded for so long burst at last. Jenny lowered her head to the table and wept, violent sobs tearing at her throat.

She'd done it now. Opened the floodgate that would let the nightmare deluge her nights with terror once again. All the same, she felt a sense of relief. Red hadn't shied away or drawn back in disgust.

She heard his chair scrape across the floor, then felt him kneel beside her, stroking her hair with his calloused hands. "But it's all over now, my girl. You've gone through a terrible time, but it's behind you."

He continued stroking her head until the storm subsided. "Somehow, God delivered you from the clutches of evil men and—"

Jenny raised her head enough to prop it on her folded arms. "Not God. A man named Michael."

"Like the archangel himself!" Red's face shone with a radiant light.

"No, but he's the only man who ever cared for me as a person since my pa died." She pressed her fingertips against her swollen eyelids, then looked straight at Red. "And except for you and my pa, he's the only man I've ever trusted."

"Ah, I'm beginning to understand." Red sat back on one heel and regarded her with eyes that mirrored her own pain. "You've suffered, and so you've closed the door of your heart to anyone, for fear some miscreant will take advantage of you again."

Jenny sniffed. "I guess that about sums it up. Now you know why I can't trust anyone. Ever."

"That's where you're wrong, lass." Red's eyes regained their sparkle. "What you need more than anything is to trust again, and trust the only One who's worthy of your confidence."

"But I do trust you, Red. I just told you so."

"Not me, lass. I'm honored to know you feel that way, and I'll do my best to live up to your faith in me. But try as I might, there's always a chance I may let you down. I'm only human after all."

"Then who—"

"God, Jenny. He's the only One you can count on never to leave you, never to let you down."

"Not again, Red. I can't take any more of that right now." She stood and crossed the room to distance herself from Red's quizzical look. "Don't you see?

Some people are good enough for God, some aren't. I don't know how He decides, but it's obvious I'm not one He's chosen to love."

Red stared at her, then drew himself up. "If you're thinking I was born some kind of saint, you're wrong as wrong can be. Maybe next time I'll tell you some different stories of my younger days." The corner of his mouth quirked up in a half smile. "Then again, maybe I won't."

He pushed himself to his feet, moving with the stiffness of his years. "I won't keep trying to convince you. I'm not the one who can make you believe God loves you. Only the Lord Himself can do that." He settled his new hat on his head and started for the door, then turned back. "But you can know one thing for sure: I'll be praying for you."

※

Jenny climbed into her bed that night with Red's words echoing through her mind. She trusted him in other things; could she trust him in this as well? What if his assertion that God loved her—as impossible as that seemed—was true?

She considered the possibility. What difference would God's presence make in her life?

Jenny rolled to one side and scooted down a bit so she could see the Big Dipper through her window. God created those stars and all the rest. Did He live among them, up on some lofty plane where He could look down and consider all His works?

Supposing the Maker of the universe did decide to take her as one of His own, what then? Could she hope to feel as pure as Elizabeth and Michael, as confident in His love as Red?

What would that mean to her? She wrapped one of her long blond ringlets around her finger and pondered the concept of truly feeling clean. Teardrops gathered in the corners of her eyes at the thought of never caring what other people thought about her or her past.

If it were possible. . . But it wasn't. Reality jolted her to her senses. According to Elizabeth and Michael, God never changed. Did that mean she had imagined His love when she was a little girl gazing up at this same night sky with her mother's soft lullaby in her ears?

Wasn't He supposed to be in control of all things? Then she had to believe He allowed her family to meet such hideous deaths and her to witness it. The power to create the universe, and He hadn't lifted a finger to avert the tragedy that set her life on its cruel path. What kind of love was that?

And God was holy. She knew that much. Holiness couldn't exist in the presence of wickedness. That would most certainly include the kind of goings-on that were considered normal behavior at the Nugget Saloon. It included Jenny, herself. No matter that she'd spent her weeks there warding off advances from leering customers. No matter that she'd earned Burleigh Ames's wrath by refusing to take any of the men upstairs to her room. She had been pawed and grabbed at, despite her best efforts to protect herself. Even against her will, the groping hands had left their mark. And left her tainted.

Tainted with a stain that blemished her soul forever and left her unworthy to even think of being welcomed into God's presence. He would have to change His very nature to accept her as she was today, and God didn't change.

A low moan escaped her throat, and Jenny gathered the sheet tight under her chin despite the sweltering temperatures of the hot summer night. She couldn't bear to throw the layer of fabric back and further expose herself to the all-seeing eye of the Almighty. She closed her eyes and forced a swallow down her dry throat. She knew who she was, no getting around it. Better to accept that fact and do what she could to make her life as tolerable as possible than to dwell on what could never be.

Chapter 11

Aand how is my lovely partner this morning?" Evan's cheerful greeting set Jenny's teeth on edge.

"Fine." She pushed open the office window to take advantage of any breeze the day might offer and forced a bright smile, well aware that she looked anything but lovely. A sleepless night as the unwilling hostess to a myriad of dark thoughts had taken care of that.

"As a matter of fact, I heard some exciting news yesterday." Maybe setting her mind on the positive things in her life would let her ignore the emptiness that threatened to engulf her these days whenever she let down her guard.

Evan sprawled in the chair and leaned his elbow against the desk. "I'm up for some excitement. What did you hear?"

"You remember Red Dwyer?"

"The scrawny little miner who looks almost as weather-beaten as his burro does?"

Jenny shot him an exasperated look. "Underneath that rough exterior, he's a gentleman through and through. I've known far too few of those."

Evan held up his left hand in a lazy gesture. "I stand admonished. Now take that scowl off your face and tell me what your little leprechaun had to say."

Excitement bubbled up inside Jenny despite her fatigue. "I grubstaked him awhile back. He came back yesterday to tell me he's located a silver strike he thinks will be very profitable. And," she added with a broad smile, "he's decided to make me his partner. I now hold an interest in a silver mine. Even if nothing comes of it, that's still a pretty thrilling thought."

"You mean the old codger actually found something worthwhile?" Evan lowered his head and stared at the floor, then looked straight at her, his eyes snapping with enthusiasm. "If this turns out to be more than the fevered imagination of one more prospector who claims he's found the mother lode, you're going to need more partners than just the two of you."

Jenny watched him, biting back a cry of dismay. Evan always had his eye on the main chance. What could he be up to now?

"Red's a nice enough fellow," Evan continued, "but face it, he's never struck it rich before. He'd hardly know the best way to go about developing the claim, if it's anywhere near as rich as he says. And you. . ." He gave Jenny a half smile and shrugged. "You're a wonder at running this restaurant, but working a mine is a different proposition altogether. You both need someone with a more diversified background, someone with the connections to make the most of this opportunity."

Jenny directed a cool glance his way, certain she knew where this was headed. "And that someone would be. . . ?"

Evan swept his hands apart and bowed with a flourish. "I know what it takes to deal with investors, and I have the connections to make it happen." He stepped toward her, his eyes glittering. "Take me into the partnership, Jenny. I can help."

Help whom? She recognized the truth of the words the moment they flashed into her mind. In the time she'd known him, she'd learned one thing about Evan: His first and last motive for taking any action was based on what he considered best for Evan Townsend. Offering to help out of a spirit of altruism simply wasn't in his nature.

"I don't think so, Evan." She turned and looked out the window. "Thank you for the offer, but Red said he already has someone lined up." *Someone he barely knows and I haven't even met.* Which would be better, the stranger, who might or might not live up to Red's expectations, or Evan, whose motives she knew all too well?

Evan stepped up close behind her. "And who's this person he's taken on? What do you know about him?"

Only that Red trusts him, however wise or foolish that may be. She kept her misgivings to herself and lifted one shoulder. "I'm supposed to meet him soon. I'll be able to tell you more about him then."

The air Evan hissed out between his teeth stirred the ringlets against the back of her neck. "I guess I'm too late, aren't I?" He chuckled, seeming to regain his typically easygoing manner. "Let Red know about my offer, will you? The time may come when you need me, and for you, I'll be willing to step in and help."

"I'll do that," Jenny agreed, grateful for his capitulation, even more grateful when he picked up his hat and left the room.

⁂

"He's coming, Jenny." Red peered through the kitchen doorway. Excitement radiated from him, making his face look like that of a child on Christmas morning. "He'll be here in just a moment."

"Who's coming?" Jenny removed four apple pies from the oven and set the heavy pan on the counter.

"Andrew Garrett," Red announced, giving the Rs a fine roll. "Our new partner," he added in answer to Jenny's blank expression.

"Oh. Oh!" What a day for Jacinta's youngest to develop croup! Jenny hadn't realized how used she'd become to being free of the cooking duties. She shut the oven door and wiped the back of her hand across her forehead. "Let me just cover these pies."

Red glanced over his shoulder and smiled. "Be out as soon as you can, lass.

He's just arrived." He hustled off toward the outer door.

Jenny quickly tossed a clean cloth over the pie pans, then thought of her appearance. "Wonderful," she muttered, smoothing back the damp strands of hair the blistering Tucson heat had left dangling along the sides of her face. "I can just imagine what I look like. If his knowledge of mines isn't any better than his timing, we are not off to a good start." At least he managed to come between the breakfast and lunch crowds. She yanked off her apron and hurried out into the dining room.

Red stood near the door in animated conversation with a tall, sandy-haired man. He beamed when he saw Jenny cross the room toward them. "Here she is now," he said to his companion. "Andrew, meet Jenny Davis, the third partner in the Silver Crown Mine."

The stranger turned and looked at Jenny with piercing blue eyes. Eyes she remembered from one brief encounter in Elizabeth's restaurant. Eyes she'd seen in her daydreams ever since.

Did he remember, too? But why should he? They had only exchanged a fleeting glance, nothing that would probably matter to him, even if the moment had branded his image in her soul.

She struggled to compose her features and forced herself to keep moving as though she didn't feel like she'd just been struck by a bolt of lightning. With her attention focused on her daydream come to life, her feet tangled in a chair leg. She scrambled for balance but succeeded only in stumbling again. With a cry of alarm, she pitched forward.

Andrew jumped forward and caught her elbow in a strong grip. A tingling shock jolted through Jenny's arm. She regained her balance and pulled away, placing the fingertips of her other hand on the arm he had touched.

Andrew seemed as affected by their contact as she did. He stared at Jenny, his gaze probing hers with a long, measuring look. "Did I hurt you?" he asked in the deep voice she remembered from Prescott.

Jenny shook her head but couldn't speak. Standing in his presence, close enough to see the details of his face, she could only stare. She drank in his appearance with her eyes, filling in the gaps her memory had missed. At the moment, she wanted nothing more than to give in to her fancies and lose herself in the blue depths of his gaze.

"You're sure you're all right, lass?" Red's forehead bunched into a mass of fine wrinkles. "You look a wee bit shaken."

The solicitous query brought her back to her senses. "No. I mean, yes. I'm fine." Jenny tore her gaze away from Andrew and gave Red a wavering smile.

"That was quite a stumble," Andrew said. "You're certain I didn't hurt you?" He reached out as if to touch her arm again.

Jenny pulled back quickly. "I'm fine," she repeated. "Shall we sit down?" She led the way to a table before the other members of the newly formed partnership could question her well-being again. Let them think she'd been shaken up by her near fall. Not for the world did she want them to see how close she'd just come to throwing her hard-won dignity to the wind.

Andrew hadn't hurt her, only set her emotional equilibrium spinning out of control. And that could prove just as dangerous as a physical tumble, maybe even more so. Jenny seated herself with aplomb and donned a mantle of cool reserve. She would have to be on her guard around this man.

Andrew followed his new partner, trying not to show the surge of excitement he felt when he recognized her as the captivating young woman from Prescott. In the fleeting moment when their gazes had locked during their first encounter, she had left an impression that haunted his memory ever since. Rather than throwing himself into his work in Tucson with his usual fervor, he'd found himself uncharacteristically impatient, chafing at every delay. Now he understood why: His physical self had been going about his work here, all the while his mind had been set on returning to Prescott to look into those aquamarine eyes once again.

And here she was, in Tucson! Who would have thought that joining forces with Red Dwyer would lead him to her? Why hadn't he seen her before? No matter. The important thing was that he saw her now and planned to keep on seeing her for a long time to come.

Lord, I don't know how You managed to bring her here. Or why, for that matter. But if I enter into Your plans in that regard, I want You to know I'm more than grateful.

He sat across the table from her to put himself in direct line with those amazing blue-green eyes. Or were they more turquoise? Her hair, too, defied a quick description. Just when he'd classified it as golden blond, a ray of sunlight streaming through the window sent copper glints shimmering through her curls.

It would take time—and a lot of study—to sort it all out. And that would be just fine with him. They would have much to talk about in getting the partnership set up. Plenty of plans to make. And knowing that Miss Jenny Davis had an interest in the mine made him all the more determined to see it succeed.

She gave Red a warm smile. "Where do we begin?"

"Ask Andrew," he replied. "He's our expert."

Jenny turned and looked straight into Andrew's eyes, and he braced himself for another heart-stopping shock. This time, though, it didn't happen. Jenny wore the same smile she'd directed at Red, but something was missing. The smile was there, but her eyes held a shuttered look, as though she'd lowered a protective shield.

"Well, Mr. Garrett, what do you suggest?" Her tone was polite but decidedly cool.

Andrew blinked and tried to get his thoughts back on track. What had just happened? Had he imagined that electric charge when he touched her? Surely she had felt it, too. He would have sworn to it only moments before. Now she looked at him as though she'd never seen him before, showing no sign of the kinship they'd seemed to share.

"I'll need to ride out to the claim with Red and give it a good looking over first. After that, I'll have a better idea of what we'll need to begin work." He hoped his inner turmoil didn't show. Trying to make sense of this situation was like chasing after a pile of dry leaves scattered by a sudden gust of wind.

An unwelcome thought struck him. Maybe she didn't remember their earlier meeting. Perhaps their connection when he touched her had been a figment of his imagination.

All right, then. He could accept that. In his mind, their acquaintance had already been of long standing, but he couldn't expect her to have the kind of feelings he'd already allowed to build up in his mind for someone she'd just met. He would have to take a few steps backward in his thinking and start afresh. He realized Jenny was speaking again and leaned forward to catch her words.

"I was talking to Evan earlier," she said to Red, the cool tone still in her voice. "He said he'd be more than willing to come into the partnership if we needed his help. I told him you already had someone in mind, but I promised I'd let you know."

"No need for that," Red replied with a grin. "We have the expertise of the esteemed Mr. Andrew Garrett on our side, and that should be quite enough." He slapped Andrew on the shoulder to punctuate his words.

"That's fine," Jenny said quietly. "I just wanted to let you know he offered."

Who's Evan? Andrew's mind probed the possibilities while Red went on enthusiastically about their future prospects. Could Evan be Jenny's brother? A suitor? Or worse, a fiancé? Red hadn't mentioned any such person, but that didn't mean anything. One didn't introduce a new business partner by outlining the details of his or her private life.

Lord, I don't know who this person is, but I'm already prepared not to like him very much. Help me to keep a right attitude in this and try to see what You're doing.

Chapter 12

By the time the arrival of lunch customers sent Jenny flying back to the kitchen to dish up new orders, the trio had established a beginning plan of action. Still to be decided was whether they wanted to sell shares to raise more capital. She mulled over the idea while she moved from the stove to the counter and back again.

Red was trustworthy; of that she had no doubt. Less certain was his wisdom in bringing Andrew Garrett into the partnership on such short acquaintance. The image of Andrew's face floated before her eyes while she stirred the gravy and set more bread dough out to rise.

Not until the last of the lunch customers left and she was ready to close down for the afternoon did she have a moment to herself to try to piece her scattered thoughts together. She poured herself a glass of water and sat next to an open window to catch as much of the slight breeze as she could.

What was it that Red saw in Andrew that sparked his trust? What did she herself know about Andrew Garrett? An overheard conversation and tender feelings from her daydreams didn't count, she reminded herself. She needed to know the real man, not the paragon of virtue she had built up in her mind.

His eyes were the same as she remembered. Deep blue, with a steady gaze that could make her heart stand still in her chest. That much, at least, hadn't been a product of her imagination.

And that voice. Even in memory, its rich timbre made her insides feel like melted butter. The same firm tone she had heard through Elizabeth's kitchen door in the altercation between Andrew and Earl Waggoner, the unscrupulous mining agent. She remembered Andrew's ire upon realizing Waggoner meant to bilk the miner he represented. That should count in his favor, she decided, pressing the cool glass of water against her forehead. But did one noble deed mean he could be trusted in all things?

The outside door to the office slammed. Jenny jumped and let out a little cry, her hand pressed against the base of her throat.

"Oh, are you still here?" Evan appeared in the office doorway, pushing a shock of his dark hair back off his forehead "I didn't mean to frighten you." He crossed the room and pulled up a chair close to hers, his relaxed smile putting her at ease again.

"It's all right. I just had my mind on other things."

Evan tilted his head to one side. "Thinking about your silver mine? You aren't getting ready to pull out on me, are you?"

"Hardly!" Jenny laughed. "From the discussion I had with Red and Andrew, it seems there's far more to establishing a mine than just going out and digging. It may be months, maybe even years, before we see a profit."

Evan lounged comfortably in a chair and stretched his legs out before him. "So you finally met the mystery partner, did you? What did you think of him?"

"Red seems quite taken with him," Jenny hedged, unwilling to admit her own doubts.

"That isn't much of an answer." Evan narrowed his eyes and regarded her thoughtfully. "Considering that you were ready to leave Prescott and travel here with me after only a few minutes of conversation, I'd say you're a woman capable of sizing up a person pretty quickly. If you still aren't sure of this fellow after your business discussion, that says something, doesn't it?"

Jenny evaded his gaze. "It really isn't the same."

"Did you tell Dwyer I was interested in coming in on the deal?"

"Yes. He wants to keep things as they are." She gave him an apologetic smile. "I'm sorry, Evan."

He raised his hands, then dropped them back in his lap. "I was only trying to help. It's a shame Dwyer didn't see it that way." He leaned forward with his elbows on his knees. "You don't think there's a hidden reason Dwyer didn't want me to come in on the deal, do you?"

Jenny frowned. "What do you mean?"

"Has either of them asked you to invest more money? Maybe, just maybe, this Garrett fellow isn't all he's made himself out to be." He wagged his forefinger at Jenny. "There are a great many unscrupulous men in the world. Some of them wouldn't think twice about taking money from an innocent investor, even one as lovely as yourself." His eyes lit with a smile for a moment, then turned somber again.

"Be on your guard, that's all I ask. And if you hear anything that gives you the slightest reason for doubt, I want you to come to me with your concerns. Will you do that?"

Jenny's lips parted in an amused smile at his earnest words. "You mean you'll be willing to give me advice on my investment as a bonus to our business relationship?"

Evan's expression softened. He scooted his chair forward until his knees almost touched hers. Reaching for Jenny's hands, he clasped them in his own.

"I've been meaning to talk to you about that. . .our relationship, I mean."

Jenny's fingers grew rigid in Evan's grip. More than anything, she longed to snatch them out of his grasp, but forced herself to hold still and hear him out. "What do you mean?"

Evan stroked circles on the backs of Jenny's hands with his thumbs and cleared his throat.

Jenny's fingers tensed even more, as though they would start twitching at any moment. She fought down the ridiculous impulse, wishing Evan would get on with it. Never before had he seemed at a loss for words.

"I've given it a lot of thought," he continued, his confidence seeming to return. "We make a good team, you and I. I think it's time to make our partnership a permanent one."

"Permanent?" Jenny drew her brows together, trying to comprehend his meaning. "What could make it any more permanent than what we have now?"

Evan's mouth turned downward in a rueful grimace. "You're not exactly being flattering, my dear." He cupped her chin in one hand, keeping the other wrapped around her fingers. "What I'm saying, Jenny, is that I think we ought to get married. What do you say?"

"Married!" Jenny's whole body stiffened, and she felt her arms start to tremble. "Evan, I—"

"Don't tell me it hasn't crossed your mind," he murmured, leaning forward to brush his lips across her temple. "We're a lot alike, you and I. With your head for business and my nose for new opportunities, we could control half the money in this territory. And how lucky for me that this brilliant business mind comes wrapped in such a desirable package."

He lifted her chin and lowered his lips to hers.

"No!" Jenny yanked her left hand free and planted it in front of Evan's lips.

She drew back and tugged her right hand, but Evan didn't loosen his grip. He sat quite still, studying her with steely gray eyes, keeping her hand pinned in his grasp.

"Is this some obligatory demonstration of maidenly modesty? I can feel you trembling." A low chuckle rasped in his throat. "I think you want this kiss as much as I do."

Jenny shook her head mutely. Fragments of memories shot through her mind: other hands holding her against her will, other voices declaring their intention to have a kiss. She pulled her hand again, and this time Evan let it go free.

"Very well." He leaned back in his chair and gave her a lazy grin. "Whatever the reason, I'm willing to hold off—for a time, at least." He reached out his hand to caress her hair but drew back when she flinched. "I'll give you time to think it over, but my offer still stands, my beautiful Jenny."

Jenny stood without a word and exited through the front door, leaving it standing open behind her. *Let him lock up.* All she wanted at that moment was to escape his clinging hands and the memories they stirred.

She walked quickly along the dusty street, skirting a group of little boys playing with a ball. Her head throbbed with questions. Whatever had possessed Evan to make such an outrageous proposal? She scrubbed her hands back and forth, trying to rub away the sensation of being imprisoned within his grip.

Safely home again, she closed the door and leaned against it, pressing her fists against her temples. Had she done anything to encourage such behavior? She couldn't think of anything—word or action—that would have given Evan cause to think she'd welcome his advances.

But then, hadn't she been the recipient of unwanted advances before? And none of them her conscious doing. Did she emanate some kind of inviting signal unbeknownst to herself?

What made Evan ask that preposterous question? While receiving an offer of marriage had to rate higher than being pawed by drunken saloon patrons, she wasn't ready to give up her independence. After working so hard to achieve that goal, she wasn't about to relinquish it now.

Not to Evan, not to any man.

With a low groan, she sank to the floor and cradled her head against her knees. What was it about her that seemed to bring out men's base desires?

Chapter 13

Hands. Clutching hands. Grabbing at her, plucking at her hair, her arms, her waist. Jenny tried to slap them away, thinking at first they belonged to Evan. Then Martin Lester's leering face appeared, and she realized the nightmare had returned. She struggled to waken, but the hated dream prevailed, pulling her down into its tangled depths.

Once again she relived the horror of being bundled into the burlap sack, of feeling like she was about to be shaken apart during the jolting ride in the wagon bed. Of being spilled out on the cabin floor like so much baggage. Martin Lester's drunken leer and Burleigh Ames's dark anger. . .

"What about selling her again?" No matter how many times she heard Martin Lester's suggestion, it never failed to renew a debilitating fear inside her. "Maybe down in Mexico this time. Or we could trade her to the Indians."

"Yeah." Burleigh Ames's gaze lit up with anticipation. "Yeah, that'd work." He glared at Jenny with hate-filled eyes. "But I vow I'm going to get some satisfaction first for all this grief." He wiped his mouth with the back of his hand and hitched up his belt.

"Hold on," Lester protested. "What have you got in mind?"

Ames shoved Lester to one side. "I'm not letting her go until she's paid for what she's done."

Jenny watched him make his way toward her, one slow, heavy step at a time. He grabbed her shoulder with one meaty hand and jerked her upright. "Come here," he said, his voice low and tight. "Let's see what it's like to kiss you."

Caught in his viselike grip, Jenny could only turn her head to one side. His mouth grazed her cheek.

"Hold still!" he bellowed, trying to pin her shoulders and force his lips to hers at the same time.

Jenny squirmed and pushed against his chest with all her might.

"Grab her hair and hold it tight!" Ames shouted.

Lester's fingers twined through Jenny's hair and twisted it into a tight knot. Burleigh Ames drew his lips back in a triumphant smile and leaned closer.

Jenny clamped her teeth together.

With a howl of pain, Ames flung her away from him. She flew as far as the length of Lester's arm, then jerked to a stop, caught by his hold on her hair.

Ames cursed. "Maybe I'll just kill her now and save us all a lot of trouble."

"You don't want to do that," Lester whined. "I don't intend to hang for no murder." He swung Jenny around by her hair and shoved her toward the cookstove. "Get over there," he ordered. "If you can't be of any other use, at least you can fix us some supper."

Jenny caught herself on the stove's edge. She had won. . .for the moment. But another time of testing would come. And another, and another. How long could she expect to hold out?

Once again, her heart sent up a desperate plea: "God, help me. Please, please help me!"

Jenny bolted awake, her gaze darting frantically around the dark room, straining to discern any hidden danger that might be lurking there. She pushed herself upright and scooted back against the headboard of her spool bed, wrapping her arms around her knees and listening for any telltale sounds. Only her ragged gasps broke the silence. A faint breeze wafted through the open window and she shivered, realizing for the first time that her sheet was soaked with sweat.

❦

Andrew dodged a trio of chickens pecking in the dust of Camino Real and turned down Calle del Arroyo in the direction of the Pueblo Restaurant. He strode at a steady pace, the same tenacity that helped him sift through endless assay reports in search of prime investments now standing him in good stead as he took on what might prove to be his biggest challenge yet: winning the confidence of Jenny Davis.

No matter how hard he'd tried to get in her good graces, the wall of hostility he'd sensed in her had only grown stronger.

But that was about to change. It had to. A successful partnership couldn't exist with that kind of strain between them. And he certainly couldn't entertain hopes of a budding romance if she wouldn't even give him the time of day.

He glanced at the sun overhead, an hour past its zenith. He had timed his visit to coincide with the end of the midday meal, hoping he could be her last customer of the afternoon. If only the two of them were in the restaurant, she'd have to talk to him, to tell him to leave if nothing else. At this point, almost any form of conversation would be a breakthrough.

Pushing the door open, he entered the dining room, grateful for its relative coolness after the midsummer heat outside. Manuel glanced up from serving a plate of fried chicken to another customer and favored him with a brilliant smile.

"Welcome, Señor Garrett," he said, hurrying to Andrew's side. "Did you come just to talk to Señorita Davis, or do you want to eat also?"

"I could use a good meal." Andrew smiled, heartened by the boy's contagious exuberance. "What's on the menu?"

"Fried chicken, roast beef, and pork chops. All cooked by my mother. All very good. What would you like?"

Andrew made a show of giving the list serious consideration. "I believe I'll try the roast beef."

"Bueno. That is a good choice."

"You recommend it, do you?"

"It is all we have left." Manuel flashed him an impish grin. "You are our last lunch customer."

Andrew chuckled at the boy's saucy rejoinder and settled himself in a chair while Manuel hustled off to the kitchen. He glanced around the dining room. No sign of Jenny, but he knew she would be somewhere on the premises, most likely in her office. And it looked like his timing had been right on target. Only three other diners remained. It wouldn't take much effort to linger over his meal and make sure he was the last one to finish.

Manuel served the roast beef with a flourish. Andrew smiled his thanks and bowed his head before concentrating on his food, one slow bite at a time.

One by one, the other diners left, until Andrew alone remained. Manuel darted back into the room to wipe the table left by the last vacating customer. "You are almost finished, Señor Garrett? Yours are the only dishes left to wash before we close the restaurant."

Andrew mumbled an apology and hurried through the last few bites of roast, berating himself for keeping Manuel and his mother from finishing their work.

He laid his napkin next to his plate, then stood, hesitating. He'd been so certain he could catch Jenny if he only stayed around long enough, but apparently it was not to be. He straightened his jacket and turned to leave.

Jenny opened the door to the office at that moment and the two of them stood staring at each other. Andrew saw her start to turn, then check herself, as though her first instinct had been to whirl around and slam the office door in his face. With her wide eyes and parted lips, she looked like a startled doe poised for flight. Then she pulled herself erect and the aloof mask dropped over her face.

"Did you want something?" The quaver in her voice didn't match the coolness of those aquamarine eyes. Her obvious uncertainty tugged at Andrew's heart.

"I just finished eating. A wonderful meal, I might add." He dropped his plan of compelling her to talk to him, during this visit at least. How could he force a confrontation and still call himself a gentleman?

He took a step toward the door and saw her shoulders sag in relief. Obviously, he'd made the right decision. A skittish quarry like Jenny wouldn't be won over by heavy-handed methods.

Quarry? The thought stung his conscience. This woman was not a prey to be stalked and hunted as a trophy. That kind of thinking belonged to a mentality that saw women only as objects of pleasure, a mentality Andrew abhorred. But the fact remained that the more Jenny pulled away, the more he felt drawn to her.

He had gleaned a few personal details about Jenny from Red. The old miner had been sparing in his comments, but said enough to let Andrew know Jenny was without a family. Andrew knew she had recently relocated to Tucson from Prescott. If she had no family, she must have come there on her own.

Or with Evan Townsend. From Red, he had learned of Evan's half interest in the Pueblo Restaurant. Could Evan and Jenny be more than just business partners? That might explain her coolness toward him. A sick feeling twisted in his stomach at the idea, but he put that thought away. Whatever the reasons for Jenny's reserve, he could not believe she was romantically involved with Townsend. A light of purity radiated from Jenny. She was blameless in that regard; he had no doubt of that.

And talk about courage! He couldn't imagine the kind of spunk it took for a young woman to strike out on her own like that. It showed a strength of character he deeply admired. The kind of character he hoped to find in a wife someday. And could Jenny Davis someday be that wife? The thought tantalized him. *I guess I'll just have to wait and see what You have in mind, Lord, won't I?*

Jenny waited until the door closed behind Andrew, then moved to slide the bolt in place. She let her body sag against the wooden plank, glad for the safety it represented.

Last night's dream still lingered all too vividly in her mind, the memory of those grasping hands all too fresh. Her office had proven a welcome hideaway, its sense of sanctuary almost allowing her to forget the whole ordeal. Then she'd opened the door and come face-to-face with Andrew Garrett.

Had her face betrayed her anxiety at seeing him? She knew in her heart he wasn't of the same stripe as Martin Lester or Burleigh Ames, but something about his commanding presence and steady gaze made her feel vulnerable, as though he could see straight into her heart.

A knock vibrated the wood under her shoulders. Jenny jumped back, her hands pressed against her cheeks, then forced herself to relax, laughing at her foolishness. The last time this happened, it had only been Red on the other side of the door.

She debated a moment, then squared her shoulders and slid the bolt back. She would not let her bad dreams get the best of her. They filled her with horror enough during the night hours, and she could do little about the effects that lingered on into the day. But if she allowed them to control her whole life, then Lester and Ames had won after all.

Determined to conquer her fears, she swung the door wide with her head held high.

A stranger stood on the other side of the threshold, and Jenny's brave resolve melted away like a skiff of late spring snow.

"You don't remember me?" the stranger asked.

Jenny blinked, sensing a spark of recognition but unable to place the man.

"I need to leave this with you." He held out an envelope. "Would you please see that Townsend gets it?"

Jenny's memory clicked into place the moment her fingers touched the envelope. "Of course!" She looked up at the hatchet-faced man with a smile. "You left a message for him once before."

"You do remember me, then." His eyes held a glint of triumph. "I would hate to think I'd failed to make any impression at all on such a pretty lady."

He stepped back with a half bow, and Jenny closed the door on both him and his obnoxious flattery. She fingered the envelope curiously. It wasn't thick enough to hold a pile of greenbacks. At least it wasn't someone coming to deliver some of Evan's gambling winnings, she thought grimly.

She twisted the envelope gently. No, it was much too thin to hold any substantial amount of cash. It didn't feel like it contained more than a single sheet of paper.

Why would that man continue to deliver messages to Evan at the Pueblo when he looked like he would be more at home among some of Evan's saloon cronies? She shrugged. The envelope and its strange bearer were Evan's business, not hers. She had enough to think about between the restaurant, learning about her mine investment, and trying to figure out how she felt about Andrew.

Without a sound to announce his presence, Evan stepped through the office doorway. Jenny shrieked and lurched back against the front door.

"Jumpy today, aren't you?" Evan asked, his gray eyes glowing with suppressed mirth.

Jenny tried to laugh and smoothed her hair back with shaking hands. *What's going on today? Every time I turn around, someone's popping up unexpectedly.* "I'm just getting ready to leave," she said. "I had a couple of customers stay later than usual."

"My good fortune." Evan moved nearer to her and slouched against the wall, a pleased smile warming his chiseled features. "I was hoping I'd get to talk to you. . .alone."

A prickle of unease ran up Jenny's arms. Hadn't he caused her enough distress already with his audacious proposal and the nightmare it set off? The dream had haunted her throughout the day, making it impossible to concentrate or accomplish anything worthwhile.

Why, she'd barely been civil to Andrew. What must he have thought when she stared at him in the same way she'd look at a toad in her bedroom? Hardly the way to cement a solid business relationship.

She remembered the envelope in her hand. "I'm glad you stopped by," she said. "I needed to give you this. That same man dropped it off for you just a few moments ago." She held the envelope out to him, hoping the change of subject would divert his attention.

Evan straightened and moved nearer, so close the scent of bay rum tingled her nostrils. He took the envelope and tossed it negligently on the nearest table, then planted his hands against the door, one on either side of her.

Jenny drew back, pressing her shoulder blades against the unyielding door. Her heart raced and her legs quivered so, she feared they would refuse to hold her up.

Outwardly, she tried to maintain a semblance of calm. Not for anything did she want Evan to know how his approach chilled her. She lifted her chin and stared into his eyes. Eyes the color of a cloudy day, with a gleam that had surely set many a young woman's heart aflutter. Why didn't they have that effect on her? Granted, her heart was pounding at an alarming rate, but it was a speed born of near panic rather than infatuation.

Holding her arms rigid, she fought down the urge to shove him away and make her escape out the back door. If she ran now, he would always have the upper hand.

"What did you want to see me about?" she asked, pleased at the cool note she injected into her voice.

"Do I have to want to see you about anything specific, Jenny?" He trailed the fingers of his right hand along her cheek, then cupped her shoulder. "Maybe I just wanted to enjoy your presence, nothing more."

She forced a smile to her lips. "Well, you've seen me. But it's been a long day, and I didn't sleep very well last night. If you'll excuse me, I need to be getting home. It's siesta time, you know."

A look of irritation flashed across Evan's face, to be replaced by a regretful smile. Rather than stepping back to release her, he bent his head nearer to hers. "Ah, Jenny. You do have a way of keeping a man humble, don't you?"

Without warning, he pulled her into his arms and crushed his lips against hers. Jenny struggled to push him away, but he wrapped his left arm around her, clamping her arms tight against her sides.

Panic seized her, and she acted purely on instinct rather than thought. Twisting from side to side, she attempted to evade the unwanted embrace. In response, Evan moved forward, pinning her between himself and the door.

A dark fog swirled through Jenny's mind, threatening to engulf her. Just when she thought it would overtake her entirely, Evan released his hold and stepped back, a satisfied grin creasing his face.

"I know I promised you time to think things over, but I wanted to give you a convincing reason to say yes."

Jenny stared at him, her chest heaving, her whole body shaking so hard she could barely stand. "And you think that speaks in your favor?"

He threw back his head and laughed. "Don't tell me you didn't enjoy it. Why can't we be honest with each other? For whatever reason, you're determined to hold on to this pose of outraged virtue, but you don't have to keep up that pretense with me. I've known too many other women to believe in that for a moment." He lowered his voice to a low purr. "Go ahead, Jenny. Why not give in to your feelings?"

You have no idea what I'm feeling right now. Before she could stop herself, Jenny's hand flashed out and struck Evan full on the cheek. He fingered the bright red imprint her fingers had left, his eyes clouded with a look of disbelief.

Jenny folded her arms across her chest in an effort to stop their trembling and drew herself erect. "Don't do that again. Ever. Do you understand me, Evan? I don't need more time to think about your proposal; I can give you my answer right now, and it's no. I came here to be your business partner, nothing more, and I have no intention of changing that."

She fumbled for the bolt behind her and pulled it back, keeping her eyes on Evan all the while. "I'm going home now. I think it's best if we try to forget what just happened and keep things as they were. You tend to your other businesses and I'll run the restaurant. I'll keep you informed about anything you need to know, but the less we have to see each other, the better."

Evan only stared at her, his eyes taking on the hue of dark thunderclouds. More shaken than she wanted to admit, Jenny let herself out of the restaurant and hurried home.

She bolted her door behind her and managed to cross the room to the sofa before her tottery legs gave out. Sinking back against the cushion, she dug her fingers into the upholstery and looked around at the room she had decorated with such care. Where was the security she once felt within these walls?

Gone, she realized. Dissipated like a puff of smoke after Evan's advances. She trembled again, but this time in anger instead of fear. Back in Prescott, he had offered her a business opportunity and a new life, a chance at a new beginning. How dare he ruin it with his disgusting overtures?

Jenny dropped her forehead onto her knees, her anger giving way to despair. Had she traveled all this distance to escape her past only to find herself enmeshed in the same kind of vile trap. . .with no one to come to her rescue this time?

Chapter 14

Bright sun streamed through the bedroom window. Jenny turned her head to escape its glare, and she wrapped her fingers around the bedpost, wishing she could squeeze it hard enough to chase away the pounding in her head.

Lack of sleep and the memory of Evan's behavior the day before had combined to give her the headache of a lifetime. Telling herself that morning would bring a diminishing of the pain, she had endured the incessant throbbing throughout the night hours, only to find no relief when dawn finally arrived.

Instead, she found herself unable even to get out of bed and stand. For the first time she could remember, Jenny stayed home instead of going to work. Manuel had rapped on her door, then her bedroom window, about seven, calling to her in a worried voice. After being reassured she was not on death's doorstep, he agreed to return to the Pueblo, giving Jenny his word that he and his mother could handle everything for the rest of the morning.

After he left, Jenny slipped into a restless doze and a light sleep. When she awoke, the pain seemed to have eased somewhat. Her stomach growled, and she knew she needed to get some food before hunger created its own problems.

Gingerly, she swung her legs over the side of the bed and eased herself into a sitting position. So far, so good. The throbbing quickened with the increased rhythm of her heartbeat, but it soon settled down to a dull pounding. Holding one hand to her forehead, Jenny slid off the mattress.

With faltering steps, she made her way to her tiny kitchen and sliced off a chunk of cheese. The combination of food and movement seemed to work. She felt her headache loosen its grip with every passing moment.

She risked a glance out the window, shielding her eyes with her hands as she did so. Too late now to do much good down at the restaurant. Manuel and Jacinta would be shutting down for the afternoon before she could get dressed and make her way there.

Jenny caught sight of the papers stacked on top of her cylinder-front desk. Her pulse quickened, and this time her headache didn't follow suit.

Retrieving her robe from its hook behind her bedroom door, she slipped it on over her nightgown and slid into her desk chair. She'd spent so much time on the restaurant's books, she had neglected keeping up with her own finances of late. She might as well catch up on those and feel she hadn't completely wasted the day.

An hour later, Jenny's headache had dissipated completely, replaced by excitement and a sense of wonder. She stared at the column of figures on her paper and tallied them up again for the third time.

She came up with the same total she'd gotten twice already. Could it be possible? She knew the restaurant had been bringing in a steady profit, but she hadn't bothered to tote up her own accounts for some time. When she left Prescott to start her new life in Tucson, she'd dared to dream that eventually she might earn enough to make a comfortable life for herself, but the figure that stared back at her surpassed her fondest hopes.

And that reflected the result of only a couple of months in business. If the restaurant continued to do that well throughout the coming year. . . Jenny pulled out a fresh sheet of paper and covered it with new figures, projecting what might lie ahead.

Her heart pounded and she caught her lower lip between her teeth. If business at the Pueblo did no more than keep pace with what it had done since it opened, she would be in a very comfortable position in another few months. The income from the expansion of the restaurant would only add to it.

And if the Silver Crown lived up to even a fraction of Red's expectations. . .

Jenny sank back into her chair, overcome. Without her even being aware of it, she had somehow become a woman of modest means and had every reason to anticipate her income growing even more.

She closed her eyes and let herself dare to dream of the possibilities that would open up. With that kind of income, she could build a bigger house, if she chose.

No, she decided, looking around her cozy little adobe, that wouldn't be necessary. This was her home, and a home was what she wanted, not a showplace. She might, however, add another room or two and pick up a few more pieces of quality furniture.

So what would she do with her money? It seemed ridiculous to work so hard to amass such a sum but have no idea how to use it. Some of it should be saved, she supposed. She wouldn't stay young and strong forever. But did she need to hoard all her money for a time that lay in the distant future?

Jenny left her desk and paced the room. New clothes were probably in order, but what after that? She halted abruptly in the center of the room when a bold idea shot into her consciousness.

Could she do it? Why not? She stood still a few moments longer, assessing the possibilities, then gave a decisive nod. Hurrying to her bedroom, she donned her favorite dotted-Swiss dress and dressed her hair, exulting in the fact that her headache had completely disappeared. She checked her appearance in the mirror glass one last time, then snatched up her reticule and headed out the front door. The only questions now were whether she would find Evan at the restaurant, and whether he would go along with her newly hatched plan.

"You want to what?" For once, Evan was shaken out of his typically unruffled calm.

Jenny tightened her grip on her reticule. "I want to buy your share of the Pueblo," she repeated. "It's a good investment for me, and it will give you the capital you need to finance whatever business venture you sniff out next."

Evan wagged his head slowly from side to side, his gaze sweeping the dining room. "What brought this about? I thought things were—" He broke off in midsentence, and a look of understanding dawned in his eyes.

"This is about yesterday, isn't it? It's your way of putting me in my place, am I right?"

"This is a separate issue." Jenny spoke in clipped tones. "I'm a business-woman, remember? I see this as a sound opportunity, one that will benefit us both." She held her voice steady, hoping he wouldn't guess how much she hoped he would agree to her plan. Not only would buying Evan out give her sole ownership of the Pueblo, it would also mean he would no longer have any right to come and go as he pleased. Never again would she have to wonder when he would appear next—and whether he would try to accost her. She watched his eyes, trying to gauge his reaction.

He tilted his head and gave her a long, considering look. "What if I promise to stop badgering you?" he asked. "We'll go back to the way things were originally and try to forget there was ever any unpleasantness between us. What do you say?"

Forget? Did he really imagine she could put the kiss he forced upon her out of her mind like nothing had ever happened? "I don't think you understand, Evan—"

"No, it's you who doesn't understand." His eyes narrowed and took on a steely light she hadn't seen in them before. "You want things on a strictly business basis? All right, here it is: You've made your offer; I decline to accept it."

A sense of foreboding trickled down Jenny's spine. "But why?"

"Let's just say I don't like to be thwarted. You've already made it plain that you find my attention distasteful. Now you want to be rid of my company altogether. That's hardly flattering, my dear."

Jenny felt her face flush. "I didn't say—"

"You didn't have to. That light in your eyes when you broached the idea made it plain enough. You can't wait to be rid of me. Well, I'm not going to make it that easy for you." His lips parted in a slow, cruel smile. "You're stuck with me, Jenny. Stuck good and proper. You can't buy me out unless I agree to it, and I don't. Is that clear enough?"

Jenny forced her stiff lips to frame an answer. "Perfectly."

Evan clenched his fist, then flexed his fingers. "We're partners, Jenny, in business if in no other way." He held up his hand as if to stave off her protest.

"I told you I'd leave off pressuring you, and I'll abide by that. For now anyway." The corner of his mouth tilted up in a pale imitation of his usual easy grin. "Believe it or not, I can be a man of honor. I'm just wondering whether you demand the same hands-off policy from your other business partners."

Once again, Jenny's hand flashed toward him.

Evan caught her wrist before her hand made contact with his cheek. He pushed her hand aside and stepped back out of her reach. "Oh-ho, so that's the way the wind blows, is it? I wouldn't have thought it of you."

Jenny floundered, trying to follow this turn in the conversation. "What are you talking about?"

Evan moved away from the wall and stood before her, his hands on his hips, head tilted to one side. "It's him, isn't it? That Garrett fellow."

He stared at her like a scientist inspecting some strange new species, then gave a decisive nod. "That explains it, then. There had to be some reason you didn't want to have anything to do with me. I've known too many other women to seriously think there's any deficiency in my charm," he added with a lopsided grin, "but I'll admit you shook my self-confidence."

A more somber expression spread across his face. "Just how far has this thing with Garrett gone?"

Jenny bristled. "There is nothing between me and Andrew Garrett—or anyone else. He's a partner, that's all, just like you and I are. No less and certainly nothing more."

Evan regarded her with a quizzical expression. "Your lips say one thing, but your eyes tell me something else." He reached out his hand as if to touch her cheek but drew back when she flinched. "Not to worry, my dear. I won't trespass beyond the boundaries you've set. But don't expect me not to wonder what Garrett's great attraction is. You've dealt a blow to my masculine pride, you know."

He straightened his jacket and brushed down his sleeves. "Just remember, when you decide you've made a mistake, you can come cry on my shoulder. If I'd had any notion before of selling you my share of the business, it's gone now. I wouldn't miss this for the world."

Despite her mounting anger, Jenny couldn't help asking, "Miss what?"

Evan smirked. "Seeing the look on your face when you find out your hero isn't all you thought he'd be and you realize that I'm your best hope for happiness after all." He caught sight of Jenny's look of scorn, and a low chuckle rumbled through his chest. "Is it that frightening a thought? Just wait until you find out what kind of man Andrew Garrett really is. I'll look positively angelic in comparison." He reached for the door handle.

Loathing her weakness, Jenny caught at his arm. "Wait a minute, Evan. What do you mean, what kind of man Andrew really is? What do you know about him?"

Evan turned slowly. "Nothing. Not directly, anyway. Just some talk I've heard around town. Surely you've heard some of the whispers."

Jenny shook her head. "What whispers?" She could barely choke out the words.

"All right." Evan lifted his hands in surrender. "I didn't want to say anything until I was sure, but I guess you deserve to know. After you told me you didn't really know anything about Garrett, I made it my business to do some checking up on him." A sad smile twisted his lips. "Despite what you think of me, I do have your best interests at heart."

A cold knot formed in Jenny's chest. "And what have you learned?"

Evan shook his head sorrowfully. "I've turned up some distressing things. It seems your Mr. Garrett is involved in a number of shady activities."

The knot grew tighter. "Such as?"

A long sigh whistled from Evan's lips. "Since he came to town, a lot of mining stock has been traded. There's nothing wrong with that in itself," he hastened to add, "but unfortunately, these mines only exist on paper."

"Andrew is selling phony mining stock? I don't believe it." Even as she spoke the words, a riot of thoughts whirled through Jenny's mind. Andrew was a mining engineer, an expert in his field. That put him in a perfect position to do exactly what Evan suggested. The knot of dread became a wave of cold fury. She'd seen the same thing happen back in Prescott and knew the havoc it could wreak.

Evan broke into her thoughts. "There's more."

Jenny's shoulders sagged. What more could there be?

"I'm afraid his name has been linked to a couple of incidences of claim jumping, too. I have no proof, of course. Not yet, anyway." He strode over to her and clasped her hands lightly in his. "I'm sorry to lay this burden on you, but I thought you ought to know the kind of man you're dealing with before it's too late."

Jenny pulled her hands away, not interested in the kind of comfort Evan offered. "They're rumors," she said. "Unsubstantiated rumors."

"True enough. And I hope they turn out to be false, for your sake." He turned toward the door. "But talk like this seldom begins without reason, or so I've always found."

He swung the door open. "Just remember, Jenny, I'll be here if you discover your shining knight is really quite tarnished after all."

Chapter 15

*W*orthless mining stock. Claim jumping. Jenny stared at the closed door long after Evan left, his allegations echoing in her mind.

Could Andrew truly be involved in such activities? She went back over the times they had been together, trying to measure the man she knew against Evan's intimations. What she knew about Andrew was precious little, she realized. Only what Red had told her and the few impressions she had gleaned on her own.

And that overheard conversation in Prescott, when Andrew refused to cheat a miner he'd only met once and would probably never see again. Did that line up with a man who would defraud investors or steal another man's claim?

Jenny shook her head slowly, trying to picture Andrew taking part in anything like that and finding it impossible to do so. Where had those stories come from? Granted, Evan himself had classified them as rumors, but they had carried enough weight to linger in his memory.

What if the stories proved to be true? What if both she and Red had been duped? The partnership could be dissolved, she supposed, and she and Red could go back to the way they'd been before Andrew became a part of their lives. Nothing significant would have changed.

Nothing? You're a liar, Jenny Davis. Jenny clenched her fists and felt the dampness on her palms. *This is what comes of letting your guard down, of thinking for even one moment that you could allow yourself to trust.*

She pivoted on her heel and strode purposefully toward the kitchen. Too late to think about an afternoon siesta now. She might as well make some good use of her time. Paring vegetables or rolling out piecrusts, perhaps. Something to make it up to Jacinta for having missed work that morning.

Try as she might, she couldn't keep visions of Andrew's face and warm smile out of her thoughts while she worked. Why couldn't she get him out of her mind? Why had he claimed a place in her heart ever since she first heard his voice in Prescott? Without her being aware of when it happened, Andrew had become a part of the fabric of her being. She couldn't imagine the hurt it would cause if he were torn out of her life.

Which was exactly what would happen if the real Andrew turned out to be the man Evan described, and not the man of her daydreams.

Jenny scooped the curled potato peelings into a heap and put them in the trash. She should have known better. She *had* known better; she'd just chosen not to remember. And look where that lapse had gotten her.

201

All right, then. Jenny squared her shoulders. From here on out, the walls around her heart would go back up, as strong as the adobe walls that had encircled Tucson. Everything—from Evan's unwanted advances to the possibility of Andrew's duplicity—only went to prove that, barring a few exceptions like Michael and Red, men were men and simply couldn't be trusted. The sooner she convinced her heart of that, the safer she would be.

"I got your message." Red stood in Jenny's doorway, a worried expression on his face. "Is anything wrong?"

Jenny led him to a bench on the east side of her house where they could take advantage of the late evening shade it afforded. She sat on one end of the bench and twisted her hands together. "I think we should take a second look at Andrew."

Red gave her a shrewd glance. "What's happened, lass? Why this sudden concern?"

"It isn't so sudden, but I've reason to think my doubts may have been justified." She repeated what Evan had told her. "I've never been entirely comfortable with the way Andrew came into the picture. You were the one who persuaded me he was trustworthy, remember?" She clapped her hand over her mouth. "I'm sorry! I didn't mean that the way it sounded."

The wiry miner chuckled. "No offense taken. I know what you meant." His expression sobered. "But I think your Mr. Townsend has gotten his facts wrong. I haven't known Andrew long, and that's the truth. But he and I have spent a good many hours talking. The Bible says that out of the heart come the words a man speaks. From everything I've heard Andrew say, I have to believe his heart is right before God. I'll stand by him until that's proven otherwise."

"I'd like to believe that, Red. I really would."

"Then keep on trusting, won't you? You haven't done so badly by taking this old prospector on faith, have you now?"

Jenny gave a shaky laugh. "I can't argue with you there. You've been a wonderful friend, and I have to admit you knew exactly what you were talking about when you said you'd found something that would make us secure for the rest of our lives."

For the second time, Red's smile dimmed. "For someone who's so cautious about putting their confidence in other people, you're awfully quick to stake your hopes on what that mine may bring."

Stung by his words, Jenny retorted, "It seems to me you've been awfully happy at the prospect of living the rest of your life in ease."

"Excited by the discovery, yes. But happy? All the silver mines in the world won't bring you happiness, you know. That has to come from within."

"What are you talking about? I'm happier now than I've been in a long time."

"Are you, now?" Red's keen eyes studied her. "I've seen you smile when the mood strikes you and even laugh on occasion. But I'd be lying if I said I've ever once seen you glow with a soul-deep happiness from within."

Jenny shifted on the bench and tilted her chin. "I'm doing just fine, thank you. I have a prosperous business and a home of my own." She reached out to touch Red's arm and a small smile curved her lips. "And I have you as a friend. What more could I want?"

"Peace." Red let the word hang between them a moment before he continued. "And I'm not talking about the contentment you feel when everything seems to be going your way. I mean a peace that stays with you even when it looks like your whole world is going to fall apart." He leaned toward her. "The peace that comes from having God in your life."

He settled back against the adobe wall and fixed her with a rueful smile. "I can see by the look on your face that I've overstepped the boundary again. Don't worry. I won't be preaching at you." He planted his hands on his knees and pushed himself to his feet. "But if you ever decide you want to talk about it, I'll be pleased to tell you more. And if I don't happen to be around, take the matter up with God Himself. He's always ready to add another beloved child to His family."

Jenny stayed on the bench long after the shadows lengthened and the sun dipped below the horizon. She—as a part of God's family? Red didn't know what an impossible thing that would be.

Jenny massaged her temples with her fingertips and tried to focus on the papers on her office desk. If she didn't work faster, she'd never have that order finished before fatigue overtook her. With Manuel and Jacinta already on their way home, the task should have been completed quickly in the quiet of the empty restaurant, but she couldn't seem to concentrate.

She pressed the heel of her left hand against her forehead and winced. The headache she had successfully fought off the day before threatened to return, its persistent throb increasing with every beat of her heart. The pain had disappeared shortly after she conceived the plan to buy out Evan's share of the business, she remembered crossly. If only he had acquiesced, surely the ache would have stayed away. It hadn't threatened again until after his refusal.

And her conversation with Red. Even now, his insistence that she needed God to be truly happy stirred feelings she thought she had buried long before. She pushed them to the back of her mind. She would deal with them later, if she decided to address the issue at all. Between Evan's contrariness, Red's tenacious prodding, and her doubts about Andrew's integrity, her mind already felt pulled in too many different directions.

Skrrr. Jenny sat bolt upright, recognizing the scrape of the back door opening, then the click of the latch. Who could be coming in at this hour? And what could they possibly want? Without making a sound, she rose from the desk and glanced frantically around the office, desperate to find something she could use to protect herself. A silver-streaked chunk of quartz, a gift Red brought from the Silver Crown, lay on a shelf. She snatched it up and held it tight, her arm cocked to swing at a moment's notice.

Scarcely daring to breathe, she slipped through the doorway into the dining room and threaded her way through the tables and chairs toward the kitchen. At the kitchen door, she paused, wondering if she should have simply made an escape through the office door. Too late now. Heavy footsteps approached the door from the other side. Jenny drew back her hand, ready to strike.

The door swung wide and she gasped. "Evan!" Her fingers went limp and the chunk of ore dropped to the floor with a *thump*.

"What's this?" Evan's eyes widened in surprise, then crinkled at the corners. "Did you think I was a burglar?" He laughed and shook his head. "Poor Jenny!" Glancing down at the fist-sized rock, he scooped it up and hefted it in his palm, a more sober expression crossing his face. "Poor *me* if I'd really been a burglar. That would have packed quite a wallop." He started to hand it back to Jenny, then set it on a nearby table instead. "Remind me not to rile you," he said with a grin.

Jenny's knees buckled, and she dropped into a chair, propping her head up with one hand. "Don't rile me." She gave Evan a shaky smile in return. "What are you doing here so late?"

"I might ask you the same thing," he retorted, perching on the edge of the table behind him. "You stayed home yesterday because you didn't feel well, and today I find you down here slaving away into the evening hours. Your devotion to duty is admirable, but please don't work yourself into an early grave."

Jenny covered her mouth to hide a yawn. "I just wanted to catch up on the work I missed doing yesterday. I need to finish putting together the order for next week's supplies."

"Then I've come at an opportune time for us both." Evan pulled a slip of paper from his shirt pocket and tossed it on the table in front of her. "I'm heading out early in the morning, so I thought I'd leave this on your desk tonight. I never intended to frighten you like that," he added.

Jenny pulled the paper closer and studied Evan's scribbled notation. "What is this?"

"A rancher who's trying to develop a new market for his beef will sell to us at a discount. If we agree to buy all our beef from him, he's willing to give us a price well below anything else we can get locally. He'll be staying at Hodges House until tomorrow afternoon."

"Wonderful!" Jenny felt her headache recede. "I'll contact him first thing in the morning." Remembering the other part of Evan's comment, she asked, "Where are you off to this time?"

"Yuma first, then up the river to Ehrenberg. I'll be back in a couple of weeks."

"I'll expect you when I see you," Jenny said, feeling more lighthearted than she had in days at the prospect of Evan's prolonged absence.

❧

Andrew looked up into the flickering light of the oil lamp and pinched the bridge of his nose between his thumb and fingers. He remembered lighting the lamp when the shadows had started creeping across the pages he was working on but hadn't noticed when the sun set completely. He snapped open the cover of his pocket watch and whistled when he saw the time. No wonder his eyes felt like they had grains of sand embedded under their lids.

He stood and stretched his arms wide, then rolled his neck from side to side. Working into the night hours hadn't been his plan, but the results were well worth it. He braced his hands on the desk and leaned over the papers there, studying his outline one more time.

As far as he could see, the schedule he'd drawn up for developing the mine was a good one. From everything he'd seen so far, the Silver Crown had all the makings of a big strike. Until the problems with the Apaches were resolved, work couldn't begin in earnest. But once they'd crossed that barrier, Andrew suspected a fortune could be in store for him and both his partners.

He thought about the Silver Crown's other owners while he carried the lamp to his bedroom and set it on the bedside table. He'd felt an immediate connection with Red the first time he'd met the feisty Irishman. Maybe it was due to the prospector's unfailing sunny attitude. More likely, it had to do with their bond as followers of Christ. At any rate, he hoped things worked out so they could get started on the mine soon. It would be grand to know that Red would be able to see his lonely years of prospecting bear fruit at last.

And then there was Jenny. Andrew pulled his shirt off and tossed it on a chair in the corner. Would knowing she would be financially secure for the rest of her days lighten her heart? He would love to do something to sweep away that terrible sadness in her eyes.

He slipped beneath his sheet and laced his fingers behind his head. What could have created such sorrow in her? What tragic circumstances could have befallen such a young woman to have left such an imprint?

He blew out the lamp, then rolled over and punched his pillow into a fluffy mound. According to Red, Jenny wasn't a believer. Had whatever left its mark on her sweet face managed to turn her heart against the things of the Lord as well? With all his heart, Andrew longed to find a way to restore her joy.

But he'd have to do that as a friend, nothing more. Jenny's lack of belief meant he couldn't take their relationship into a closer realm, much as he would like to. He closed his eyes, only to see Jenny's face. He opened them and found her image hovering in the darkness of his room. Scrubbing the vision away with the palms of his hands, he wished he knew how to handle his growing feelings for Jenny. Instead of Red's information putting a damper on his emotions, they seemed all the stronger for knowing he couldn't pursue her.

Better pull the reins up tight before this horse runs away with you. He pulled the pillow up around his ears and started praying for her instead, asking God to move in Jenny's life in such a way that she would see her need for Him.

Chapter 16

Red burst through the office door, beaming and waving a sheaf of papers over his head. Andrew followed him inside, his gait more subdued but his smile every bit as wide as Red's. "Look at these, Jenny," Red exclaimed. "We're on our way!"

"And good morning to you, too," Jenny said, laughing. "What's gotten you in such a dither?"

"What's got me dithery? Why, it's the fine handiwork of our esteemed partner, my girl. Andrew spent all night on these plans, and just see what a grand job he's done." He bent to spread the papers out across the desk.

Jenny cast a sidelong glance at Andrew, and she watched the warm light in his eyes fade under her frosty scrutiny. Uncertainty replaced his earlier eager expression.

"Would it bother you if I run along now and let the two of you discuss this on your own?" he asked. "I need to deal with some other things I've been neglecting."

"What?" Red expostulated. "Leave us now, just when—"

"It's all right," Jenny cut in. "I'm sure Mr. Garrett has pressing business to attend to." She heard the coolness in her tone and knew Andrew had recognized it as well by the way he swung around and headed for the door.

"Thank you for all your hard work," she called after his retreating figure, hoping to salve her conscience and erase Red's look of bewilderment.

"Now, what was all that about?" Red demanded as soon as the door closed behind Andrew.

"Nothing at all. The man said he had things to do. I had no desire to keep him from them." She stepped nearer to the table, keeping her eyes focused on the papers in order to avoid Red's penetrating gaze. "Are you going to explain these to me?"

"I might," he said, folding his arms across his chest and perching on the edge of the desk. "And I might not." Jenny risked a quick peek at him through lowered lashes. He glared at her with an expression that reminded her of an exasperated schoolmarm determined to ferret information out of a misbehaving student. "I'd like to know why you sent young Andrew packing."

"I didn't," Jenny protested. "He's the one who said he had to leave." She lifted her chin and stared straight back at Red.

He shook his head sorrowfully. "Jenny lass, this has something to do with those groundless stories, doesn't it?"

"Of course not," she began, then halted and took a deep breath. "I suppose it does," she admitted. "You know I've had reservations about him from the first. The concerns Evan shared only served to reinforce them." Taking the offensive, she dared to add, "Someday you may thank me for protecting our mine."

Red snorted and slid down off the desk. "And someday I may sprout wings and fly." He stirred the stack of papers with his forefinger and fished two sheets from the pile. Scooting the other papers aside, he laid those two out for Jenny's inspection. "Let me show you briefly what your suspicious character spent all night working on. If that doesn't convince you he's on our side, I don't know what will."

Jenny's shoulders slumped. "All right, show me."

For the next hour, Red went over the details Andrew had labored over, his voice becoming more animated with every new idea he showed Jenny. After he laid the last sheet of paper atop the stack, he turned to her with a look of triumph. "We'll have to bide our time for a wee bit before the majority of the work can commence, but if this yields what Andrew and I expect it to, we'll all be in clover the rest of our days. How does that strike you, Miss Too-Suspicious-For-Your-Own-Good?"

Jenny ignored the jibe. Her heart beat wildly. She had dared to dream of the mine's success, but to see those dreams put down in black and white and by someone who knew what he was doing. . .

"It's amazing," she breathed.

" 'Tis more than that. It's an outright blessing. The Lord knew I needed something to keep me in my old age and saw fit to provide it."

Jenny ignored his reference to God's provision and allowed excitement to take hold of her in spite of herself.

"And as you see," Red went on, "it'll benefit all three of us equally. Andrew has been very careful in that regard. He thought of things neither you nor I would ever have come up with."

Andrew again. Jenny said good-bye to her happy daydreams and came back to the world of reality. "Red—"

"Now, don't be getting your back up like that. Every time I mention the lad's name, you fluff up like a hissing cat."

"I'm just trying to be realistic. He seemed to appear out of nowhere." *Nowhere except my memory.* She cut that thought off sharply. "He didn't know us; we didn't know him. Think about it for a moment: Why would anyone offer to jump into a partnership with two perfect strangers for no good reason? It doesn't make sense."

"Unless you add God to the mix," Red said. "I keep telling you, Andrew is a follower of Christ, the same as me. God brings His people together as He sees fit to accomplish His purposes. When you look at it that way, it makes all the sense in the world."

"Not to me, it doesn't." Jenny sighed. "I don't mean to be obstinate, and I know beyond a doubt that your heart's in the right place. But in my experience, things just don't happen that way. I'll believe it when I see it—once the mine is in operation and I know my future is secure."

Red tilted his head to one side, making him look more like a leprechaun than ever. "But is it?"

Jenny gaped at him. "Of course it is, assuming Andrew's assessment is even halfway accurate, and if he's the honest man you believe him to be. We'll never suffer want again as long as we live."

"Mm." Red pursed his lips and regarded her thoughtfully. "And after that?"

"After what?"

"After this life is over, how secure will your future be then?"

"After—Red, what are you talking about?"

"I think you know what I mean, lass. None of us will live forever. All of us have to face God at some point. What then?"

Prickles of apprehension ran from Jenny's shoulders to her wrists. She slid her hands up and down her arms, trying to rub away the disquieting sensation. She attempted a laugh. "How did we get from the subject of mining to theology?"

Red took up a stance in front of the window. "The Lord Jesus told us not to put our confidence in treasures here on earth, but in the treasure we store up in heaven instead. There's nothing wrong with appreciating God's provision here, but I fear that's where your whole heart is focused. And there's more, Jenny. So much more."

"Can we just drop the subject, Red?" Jenny pressed her fingertips against her temples, wondering if another headache were coming on. "It seems to me this whole thing started when the conversation turned to Andrew, and it proves my point. Even setting aside the allegations Evan brought up, the man is a distraction. If he can set us at odds with each other even before the mine is opened, what will happen when things really get under way?"

Red scooped the papers into a pile and tapped the edges to square the stack. "Sure," he said in a tone lacking his usual enthusiasm. "We'll drop it. For now." A glimmer of humor returned to his eyes. "And I'll be agreeing that young Andrew Garrett is a distraction of the worst sort, but not for the reasons you've named. I think our Andrew has become a distraction to you in a special way—a distraction of the heart."

He sobered again. "Just be remembering what I've said. Regardless of what your high-and-mighty Mr. Townsend says about him, I'd stake my life that Andrew Garrett is a fine and honorable man." He tugged at his coat lapels and tucked the papers under his arm. "You need to give him a chance." He shut the office door quietly on his way out.

Jenny returned to her ledger entries, but the figures swam before her eyes. *Give Andrew a chance,* Red had said. She didn't dare. One fleeting encounter in

Elizabeth's restaurant had impressed him so deeply on her mind, she feared she would never be able to be free of him. What chance did her heart have if she opened it up to him?

❧

Andrew stood in the sparse shade of a paloverde tree and watched Red exit the Pueblo Restaurant. The miner paused and heaved a long sigh, then walked in Andrew's direction. Andrew let out his own sigh, one of relief. He had correctly guessed the path Red would take. When his friend drew even with the paloverde, Andrew stepped out with a casual air and fell in step beside him.

They walked in silence for a few moments, then Red spoke. "And what is preying on your mind, may I ask?"

Andrew avoided the other man's gaze as they turned north along Camino Real. "What makes you think I have anything special on my mind?"

Red rubbed one hand across his jaw. "Let me see now. You left Jenny and me in a hurry, saying you had important things to do. Instead, I find you waiting outside under a pitiful excuse for shade on a blistering hot afternoon, right along the path that will take me back to my digs. And you seem to have a desire for my company. All signs of a man with a heavy weight on his shoulders, I'd say." The miner's seamed face crinkled into a broad grin. "She is a lovely lass, isn't she?"

Andrew started. "Who?" The moment the word left his lips, he knew he'd made a mistake.

Red laughed long and loud. "Oh, Andrew, my boy, it's a good thing you set your mind to be a mining engineer. You'd never make it on the stage. 'Who,' he says. Why, our Jenny, of course."

Andrew felt a flush begin at his collar and work its way upward toward his hairline. "That obvious, is it?"

"So you're admitting it freely, are you? Good lad. That saves me the trouble of prying it out of you." Red chuckled at Andrew's chagrin and clapped the younger man on the shoulder with his work-hardened hand. "Don't be looking so downhearted. I don't believe the lady has found you out, if that's what you're worried about."

"That's a good thing. It would only give her one more thing to despise me for."

Red shot him a sidelong glance. "And why should the lady despise you?"

"That's what I wanted to talk to you about," Andrew admitted. They stepped inside Solomon Warner's store, and each ordered a bottle of sarsaparilla. When the genial owner had handed over their drinks, they carried the bottles outside and resumed their walk.

"What have I done to put her off so?" Andrew asked.

Red took a long swallow of his drink. "Before we go any further with this, let me get one thing straight in my mind." He peered at Andrew soberly. "You realize, don't you, that our Jenny isn't a believer? Anyone with an eye to see can tell you have feelings for her. But there's a danger there, lad. Don't let your heart go further than where God is leading. You don't want to become entangled in something that will only bring both of you heartache later on."

"I know." Andrew stared at the line of trees bordering the Santa Cruz River and set his jaw. "I know, and I realize it means I can only be a friend to her. But I want to do at least that much. I don't know what's happened in her life, but I have a feeling she needs all the friends she can get."

"Aye." Red took the last swig from his bottle and nodded agreement. "You're right about that."

"Then why is she so cold toward me? I've seen warmer glances from a dead fish than the one she gave me this morning." Just speaking the words made him feel the rebuff afresh. "It isn't as though I've given her any reason to dislike me. None that I know of, that is. But every time I come around, she pulls away, and I don't understand why."

Red looked off into the distance but kept silent.

"Every time I look into her eyes. . .have you noticed? Even when she's smiling, her eyes seem to hold such sorrow. She reminds me of a lost little girl."

"Aye, lad." Red nodded slowly. "She's that, all right. Lost and alone and without a Savior."

"But why? What's happened to make her that way?" Andrew tried to catch Red's gaze, but the older man's glance skittered past his and focused on a point across the river. Andrew went on, feeling as though he was picking his way through a maze. "You know something, don't you? Something you haven't told me?"

The miner knotted his hands, then spread them out flat against his thighs and turned toward Andrew. "I can't be telling all I know. It was told to me in confidence, and I intend to keep it that way. But I'll say this much, since you've guessed some of it on your own: She does have reason to shy away from men. Good reason. And I suspect she feels special cause to be apprehensive around you."

The words hit him like a blow. "Me? What are you getting at?"

Red's posture relaxed, and he gave Andrew an impish grin at variance with his earlier solemnity. He took his time choosing his words. "Only that being able to trust comes hard to Jenny." His grin grew wider. "And she may feel she has as much reason to mistrust herself as anyone else."

Andrew felt his forehead pucker. "Meaning?"

Red shook his head. "If your aim was no better than your thinking, you wouldn't be able to hit a hole in a ladder. Meaning, my dense young friend, that your feelings for her are not entirely unrequited. Do I need to spell it out further?"

"Are you saying. . . ?"

Red raised his arms and looked up, as if beseeching help from heaven. "It's a good thing God loves the simpleminded. The girl cares about you. Can I say it any clearer than that?"

A warm spring of hope bubbled forth inside Andrew. And that was where the danger lay, he reminded himself. He wouldn't—couldn't—let those feelings take control. "What makes you think so?" he asked cautiously.

Red let out a loud guffaw. "Being in the same room with the two of you is like standing in a field where lightning is about to strike. There's the same kind of spark, the same tingling feeling that sends my hair standing on end. Good thing I'm only a bystander. I don't think I could take the full force of it."

Joy surged through Andrew, then died away as quickly as it had come. As a follower of Christ, he couldn't link his life with that of an unbeliever. As much pain as it would cause him to deny his deeper feelings for Jenny, he would have to do just that and concentrate on being her friend, nothing more. To do otherwise would be totally unfair to both him and Jenny. "God has given me a mixed blessing. . .and a very tough assignment."

"Aye, lad." Red gave him a look full of sympathy. "I know it won't be easy for you. But remember, we have a partnership to think of, and don't think for a moment that it came about by chance. I don't believe in chances. God had a purpose for bringing the three of us together, and I'm looking forward to finding out what it is. Maybe it's only to stand by young Jenny and show her there is still room for trust and hope in this world." His eyes took on a mischievous gleam. "Or maybe He has plans yet for an even greater partnership for the two of you someday. Whatever the case may be, I think it'll be worth watching this play unfold."

He turned the empty bottle in his hands and fixed Andrew with a piercing gaze. "Are you willing to walk this path not knowing what God has in mind in the end, even if it means friendship is all you'll ever have between you?"

Am I? The question made Andrew take a long look at the innermost motives of his heart. Could he stand back and offer Jenny his friendship, knowing he might never have anything more? Could his love for Jenny be refined in the fire of self-denial until it shone forth as a reflection of God's love for her? He nodded slowly, meeting Red's gaze. "I'm willing." *But I'll need Your help, Lord, and a lot of it.*

Chapter 17

M anuel bustled up to the corner table where Jenny was working. "My mother wishes to know if she can leave a few minutes early and let me finish cleaning the kitchen for her. *Mi abuela*, she's sick and my mother is worried about her."

"Your. . .oh, your grandmother," Jenny said, recognizing one of the Spanish words she had picked up from her employees. "Of course, Manuel. Tell her to go, and I'll help you clean up."

"It is not necessary." He puffed out his small chest. "I am a good worker."

"A very good worker," Jenny agreed. "Now go tell your mother she can leave. And have her take some of that barley soup. It ought to be good for your grandmother." She watched Manuel scurry back to the kitchen, her thoughts returning to the dilemma posed by Evan's allegations against Andrew.

To her surprise, the doubts raised by those allegations wrestled against an unexpected desire to believe Andrew Garrett was everything he purported to be. The struggle haunted her waking moments and interrupted her sleep at night. How could she believe such outrageous claims? But how could she give Andrew the trust necessary for their partnership to succeed unless she knew for sure whether they had any factual basis?

I have to know. Despite Red's confident assertions, she couldn't just accept Andrew's innocence on faith. She needed proof—needed it now, before too many more sleepless nights took their toll. But how could she hope to get it?

She couldn't very well go up to Andrew and ask. Nor could she follow him and keep watch, hoping to pick up information that would prove or disprove his innocence once and for all.

She made another entry in her ledger, then laid her pen down and considered her options. What if she could find someone to act for her? Someone she could trust to investigate without letting Andrew know of her interest. She turned the idea over in her mind. The more she thought about it, the more she wanted to do it. But where could she find someone she could trust who was clever enough to pursue Andrew unnoticed?

Manuel cleared away more of the lunch dishes, slipping in between the tables with grace. Jenny stared after him, an audacious thought forming in her mind. *No.* She couldn't possibly. The idea was ridiculous. And yet. . .

He returned and started wiping off the empty tables. Jenny watched him work. Small for his age, he could easily give the appearance of a little boy interested in nothing more than childish pursuits, thereby keeping him from danger. Clever? Without a doubt. And his ability to hear conversations, whether or not they were directed at him, was legend around the Pueblo.

Would he be willing to perform such a task? She thought of his glee whenever he passed along some tidbit of information he'd overheard from one of their customers. He'd love it. Now all she had to do was convince him he had to stay safe.

After she ushered their last customer out and dropped the bar on the door in place, Jenny swept the dining room, over Manuel's protests. "Let me help," she told him, trying not to laugh at his offended scowl. "We need to finish quickly. There's something I need to talk to you about."

A gleam of curiosity replaced Manuel's frown, and he peppered her with excited questions. "Is something special going to happen? You are planning a party, perhaps? Can you tell me about it while we work?"

"No, no, and no," she replied to his entreaties. "Let's get this work done so we can talk."

With the cleanup finished in record time, she carried a cup of coffee and a glass of milk to a table and gestured for Manuel to sit down across from her. "I have a job that needs to be done by someone I can trust," she began, scooting the milk over to his waiting hands. "Would you be interested?"

He lifted the glass to his lips and swallowed deeply before setting it down again. A milk mustache decorated his upper lip. "What kind of job?" he asked. "Something you need a strong man to do?"

Jenny took a sip of coffee to hide her amusement. The combination of masculine pride and the white streak above his mouth would be her undoing if she weren't careful. "Definitely," she told him. "I need you to get some information for me."

The boy's expression clouded. "Why do you not just ask for it yourself?"

Why, indeed? Jenny pondered the best way to answer and decided to be candid. "It's information about a person. Information he might not be willing to give me if I asked."

"Ah!" Manuel's eyes lit up. "It is something secret, then?"

"It could be. I'm not certain exactly what we may find." She studied the little boy's face. "Do you think you'd like to try?"

"It sounds exciting," Manuel said. "What do you want me to do?"

They had arrived at the sticky part. "Do you know Mr. Garrett?"

"Ah, Señor Garrett! He is the tall man, sí? The one whose eyes glow like candles when he looks at you?"

Jenny stared, dumbfounded. "What are you talking about?"

"And when he comes into the room, your face does this." Manuel twisted his own features into a look of unbridled rapture. "That is the one, yes?"

Jenny pressed her hands against her cheeks, feeling them grow warmer by the second. "I do no such thing!"

"Ah, but you do, Señorita Davis," Manuel continued, unperturbed by her agitation. "My mother has noticed it, too. She told Aunt Rosa only the other day that she would be surprised if you two were not married before the year is out." He looked at Jenny with a happy smile. "That is the man you mean, is it not?"

"No. That is, I don't. . . Yes, I suppose it is." Surely she didn't look as calf-eyed as Manuel's imitation would have her believe. "But it isn't what you think. It isn't like that at all." She straightened her shoulders in her most businesslike manner. "I need you to find out everything you can about Mr. Garrett. Follow him if you need to, but don't let him catch you at it. Or if he does, make sure he doesn't suspect what you're up to. Do you understand?"

Manuel nodded gravely. "You think he may have another sweetheart, and you wish to know for sure."

"No!" Jenny looked at Manuel in horror. "I barely know the man. I don't know whether he has a sweetheart, and I don't care one way or another. I simply need to know what he's up to. Businesswise, that is."

Manuel crinkled his forehead. "But you and he do business together, no?"

Jenny searched for a way to explain. "It is possible," she said, choosing her words with care, "that Mr. Garrett may be involved in selling stock for mines that don't exist. I don't know this for sure, you understand, but I would like very much to find out whether it is true."

"Aah." Manuel released a long, happy sigh. "You wish me to be a. . .a spy, is that the word?"

"That's the idea," Jenny agreed reluctantly. "But I don't want you to do anything that would put you in any danger. Do you understand, Manuel? I want you to be very careful, or I won't let you do this at all."

Manuel drew himself up with every indication of wounded dignity. "Of course. He will never know what I am about. I will be like the cougar that stalks its prey."

"Better be more like a little mouse that hides in a corner," Jenny replied. She felt a sudden prick of doubt about the wisdom of this course of action. "Do you think you can handle it?"

Manuel rose and placed his hand over his heart. "Señorita Davis, I will be the finest spy ever."

❧

Andrew shielded his eyes from the glare of the afternoon sun as he wended his way back to his rented house. Once he went over the assay reports he had tucked in his coat pocket and sent in his final report, his obligation to the Denver Consolidated Mining Company would be completed. The prospect of being free to concentrate on his own interests here in Tucson—business and personal—put a spring in his step.

A lumbering freight wagon bound for Lord & Williams's warehouse rounded the corner and headed toward him. Andrew pressed against the wall of the building behind him to let it pass on the narrow street. He had just started on his way again when he heard a voice call his name from a small plaza up ahead. Andrew squinted against the sun and grimaced when he recognized the three men who hailed him with genial smiles.

"Garrett!" the tallest one called again.

Andrew sighed and crossed the road to join the three where they clustered underneath a mesquite tree. A small boy pattered up behind him and squatted in the dirt at the base of the tree. Andrew took a second look at him, recognizing Jenny's helper, Manuel. *Where did he get those ragged clothes?* Andrew wondered. He'd never seen him wear anything like that around the restaurant.

Manuel paid no heed to the men around him but scooped up a pile of mesquite beans and laid them out in an intricate pattern, apparently intent on some child's game. *Cute kid,* Andrew thought. He wished he could spend time talking to him instead of the men now grinning at him eagerly.

"Have you had a chance to look over the papers we gave you?" The tall man apparently served as the spokesman for the group. The others merely watched Andrew, awaiting his answer.

"I'm sorry, gentlemen. I'm afraid the claim you're offering just doesn't fit the criteria the Denver Consolidated has set."

All three men shook their heads in disgust, then the leader spoke. "You're making a mistake. That's a prime claim sure to make money for whoever owns it."

"Sorry," Andrew said again. "There's nothing I can do. Good day." He gave a curt nod and continued on his way. He'd gone over their papers, all right, and every instinct he possessed told him the claim was likely to be fraudulent. The assay report they'd given him didn't line up with what he saw on reports from the neighboring claims. He wasn't about to risk the group's money on something as suspect as that.

If he had his way, every seller of bogus mining stock would be run out of town on a rail. They preyed on the dreams of the gullible but only enriched themselves. Human nature being what it was, he knew there would always be both cheats and willing victims.

But he didn't have to like it.

"Señorita Davis!"

The sharp whisper caused Jenny to look up from her comfortable seat on her sofa. She rose and crossed to the door. "Who is it?"

"It is I, Manuel. May I come in? I have news."

Excitement coursed through Jenny when she remembered the job she'd given him. "Of course!" She drew back the bolt and swung the door open wide.

Manuel looked over his shoulder, then flitted inside like a shadow of the night. He stood tall and erect before her, eyes flashing with pride. "I have found the answers you wanted."

Jenny peered up and down the street before she closed and bolted the door again. She sat down on the sofa and patted the cushion beside her. Manuel shook his head and stood ramrod straight before her, like a soldier reporting to his commander. Jenny half expected him to salute. "What have you found out?" she asked.

"I will tell you about my day," Manuel began. "I left the restaurant after we closed for the afternoon. You told me I could leave early to begin my duties," he reminded her. "I went first to the house where Señor Garrett lives and waited across the street. Soon, he came out and I followed him. He went into the assay office, then came back out again. I stayed behind him until he joined some other men. They talked for awhile, then Señor Garrett left."

"And no one noticed you?"

"They saw only a small boy playing in the dirt." He dropped his military air for a moment. "I have decided it is not so bad not to be tall. It can sometimes be a. . .a. . ."

"An advantage?"

"That is something that helps? Yes, then. An advantage. My cousin Rafael could not have done this," he said solemnly. "He is too big. And he is not as smart as I am, either. He would just stand there and look at the men and make them wonder what he wanted. But I," he said, puffing out his chest, "I crouch down into a little ball to look even smaller. And I look all the time at the ground, never at them." He beamed at his cleverness.

"That was very wise of you," Jenny told him. "What did you hear?"

"They talked for only a moment, then Señor Garrett left."

"And you followed, of course."

"No, Señorita Davis." He lifted his chin proudly. "I stayed."

Jenny's mouth fell open. "But why? You were supposed to find out what Andrew is doing."

"I was getting ready to follow him," Manuel explained. "I waited until he walked down the street, then before I could move, I heard something. Something that made me choose to stay."

"Don't drag this out, Manuel. What was it you heard?"

"Something one of the other men said. He was bragging to the rest, talking about 'unloading more of that worthless mining stock,'" he parroted.

Jenny blinked. "The other man? Not Mr. Garrett?"

Manuel nodded. "I learned many things this afternoon. There has been much selling of this mining stock you talked about. They wait for new people to arrive on the stage, then offer them a share in a mine. The newcomers do not know there is no mine, only a piece of paper. The man who bragged even said he told the people the quality of the ore had been verified by Señor Garrett." He wrinkled his brow. "Whatever 'verified' means."

Jenny sagged against the sofa cushion. "Then it's true. He really is involved in this."

Manuel's dark eyes gleamed and he bounced up and down on his toes, looking less like a professional spy and more like an excited little boy. "The stock is being sold, that is true. But it is not Señor Garrett who does this." He peered over each shoulder, then leaned toward her and lowered his voice to a dramatic whisper. "It is Señor Townsend."

"Evan?" Jenny's voice came out in a croak.

Manuel nodded eagerly. "Sí. He makes up the new papers for them to sell and tells them how much to ask for. The men I listened to call him their boss. They said it is his idea to use Señor Garrett's name to make people feel safe in buying." His face clouded. "Did I not do well, Señorita Davis? Why do you look so upset?"

"You've done a fine job, Manuel." Jenny parted her stiff lips and tried to shape them into a smile. "That information clears up a lot of things for me. I just need to decide what I'm going to do about it."

Chapter 18

Jenny beckoned to Manuel from her office doorway. She waited until the boy scampered into the room, then shut the door with a quiet click. She knelt to his level and spoke in a low voice. "Do you think you could spend more time listening to those men without them knowing what you're doing?"

Her chest tightened when he gave an eager nod. If any harm befell Manuel, she'd never forgive herself. But the more she thought about what she'd heard about Evan's part in the mining stock sales, the more she wanted to know the whole story. She had to find out what was going on, and this looked like her only chance.

"Promise me you'll be careful," she ordered.

Manuel paused at the door and flashed her a happy smile. "Don't worry. I am like the little mouse, remember?"

Three days later, Jenny found herself in possession of more information than she ever dreamed could be gleaned in such a short time. Manuel's keen hearing and knack for blending into the background had proven invaluable. From the overheard comments he relayed in his daily reports, she had pieced together an astonishing list of criminal doings by Evan and his associates.

Sitting at her desk, she pulled out the notes she had taken while listening to Manuel repeat what he had heard. She stared at the incriminating evidence spread before her. Manuel's discovery of Evan's involvement in the sales of bogus mining stock had given her a starting point for her investigation, thus opening a veritable Pandora's box of illegal activity. Jenny fumed, her anger at his betrayal growing by the minute. Everything Evan had accused Andrew of doing reflected some wrongdoing he himself was engaged in.

She gripped the edge of the desk with both hands, trying to contain her fury. She had recognized Evan's desire for easy riches from the start. But she had never, not for one second, suspected him of being capable of this kind of amoral action.

Was she more upset with Evan or herself? She had called herself a hard-headed businesswoman. How foolish she had been! Anyone who could so readily fall prey to his easy lies had no right to pride herself on her acumen.

She rose and paced the room from the desk to the far wall and back again, then stopped abruptly in midstride. If Evan's character was so corrupt, could she trust any of the aspersions he had cast on Andrew?

For the first time in the dark days since she'd learned of Evan's perfidy, Jenny felt a flicker of hope. Could it be that Andrew Garrett was every bit the man of honor Red believed him to be? A man more like the hero of her imagination than she ever dreamed possible?

Manuel tapped on the door frame and poked his head inside the office. "Señor Townsend is coming. I saw him just now when I went to sweep outside."

Jenny stiffened. "He's here now?"

"He is talking to some other men down the street." Manuel jerked his head in the direction of Camino Real. "It may be some time before he gets here, but I thought you would want to know."

"You did the right thing," she told the boy. "Run along now and take care of the customers. I'll handle Mr. Townsend. And thank you for letting me know."

Manuel returned to his duties. Jenny stepped to the window and took a series of deep breaths. She could not afford to lose her temper now. She would need every shred of self-control at her command when she confronted Evan.

Gathering the papers on her desk into a neat stack, she slid the collection of notes into a drawer and pulled out another sheet on which she had made an organized list of her findings.

She had just squared the paper on her desk when she heard Evan's voice out in the dining room. Drawing a long, shaky breath, she pushed back her chair and stood facing the door.

"And how is my beautiful partner today?" Evan breezed into the office and tossed his hat toward the row of pegs on the wall. The hat arched through the air and came to rest on the center peg. Evan grinned. "Perfect." He beamed at Jenny, then seemed to notice her lack of response for the first time. "Is something wrong?"

"Quite a lot, I'm afraid. Please close the door, Evan. We have some things to discuss."

"Aah," he said, complying with her request. "I have the feeling I'm in your bad graces once more. What is it this time? Have I failed to report on time again?"

Jenny clenched her teeth. "Nothing so minor as that." She made a conscious effort to relax her jaw and summoned all her courage. "Evan, I know."

His look of innocence would have done credit to an actor on the stage. "Know what?"

"Everything." Her throat tightened. "Look here." She jabbed her finger at the paper on the desk. "Sales of phony mining stock, claim jumping—the very things you accused Andrew of doing. I even have the names of some of your victims here. And what's this, Evan? Undercutting bids to sell supplies to the army?"

Evan bent over the sheet, his confident expression slipping for a moment before he turned to her again with his smile back in place. "But none of this has anything to do with the restaurant. What has you so upset?"

"Stop it! I'm tired of being treated like one of your gullible victims. I'm not a brainless ninny, to be lied to whenever you please. I'm your partner, remember? Partnership implies the need to be able to trust one another." She swept her hand toward the list of offenses. "How can you possibly expect me to trust you about anything now that I know about all this?"

Evan stepped back and appraised her with cool detachment. "Have I proven untrustworthy as far as the Pueblo is concerned? Have I embezzled funds or cheated you in any way?"

"N—no. At least not as far as I know," Jenny added.

"Haven't I let you run the business as you see fit?"

"Well, yes, but—"

He spread his hands wide apart. "Then what's the problem?"

Jenny stared in disbelief. "The problem, Evan, is that I *know* about these things. Before, I wasn't aware of what you were up to, but now I am. That changes everything. I can't continue in a partnership with someone who'll drag my reputation down along with his."

Evan leaned back against the door frame. "So what are you suggesting?"

"The same thing I suggested before. I want to buy out your share of the business."

"All right. Pay me a thousand dollars, and it's yours."

Jenny gasped. "You can't be serious."

"Oh, but I am, sweet Jenny. The question is, are you? How badly do you really want to buy me out?" His eyes held a gleam of triumph.

Hot bile stung Jenny's throat. "I'm very serious, but that price is outrageous. You know this property isn't worth more than three hundred."

Evan raised one eyebrow in mock sympathy. "Then I'm afraid you're stuck with me for the time being."

The door to Jenny's office stood open. Andrew tapped on the frame and peered inside, waiting until Jenny looked up. "Red wanted me to stop by and ask you—"

He stopped short. "Is anything wrong?"

Jenny shook her head mutely, but the smudges on her cheeks told him otherwise. Andrew took a step inside and reached out to wipe an errant tear away, then drew his hand back. She wouldn't thank him for pointing it out.

"Nothing's wrong," she said. "Nothing you can do anything about, anyway."

Feeling daring, Andrew pulled a chair up close to hers. If she asked him to leave, he would. But she hadn't, not yet anyway. "Would you like to tell me about it? Maybe it would help to talk it out with a friend, or partner to partner, if you'd rather look at it that way."

She waited so long to answer that he felt his hopes rise. Then she shook her head again, more decisively this time. "It's something to do with the restaurant.

Nothing you need to concern yourself about. I need to handle this myself." Her mournful expression softened a bit. "Thank you for asking, though. I appreciate the offer."

There seemed to be no reason for him to stay any longer. He pushed himself to his feet. "All right, I'll be going now."

"Wait. What did Red want you to ask me?"

"He was wondering if we could all meet again tomorrow afternoon. Don't worry about that now, just take care of whatever is bothering you first." He replaced the chair, then paused near the desk. "I just want you to know that I'd like to be your friend. Please feel free to call on me if you ever need any help." He reached out and gave her arm a brief squeeze.

There it was again—that lightning-bolt feeling that surged between them. Andrew left the restaurant feeling unnerved. For the first time since he had arrived in Tucson, Jenny had looked at him with something other than disdain. Would he have that same feeling every time they came in contact? He didn't know, but he wouldn't mind finding out.

❧

Jenny stood at the window and watched Andrew walk away down the street. She rubbed her fingertips lightly over her arm. Did he have any idea how his touch affected her?

She walked back to the desk, sat down, and cradled her head in her arms. Was it possible to know another human being? Really know them? She had staked everything on building a new life in Tucson, basing her decision on the assumption that Evan's offer held the key to a brighter future. How could she have been so wrong?

Had she been wrong about Andrew, as well? The fragile hope that sprang up within her at the prospect that he might be the kind of man she secretly wanted him to be disturbed her. No, more than that. It frightened her.

If the flesh-and-blood Andrew proved to be as worthy of her trust as the man of her dreams, she might be tempted to drop the walls that had protected her for so long. Walls that seemed to be crumbling bit by bit ever since the probability of Andrew's innocence arose. More to the point, did she *want* to keep those barriers in place? That possibility bothered her even more.

❧

"Did you hear?" One of the Pueblo's regular customers sidled up to Jenny on his way out the door. "There's some big stir down at the sheriff's office. Seems a few of our local citizens have been busy selling stock in phony mines, and someone's complained about it. They'll have their hands full trying to sort this out. I've seen it happen before up San Francisco way."

Jenny nodded her thanks and tried to conceal her shock at the news. Not until she reached home that afternoon did she allow herself to focus on what this might mean for her.

She dropped onto her sofa and buried her face in her hands. What an ironic twist her life had taken! She had put her trust in one man and doubted another, only to find that the one she doubted had proven to have a sterling character while the one she trusted—her partner, no less—turned out to be a swindler.

And now that she knew it, what was she supposed to do about it? Being Evan's partner, her name had been linked to his since the day she arrived in Tucson. His illegal activities, if they ever came home to rest, would reflect on her as well.

Conscience demanded she dissolve their business relationship and sever her association with Evan. But how could she do that when she couldn't possibly meet the price he'd named?

She saw only one other possibility: turn the business over to Evan and return to Prescott. Elizabeth and Michael would offer her a warm welcome. She could return to her little room in the back of the Capital Restaurant & Bakery and pick up her life at that point again.

It would be like she'd never left. She would go back to waking up every morning looking forward to Elizabeth's companionship and Michael's teasing banter. To a routine she knew so well she could perform every bit of it by rote.

Back to wondering what she'd face every time she set foot out on the streets of Prescott. To bracing herself for the next round of insults.

How could she give up the self-respect she had fought so hard to win? The thought of having to admit defeat and return to the wagging tongues of Prescott was more than she could bear.

What if. . . For the first time since her confrontation with Evan, Jenny's hopes rose. The sheriff was even now investigating the mining stock fraud. When the law uncovered proof of Evan's crooked scheme, surely she would be able to acquire full ownership of the Pueblo and get her life back on track. Hope fluttered and died when another thought entered her mind. Would Evan's exposure help or hurt? Would their connection mean her reputation would once again be destroyed through no fault of her own?

Not again. Oh, please, not again.

She clenched her fists and sat bolt upright. That wouldn't happen. Not if she could help it. Hurrying to her cylinder-top desk, she sorted through the stack of notes she had brought with her from the restaurant. No doubt about it, they gave clear documentation of Evan's nefarious doings. She would give every scrap of knowledge she possessed to the sheriff. Doing so would put as much distance as possible between her and Evan's misdeeds and let everyone know she had no connection with any of it.

Jenny pored over her notes, fixing each point in her mind. When she felt sure she could recite every detail, she looked through her wardrobe and selected a dark blue dress with matching bolero jacket. Its demure lines projected the respectable image she wanted to portray. She reached for her reticule and checked her image one last time in the mirror on her bedroom wall.

A sharp rap summoned her to the front door. Jenny hesitated, wanting to avoid any interruption that would delay her visit to the sheriff. But it might be Red or Manuel. Or Andrew. She opened the door.

A tall, sober-faced man stood on her doorstep. He tipped his hat and gave her a brief nod. "Miss Jenny Davis?"

Jenny nodded warily. Then she saw the badge on his vest and brightened. "You're the sheriff?"

He seemed taken aback by her obvious pleasure. "That's right. Tom Randolph. I'd like to talk to you."

How had he known? Jenny put the question from her mind. It didn't matter. The important thing was that he was here and they could discuss her knowledge of Evan's activities. "I'm glad you came. I understand you're investigating the sale of fraudulent mining stock. I was just on my way to your office."

Again, Randolph seemed confused by her response. "I must say I'm surprised to find you so eager to talk to me."

Jenny gave him a puzzled look. "Surely you're interested in any information that would lead you to the culprits."

"Yes, ma'am. But I don't usually come across this kind of cooperation from the person I'm investigating."

Chapter 19

Jenny couldn't force a single sound from her throat. Surely she hadn't heard him correctly.

Randolph studied her for a long moment, then said, "Why don't we just walk on down to my office? We can carry on the rest of our conversation there."

He cupped Jenny's elbow in his hand and walked beside her along the dusty road. On the surface, she supposed, he looked like any gentleman escorting a lady down the street. But she could feel the iron in his grip and knew he acted the part of the gentleman only so long as she cooperated.

Her feet moved in step with his; her mind ran miles ahead. Once again, she was in the control of a man without being sure of his intentions. When she had been in the clutches of Martin Lester and Burleigh Ames, she'd prayed for some representative of the law to come along and save her. Now she was in the hands of the law, and who could rescue her from that?

But did she need rescuing? She swung her head slowly from side to side. It couldn't be. Whatever he'd meant by that comment about investigating her, surely she had taken it wrong.

They passed the Pueblo, where Manuel stood outside, sweeping the doorway in preparation for the evening customers. He looked up and beamed when he saw her approach, then frowned in confusion when she didn't smile back. His gaze darted between the badge on Randolph's vest and his hand on Jenny's elbow, then Manuel's mouth formed a silent O. Casting an apprehensive glance over his shoulder, he turned and ran off in the opposite direction, his bare feet kicking up puffs of dust.

❧

"I've told you everything I know." Jenny stared at Randolph, seated on the other side of the sheriff's desk, and passed her hand across her forehead to push the damp bangs back off her brow. "I've given you names, dates, and places. I don't understand why you persist in thinking I'm a part of this."

Randolph stared back. Without taking his gaze off her, he leaned back in his chair and propped one booted foot on the corner of a half-open drawer. "That's just it, ma'am. You've given me too much information, if you see what I mean."

"No, I'm afraid I don't," Jenny snapped, exhausted from the long afternoon of relentless questioning. "I've come forward like a good citizen and given you the information you need to solve this case and more besides. As I told you, I was just on my way here to see you when you showed up at my door."

"Mm-hm." Randolph's simple remark didn't carry any inflection, but Jenny could read the unbelief in his eyes. "If you'll pardon my saying so, ma'am, I find that hard to believe."

Jenny bit back the hot reply that sprang to her lips, wishing she could shake herself awake from this living nightmare.

◈

Andrew's long-legged stride ate up the ground between his rented house and the sheriff's office. When Manuel's steady pounding roused him from his afternoon nap, he'd been too groggy at first to take in the boy's frantic babbling.

"Señorita Davis," Manuel kept repeating, his eyes wide with panic. "The sheriff has her. She needs your help."

By the time Andrew sorted out Manuel's meaning, he was wide awake. Without taking time to do more than tuck his shirttail in and comb his fingers through his hair, he set out downtown to see what he could make of this business. Jenny, under arrest? For what? It didn't make a lick of sense, but there was no denying Manuel's sense of urgency.

He rounded the corner and made straight for the sheriff's office door. He shoved it open without knocking and marched inside.

Jenny sat ramrod straight on a chair facing the sheriff's desk, her dark dress making a marked contrast to the pallor of her face. Her eyes, wide blue-green pools of anxiety, lit up at the sight of him, but she didn't otherwise react to his entrance.

"What's going on?" he demanded, every protective fiber of his being springing to the fore.

The sheriff unfolded his long, lean body and rose from the chair behind the desk. "And you would be. . . ?"

He returned the man's steady gaze. "Andrew Garrett. I'm one of Miss Davis's partners in the Silver Crown Mine."

The lawman tilted one eyebrow upward and looked back at Jenny. "A newly expanded restaurant, the purchase of a house, and now a silver mine? Quite a bit of money at your disposal, wouldn't you say?"

"Money that I came by through my own hard work," Jenny retorted. She held her head as high as ever, but Andrew could see her shoulders trembling. Whatever was going on here, it was clear to him that she had been pushed to her limit.

"Are you finished with Miss Davis?" he asked. "If so, we have some personal business we need to discuss."

The sheriff shifted his gaze to Andrew and gave him a long, appraising look. "The two of you wouldn't be planning to head out of town anytime soon, would you?"

"Sheriff Randolph, I resent your implication." Jenny's voice held a note of defiance, even though Andrew knew she must be exhausted. "I'll be available if you have anything further to discuss with me."

"Oh, you can count on that," Randolph drawled. He narrowed his eyes and leaned over the desk. "I don't have anything solid to hold you on, only my suspicions. . .and you've given me plenty of those. I want you back in this office tomorrow morning at nine to answer some more questions, is that understood?" He straightened and rocked back on his heels. "If you're really the innocent party you claim to be, that shouldn't be a problem."

"I'll be here." Jenny's body quivered, but her voice held firm.

"So will I," Andrew said. He helped Jenny to her feet, alarmed by her fragile appearance. "I'm her partner, remember? She won't be here without me."

What has she gotten herself into, Lord?

"Good morning," Tom Randolph greeted Jenny when she walked into his office with Andrew promptly at nine the following morning.

Jenny seated herself in the chair she had occupied the day before and gave the lawman a level glance. A night to reflect on the previous day's proceedings had given her a new perspective. Trying to see things from the sheriff's point of view, she could understand why he might look askance at anyone who possessed such detailed knowledge of criminal activity yet proclaimed her own innocence. No wonder her sudden spate of information had taken him off guard.

She'd had time now to think things through, to plan how to act rather than react. Undoubtedly he'd done some thinking about his own attitude as well. Today they could both start fresh and have the whole misunderstanding ironed out in no time.

And then there was Andrew. Just the thought of him being there sent a warm glow through Jenny. She had treated him abominably, yet he'd rushed to her aid without a second thought the moment he knew she was in trouble. His presence today meant more to her than he could possibly know. Red would have come if she'd asked him to, but Andrew had chosen to be there—insisted on it, in fact. He'd told her once he wanted to be her friend. That knowledge gave her the courage to straighten her spine and speak to Sheriff Randolph without a quaver in her voice.

"I assume that since you've had time to think things over, you no longer believe I'm guilty?"

Randolph took a seat behind his desk and regarded her a moment without answering, then leaned forward, his gaze boring intently into hers. "What do you know about rigging bids for army supplies?"

Taken aback by the sudden question, Jenny faltered. "Only what I told you yesterday, that I have reason to believe Evan Townsend has done exactly that."

"Miss Davis, do you know a man named Zeke Waterford?"

Jenny shook her head, trying to follow the abrupt change of direction. "I don't know anyone by that name."

Randolph's gaze never wavered. "He's a tall fellow, thin, with sharp features."

226

"I still don't—wait a minute." A picture formed in Jenny's mind. "That sounds like the man who stopped at the restaurant on two occasions. He left an envelope for Evan both times, but I never knew his name."

Randolph made a quick note of her response. "He's been arrested for his part in the bid rigging. One of my deputies caught up with him last night. He admits his involvement, but said he gave the information directly to you. He never mentioned Townsend."

"You mean that's what was in those envelopes?" Jenny asked. "Well, yes, he did hand them to me, but I gave the envelopes to Evan without opening them. I had no idea what was inside."

"What about Harvey Green?"

"The rancher? I ordered some beef from him for the restaurant. What of it?"

"You were seen passing money to him in the lobby of the Hodges House."

"I told you," Jenny said, her voice rising, "I was paying him for the beef I ordered. Beef from his ranch."

"There is no ranch." Randolph leaned his elbows on the desk and steepled his fingers. "Your connection with Green is what drew our attention to you in the first place. Green's only involvement with cattle is in rustling them and selling them off as his own. His big mistake was in trying to palm some of them off on the army by being the lowest bidder—information provided by you, Miss Davis."

Jenny clutched at the seat of her chair with both hands. If she let go for an instant, she feared she would topple off onto the floor. "It's Evan," she whispered. "I gave the envelopes to Evan. And he's the one who told me to order the beef from Harvey Green."

"So you say." Randolph's grim expression didn't alter. "Let's see what someone else has to say, shall we?" He stepped to a hallway at the back of the room and called out, "Come in, Mr. Townsend."

Evan stepped in and took up a position near the desk.

"You heard what Miss Davis had to say?" Randolph asked.

Evan nodded. "I heard it all." He turned to Jenny. "Why? If you needed money, you should have come to me. I'm sure we could have worked something out. You didn't need to go to such lengths. And I don't understand why you felt it necessary to use my name to cover up your own misdeeds." He dipped his chin and looked at her with a sorrowful gaze. "What have I ever done to you?"

Her grip on the chair loosened, and the floor rose to meet her.

❦

Andrew rushed to catch Jenny before she hit the hard plank floor. He scooped her up and cradled her in his arms. "Where can I put her?" he asked.

"Back here." Randolph led the way to an empty cell containing a cot. Seeing Andrew's glare, he protested, "This is a jail, not a hotel. It's the only place available."

Andrew growled under his breath but laid Jenny down on the thin mattress. He patted her cheeks and chafed her wrists until her eyes fluttered open.

"Andrew?" Her blue-green eyes looked at him uncomprehendingly. "Why am I. . . .*where* am I?" She looked around at the surrounding bars and bolted upright, her mouth hanging open in a silent scream.

"It's all right." He gripped her shoulders and turned her to face him. "It's all right," he repeated, praying it was true. He pulled Jenny toward him, and when she didn't resist, he sat on the edge of the cot and wrapped his arms around her. "Shh. Take it easy." He stroked her hair as though comforting a child. "The sheriff wants to ask you a few more questions, but I won't let that happen until you're ready."

"The sheriff," she murmured. Then she stiffened. "Evan! He was here, wasn't he?" She pulled back and looked at Andrew for confirmation. "Where is he now?"

"He left just after you passed out," said Randolph, striding into the cell. "Said he had some other business he needed to see to." The sheriff propped his hands on his hips and looked at the two of them. "Are you ready to do some more talking?"

"I think she's had enough for one day," Andrew began.

Jenny laid her hand on his arm. "No," she said, "I want to be done with this." She struggled to her feet, and he helped her walk to the outer room, marveling at her courage. This woman couldn't be guilty of the charges Randolph kept heaping at her feet.

Could she? He didn't believe it, or at least he didn't want to. But the tiny seed of doubt planted by the mounting evidence and Jenny's inability to refute the claims refused to be uprooted entirely.

The one thread of hope that Andrew clung to like a lifeline was Evan's earlier denunciation. Every instinct Andrew possessed told him the man could not be trusted. If Evan said Jenny was guilty, it gave Andrew reason enough to think the opposite might well be true.

❧

"You're sure you're up to this?" Randolph's rumbling voice held a note of genuine concern.

"I'll be fine," Jenny replied. She took a sip of the water he brought her at Andrew's request. "What else do you want to ask me?"

Randolph tapped his fingers on his desk and considered the notes before him. "You still contend you had nothing to do with any of this—the mining stock, rigging those bids?"

"No." Jenny felt her former indignation return. "And I'm no rustler or claim jumper, either."

"Settle down, now. I didn't say you were."

"No, but your implications have been clear enough. I'm the one who provided the information you were looking for about the mining fraud, remember?"

"You see, that's just the problem." Randolph scrubbed his face with his hand. "I never said a thing to you about the mining stock. You're the one who brought that up, remember?"

"But you asked me—" Jenny stopped, remembering his earlier comments. No, he hadn't. His interest in her lay in her supposed involvement with Harvey Green. She had been the one to draw Randolph's attention to a possible connection with the sales of bogus mining stock. In her eagerness to bring Evan to justice, she had turned the eyes of the law on herself.

The door opened before she could say another word, and a portly man strutted in. He walked over to the sheriff and stuck out his hand. "Randolph? I'm the new owner of the Red Slipper Saloon. I understand you're the one I need to see about paying my taxes." His gaze fell on Jenny and a delighted smile split his face. "Well, look who's here!"

Jenny stared at him, her mind a blank. "Do I know you?"

The man's ample belly shook with his guffaws. "Know me? Why it's Adrian Vance. From Prescott, remember?" He turned back to Sheriff Randolph with a jovial chuckle. "I'll never forget this one, I can tell you that. The prettiest songbird who ever lightened the hearts of thirsty miners."

No. This couldn't be happening. Jenny laced her fingers together in a white-knuckled grip and fought back the waves of darkness that threatened to overwhelm her. She would not faint again. No one in Tucson knew of her days at the Nugget, save Red. She had left that life behind her. Or thought she had, until this talkative man showed up. She shot a quick glance at Andrew and saw his stunned expression.

Vance grinned at her again. "It's no wonder I didn't make much impression, with all those young bucks wanting your attention. I'd be a pretty poor choice in comparison, wouldn't I?" His chest shook with laughter again. "No matter." He sketched a wave at Randolph and walked back to the door. "I can see you're busy now, so I'll come back later. It was a pleasure meeting you, Sheriff. There's always a drink waiting for you at the Red Slipper. And you," he said, pointing a pudgy finger at Jenny, "if you're ever in need of a job, be sure to look me up."

Vance exited an a heavy silence settled over the room. After a moment, Randolph got to his feet and reached for the large ring of keys that hung near his desk. "I hate the thought of locking up a lady," he said. "But under the circumstances—"

"That's exactly the word for it." Andrew stepped forward. "Circumstantial evidence is all you have."

"But I need to be sure she's around to answer any more charges that may come up," Randolph said.

"Miss Davis has a business to run," Andrew told him, helping Jenny to her feet. "If you need to speak with her, you'll find her either at home or at the Pueblo Restaurant. If you want more assurance than that, I'll vouch for her."

The two men locked gazes, then Randolph put the key ring back on its hook. "All right," he said. "But you see that she checks in with me tomorrow."

Chapter 20

"I have to get back to the restaurant," Jenny said. "I need to help Jacinta and Manuel."

"You need to go home and rest," Andrew countered. He took her elbow and steered her through the streets in the direction of her home.

Jenny complied, too tired to argue. "Thank you for standing by me today," she told him.

"I said I wanted to be a friend to you, and I meant it." Andrew squeezed her elbow and gave her a warm smile, then his gaze turned sober. "Randolph isn't going to let go of this anytime soon, you know. You're going to need more than just my friendship to see you through this."

"What do you mean?" she asked, although she had an uneasy feeling she knew the answer.

"I mean Jesus," Andrew answered, confirming her suspicion. "You need Him as your Savior. We all do. But right now you also need someone to help you carry this burden, and He's the best one to do that."

"What if He doesn't want to?" The words were out before she could stop them.

Andrew halted in the middle of the street and caught her hands in his. "He does, Jenny, you can trust me on that. He loves you." He opened his mouth again as if to add more, then pressed his lips together. "Think about that while you're resting this afternoon."

Red jumped up from the bench outside her door when they approached the little adobe house. "How are you, lass? Did that bully of a sheriff come to his senses?"

"I sent Manuel over last night to tell Red what happened," Andrew said in response to her questioning look.

"I'm all right, Red. A little worse for wear, perhaps, but doing well enough." She propped her hand on the doorpost, glad of its support. "I really do need to get back to the restaurant."

"Not on your life." Andrew folded his arms and set his jaw. "You're going to go inside and lie down. Red and I are going to sit out here and make sure no one comes by to bother you. And to make sure you don't get any notions about sneaking out and going to work."

She tilted her head and mustered up a weak smile. "Afraid I'll run away and leave you to face Randolph alone?"

"I have no doubt at all about you keeping your word." His gaze bored into hers with an intensity that made her knees go limp. She nodded, too shaken to resist further, and went inside. Alone in her room, she took off her dress and laid it across a chair, then stretched out on the bed. She felt her eyelids close as soon as her head touched the pillow.

When she woke, the sun had traveled far down in the western sky. Jenny lay still for a moment, wanting to savor the first moment of peace she had known that day.

Red's and Andrew's voices filtered in through the curtains of the open bedroom window. "So now you know the whole story," Red was saying. "I wouldn't have told you if that fat saloon keeper hadn't opened his mouth and given things away."

"It explains a lot," Andrew said. "No wonder she doesn't trust anyone." He paused a moment, then went on. "I talked to her about needing Jesus."

"Did you now?" Excitement was evident in Red's tone. "And what did she say?"

"She has the notion He wouldn't want to help her. And from what you've told me of all she's been through, I'm beginning to understand why. It's a wonder she believes anyone truly cares for her."

Jenny heard him heave a deep sigh. "I wish I knew people as well as I know rocks," he said. "Rocks don't lie to you."

"Don't be giving in to doubt, yourself," Red cautioned. "Keep on believing in our Jenny. She needs true friends who'll stand by her, no matter what. If she doesn't see Jesus for who He is, you'll have to show Him to her by your actions."

Jenny lay in her bed long after the sunlight paled and the two men crept away from their post for the night. She watched the shadows lengthen across her bedroom floor.

So she could now add Andrew to the list of those who thought all her problems could be solved by God. Did he think she wouldn't welcome that? Didn't any of them—Andrew or Red or Elizabeth or Michael—realize she longed for an acceptance she knew could never be hers?

She pushed herself up off the mattress and donned her nightdress. Tucson was no longer her haven, no more a sanctuary in which she could hide from the echoes of her past. Adrian Vance's coming had changed all that. Her hands trembled as she reached for her hairbrush. She could almost hear his booming voice describing her history in Prescott to Sheriff Randolph and Andrew.

Andrew. Her fingers tightened on the brush handle when she remembered his stricken look upon hearing Vance's words. Yes, he'd told her he wanted to be her friend, but wasn't the whole purpose behind that to persuade her she needed to turn to Jesus?

Her eyes welled with tears, and the brush clattered to the floor. Everything she had worked so hard to achieve threatened to crumble around her in ruins.

First the restaurant, then her reputation, and now Andrew's regard.

She slipped to the floor and wrapped her arms around her knees, the ache of loneliness stabbing at her like a heavy blade. She had gained valuable experience running the Pueblo; she could duplicate that success elsewhere if she had to. And assuming the next few days didn't find her in Sheriff Randolph's custody, she could start anew in another town, one so far away that no one from Prescott or Tucson would ever find her.

Those things would cost her in time and trouble, but the pain that tore at her heart the most came from the thought of losing Andrew's friendship.

Jenny let out a low moan and hugged herself tighter, trying to alleviate her misery. She had pushed Andrew away for most of the time she'd known him. How could his loss now feel like such a blow? Whether it made sense or not, without Andrew, she felt more alone than she'd ever been.

"God, help me!" The cry burst forth before she realized she was going to utter it. The words hovered in the air, mocking her. Hadn't she cried out the same plea dozens of times before?

That didn't matter. Nothing mattered now except her knowledge that the only hope she had lay in the slim possibility that God would listen this time.

"God, I need You. I know I'm not good enough for You, but Andrew says You love me. So does Red. So does Elizabeth. If that's true, if You love me in spite of all the things that have happened and all the things I've done, won't You let me know it?"

A faint stirring fluttered in her heart, a whisper no stronger than the brush of air from a butterfly's passing. *Could it be?* Jenny gathered up her courage and whispered, "Is that You, God? Are You listening?" The flutter grew more insistent, spreading throughout her innermost being until it filled her with a flood of joy.

"You do love me! I believe it now. Thank You so much for not giving up on me."

Tears streamed down Jenny's cheeks. From the brink of ruin, she had been lifted up to a pinnacle of belief. Whatever happened in the morning, whatever new treachery Evan might devise, this certainty of God's love was now hers, and nothing could take that away.

❧

Jenny stepped into Sheriff Randolph's office the next morning with a light step and her head held high. The sense of forgiveness that filled her soul still amazed her. She smiled at Andrew, who had accompanied her once again. He looked perplexed by her calm demeanor but smiled back.

Even the sheriff seemed startled by the change. "You look happy today, Miss Davis. Did you find out something that will prove your innocence?"

"No, Sheriff. I found peace." Randolph stared as though he thought she'd lost her mind, but Jenny didn't care. It was true. Becoming a child of God hadn't made all her problems go away as she once believed. The problems still existed. But now she had a place to take them. She looked at Andrew again and caught the hopeful look in his eyes. She appreciated Andrew's continued support more than she could ever tell him, but even if he changed his mind and left her on her own, she now had another Friend who would help her through her ordeal.

Randolph cleared his throat. "And just where did this peace come from?"

Jenny smiled. "I won a battle last night, Sheriff. Or rather, I lost a battle and wound up the winner." His look of utter confusion made her chuckle. "I've fought against God for years," she explained. "All the people I loved most told me He loved me and wanted to make me His child, but I knew they were wrong. You see, I thought I wasn't good enough for Him. And I was right! I wasn't. But the amazing thing is, He loved me anyway. I couldn't see that until last night, when I didn't have anyplace else to turn."

"I. . .see." Randolph shifted in his chair. "The investigation is still continuing. Check back with me tomorrow."

"I'll do that," Jenny assured him. "And if you need me any other time, you know where to find me."

Andrew sat at a corner table in the Pueblo Restaurant and watched Jenny through the office doorway. She sat serenely at her desk, apparently unperturbed by the storm that raged around her. Did she have any idea of the way her face glowed? Randolph might be dubious about the change in Jenny, but the joy that radiated from her convinced Andrew beyond a doubt.

Speaking of doubt—the memory of the skepticism he'd voiced to Red only the night before came back to haunt him. Hadn't he doubted her, too? If only there were some way he could make up for his lapse in faith, some way to clear Jenny's name without question.

Manuel sauntered up to the table and handed Andrew a cup of coffee. "She is going to be all right, is she not?" he asked in a worried tone.

"I think so. But if we could get some proof that would convince the sheriff she's innocent, it would sure help."

Manuel's face lit up. "You need help finding proof? I am very good at that. I helped Señorita Davis find the information about Señor Townsend."

Andrew turned his attention to the grinning boy. "You did?" A plan began to form in his mind. Maybe there was a way to help Jenny after all. "Manuel, do you think you could help me find a man?"

Chapter 21

An insistent pounding jerked Jenny from her sleep. She sat up and looked around, disoriented for a moment in the dark room. The pounding came again. Jenny jumped out of bed and pulled her robe from its hook. Belting it around her waist, she padded toward the front door.

"Who is it?" she called in a low voice.

"It's Evan. Let me in. I need to talk to you."

"Are you out of your mind? It's the middle of the night."

The pounding persisted. "I'm going to stand here and keep knocking, Jenny. If you don't open up, the whole street will know I'm out here."

Jenny waited in the dark living room a moment longer until the hammering on the door convinced her Evan had every intention of making good his threat. She fumbled for a match and lit a lamp.

"Will you be quiet?" she said. "Quit knocking. I'm going to open the door." She slid the bolt back as she spoke. Evan nearly bowled her over in his haste to enter the room.

"What is wrong with you?" she blazed at him. "Isn't it enough you've dragged my name through the mud? Now you show up at this hour—you're going to destroy what little is left of my reputation."

"I wanted to tell you I'm sorry," he said. "I couldn't stand to wait until morning to get that off my conscience."

Jenny held the lamp higher and looked at him more closely. The light showed dark circles under Evan's eyes that hadn't been there before. Could he be telling the truth for once?

"All right, you've told me. Now go away. I'm near to being arrested, Evan. For something you've done. I'm afraid your apology won't do much to change that."

He held up one hand. "No, wait. That's why I wanted to see you tonight. To tell you I'm sorry and that I want to make it right."

Jenny eyed him narrowly and waited.

"I know I've put you through a rather bad time." Evan caught her angry gaze and flinched. "All right, a terrible time. And I am truly sorry. I'm going to talk to Randolph in the morning and tell him that you had no part in any of it. It was all my doing."

Jenny set the lamp down before she dropped it in her shock. "You'd do that for me? Why?"

"Call it an acute attack of conscience, if you will." The smile he gave her ooked more like the Evan she knew. "I just know that I can't go on any longer knowing I've caused you such grief. And to show you I really mean it, I'm willing o sell you my half of the business."

"For a thousand dollars? You know I can't possibly come up with that amount."

"No, not a thousand." His face twisted in a wry grin. "You said the place wasn't worth more than three hundred. I'll go along with your estimate. Give me a hundred and fifty, and we'll call it even."

Jenny stared at him. "Are you serious?"

"Absolutely." He drew a folded paper from his inner coat pocket. "And to prove it, I've brought along a bill of sale."

"You mean you want to do it tonight?"

"If you have the money here at home, why not get it over with right now? Then we'll be square."

"Well, I suppose. Wait right here." She left Evan in the dark living room and carried the lamp to her bedroom, where she pulled her savings from a niche in the wall behind her bed. She sorted out a small stack of bills, then went back to Evan. "Go ahead," she told him. "Count it."

"No, I trust you." Evan pocketed the cash and scribbled his signature at the bottom of the bill of sale. "There we are, everything tied up nice and neat. I'll be going now. How about meeting me at the sheriff's office at nine?"

"Nine will be fine." She closed the door behind him and leaned against it, filled with wonder at what had just transpired. The restaurant was hers, truly hers! And tomorrow Evan would clear her name.

❦

The following morning, Jenny walked the familiar path to Sheriff Randolph's office by herself. No point in bothering Andrew today. She wouldn't need a protector this morning. Today was the day she would be exonerated. She strode up the steps with a confident air and rapped on the door before pushing it open.

"Is he here?" she asked the moment she set foot in the room.

Randolph looked up from behind his desk. "Is who here?"

"Evan. Evan Townsend. He said he'd meet me here at nine."

A baffled expression spread across the sheriff's face. "And why would he do that?"

"He was going to take responsibility for—" A commotion behind her made Jenny whirl around. The door burst open and Andrew appeared, pushing a stocky, balding man before him.

Jenny gasped. "Harvey Green!"

"What's going on?" Randolph demanded.

Andrew, grim-faced, shoved the man toward the sheriff. Manuel scooted into the room behind him. "Have you been looking for this man, Randolph?"

"Yes," the sheriff began, "but I want to know—"

"Good. He has something to say to you." Andrew prodded the heavyset man between his shoulder blades. "Go on. Tell them what you told Manuel and me."

Green glanced at the sheriff, then dropped his gaze to the floor. "You've got me dead to rights," he muttered. "I know I'm headed for Yuma and hard time, but I ain't going alone." He flung his head back and stared directly at Randolph. "Townsend's going with me. He's the boss; he can take his share of the blame."

"Townsend?" Randolph echoed. "You're sure?"

Green spat on the floor. "I ought to know who gave me my orders, hadn't I? The whole thing was his idea from start to finish. The rustling, rigging those bids for the army, all of it."

"What about her?" Randolph jerked his head in Jenny's direction.

Green's lips curved in a sly smile. "That was his idea, too. He had her pay me for beef for their restaurant and the money wound up right back in his pockets. If any of this came to light, I was supposed to vamoose so she could take the blame instead of Townsend."

"So what do you think, Sheriff?" Andrew asked.

Randolph lowered his head a moment, then looked straight at Jenny. "Sounds like everything you said was true, Miss Davis. You're free to go."

Relief made Jenny's head light. She smiled her thanks at the sheriff. "I'm happy to hear that, but I'm even happier to know Evan was ready to tell you himself."

"Townsend? What do you—" The sheriff's comment was cut off when the door crashed open again. This time it was Red who entered the crowded office.

"Sheriff, I need a word with you. Andrew told me what Jenny said about Townsend being the mastermind of all these evildoings. I went to confront the man this morning, and. . ." He paused dramatically. "He's gone, Sheriff. Gone! Saddled his horse and set off for parts unknown sometime during the night."

Chapter 22

Jenny folded her dark blue dress and laid it neatly atop the others in her trunk. She reached for the dotted-Swiss, then paused to brush away the tears that filmed her eyes. Her dear house, the home she'd loved—how much it meant to her! She would leave a piece of her heart here in Tucson when she left.

It couldn't be helped, though. She heaved a shaky sigh and smoothed the dotted-Swiss out on the bed. She now carried another stain on her name. True, she had been cleared of wrongdoing in the eyes of the law, but she knew well enough that there were plenty of people who would always remember her suspected role in Evan's crimes. She couldn't go through that again.

She settled the dress in its place in the trunk. Only her smaller belongings still waited to be packed. She rested her arms on the windowsill and gazed outside. Who would tend her rosebush next summer? The thought left her even more melancholy. At least she knew the restaurant would be in good hands under Jacinta's supervision. It would bring in continued income to support the Ochoa family, and with the profits that would be sent Jenny's way, she could live comfortably wherever she went.

In a way, she looked forward to it. *I do,* she insisted, trying to stifle the voice of doubt. It would be a chance for a new start, just her and the Lord. Having time to spend getting acquainted with her Savior was the bright spot in the days ahead. Even if it meant leaving Tucson and the restaurant.

And Andrew. She stifled a sob at the thought of never seeing him again. *It's all for the best.* If only she could convince her heart of that. He would have her eternal gratitude for the way he stood by her in her darkest hour and the effort he made to clear her name. If the circumstances had been different. . .

"But they aren't," she said aloud. "And you might as well get used to that fact."

A knock at the door interrupted her musings. She pulled it open, expecting to find Manuel with the additional shipping crates she'd sent him after. Instead, Andrew stood on the doorstep, holding his hat in his hands. "Good morning," he said, giving her the smile that always made her knees tremble. "May I come in?"

Wordlessly, Jenny backed away from the door. Andrew entered and looked around the room, his gaze landing on the stack of boxes. He glanced back at Jenny. "What's going on?"

"I'm packing," she said, turning away to avoid his gaze. "I've decided to see what California is like."

"You're moving there? Leaving the restaurant?"

"In Jacinta's capable hands. Don't worry." She forced a laugh. "You'll still be able to enjoy her cooking."

Andrew took a step toward her. "It isn't Jacinta's cooking I'll miss." He moved nearer and took her hand. "Why leave just when God has worked everything out for you?"

Her fingers felt the tingle she always experienced whenever he touched her. "People don't forget when someone has been hauled up in front of the sheriff day after day. There'll be talk, Andrew, and lots of it. I've been through this before, and I can't do it again."

"You mean you're running away?" He brushed her cheek with the back of his hand and shook his head. "You can leave Tucson, Jenny, but you can't run away from yourself. You just carry the same problems with you from place to place. The best thing you can do is stay here, hold your head high, and keep going."

Jenny shivered at his touch. "I can't face down the rumors on my own." She raised her gaze to his face, only inches away.

"You don't have to do it alone," he murmured. "You have God—and me."

Jenny stared into Andrew's eyes, so close to hers. For the first time in her life, she didn't want to run away from a man's embrace. What would it be like to feel Andrew's lips on her own? The thought took her breath away. "I know," she whispered. "You've truly become my friend."

A low chuckle shook Andrew's chest. "I'll always be your friend. But I want to be more than that. Much more." His breath stirred the ringlets at her temple. "Don't go, Jenny. Don't leave Tucson, and more importantly, don't leave me. Won't you stay here with me. . .as my wife?"

Jenny raised her hand and pressed her fingertips against Andrew's cheek. "You know everything that's happened, and you still want to marry me?"

"More than anything in the world." He bent until his lips almost touched hers. "Will you have me?"

A wellspring of joy bubbled up inside Jenny, filling her soul until she thought she would burst. "I'll be your wife," she said, twining her arms around his neck, "and your best friend. Forever."

She raised her face to bridge the tiny gap between them. The touch of Andrew's lips on hers was everything she had longed for, and more.

Chapter 23

Jenny stared into the full-length mirror and checked her appearance for the tenth time in as many minutes. The pale aqua dress brought out the highlights in her eyes and set off her copper-blond hair to perfection. A quiver of excitement ran through her, and she clasped her hands tight against her waist.

Her wedding day. Who would have believed it? But then, who could have imagined all the changes that had come into her life in the space of a few short months?

A radiant smile lit her face. God could, that's who. Elizabeth had been right all along. If only her dear friend could have been there to share this special day with her! But Elizabeth's condition made it impossible to undertake such a journey anytime soon, and neither Jenny nor Andrew wanted to put the wedding off until after the O'Roarkes' baby arrived. Instead, they would travel to Prescott for a visit as part of their honeymoon trip.

Jenny pressed her fingers to her lips and felt the sting of tears. After all the years of hiding from the world, she now had friends who truly cared for her: Elizabeth and Michael, Red, Manuel and his family. . .and Andrew, her dearest friend in the world and soon to be her life's mate. And a heavenly Father who loved her even more than they did. Truly, her cup of joy was filled to the brim.

A light tap interrupted her musings, and the bedroom door swung open. Jacinta stepped into the room carrying a wrapped bundle. Her forehead puckered when she saw Jenny wiping traces of moisture from her cheeks.

"You are all right, Señorita Davis?"

"I'm fine. Just a little emotional I guess."

Jacinta moved nearer and held out the bundle. "For you. *Un regalo*. A gift." She pulled back the paper wrapping to reveal a length of delicate lace fabric.

Jenny gasped. "It's beautiful!" She stood still while Jacinta unfolded the shawl and draped it over Jenny's head. The wisp of fabric settled over her shoulders like the touch of a butterfly's wing.

"*Gracias*," she whispered, and pulled Jacinta into a hug.

She had been wrong. Her cup of joy now overflowed, along with a fresh round of happy tears.

"Are you ready, lass?" Red stood just outside the doors of the tiny adobe church, looking as jittery as if he truly were the father of the bride.

Unable to speak, Jenny merely nodded and took his arm. Together they stepped into the cool dimness of the sanctuary. At the end of the short aisle stood Andrew, and beside him Manuel, resplendent in his white shirt and trousers. Red escorted her the rest of the way then placed her hand in Andrew's and bent to kiss her on the cheek before taking his place in the front pew.

Jenny stared up into the eyes of the man to whom she had pledged her heart as she listened to the opening words of the service that would bind them together for the rest of their days.

After the ceremony, the small cluster of guests gathered at the restaurant. Amid the gaiety, Jenny slipped away to her office, closing the door gently on the sounds of the joyous celebration.

She picked up a sheaf of papers from the desk and flipped through them one by one. A waft of air brushed her cheeks when the door opened and closed again, and Andrew moved to stand behind her.

"Is everything all right?"

Jenny nodded. "Just making sure everything is in order. It's going to seem strange, not coming in here every day."

Andrew laced his fingers in front of her waist and bent to nuzzle her cheek. "Any regrets?"

Jenny turned in the circle of his arms, feeling the familiar quiver his presence always brought. "None at all. Jacinta is thrilled at the idea of having her own restaurant. She'll make a success of it, I know.

"As for me. . ." She slid her hands up the front of Andrew's coat and framed his face between her palms. "I have everything I could possibly want—a new life, new hope, and a husband I treasure. I couldn't ask for more."

"Well. . ." Andrew tightened his embrace and lowered his face toward hers. The look in his eyes set her heart racing. "We could ask for a son. Or a daughter."

A soft smile curved Jenny's lips. "How about one of each?" Her eyelids fluttered closed, and she lost herself in the wonder of his kiss.

Road to Forgiveness

Dedication

*Many thanks to Terry Schultz,
Arizona State Livestock Officer,
for answering my questions and
giving me some good ideas.*

Chapter 1

Tucson, Arizona Territory—March 1898

A cloud of dust mushroomed over the top of the rise ahead. Jacob Garrett spurred his horse up the low slope. Dust didn't billow up like that on its own on a windless day. A shrill whinny mingled with a man's frantic yells, heightening Jacob's sense of urgency.

He topped the rise and took in the scene at a glance. A calf lay on its side in the sandy dirt. A rope stretched taut from the calf's neck to the saddle horn of a sweat-soaked dun who backpedaled, eyes wide and nostrils flaring, putting all his effort into breaking away from the dead weight that anchored him to the spot.

On the opposite side of the calf, a cow shook her horns and pawed another puff of powder-fine dust into the air. A man crouched behind the calf, using it as a living shield between himself and the cow. She made a quick sidestep to the right, then the left, as if sizing up her intended target.

Jacob jerked his rope from his saddle and began to build a loop while he circled behind the threatening animal. With a quick flip of his wrist, he pitched the loop and turned his horse as the rope caught the cow's right hind leg. He spurred his horse forward and jerked the cow off her feet.

The steel-dust gelding pulled back to keep tension on the rope, and Jacob sprang from the saddle and hurried over to kneel on the cow's neck.

"Afternoon, Gus." He nodded to the gray-haired rancher, on his feet now and slapping the dust off his chaps. "If there's something you needed to do to that calf, you'd better do it quick, while I have his mama on the ground."

"I already finished doctoring him." Gus yanked the piggin' string loose. The little calf staggered to his feet and trotted over to his mother. "All I needed to do was smear some salve on a cut to keep the flies off. I was ready to let him up when she pitched her fit. No patience at all. Ain't that just like a woman?"

"If you wouldn't mind pulling my rope off her leg, I'd like to get up pretty soon. She's getting a mite testy."

Gus hobbled over to the cow and loosened the rope. "Give me a minute to get back on my horse, will you? I'm not as spry as I used to be."

Jacob held the struggling animal's head while Gus mounted the dun, then jumped back and raced for his own saddle.

The cow scrambled to her feet and gave them a belligerent glare before checking her calf for signs of ill-treatment.

"Whew!" The grizzled rancher pulled a dark blue bandanna from his hip pocket and swiped his forehead. "That was closer than I care to come to eternity anytime soon. Glad you happened along when you did."

"Glad I could save you from being stomped into the dirt. I was just out riding; I didn't expect to get a chance to play hero."

Gus grinned and settled his hat on his brow. "Want to come back to the house for supper? Martha's fixing your favorite tonight."

"I wish I could, but I need to talk something over with my folks."

Gus raised a white tuft of an eyebrow. "It must be something pretty important to lure you away from Martha's pot roast."

"You could say that." Jacob stared off toward the Rincon Mountains. He might as well confide in Gus, after all the man had done for him. He slid an envelope from his vest pocket. The letter felt unaccountably heavy in his hands. "I got this today."

Gus studied him but said nothing.

"It's from Dan O'Roarke. Remember him?"

"O'Roarke? Isn't that the fellow from up Prescott way? The one you brought by my place last year?"

"That's him. The one with the ranch up near Coyote Springs. I've known him all my life. His parents and mine have been friends for years." Jacob tapped the envelope on his saddle horn. "He's asked me to come up and work for him."

Gus's pale blue eyes gleamed. "That'll be a fine opportunity for you. Even if it means I'll be losing your help. I have to admit I've gotten kinda used to you coming around every now and then."

"If you hadn't taken me under your wing when I was a green kid, I wouldn't have known a heifer from a steer. You taught me everything I know about livestock." Jacob's voice thickened. "As a matter of fact, knowing I learned from you is what made Dan decide I knew enough about working stock to be a help instead of a hindrance."

"I'd have made you the same kind of offer if I thought you'd take me up on it." Gus leveled a knowing look at Jacob. "But I have a feeling your heart isn't set on staying around Tucson."

Jacob grunted assent. "You're right about that. My folks don't know it yet, though." He slid his thumb along the edge of the envelope. "I guess it's time I told them."

⁂

Jacob listened to the saddle leather creak in time with his horse's footsteps as the steel-dust ambled along. He resisted the impulse to touch his heels to the gelding's flanks and urge him into a lope. Instead, he settled back in his saddle and took note of the desert that stretched out for miles around him.

Some might describe the balmy Tucson weather as paradise on this early spring day. But this was March. In another couple of months, the temperatures would soar up to a hundred degrees and more, making it seem less like paradise and more like living next to the blast furnaces at one of his father's mines.

"I have learned, in whatsoever state I am, therewith to be content." The verse from the fourth chapter of Philippians sprang into his mind without warning. The apostle Paul had found contentment, even in the midst of persecution and imprisonment. Why couldn't he do the same? His parents could certainly make the same statement.

How had they managed to adjust to the searing heat after spending their early years in the cool forestlands of Colorado and northern Arizona? Jacob never could figure that out. But adapt they had. They both loved it here. He rocked along, taking note of the different types of cactus within his view: the saguaro, the deceptively fuzzy-looking cholla, the spindly ocotillo. *Everything around here has thorns.* But his mother would find beauty in each one, and because she did, his father would see the beauty, too.

Jacob appreciated the majesty of his surroundings when his mother pointed them out to him, but in his eyes the landscape rolled out as a vast barrenness, something like the wasteland his soul had become of late. For twenty-five years, he'd tried to live the life his parents had built up and loved. But that was their life, not his. More and more, he knew he needed a change. Now he just had to convince them of that.

The house and barn came into view all too soon. On any other day, the sight would have calmed his spirit. Today, though, he carried news that made him feel like a traitor.

Jacob took his time unsaddling his gelding, brushing him down, and tossing him some hay. Cap munched greedily at the brittle green stems. Long before Jacob was ready, he heard the call for supper.

"Better get this over with," he told Cap. The steel-dust pulled at another mouthful of hay. Jacob slapped him gently on the withers and turned toward the house with a twinge of envy. At least one of them would enjoy their supper tonight.

※

"Seconds, dear?" Jacob's mother held out the steaming platter of roast chicken.

Jacob served himself, then passed the dish to his father at the head of the table. Truth be told, he had no interest in a second helping of chicken. Or string beans or even some of his mother's fluffy rolls. But the longer he dragged out the meal, the longer he could put off springing his news.

His father helped himself and set the platter on the table. "Everyone in town seemed to be talking about the situation in Cuba today. If you can believe what's in the newspaper, those people down there are being grievously mistreated by the Spanish."

His mother's fork clinked against her plate. "Is there more talk of war with

Spain? President Cleveland always insisted that would never happen."

"True enough," his father agreed. "But McKinley is being pressured to take a different stance. I'd say it's only a matter of time."

Jacob chewed slowly, grateful for the diversion. He dawdled as long as he could before lifting the last bite to his mouth.

His father took a swallow of water and leaned back in his chair. "So what's on your mind, son?"

Jacob nearly choked on his chicken. He reached for his water tumbler and took a hearty swig to help the bite go down, then coughed into his napkin until he recaptured his breath.

He shot a rueful smile toward his father. "I guess there's no point in asking what you mean, is there?"

Jenny Garrett looked at her son and gave a soft chuckle. "We've raised two children, Jacob. We know the signs. And I once owned a restaurant, remember? Of all the meals I served, I never once saw anyone trying to sop up gravy with his green beans until tonight. I'd second your father's guess that your mind is somewhere else."

Jacob held up his hands. "All right, I give up. Guilty as charged. I have something to say, and I've been trying to figure out how to break it to you. I thought I was keeping a pretty good poker face. Evidently, I didn't do such a good job of it."

He drew a deep breath and removed the envelope from his pocket. Pulling a sheet of paper from the envelope, he spread the letter out on the table. "I got this today. From Dan O'Roarke."

His mother clapped her hands. "How nice. Did he say anything about his parents? We haven't heard from Elizabeth and Michael in ages."

Jacob cleared his throat. "Actually it's more than just a friendly letter. Dan asked if I wanted to come work for him."

His mother beamed. "I think that's a fine idea. Don't you, Andrew? You'll enjoy spending the summer up there. I know how you hate the Tucson heat."

"Actually, Mother, it would be more than just this summer."

She studied him more closely and seemed to read something in his expression. "You mean you're thinking of leaving here for good?"

Here it comes. Jacob took a deep breath and plunged ahead. "I've done my best with every job Dad's given me to do in the mines, and I've tried to make a go of it."

A puzzled look shadowed his father's face. "You've done far more than try. You've learned the business well. As a matter of fact, I've been gearing up to put you in as manager of the new copper mine we'll be opening down by Bisbee. I hope you don't think I haven't been pleased with your work."

"No, Dad. That isn't it at all." He clenched his fists under the table. They weren't going to like what he had to say, not one bit. "I don't want to spend the rest of my life looking for ore in the desert. That isn't where my heart lies. I grew up hearing the stories about how you and Mother and Red Dwyer started the Silver Crown and built it up into the mining company you have today. How finding a strike is one of the most exciting things in the world for you." He shook his head, feeling like the worst kind of deserter. "But that isn't the way I'm made. I get that same feeling spending my days outside on horseback, not on the business end of a pick."

His father nodded slowly. "I can understand that, son. If ranching is what you want to do, your mother and I would be happy to set you up with your own place down here."

"I'm sorry, Dad. If I thought it would work, I'd jump at the chance. But there's something in my soul that needs trees instead of cactus, green hills instead of brown desert. And I really want the opportunity to get out on my own and find out what I'm made of."

His mother and father exchanged a glance full of meaning. After a long silence, his mother sighed. "We went our own way; we can't very well ask him not to, can we?"

"That's what I love about you, Jenny. You always seem to know what I'm thinking." Jacob's father turned to him. "We know you'll do your best, son. I believe God has some mighty plans for you. You need to go out and discover what they are." He gripped Jacob's hand in a firm clasp. "You have our blessing. And you know there will always be a place for you if you ever decide to come back here."

Jacob returned his father's grip, grateful beyond measure for their support. "Thank you. Both of you. I'll have to hurry to pull everything together in time. Dan wants me up there next week."

Chapter 2

Lonesome Valley, Arizona Territory

Hallie! Where are you, girl?" Burke Evans's bellow broke the stillness of the spring afternoon.

Hallie Evans scrambled down from her perch on the water tank catwalk and hurried toward the weathered ranch house. When her father roared like that, he expected an immediate response.

Inside, she paused a moment to smooth her skirt and give her eyes time to adjust to the relative dimness. "I'm here, Pa."

Her father's heavy footsteps clumped across the plank floor. "Edgar Wilson stopped by on his way home from Prescott. Get us some coffee, would you?"

"I'll be right there." A glance out the front window showed her Mr. Wilson's sorrel mount tethered to the rail. *How did I miss hearing him ride up?* She ducked into the kitchen, where she checked the contents of the coffeepot on the back of the stove. Her father insisted on having a steady supply of coffee at the ready throughout the day. If he hadn't gotten into too much of it since lunch. . . Good, the pot was still nearly full.

Hallie set the coffeepot and two mugs on a tray, glad she wouldn't have to keep the men waiting. Edgar Wilson had even less patience than her father. Two short-tempered men in need of coffee would not make for a pleasant afternoon. For good measure, she opened the pie safe and added two servings of dried apple pie to the tray. From the ominous tone of the voices rumbling from the front room, those two could use all the sweetening up she could give them.

"Where have they gone, and who's taking them? That's what I want to know." Wilson's harsh words rolled over Hallie when she pushed through the swinging door. The neighboring rancher stood before the empty fireplace, every line of his bearing shouting outrage.

"Here's your coffee." Hallie set the tray down on a low table and slipped back through the swinging door, then through the kitchen, and back outside. It wasn't wise to be around when Wilson and her father got started. She propped the back door open so she could hear if he should call her again. A week ago, they would have had the house shut tight against the late winter chill, but the past few days brought warmer, almost balmy weather. The fresh air would help chase away the stuffiness after being closed up for months.

How far could she go and still be within earshot? The catwalk beckoned, her favorite spot from which she could view the length of Lonesome Valley like a princess from her high tower. But if her father called, it would just mean rushing down the ladder again. She settled for dragging a sturdy chair across the packed earth and setting it beneath the raised platform the tank sat on. That would still provide a degree of privacy and relief from the sun's glare, but she could jump and run as soon as her father summoned her.

Despite his brusque, heavy-handed ways, she loved him dearly. Since her mother's death eight years before, it had just been the two of them. Some fathers might have lamented being saddled with a lone daughter, but not hers. The lack of a son never seemed to bother Burke Evans. If anything, he seemed to treasure their relationship as much as she did.

Hallie drew her feet up onto the wooden seat and folded her arms atop her knees. Resting her chin on her arms, she stared out across the rolling valley. Fawn-colored hills stretched out in a broad sweep to the mountains in the near distance, Mingus Mountain to the east, the Bradshaws to the south. Their solid bulk surrounded her valley like a pair of mighty arms, shielding the range her father had claimed as his own—the Broken Box Ranch, the only home she had ever known.

This land was a part of her, its texture intimately woven into the very fiber of her being. For as long as she could remember, she had watched its many moods unfold. And for as long as she could remember, its familiarity never failed to calm her, to fill her with a sense of peace and satisfaction.

Her land. Her home. And yet. . .

A vague longing surfaced, one that filled her consciousness more and more often of late. Why didn't the majestic panorama provide the same satisfaction as before? What had changed? It couldn't be her beloved mountains. Their solid bulk stood just as imposingly as it had for untold centuries. The foothills, the valley—they remained the same as they had always been. No, if there was a difference, it must be within her.

A soft sigh escaped her lips. "What's the matter with me?"

A shadow fell across her lap and a voice grated near her ear. "Not a thing that I can see."

Hallie started and whipped her head around to see who had invaded her private moment. All her peaceful feelings scattered to the winds like dandelion fluff at the sight of Pete Edwards, her father's top hand, standing behind her. She fought to untangle her legs from her skirt and struggled to her feet.

Pete watched her with a slow smile that made her bring her hand to her neckline to make sure the buttons of her bodice were fastened. He spread his legs wide apart in a bold stance and folded his beefy arms, obviously enjoying her discomfort. "Need a hand?"

"No, thank you." Hallie looked at Pete with distaste. With his stocky build and self-assured air, he could almost pass for a younger version of her father. Their demeanor, though, could not have been more different. Her father's expression often looked as if it had been carved from a block of granite, but Hallie never doubted the depth of his love for her. Pete, on the other hand, generally sported a smile, but it held all the warmth of a coyote's grin when eyeing a cottontail.

Right now his smile set warning bells off inside her head. "Excuse me. I need to go inside now." She angled to her left, intending to give Pete a wide berth.

He took a step to his right and blocked her way. "You don't have to be coy, Hallie. I know you like me."

Hallie caught herself in midstride and shifted to the right. Pete followed suit. "Darlin', if you want to dance with me, just say the word."

Hallie flushed, and he let out a low rumble of a laugh. She felt the sting of tears.

Pete's broad face split in one of his coyote smiles. "Face it, Hallie. You can't get away from me unless I let you. You might as well give up and admit how you feel about me."

I can't tell you what I think of you, Pete Edwards. My mother raised me to be a lady. Hallie's glance darted from Pete to the kitchen door. Even listening to her father and Edgar Wilson haranguing would be better than this. "Leave me alone, Pete."

In answer, he spread his arms wide and took a step toward her. Hallie darted toward the left, then scurried to the right. The abrupt change in direction caught Pete off guard, and she slipped past him.

Her moccasins churned up puffs of dust as she raced toward the house. Behind her, Pete's taunting voice rang clear: "You can run away this time, but there'll be another. I know where to find you when I want you."

Hallie slammed the kitchen door shut and bolted it behind her. Wrapping her arms around her waist, she slumped to the floor and bent her head to her knees. "Thank You, Jesus."

With no thought but seeking the safety of her father's presence, she jumped to her feet and hurried to the front room, only then remembering they had a visitor. To her relief, Edgar Wilson stood on the porch, taking his leave.

"I'm telling you, Burke, this is a bad business." The lean rancher's eyes flashed. "We can't take it lying down."

Her father pounded his fist into his palm. "I don't intend to. If these fellows keep messing with me, they're in big trouble. Count on it." He stepped back into the doorway. A grim expression hardened his features.

Hallie held herself in check until he closed the door, then ran to him. "I need to talk to you."

Her father turned away from the door and looked at her. "It's a good thing Wilson stopped by."

"Pa, please. I don't know what to do."

Her father rubbed the back of his neck with a calloused hand. "I don't, either. It turns out I'm not alone. Wilson's been losing cattle, too."

"This is getting out of hand—"

"I know. I kept trying to convince myself it was due to natural causes—a mountain lion, maybe. But it doesn't look like that anymore. We never came across any carcasses, for one thing. And with stock going missing from both our places. . ." He shook his head slowly.

"It's getting so I'm afraid to go outside the house anymore."

Her father set his mouth in a grim line. "If someone's stealing cattle, I can tell you one thing: They're going to pay for it." He raised a meaty fist and slammed it against the wall. The window glass rattled in its frame. "I haven't spent twenty years building up this ranch to hand the profits over to some no-account too lazy to do an honest day's work."

Hallie grabbed his arm and hung on tight. "Pa, it's about Pete."

Her father's head jerked around. "Pete? What are you talking about?"

She finally had his attention. The relief made her weak. "He keeps waylaying me whenever he catches me outside. I've asked him to leave me alone—more than once—but he won't. Could you talk to him, maybe tell him to keep his distance? I know he'll listen to you."

Her father bristled. His eyes took on a glint that made Hallie take a quick step back. "What do you mean, keep his distance? Has he touched you?"

"No, nothing like that. He just. . .comes up on me and talks to me. No matter what I tell him, he won't stay away. I really need your help, Pa."

Her father's bark of laughter grated on her ears. "So you've finally come out of your dream world long enough to realize you're a grown woman now." His tone softened, and he patted her arm awkwardly. "You're a fine-looking girl, Hallie. You take after your mother that way. You can't blame Pete. He'd be less than a man if he didn't notice. Don't take on about it. It's nothing serious."

The forbidding expression returned to his face, and he pointed a meaty finger at her. "Don't you go getting all uppity and running off my best hand, do you hear me? Pete knows nearly as much about raising cattle as I do, and with the problems I'm facing now, I need his help more than ever."

Hallie's jaw sagged. "But, Pa—"

"Maybe I've made a mistake, letting you have the run of the range. I don't need you being out there causing problems and getting my men all stirred up."

"Pa!"

Burke strode off. "I'll be in my office. Call me when supper's ready."

Hallie stared after him, a feeling of helplessness spreading through her. A leaden weight settled in her chest. Choking back the tears that threatened to flood her eyes, she went to the kitchen to start the evening meal.

She pulled a slab of meat from the cooling box and began to cut it into chunks for stew. Her earlier discontent stirred within her again, a longing for something she couldn't define.

One thing she knew beyond a doubt: Whatever she was longing for, it had nothing to do with Pete Edwards.

Chapter 3

Jacob squinted and tipped his hat brim farther down over his eyes. After nearly a week on the trail, he felt more than ready for the trip to end. Time to get down to business and put some of his dreams into action.

He checked the sun's position. If he hurried, he ought to be stepping up onto Dan's front porch just in time for supper. And if Amy was still as good a cook as he remembered, that would be a goal worth shooting for. He grinned and tapped the horse's flanks with his heels to push him into a trot down the length of Lonesome Valley toward Coyote Springs.

Lonesome Valley. The name suited the place, he'd always thought. A wide, rolling plain flanked by mountains on three sides. Lush grass waved in the light breeze, in stark contrast to the desert terrain he'd climbed out of the day before. Buckbrush and manzanita scattered across the valley floor, giving way to the cedars that covered the foothills and the pines crowning Mingus Mountain. This land promised a host of surprises, enough that it would take years to discover them all. Spending years—or the rest of his life—in this spot would suit him just fine.

Clouds hung low in the sky, forming a backdrop for the mountains. Where the clouds broke, golden light splashed over the ground below, as if an artist had dabbed it with a paint-laden brush.

Jacob reined his mount to the right, veering off the main road and heading toward Dan's ranch. The steel-dust pricked up his ears, seeming to sense his rider's eagerness to reach their destination. "We're almost there, boy." Jacob patted the horse's neck. "Just a few more miles and it's a rubdown and some oats for you." *And a new life for me.*

An hour later, he spotted a herd of cows dotting the hillside. He stopped to give his horse a rest under the only tree in the area while he looked them over. *A fine-looking bunch*, he thought. They'd wintered well, with a full contingent of wobbly-legged newborn calves at their sides. Off to the right, a massive white-faced bull pawed the earth, showering his red coat with dust.

Jacob pursed his lips in a soft whistle. Dan's letter said he intended to improve the quality of his stock. If he'd gone to the expense of bringing in a registered Hereford bull to build up the strain, he meant business.

Excitement flickered through him. Big things were happening here, and he would be a part of bringing them to life. He leaned forward and stroked his horse's neck. "Rested up, boy? Let's go get some dinner."

"Uncle Jacob?"

The voice seemed to come out of thin air. Jacob twisted from side to side in his saddle, looking for its source.

"Up here," the voice called.

He craned his neck to look up into the branches of the alligator juniper. Dusty boots, spindly legs, and a flounce of skirt dangled six feet above his head. Atop the calico dress, he spotted a crown of coppery-gold curls. Jacob felt his eyes bulge. "Catherine?"

"Uh-huh." Dan O'Roarke's eight-year-old daughter began to pick her way down from limb to limb. When she reached his level, she crouched on a branch and looked him in the eye. "Will you give me a ride home?"

"Why, sure." Jacob reached out and pulled the little girl into his arms, then scooted back onto the cantle to make room for her in front of him.

Catherine snuggled back against him as though they were getting ready to set out on a pleasure ride. "Thanks, Uncle Jacob. I was getting tired of sitting up there. My legs were starting to get stiff."

Jacob shook his head. "How did you get up there in the first place?"

"I climbed."

"I meant, what were you doing up there?"

"Oh, that. I got off my horse to. . .well, you know." She giggled and pointed off toward a clump of nearby bushes. "And then that ol' bull started pawing the ground and my horse spooked and took off and I had to climb the tree to get away from the bull."

"He didn't come after you, did he?"

"Not until I hit him with a rock. I thought it would make him go away. It didn't. That's when I decided I'd be better off up in the tree."

Jacob's blood ran cold at the thought of what a two-thousand-pound bull could do to a little girl. He touched Cap's flanks with his spurs and urged him into an easy canter. Another thought came to mind. "How far are we from the house, anyway? It's at least half a mile, isn't it?"

"I guess so." Catherine's casual air would have done credit to an actress on stage.

"You guess so? What's a little thing like you doing so far away from home by herself?"

Catherine adopted a haughty tone. "I was fine until that bull came along. I can go wherever I want."

Jacob kept his opinions to himself as they rode on. When they neared the house, a small figure bounded off the porch and ran to meet them. Jacob recognized Catherine's brother, Benjamin.

"Where have you been?" the boy demanded. Then he added, "Hi, Uncle Jacob."

"Out riding." Catherine slid down off Cap's back and rearranged her clothing, then strolled off toward the back of the house.

Benjamin hurried to catch up to her. "Your horse came back an hour ago."

"I found her out where the cows are grazing," Jacob called. "About half a mile down the road."

Ben's eyes rounded. "Half a mile! Boy, are you going to catch it when Ma and Pa find out."

"Am not."

"Are so."

"Am not!"

"Are so!"

Their voices trailed off as they rounded the corner of the house. A few moments later, a smiling woman rushed out onto the porch, her hands outstretched in welcome. "Jacob! Catherine told me you just arrived. Welcome to the T Bar."

Jacob dismounted and stretched. "It's good to be here. Is Dan around?"

"I'm expecting him any minute. Supper is almost ready, so why don't you take care of your horse and wash the trail dust off? He ought to be here by the time you're finished." She clasped her hands together. "I can't tell you how excited we are to have you here. Dan's been talking about nothing else all week."

A weight lifted off Jacob's shoulders. He was home. He hurried to the barn and pulled Cap's saddle off, then brushed him down and settled him in a stall with a manger full of hay. After sluicing water from the rain barrel over his arms, face, and neck, he headed for the house.

Dan opened the door before Jacob reached the top of the porch steps and welcomed him with a bear hug. "Good to see you. Come on in. Amy has supper on the table."

The scent of steak and fresh-baked bread drew him toward the dining room where Amy sat, flanked by Benjamin and Catherine. "Have a seat and make yourself at home. I hope you enjoy the meal."

After Dan said grace, Jacob made quick work of his dinner. Amy's cooking was every bit as good as he remembered.

"Are you ready to start work in the morning?" Dan asked.

"You bet. What do you want me to do first? I'm ready to tackle whatever you want."

"I thought I'd take you around and show you the water holes and lay out the plans I have for this place." Dan's face took on a look of pride. "Wait until you see Imbroglio."

"Imbrolly-who?"

Everyone at the table laughed. "Alistair's Crimson Imbroglio. My new bull. He's a papered Hereford. I had him shipped in from back East."

Jacob chewed slowly, avoiding Catherine's pleading gaze. "I ran across him on the way in. He's a fine specimen, all right. He ought to do a good job for you."

Dan tilted his head. "Why do I get the feeling you're trying not to tell me something?"

Catherine pushed back her chair. "May I be excused, Mama?"

Amy frowned. "Yes, you may. But please don't interrupt. Go on, Jacob."

Both the children sidled toward the door. Jacob tried to shake off the feeling he was being marked as an informant.

"I'm not the only one who encountered Imbroglio this afternoon. I found your daughter perched up in a tree about fifty yards away from him on my way in."

"Catherine?" Dan's face darkened. "Catherine Elizabeth O'Roarke, what were you doing out around those cows?"

The only answer was the sound of feet scuttling across the floor and Benjamin's voice: "Told you! You really will catch it."

"Will not."

"Will so."

"Will not!"

Amy pressed her hands against her cheeks and gave Jacob an apologetic smile. "I'm sorry. This is no way to welcome you on your first night here."

Jacob chuckled. "Don't give it a second thought. They sound just like Emma and I did at that age. It makes me feel right at home. I'm just sorry for getting Catherine in trouble. I hate to be a tattletale."

"That child!" Amy spread her hands wide. "I don't know what we're going to do with her. She's always into something."

"She needs a strong hand, that's for sure." Dan arched his eyebrows at his wife.

Jacob decided it was time to change the subject. "She's sure growing up to be a cute one, though. Where did she get all that red-gold hair?"

"That came from my aunt Carrie," Dan replied. "According to my mother, Catherine looks exactly like her younger sister."

"But that mind of her own comes straight from your mother," Amy noted.

"True enough," Dan agreed. "But Mother isn't quite so quick to point that out." He and Amy both sputtered with laughter.

Jacob joined them, feeling more relaxed than he had in months. A yawn stretched his lips wide, and he clapped his hand over his mouth. "I guess I'm farther gone than I thought." He pushed his chair back. "Where do you want me to stow my gear?"

"You're sleeping in the guest room tonight," Dan told him. He held up his hand when Jacob started to protest. "You can move out to the bunkhouse tomorrow, if you've a mind to, but tonight you're our guest, not an employee."

Jacob hesitated. Special privileges like sleeping in the boss's house wouldn't win him any points with the other hands. But after nights of lying on the hard ground, his weary body craved the thought of sleeping on a real mattress. He nodded and followed Dan down the hallway. He could get down to business tomorrow.

"Look out! She's going under."

"Get a rope on her, Jacob."

Jacob pushed Cap as close as he dared to the edge of the mud around the water hole. He picked his way carefully, not wanting to get bogged down in the same clinging mire that held the cow captive.

He swung the loop around his head. Cap sidestepped to pull loose from the muck at the same instant Jacob released the rope. The loop fell short of the cow by a yard.

Jacob felt himself redden. Some asset he'd be to the T Bar, if he couldn't do a simple thing like roping a cow when her life was in danger. No telling how long she'd been struggling there. Long enough, at any rate, to get herself bogged down clear up to her belly with no means of getting out on her own. Long enough to wear herself out to the point she could barely hold her head above water level. Off to the side, her calf bawled plaintively.

If they didn't get her out soon, she would drown. Jacob backed his horse out to come in at a better angle. He looked up in time to see Eb Landrum's rope snake out in a graceful arc and settle over the exhausted cow's horns. Eb's horse dug in and leaned back on its haunches, holding the rope taut.

I should have been able to catch her. Jacob shook off his disgust and sprang from his saddle to wade across the mud. The bog pulled at his boots, sucking them deeper into the muck with every labored step. *Next thing you know, they'll have to lasso me to pull me out.*

The cow bellowed, a high-pitched sound that ended on a wheezing note. If they didn't get her out fast, she'd be a goner. Her calf bawled back at her and dashed back and forth. The cow's eyes rolled back until only the whites showed. Despite Eb's efforts, her nose hovered perilously near the water. *If I don't get to her soon. . .*

Jacob gave a lunge that placed him near the animal's head. "Hang on, girl. We're going to get you out of here." He reached for the trailing loop end of his rope and used both arms to shove it down into the miry clay and work it around the cow's belly. By the time he brought the loop up on the far side of the cow, he felt like his shoulders were on fire.

He dragged the free end of the rope over to him and threaded it through the loop, then tossed the end back to Buster, the other cowhand working with them. With two horses pulling and Jacob pushing, they managed to haul the cow back to solid ground.

Jacob staggered out of the mess and pulled both ropes off the cow while she lay on the ground, panting. Her baby trotted over to her and nosed her face. The tired cow lifted her head and nuzzled back.

"Think she's going to be okay?" Jacob asked.

"She should be," Eb replied. "We'll give her a few minutes to catch her

cond wind, then we'll haze her over to another water hole so she won't get
ck here again."

Buster cackled. "Have you taken a look at yourself? I've seen hogs that
oked cleaner than you."

Jacob looked down at his clothes. His denim pants were totally covered with
e slimy goo; his shirt hadn't fared any better. He pulled off his hat and raked
s fingers through his hair. From the feel of it, there wasn't an inch of him that
asn't coated with mud.

"Look on the bright side," Buster chortled. "With all that mud on you, you
on't have to worry about the flies."

Jacob chuckled and scooped a handful of sludge off his rope. "The things we
through for these knot-headed bovines."

Eb coiled his own muddy rope and hung it over his saddle horn. "Don't let
get to you. You did a fine job out there. I wish Dan had been here to see it. He
d a smart thing when he hired you on."

Jacob trudged over to Cap, feeling some of his chagrin roll away. He started
put his foot in the stirrup, then realized he was going to get his saddle caked
ith mud. But his only option would be to walk. He swung his sore body into the
ddle. At least it wasn't as bad as the caliche clay they had around Tucson. This
uff just might powder off when it dried instead of turning to cement.

Eb rode up beside him. "Roundup starts next week. It'll give you a chance
meet some more of the folks around here." He winked. "Dan better hope the
her ranchers don't try to lure you away when they see how good you are."

Jacob ducked his head to hide his pleasure. "I couldn't do any of this if it
adn't been for an old rancher in Tucson who took me under his wing." His mind
ailed back to Gus's spread. He knew the place so well, he could picture every
tail. Right about now the cactus would be blooming and the days would be
arm and pleasant.

A spring breeze kissed his mud-smeared cheek. Jacob drew in a breath of
ne-scented air. But down in Tucson the heat would just be beginning to build
. He remembered all too many summer days when a man couldn't go outside
ithout feeling like the sun was going to cook his brains.

He grinned and felt the drying mud on his face crack. Oh yes. He'd made
e right choice when he decided to take Dan up on his offer.

Chapter 4

H allie leaned against the porch rail and watched her father ride u[...] Her hands gripped the rigid wood. "Please let him agree to this," sh[...] whispered.

"I hope you're packed and ready to go." He swung his leg over the cant[...] and dismounted.

"Roundup starts tomorrow."

Hallie squeezed the rail until the edges bit into her palms. "I'm not goin[...] this year." *Please don't ask me to explain why.* She didn't know how to make hi[...] understand that the memory of Pete's constant pestering the year before ha[...] soured her on ever going again, as long as Pete was around.

Her father's look of astonishment would have seemed humorous at a le[...] serious moment. "What do you mean, you're not going? Clive Jensen packed u[...] and moved his family back to Kansas, remember? You can't keep his wife com[...] pany again this year. Where do you think you're going to stay?"

"I'm staying right here." She forged ahead to cut off his protest. "I'm twen[...] years old, Pa. I can manage on my own."

"This is foolishness, Hallie. You can ride as well as any hand. And if yo[...] don't want to work on horseback, you can help with the food. Your cookin[...] beats anything we're likely to get out there. What would you do around here [...] yourself for a week?"

Hallie strived to keep her tone light. "For one thing, I can get my sprin[...] cleaning done. It'll be lots easier to scrub cupboards and air bedding if I don[...] have to stop to fix meals. And I can clean out the bunkhouse without comin[...] across a pair of Homer's long johns draped across the door and embarrassing th[...] poor man half to death."

Her father's laughter gave her hope. "It wasn't so much knowing you'd see[...] them as finding them mended, washed, and folded on top of his bunk." He pat[...] ted her hand. "All right, Hallie. You're a grown woman. I guess you can handl[...] yourself like one. Just remember, if you run into any trouble, the shotgun's i[...] the corner."

"I'll remember." But with Pete gone along with the rest of the hands, sh[...] probably wouldn't need it for protection.

A puff of acrid smoke rose from the T Bar branding iron as it burned into th[...] calf's flank.

258

"Okay, let 'im up." Dan stepped back from the bawling calf. The two other cowboys from his fire crew released the steer calf and watched it scramble up to rejoin its frantic mother.

Jacob wiped his brow with his shirtsleeve and watched Eb drive the cow and calf over to the herd of branded animals. Looking around at the numerous teams at work, he felt thrilled at the efficiency of their labor. He shook out his loop and headed back into the gather for another unbranded calf.

He saw Buster dab a loop over the head of a brindle calf with white legs and face, then drag it to the closest fire.

"This one's a T Bar," Buster called. The ground man reached over to pull that iron from the fire and applied it quickly, while the other team members clipped the ear and applied salve to the wounds.

Jacob frowned. He could have sworn that little heifer belonged to a Seven X cow. He continued working, but vowed to stay aware of Buster's activity.

Within minutes, Buster pulled a small black calf with a white spot over its left eye out of the herd. "Here's another T Bar."

"Are you sure?" Jacob called. "I think that calf belongs to a Lazy EW cow."

Buster shook his head. "I'm sure. This is one of Dan's, no question about it."

"What's the problem?" asked the cowboy at the fire. "Do we know whose calf this is or not?"

Jacob shrugged. "I'm not trying to cause trouble, but I'm positive that calf was mothered up to a black Lazy EW cow. Buster, why don't you turn it loose and see where it goes?"

With an angry shake of his rope, Buster released the calf. It trotted back into the herd and immediately paired up with a black cow wearing the Lazy EW brand.

"Looks like you were right, Garrett." Buster stared at the calf, his mouth a grim slash. He nodded an apology to Edgar Wilson. "My mistake. I'll be more careful."

Jacob waited until the next time he and Buster were changing horses to talk to him alone. "How many calves are wearing the T Bar brand that don't have a right to?"

Buster glared. "What's that supposed to mean? In a roundup, those things happen all the time. It was just an honest mistake."

"Was it?"

The corner of Buster's mouth twitched. "What are you getting so worked up about? So Dan's got a few extra head. I thought he was your friend."

"He is, and I wouldn't count myself any kind of friend if I let his reputation get tarnished."

Buster gave a snide laugh. "You don't know how many T Bar calves are going to wind up wearing somebody else's brand by the time this week is over. If we don't get some back, we end up getting cheated. And if the scales tip in our direction, so much the better. Nobody gets hurt."

"Everybody gets hurt," Jacob shot back. He felt his features harden. "It isn't honest, and that's all there is to it. I wouldn't stand for someone taking Dan's calves 'by mistake' like that. Neither would you. And I won't stand for the T Bar growing its herd by dishonest means."

Buster glared at him in disgust. "You just keep living in your dream world. See how fast you get ahead." He mounted his horse and spurred back toward the herd.

Jacob slapped his gloves against his chaps. If Buster had anything to say about it, his stay at the T Bar wouldn't last long. It didn't matter, he told himself. Right was right, and he couldn't go along with anything less. He picked up his reins and turned to go back to roping.

"Hold it a minute, son."

Jacob pivoted on his heel. A lean man with a complexion like old leather stepped out from behind a tree holding the picket rope.

The older man studied Jacob with keen blue eyes. "I'm Fred Davenport, owner of the Diamond D. I heard what you said to Buster." The weather-beaten rancher stuck out a calloused hand. "I can't say I've seen that kind of integrity before, but I like your style, Garrett. We need more of your kind around these parts."

Jacob shrugged. "I just can't see fudging on things. It isn't the way I was raised. My parents tried to bring me up according to the Bible, and it seems to me God takes a mighty dim view of appropriating someone else's property."

Fred Davenport nodded appreciatively. "Sounds like you come from good stock, son. Dan better watch out."

Jacob shot him a questioning glance.

The rancher's leathery cheeks creased when he grinned. "If he isn't careful, half the ranchers in this area are going to be trying to steal his new hand." He laughed at Jacob's look of surprise, then turned to rejoin the men around the branding fire.

❦

"Garrett?"

Jacob looked up from braiding the hondo on a new lariat to see three men standing in the open barn door.

"I'm Lucas Rawlins, head of the Cattlemen's Association. This is Morris Atwater." He gestured to the man next to him. "I believe you already know Fred Davenport."

Jacob nodded a greeting and hooked his thumbs in his pockets. "What's on your mind?"

"Fred here wasn't the only one impressed by your honesty at the roundup," Rawlins told him. "I'd say word of what you did has pretty much spread through the area." He cleared his throat. "On behalf of the Yavapai Cattlemen's

Association, I'd like to offer you the job of range detective."

Jacob stared at each of the men in turn.

"You'd be responsible for checking brands on cattle being bought and sold and investigating claims of rustling," Fred Davenport explained. "Since you'll be doing a lot of riding, you need to keep your eyes open for outbreaks of noxious weeds or anything else that might harm the stock. But the most important thing is to stop this thieving that's been going on. We need someone we can trust, and we think you're just the man for the job. What do you say?"

Jacob turned the idea over in his mind. With that kind of work, he'd be on the trail most of the time. He couldn't think of a better way to get to know every corner of this new area he had claimed for his own. He would still be dealing with livestock. And he'd have the satisfaction of knowing he would be contributing to the growth of the territory.

It sounded like the opportunity of a lifetime, a job tailor-made for him.

But he couldn't accept. The realization hit him with a sickening thud.

"I appreciate your asking me," he began. "But I just hired on with Dan. I can't see leaving him shorthanded." He pulled his hat off and ran his hand over his hair, then settled the Stetson back on his head. "Much as I hate to, I'm going to have to turn the job down."

Rawlins looked at his companions, then back at Jacob. "We were afraid you might feel that way. I guess that's what we could expect from a man of integrity. Thanks for giving us a listen."

Jacob stood in the barn doorway and watched them ride away. He flexed the rope between his hands. "I think I'd like extra credit for turning that job down, Lord. That was one hard choice to make."

Dan came trotting up on a long-legged buckskin. He reached over and patted the snorting horse's neck. "A few more miles on this young fellow, and he'll be ready for everyday use." He nodded toward the south. "Was that Rawlins I saw riding off? What did he want?"

Jacob forced a crooked grin. Not for the world would he let his friend see how deep his disappointment ran. "Oh, they had some crazy notion about wanting me to be their range detective."

Dan's face lit up. "It's nice to know they have some sense. When do you start?"

"You don't need to worry about that. I told them no."

"You turned them down? Sounds like you're the one who's crazy."

"Come on, Dan. You know I'm not going to come up here, then go haring off and leave you high and dry."

"Listen. What we need more than anything else in this county is someone we can depend on. All joking aside, Rawlins is no fool; neither is Atwater or Fred Davenport. They know a good thing when they see it, and that means you, Jacob. You've got the kind of honesty that will keep things straight around here. The last range detective around here was more interested in lining his own pockets than cracking down on shady branding practices. I know you won't do that, and so do those men. In the long run, having you in that position will benefit me as much as anyone else in the county, even though you won't be working directly for me. It's for the good of everyone, you included."

Jacob couldn't stop a hopeful smile from spreading across his face. "You mean that?"

Dan laughed at the eagerness in his voice. "Absolutely. Now, you'd better throw a saddle on Cap and catch up to them. You need to tell those men you've changed your mind."

Chapter 5

Cap's hooves clattered over the rocky trail from the Verde Valley. Jacob pulled up to let the steel-dust catch his breath when they topped out on the ridgeline overlooking the broad expanse of grassland. Over the last week, he had been to half a dozen ranches, getting to know the local stockmen. More than one rancher brought up his concern about missing stock. His last stop had been Stuart Brannon's ranch.

Jacob thought back over his visit with the famed lawman turned rancher and chuckled when he remembered Brannon's calm reply that he hadn't lost any cattle and didn't expect to. Jacob had a feeling if anyone were foolish enough to mess with Brannon's stock, they'd be the ones hollering for help.

He slackened the reins and let Cap grab a few mouthfuls of grass while he got his bearings. If he remembered Dan's directions correctly, he ought to be at the east edge of Lonesome Valley. He would cut over to the Broken Box and make that his last stop before heading up the valley to Coyote Springs and the T Bar. Dan had been good enough to offer his guest room for Jacob's use as long as he needed it. Jacob couldn't complain about the central location—or continued access to Amy's cooking.

He held Cap down to a walk so he could take a good look around as he neared Broken Box headquarters. No one appeared in the yard when he approached.

He leaned on his saddle horn. "Hello, the house! Anybody home?"

A stocky, barrel-chested man appeared in the barn doorway. "Who wants to know?"

"It's Jacob Garrett. We met during roundup." Jacob swung out of the saddle and went to shake hands with Burke Evans.

Burke's quick grip went along with his no-nonsense bearing. "I remember. You're that young pup from O'Roarke's spread who got Fred Davenport so stirred up when you lit into Buster. I hear he talked Rawlins into hiring you to find our missing stock." Burke spat and wiped his mouth with the back of his hand. "Well, you've got plenty of them to look for. They've been disappearing by twos and threes for several months now. What do you think you're going to be able to do about it?"

"I've been out getting acquainted with the ranchers and the territory—"

"I don't know why they called in an outsider in the first place. What earthly good do they think you'll do?"

Jacob bit back a hot retort. "Why don't you give me a chance to show you

what I can do before you pass judgment?" From the corner of his eye, he saw
flash of movement. A young girl darted from the edge of the barn toward t
house, obviously trying not to be seen.

"Hallie! Come over here." Burke's voice sounded like gravel pouring over
sheet of tin.

The girl stopped abruptly and stood poised in the manner of a deer ready
take flight. Seeming to realize she couldn't pretend she hadn't heard, she cross
the yard and stopped ten feet away with her gaze focused on the ground. O
closer inspection, Jacob realized she wasn't a girl after all but a young woma
probably only a few years his junior.

"This is—what'd you say your name was again?"

It took a moment before Jacob realized Burke was talking to him. "Garret
he replied without shifting his gaze. "Jacob Garrett."

"That's right, Garrett. My daughter, Hallie."

Jacob couldn't make out the words of her murmured greeting.

"I'm pleased to meet you." Well trained by his mother, he had said tho
words a hundred times before, but never had he meant them as much as at th
moment. What was it about this girl—this woman—that made his heart rac
and his palms grow moist?

Hallie lifted her gaze to meet his. Her shy demeanor reminded Jacob
a watchful fawn. Her dark hair, held back at the sides by two combs, tumble
down her back in loose waves. A tinge of pink crept into her cheeks under Jacob
intense scrutiny. She looked down again and began tracing patterns in the du
with the toe of her moccasin. Without raising her head, she said, "Please excu
me. I need to go start supper."

Jacob watched her walk swiftly toward the house and kept on staring aft
the door closed behind her.

"So what are you going to do about it?" Burke's rough voice called him bac
to attention.

"Would you mind repeating that last part?" Jacob asked, uncomfortab
aware he'd missed everything Burke just said. He shot a quick look at the ranch
but saw nothing in his square face to indicate he'd caught anything passin
between Jacob and his daughter.

Burke planted his hands on his hips and let his breath out in an impatien
huff. "I said I'm not the only one around here who's been missing cattle. Wilson
lost nearly as many as I have. So have Miller and Ladd. I want to know what yo
intend to do about it." His stony gray eyes narrowed to slits, and his lower ja
thrust forward. He gave every indication of being a man used to getting his ow
way or knowing the reason why.

Jacob realized his first major test had come and hoped he would be up to th
challenge. "I've been hearing the same thing from the ranchers I've visited. M
first thought is to check the most obvious avenues—shipments that may hav

gone out on the railroad without proper paperwork, evidence of herds moving out of the area without any connection to a legitimate sale. If that doesn't turn anything up, I'll have to start trying to work out the trails and discover where they've gone."

"Sounds like a lot of wasted time to me. We need results and we need them soon."

Burke pivoted on his heel and headed back to the barn.

And a good day to you, too.

Jacob mounted and swung Cap back toward the road, casting one last look at the ranch house where Hallie Evans had disappeared.

Hallie hurried toward the house, her moccasined feet making whispers of sound against the hard-packed dirt. Inside, she leaned back against the door and pressed her palms against her flaming cheeks.

What a fool she'd made of herself, staring like that! *What came over me? I don't ever remember behaving like that. Mama would have been mortified if she'd been here to see.*

She squeezed her eyes shut and tried to stop the feeling that her whole world had just tilted off its axis. What had happened? Everything seemed normal up until the moment the stranger rode up while she was out in the chicken coop checking on the brood hen. Dressed in her most faded work clothes and with her hair hanging loose like a little girl's, the best course of action seemed to be to remain in the shadows of the barn.

But if she didn't get those potatoes on to boil, supper would be late. After a second glance, she'd decided the newcomer and her pa were engrossed in conversation deep enough to give her the opportunity to get across the yard unseen.

She'd almost made it, too. She would have, if her father hadn't called her over. *Of all the times for him to decide to observe the social graces.*

Sheer embarrassment fastened her gaze to the ground while she walked over to them. And if only she'd *kept* it focused there, she might not have humiliated herself. Her mother's training in deportment held true, though, and she forced herself to look up at the stranger when her father introduced him.

But he wasn't a stranger. Not since the instant their gazes locked and every thought left her mind except the desire to lose herself in the depths of his sky blue eyes. Some part of her felt like she had known him forever. His tanned face and wavy, dark blond hair seemed as familiar to her as her own features. Then came the awful moment when she realized she was staring at him, gaping like a fish.

Her cheeks burned against her fingertips. *What must he have thought?*

Not many visitors came to the Broken Box, and her trips to town were few and far between, giving her little opportunity to practice social skills. Would she have reacted as strongly to just anyone who happened to drop in unexpectedly?

Hallie felt tempted to use that excuse to explain away her feelings, but she knew there was more to it than that. A current of recognition had passed between them, a sense of connection she couldn't begin to fathom.

She moved to the window and pulled back the edge of the curtain. Peering through the crack, she watched Jacob Garrett mount up and ride away. At the edge of the yard, he glanced over his shoulder and looked back at the house. His eyes appeared to focus right on her.

Hallie gasped and dropped the curtain as though she had singed her fingers on a hot stove. Had he seen her standing there, mooning after him? She tried to console herself with the knowledge she probably would never see the man again.

It wasn't much consolation.

She waited until he was a fair distance away, then stepped out onto the porch and wrapped one arm around a post, staring at his retreating figure. Long after he and his horse dwindled into mere specks on the horizon, she watched, fixing that significant moment in her heart.

Could it be possible the hunger for something more that stirred her soul of late was for some*one* instead?

Hallie leaned her head against the post and let her thoughts take wing until the sun's rays glared directly into her eyes, reminding her how much time she'd spent dreaming.

Catching her breath in dismay, she hurried to the kitchen and started peeling the potatoes. It looked like supper would be late, after all.

Chapter 6

Jacob trotted up the steps of the red brick courthouse and walked down the hallway to an open door. A bespectacled young man sat working at a small desk. Jacob cleared his throat.

The young man started and peered up over the tops of his spectacles. "May help you?"

"Is this the mayor's office?"

"You've got the right place." The clerk gestured to the open door behind im. "Go on back. He'll be glad to see you."

Jacob tapped on the door frame, then poked his head inside. "Mr. Mayor?"

The handsome, dark-haired man behind the desk rose. "I don't hold with ormality. My friends call me Buckey."

His genial smile immediately put Jacob at ease. He reached out to shake the and Buckey offered. The mayor had a strong, honest grip and a direct gaze that nspired in Jacob an immediate liking for the man.

"Glad to meet you, sir. My name's Jacob Garrett."

Buckey's trim mustache twitched upward. "So you're the one Lucas Rawlins nd Morris Atwater tell me is the answer to their prayers."

"I'm not sure I'd go that far, but I hope to live up to the expectations they ave of me."

"Sit down." Buckey waved Jacob to a straight-backed chair. "Lucas wore ny ear out singing your praises, but he didn't tell me anything about your back-round. How long have you been in the area?"

"Just a few weeks. I was born and raised in Tucson, but I've known Dan)'Roarke and his family all my life. Prescott always seemed like a second home o me. My parents first met here, as a matter of fact."

Buckey stroked his mustache with his thumb. "Tucson, eh? Any relation to ndrew Garrett?"

The question startled Jacob. "He's my father. Do you know him?"

"Not personally, but I know of him. I have some mining interests of my own. His name is well known around the territory." He leaned back in his desk chair nd his eyes gleamed with a friendly light. "If you have half the integrity your ather is known for, I have no doubt you're the right man for the job."

"Thank you. He's given me a fine example to follow and some mighty big hoes to fill."

"You say your parents once lived here?"

"My mother did. My father was just passing through when they first me They met again down in Tucson." No point in bringing up the stories he'd hear about that dark time in his mother's life before she discovered the love of both h father and Christ. Her years in Prescott did not hold happy memories for her.

"How long ago would that have been?"

Jacob pursed his lips. "She left in '69, two years after the capital moved fro Prescott to Tucson. So that would have been. . .what? Twenty-nine years ago?"

"Before my time," Buckey said. "I didn't get up to these parts until th spring of '82, after the capital moved back up here again. Then we got into th squabble with Tucson and the powers that be decided to put both cities in the place and send the capital to Phoenix." He chuckled. "Maybe they'll keep there, maybe not. But what the people of this territory need to do is forget ou petty differences and move forward together. Seeing statehood come to Arizon: that's where my heart lies. It seems to me that thirty-five years as a territory long enough."

"I couldn't agree more." The subject of achieving statehood was dear to th hearts of all Arizonans. "I understand you used to be sheriff?"

"That's right." Buckey placed his right ankle on his left knee. "I've worn a lo of different hats since I came here: sheriff, court reporter, probate judge. I lost bid for Congress in both '94 and '96, but I managed to be elected as mayor las year." He uncrossed his legs and leaned forward on his desk. "This territory hold tremendous potential. I'm willing to do whatever I can to add a new star to ou nation's flag." A mischievous light danced in his eyes. "That was a long answer t your question about my being sheriff. Was there a particular reason you asked?

"Some of the ranchers have been missing cattle," Jacob said. "I intend to fin the thieves and bring them to justice. But I'm new here. I don't know the lay c the land. I thought you might have some ideas on the best place to start lookin; That is, if you don't think I'm out of line for asking."

Buckey smiled. "It's an intelligent man who knows when to ask for help And don't think for a moment I feel like you're asking me to do your job for you. . you'll have plenty to do on your own." He walked to one side of his office, wher a large map hung on the wall. He traced a circle with his finger. "This is the are you're responsible for, all the way north to south from Ash Fork to Bumblebe Ranch, and east to west from the Verde Valley almost to Wickenburg. These dot mark the different ranches under your jurisdiction. My advice would be to pay visit to each of the ranchers and get to know them. See who's missing cattle anc who might know something. I'm sure we've got some in the area who wouldn' hesitate to buy cheap cows and not ask questions, but for the most part there ar a lot of good solid citizens around here."

"I've already started along those lines." Jacob pointed out the ranches h had already visited. "This map gives me a better perspective on the whole layout though."

Buckey clapped him on the shoulder. "I knew you were the right man for he job. Come back anytime you want to take another look at the map or to ask me any questions. I'm glad to help. If I'm not in my office or at home, you can generally find me down at the Palace. Speaking of which. . ." He pulled out his pocket watch and snapped the cover open.

"How would you like to meet some more of our local citizenry? I'm rather partial to a few hands of faro, and there's usually a good game starting up right about now."

"I'm not a gambling man, but I'd welcome the opportunity to get to know more of the folks around here."

"Fair enough." Buckey pulled his hat from a hook on the wall and settled it on his head. "Let's head to the Palace."

It took a moment for Jacob's eyes to adjust to the dim interior. While saloons would never be his natural haunt, the Palace was well appointed, a comfortable place for local men to gather.

"Hello, boys!" Buckey wended his way toward a group of men clustered around a table in the back room.

"About time you got here," one called back. "We were about ready to send out a search party." A chuckle rippled around the table at his sally.

"Meet Jacob Garrett, formerly of Tucson, currently Yavapai County's new range detective."

"Pleased to meet you." The men shook hands with Jacob in turn.

"Any relation to Andrew of the same name?" quizzed a black-haired man on the opposite side of the table.

"My father." Jacob felt a glow of pride at the admiring response his father's name evoked. He truly did have big shoes to fill.

"Jacob here jumped right into a tough situation," Buckey announced. "Rustling has gotten beyond the two-bit stage and he's charged with finding out who's to blame. Sounds like he's already made a good start."

One of the faro players snorted. "That's more than Clive Jensen would have done."

Jacob shot a questioning look at the group. The black-haired man twisted his mouth in disgust and leaned closer to be heard over the noise of the crowd near the bar. "Your predecessor would have been more likely to turn a blind eye to such goings-on than try to do anything to stop them."

Jacob drew his brows together. "But why?"

A craggy-faced man shrugged. "Hard to tell. Some say he was getting a pay-off from the rustlers; some say he just didn't care. All I know is, he never seemed to take loss of stock very seriously."

"That's going to change," Jacob promised.

"You fellows can help get the word out," Buckey said. "Let people know we have a range detective who means business. Sometimes just knowing someone is willing to act is enough to put a stop to that kind of thing."

A general murmur of approval ran around the table. The topic of conversation turned to Spain and the political situation in Cuba, but Buckey's comment sent Jacob's mind back to his talk with Burke Evans at the Broken Box. And from that to a mental picture of Hallie Evans. The voices from the table faded out as he daydreamed of that moment their eyes met.

Jacob wondered what it would be like to spend time in the company of Burke Evans's quiet daughter. Were her gentleness and sweet spirit as real as they seemed in that brief encounter? Her large brown eyes seemed to have looked into his soul. He hoped she had seen something worthwhile.

"What are your views on the subject, Garrett?"

The question pulled Jacob back to the present with a start. He stared at the men around the table. "Sorry," he muttered. "I'm afraid my mind was somewhere else."

The man beside him guffawed and dug his elbow into Jacob's ribs. "I've seen that look on a man's face before. You had some female on your mind, if I don't miss my guess."

The rest of the group joined him in ribald laughter.

Jacob forced a tight smile. "If you'll excuse me, gentlemen, I have to get back to business." He stepped outside and left the clamor of the saloon behind with a sense of relief.

Chapter 7

Half-dozing in the saddle, Jacob gave Cap his head and let him choose his own way down the slope from Harvey Fletcher's place to the valley floor. A newcomer to the area, Fletcher hadn't met many of his neighbors. He'd been glad to see Jacob, hungry for information about the local happenings, but hadn't added anything to Jacob's store of information about the rustling.

Jacob angled across the plain. If memory served him, this route ought to cut off a good two miles and get him back to the T Bar well before sunset.

Cap whickered and pricked up his ears at the top of the next rise. Jacob straightened in his saddle and peered in the direction Cap was looking. Up ahead stood a saddled mount. On the far side of the gray horse, a figure crouched next to a struggling animal in the tawny grass.

Jacob came fully alert. Keeping the gray between himself and the kneeling figure, he urged Cap closer. He let his right hand move down to his holster, and he slipped the loop off the hammer, never taking his gaze from the person in the grass.

When he had narrowed the distance, he circled out past the gray for a better look at the person on the ground. Long dark hair streamed down the back of the slender figure.

Hallie? He slowed when he drew near so as not to spook her horse. "What are you doing out here by yourself?"

Hallie swung around, eyes wide. She relaxed visibly and put a comforting hand on the calf stretched out on the ground before her.

"I just needed to get outdoors for a while, so I took Gypsy for a ride. Then I came across this little fellow. Could you give me a hand? He has a broken leg, and I can't set it alone."

Jacob swung out of the saddle and hurried to her side. The calf's left hind leg lay twisted at an unnatural angle. The little animal's eyes were ringed with white, and it bleated pitifully.

"Shhh," Hallie murmured in a soothing tone. "It'll be all right. We're going to take care of you."

Jacob eyed the calf. "He looks pretty well done in already, and there's no telling whether it will heal straight or not. Do you think it's worth it?"

"I don't know," Hallie replied simply. "I only know I have to try. Will you help me?" She looked up at him, and he knew in that instant he'd do anything she asked of him.

"I found that cedar branch to use as a splint." She nodded toward a short length of wood on the ground. "But I can't hold him down and work on him at the same time."

Jacob knelt beside her. "You hold his head. I'll see what I can do to get this leg straight." He ran his hand along the calf's leg and winced at the thought of the additional pain he was about to cause. He glanced at Hallie's delicate features, wondering whether she was really up to the task at hand. "Ready?"

She wrapped her arms around the calf's chest and nodded. Jacob took hold of the leg below the break and pulled. The calf let out an anguished bawl and strained to get away.

Jacob glanced at Hallie. Her arms were still locked around the calf, her feet braced against the ground. She pulled back with all her might. Her lips trembled and tears pooled in her eyes, but her face bore an expression of firm resolve. She dug her heels into the ground and held on tight.

"Just a little bit longer," she told the frightened animal.

Jacob increased the pressure and felt the ends of the bone shift into place. He broke the cedar branch in half and applied the pieces to either side of the calf's leg, then bound them in place with a bandanna Hallie had torn into strips. "You can let go now. We're finished." He leaned back on one arm and wiped beads of sweat from his upper lip with his sleeve.

Hallie released her grip and bent over her charge. "There you go, little guy. The worst is over."

Watching her fingers move in gentle strokes along the calf's neck, Jacob marveled. What a combination of gentleness and strength. What would it be like to have a woman like that stand behind him? No, *beside* him. A prize like Hallie Evans should never be pushed into the background.

❦

"That's a sweet boy." A surge of relief swept through Hallie when she felt the calf's tense muscles begin to relax. "I'll fix up a nice place for you in the barn and you can rest and take it easy until you're better.

"Poor little thing, he must wonder what he did to hurt himself so badly. And where his mother is." She pointed up a nearby draw. "I saw tracks up that way, where the earth was all churned up. It looked like somebody was pushing some cows pretty hard. I wonder if the rustlers were herding them up somewhere, but this baby got hurt and they left him behind."

She stopped talking abruptly. "Oh, dear." She clamped her lips together.

Jacob glanced from side to side. "What's the matter?"

"I'm chattering. I never chatter."

His smile warmed her more than the spring sunshine. "I wish you'd do more of it. I like hearing your voice."

Hallie felt her cheeks redden. She pushed herself to her feet and glanced down at her riding skirt. The once clean fabric now sported a coating of fine dust and bits of grass.

She dusted her skirt with her hands. *He's going to think I'm some kind of ragamuffin.* She pressed her hand to her mouth. Jacob grinned.

"What?" she demanded.

"That dirt you just brushed off your skirt? It's all over your hands now. At least, it was until you wiped most of it off on your cheek."

Hallie scrubbed frantically at her face.

Jacob stifled a chuckle.

"I'm only making it worse, aren't I?"

"Here." He pulled a bandanna from his back pocket. "On you, even dirt looks cute as a bug's ear. But use this if it will make you feel better."

❧

"How is he doing?" Hallie twisted in her saddle to look at the calf riding across Jacob's lap.

"Not bad, but he will be mighty happy to get down once we get him home."

"Not much farther," she promised.

The house and barn came into view quickly—too quickly, in Hallie's estimation. She wished she could stretch these last remaining moments out for hours. Being with Jacob was like a refreshing spring rain on parched earth. He hadn't minded her chatter; in fact, he'd encouraged her to talk. And with him, she found it easy to do.

"Here we are," she said when they rode into the yard. "Let me help you get him down."

Her father strode out of the barn with an expression like a thundercloud. "What's going on?"

"I found this little fellow hurt out on the trail," Hallie explained. "Jacob— Mr. Garrett—came along and helped me set his leg."

"And he had to trail you all the way home, I see." Her father gave Jacob a hard look.

"Just long enough to drop this little guy off." Jacob slid from his saddle and lifted the calf down in one easy motion.

"Hallie could have brought him home herself. She's a good worker. You'd best be on your way now."

Hallie felt her cheeks flame. "Pa!"

Her father leveled a warning glance at her, then turned back to Jacob. "I lost another half dozen head this past week. You'd do better to spend your time looking for whoever has been stealing my stock instead of making calf eyes at my daughter."

"Pa!"

Burke rounded on her. "You just settle down, young lady. You've hardly set foot off the ranch these past few years, and you don't know the first thing about the way a man's mind works. You're easy pickings for the first young buck who comes along."

"Pa, stop!" Hallie held up her hands as though she could ward off the harsh words that fell like lashes from a whip. "How can you say such things? Don't you know me better than that? And what about Jacob? How can you cast aspersions on someone you barely know?

"You're right about one thing," she continued. "I haven't spent much time off the ranch. But anyone with half an eye could see that he's a decent, upright man." Tears clogged her throat and she subsided, wrapping her arms around her middle.

Her father's eyes bulged and his face took on a ruddy hue. "What's gotten into you, sassing back like that? You get yourself inside the house, girl. And you stay there, you hear?"

Unable to hold back her sobs a moment longer, Hallie sprinted for the front door.

Inside, she collapsed against the closed door, then slid down until she huddled on the floor in a heap. She hugged her knees and pulled her body into a tight knot.

"Why, God? Why can't he see? He's completely blind to Pete's advances, but he's ready to tear Jacob apart without even getting to know him."

Tears blurred her vision, and she pressed her forehead against her knees. With all her heart, she hoped her father's insinuations wouldn't keep Jacob from coming around again. But she couldn't blame him if they did.

⁕

Burke turned from watching Hallie's dash to the house and fixed Jacob with a malevolent glare. He took a threatening step forward, meaty hands balled into fists. "I don't know what you did to make her spout off like that. She's never done a thing like that before."

Jacob felt the hairs on the back of his neck stand on end like the hackles of a dog facing a growling bear. "Your daughter is a fine woman, one you can be proud of. You'd do well to appreciate what you have."

"You'd better not have been appreciatin' anything you aren't supposed to, or I'll send you home draped over your saddle."

Jacob had to force his clenched jaw open before he could speak. "Mr. Evans, I resent your implications. Things happened out there just as Hallie said. I came upon her while she was trying to doctor that calf. She needed help; I gave it to her. We brought the calf back so she could tend to him while his leg heals. That's the whole story. Period." He jabbed his finger toward Burke, who maintained a stony silence.

Jacob swung up onto Cap's back. "And now I'm heading out to do some more searching for your rustlers." He dug his heels into Cap's sides and left Burke Evans standing in a cloud of dust.

All the way back to the T Bar, Burke's accusation churned his stomach. *How can such a hard man have such a sweet daughter?*

"He's a decent, upright man." Hallie's words floated through his mind, the memory of her passionate defense overshadowing her father's words.

He relaxed a fraction, finally able to loosen his jaw and work it from side to side. It was almost worth listening to that diatribe just to hear Hallie champion him like that.

"How could she know what kind of man I am? We've only spoken twice." Whatever the reason, he was glad. The memory of her support would bolster him for quite a while.

The shadows stretched long through the windows and inched their way across the floor. Time to light the lamps. Past time to fix supper.

Hallie remained curled in her tight ball. Muscles cramping, head throbbing, she sat alone in her misery in the gathering dark.

The back door opened, then slammed shut. Boots tromped across the plank floor. "Hallie!" Her father's rough voice echoed through the house. "Where's my supper? I'm hungry."

He stopped in the doorway that separated the kitchen from the front room. He stood a long moment without speaking, then said in a quieter tone, "What is it? Are you sick?"

Hallie spoke without raising her head. "I'm fine."

"Then why are you just sitting there in the dark? Why aren't the lamps lit? Where's supper?" He struck a match and touched it to the wick of the lamp on the mantel. "With everything else on my mind right now, I can't be worrying about going hungry."

"You're right." Hallie planted her palms on the floor and pushed herself up. "It wouldn't do for you to have any more worries. I'll make some sandwiches out of that beef we had for lunch."

Her father hung his hat on its hook and headed for his favorite chair. Halfway there, he turned back, a worried frown creasing his forehead. "You sure you're all right? It isn't like you to slack off like this."

He walked over and put his arms around her. "Tell your old dad what's going on. All we've had is each other ever since your mother died." He ran his work-hardened hand over her hair. "I know I've been short with you lately, and I'm sorry. It's the loss of all that stock. It just burns me to no end to think someone is strolling in here and trying to ruin everything I've worked so hard to build up."

Hallie leaned against him, remembering how it felt to be a little girl and know her daddy would take on the whole world to keep her safe. She let herself relax in his embrace and wiped her eyes on the front of his shirt.

She stretched her arms around his stocky frame. "Give me a few minutes, and I'll come up with something more substantial than sandwiches. You just sit in your chair and relax until then."

His strong arms squeezed her in a bear hug. "That's my girl. I knew you couldn't stay in a pout for long. You're a sensible girl, Hallie. At least when you're not all dewy-eyed over some footloose yahoo."

Hallie stiffened and pulled away. "I'll go make your supper."

"You gettin' all fussed up again? What did I do this time? I don't understand."

Hallie stormed into the kitchen and leaned her head against the doorframe. "That's just the trouble, Pa," she whispered. "You don't understand at all."

Chapter 8

Even though it was just after ten in the morning, the heat reminded Jacob of Tucson. His horse pushed through the milling cattle as he checked the final brands of this herd. He rode over to where the buyer and seller sat their horses beneath the shade of a large walnut tree.

"Everything looks good here. Every one of them a Heart Cross brand. I'll sign off on that bill of sale, Mr. Potter, and you can be on your way." He scribbled his name at the bottom of the paper. "How long will it take you to push them up to Ash Fork?"

"Four or five days should get us there, if we don't have any trouble." Potter folded the bill and placed it in his pocket. He shook hands and rode toward his cowboys to start the hundred head of breeding stock.

Jacob mopped his forehead with his bandanna, then used it to wipe the sweat band of his hat. "You've got some good-looking stock there, Bradley. From the looks of them, I'm guessing the range is in good shape over on this side of Granite Mountain."

"This year looks good. And I'll be able to upgrade my stock after selling these heifers." Will Bradley gave a satisfied nod and reached over to pat the gangly boy on the horse next to him. "By the time this button gets big enough to take over, we ought to have quite a spread built up."

Jacob studied the ten-year-old wearing a hat nearly as big as he was and held back a grin. By the looks of him, that boy wouldn't be ready to boss an outfit for a good long time.

The boy flashed a grin at his father, then pulled a book from his saddlebag. Propping it against his saddle horn, he settled back to read.

Jacob turned a puzzled glance at Will Bradley, who merely shrugged and grinned. "He gets that from his mother. You'll never find either one of them far from a book. He got his dark hair and those bright eyes from her, too. This territory has brought me a good family, a good life. Pulling up stakes and moving out here was the best thing I ever did."

Jacob could understand his desire to strike out on his own. "Where did you come from?"

"New Mexico, up in the northeast corner of the territory. My father and uncle have a good-size spread. My sister and her family are up there, too. It was hard leaving them all, but I wouldn't trade what I have here for anything." He turned to his son. "Alexander, show Mr. Garrett what you're reading."

"It's *A Connecticut Yankee in King Arthur's Court*." Alexander's deep blue eyes lit up when he grinned. "It's all about knights and jousting and stuff like that."

Jacob chuckled at the boy's enthusiasm. "It sounds like quite a tale. That Mark Twain really knows how to spin a yarn."

"Have you found a place in Prescott?" Will asked.

Jacob shook his head. "I'm staying on at the T Bar for the time being. There's a fair amount of stock missing over that way, and I figure being on the spot might help me get a line on what's going on."

"Dan's a good man," Will said. "I'm glad he brought you up here. We've been needing someone like you."

Alexander looked up from his story. "You're staying with Mr. O'Roarke?" A mischievous grin crept across his face. "Would you tell Catherine something for me, please? Tell her I got a new pet frog, and I'll let her play with him anytime she wants."

Jacob blinked at the odd request. "Sure. I'll be happy to pass that along."

Will Bradley eyed his son. "And just why would Catherine be interested in a frog, pet or otherwise?"

"Hey, look." Alexander stood in his stirrups and pointed toward the east. "Someone's coming. I'll just ride out and see who it is." He kicked his horse into a lively trot.

"We'll discuss this later," Will called to his retreating back. He shoved his Stetson back and scratched his head. "I have a feeling I'd better check into that. Those two have been feuding since they were babies."

"You never know," Jacob replied. "They may turn out to be the best of friends someday." The two men waited in companionable silence, watching the rider approach.

"That's a Broken Box rider," Will observed. "Bernie Harrelson, if I don't miss my guess."

Jacob nodded, recognizing the thin-faced man at the same moment. *What's one of Evans's riders doing way over here?* A knot twisted in his gut.

Harrelson pulled his horse up about ten feet away. "Afternoon, Mr. Bradley." He looked toward Jacob but didn't meet his gaze, focusing instead on a point just beyond his left ear. "Sheriff Ruffner said you might be out here today, Garrett, so I rode on over. Mr. Evans sent me."

"What can I do for you?" Jacob asked, afraid he already knew the answer.

"We discovered more stock missing over the last couple of days, nearly a dozen head this time. The boss is pretty upset."

Jacob watched the cowboy swallow repeatedly, like a cow working her cud. "Is that all he wanted you to tell me?"

Harrelson's Adam's apple bobbed up and down. "He said he hoped you weren't going to just sit back and look the other way like the last fellow who had this job." He risked a quick glance at Jacob. "Those are his words, Garrett, not mine. Me and the boys know you're doing your best."

Jacob ducked his head in a curt nod. "Anything else?"

Harrelson's gaze shot back toward the horizon. "Just that you'd better find out who's stealing his cattle, and soon, if you know what's good for you." He wheeled his horse back toward the east. "I have to be getting back. The boss is going to have my hide for being gone so long. He figured you'd be sticking a lot closer to the Broken Box these days, with all the trouble that's been going on." Harrelson dug his heels into his horse's sides and rode back the way he came.

A muscle twitched in Jacob's cheek. He forced his clenched teeth apart. "That was a lovely bit of news."

"Don't let Burke get to you," Will said. "He wasn't like this years ago, back before his wife died. Most of it's just bluster, trying to cover up the hurt he's carrying around inside. He isn't really a bad fellow. He sure dotes on that daughter of his."

"I've seen them together," Jacob said shortly. "I haven't noticed much doting."

Will turned toward him, a speculative gleam in his eye. "From your tone of voice, it sounds like you might be a bit interested in his daughter."

"I'd better go see what I can do about those cattle." Jacob touched the brim of his Stetson. "Tell Alexander I'll deliver his message."

⁕

In the days that followed, Jacob found—and lost—more trails than he wanted to count. If a spring shower didn't come down at just the right time to wash fresh signs away, the tracks would lead him on a chase up into a stretch of rocky ground, then disappear. Like the ones he had just followed.

He swept his Stetson from his head and ran his fingers through his damp, tangled hair. *So much for getting into Evans's good graces by my dazzling tracking skills.* Bernie Harrelson's announcement that larger numbers of cattle were being taken at a time indicated that the rustlers were becoming bold, almost arrogant in their approach. Obviously, they didn't consider Jacob's presence on the range a threat.

He settled his hat back on his head and surveyed the slope below the rocky ledge where his most recent foray had led him. How could cattle disappear into thin air? The answer had to be out there somewhere, if only he could find it. Jacob slapped his rope against his chaps, sending a cloud of dust floating skyward. They had to know he was out here looking for them. Were they watching from some hidden spot right now, having a good laugh at his expense?

He scanned the slope and felt his heart quicken when he spotted something that caught his notice. "Let's try over there, Cap. It looks like that ground's churned up a bit."

Not just a bit, he discovered when he reached the spot, but crisscrossed by the mingled tracks of horses and at least a dozen head of cattle. "This is it, Cap,

I can feel it. Let's just meander on and follow the trail and see where this one takes us."

The steel-dust seemed to catch his sense of excitement. The horse's steps quickened as he stepped out briskly, ears alert. They followed the tracks for nearly a mile. Twice, smaller numbers of tracks joined the main group from the sides. "They were pushing a pretty good-sized group here," Jacob mused. "Looks like they weren't afraid of being noticed. They're either feeling pretty confident of their ability, or they don't have a very high regard for mine."

But this time they'd overplayed their hand. The case was about to break; he could feel it in his bones. He half-expected to run across the stolen cattle every time he rounded a hill or topped a rise. A half mile farther, the trail made a sharp turn to the right, then dipped down into a dry wash.

Jacob felt the blood pound in his temples as he followed, then reined Cap to a halt. He stared helplessly at the bottom of the wash, where those clear-cut tracks became mere dimples in the sand, giving no indication of the direction they had taken. The familiar taste of defeat burned the back of Jacob's throat.

He slammed his fist against the saddle horn. Another dead end! With the number of failures he had racked up lately, he couldn't blame Burke for thinking he was on the side of the rustlers.

The man had every right to expect tangible results from Jacob and every reason to feel betrayed when he didn't receive them. Moreover, he was Hallie's father. That didn't make matters any easier. Bad enough to look like an inept fool in front of any one of the people he had promised to serve; even worse to do so in full view of the man he hoped would be his father-in-law one day.

"I can't afford to stay on his bad side," Jacob told Cap. "I have a feeling I'm going to be seeing a lot of the man." The one bright spot he could see in all this mess was the likelihood he would be making frequent visits to the Broken Box. The opportunity to spend time with Hallie was enough to sweeten any disappointment.

Jacob rode on, turning the situation over in his mind in the hope he might come up with a new angle he hadn't considered before. Other ranches had lost stock, but none had been hit as hard as the Broken Box. What made Burke Evans such a tempting target? Jacob tried to reason out an answer, but he couldn't see any major difference between the man and his neighbors. It wasn't like he had a shortage of riders or any other lack that would make him easy pickings. It was almost as though there were some personal reason for him to suffer the most loss.

Could someone hold a grudge against Burke? Now, that he could believe. Maybe it would pay to learn more about any enemies Burke might have made, someone who wouldn't quibble about stealing his cattle.

His mind went wheeling along possible lines of investigation. Had Burke ever done someone dirt? Shorted someone in a deal? The possibilities mounted, along with Jacob's excitement. Despite Will Bradley's assurances of Burke's goodhearted nature, Jacob had already witnessed a much darker side of the man, and he'd only known him a short time. He had tried his hardest to overlook as much as possible for Hallie's sake. Anyone else getting that kind of treatment might feel inclined to get some of his own back by whatever means necessary.

He felt a stirring of excitement at this first bit of encouragement he'd had in weeks. The next thing he'd do would be to delve into Burke Evans's background.

Chapter 9

Hallie swirled a piece of soft flannel in small circles over the surface of her saddle, spreading a coating of glistening oil across the polished leather. She breathed deeply and felt the tension of the past days slip away. The mingled scents of leather, hay, and neatsfoot oil never failed to relax her and fill her with a sense of well-being. She set the oil-soaked rag aside and wiped her hands on a scrap of burlap, careful not to get any oil stains on her skirt. She lifted the saddle and prepared to hoist it onto its stand.

A warm breath tickled the back of her neck. "Hello, you pretty thing."

Hallie whirled and clutched the saddle against her chest. Pete Edwards jumped back to avoid being slapped by the swinging stirrup leathers. "Whoa, there. You nearly hit me."

"What do you want, Pete?" After the scare he'd given her, Hallie felt in no mood to soften her tone.

His lips parted in a leer, and he leaned toward her. "Why don't you set that saddle down and let me show you?"

Hallie tightened her grip on the saddle's gullet and skirt. "Get out of here and leave me alone. I have things to do, and I'm sure you do, too."

Pete snickered. "I've got something in mind, all right. Let's start with a little kiss. You've been holding me off long enough." He moved nearer, forcing her back into the corner.

Her irritation gave way to a faint prickle of fear. "I said, leave me alone." She shoved the saddle at him and sprang to one side.

Pete knocked the saddle away, and it landed in a heap on the dusty floor. He jumped over it and moved quickly to put himself between her and the doorway. They stood in a frozen tableau, with only the sound of Pete's rough, uneven breathing invading the heavy silence. He flexed his fingers, and a slow smile worked its way across his face. "You got away from me the last time, but not today. I'm tired of playing games with you, Hallie. This time, things go my way."

Terror flowed through her veins like icy water. She did her best to inject a note of scorn into her voice, knowing if she showed her fear, she would be lost. "I'm not playing, and this is no game. Move out of my way." She started toward the door, hoping sheer bravado would carry her through.

Pete spread his arms wide and moved toward her, giving her no choice but to retreat into the corner near the stalls.

Her bluff wasn't working. Hallie fought to gain control over the panic that threatened to overcome her reason. She was no match for Pete in physical strength. She could scream, but was anyone near enough to hear her? And if no one did, what then? She rejected the idea. A scream would only let Pete know how vulnerable she felt. She couldn't afford to do anything to strengthen his position.

She inched backward, frantic at the knowledge that every step she retreated put her that much farther from escape.

Pete advanced, matching her step for step. His look of anticipation sent slivers of fear plunging through her. His voice softened and took on a cajoling tone. "You know you're going to give in one of these days, Hallie. Why not now? We could have a lot of fun, you and me."

A sense of unreality enveloped her. This couldn't be happening, not in her own barn. Dread wrapped its steely talons around her heart. Hallie looked around, her mind scrambling to find some means of escape. The only exit lay through the wide barn doorway, and Pete stood square in her path.

If not escape, then defense. What could she use? Her gaze lit on a coil of rope, a pair of bridles. *Lord, help me!*

Pete made a grab for her, and she countered by ducking behind the center post. The sudden change in direction tangled her feet in her skirt, and she sprawled backward into a deep pile of hay. She lay motionless, the wind knocked out of her.

A satisfied chuckle rumbled from deep in Pete's throat. "There now. If that don't look inviting." He lunged toward her, a gleam of victory in his eyes.

"No!" Hallie's shriek reverberated from the rafters. With a burst of strength born of desperation, she dug her heels into the floor and pushed herself away.

Pete cursed and made a grab for her. His hand closed on the hem of her skirt. Hallie lashed out with her foot and saw his head snap back when her boot made contact with his chin. Pete cursed again. His lips drew back over his teeth in a feral snarl.

Hallie scrambled backward through the hay, knowing her only hope lay in breaking Pete's hold on her skirt. *Help me, Jesus.* Her hands clawed in the dust beneath the hay, and her fingers wrapped around a wooden handle. *Pa's sickle! Thank You!*

She yanked at her skirt with her free hand and heard the fabric rip. She scrambled to her feet and faced Pete, swinging the sharp sickle blade back and forth.

"Get away from me." The sickle blade flashed in a broad arc from right to left. "Do you understand? Leave me alone!" She slashed the sickle in the opposite direction. "I don't want anything to do with you." *Slash.* "Now or ever." The blade flashed again.

Pete shuffled on his hands and knees, backing another step across the floor with every swing of the blade. At the doorway, he staggered to his feet and held his hands in front of him. "All right, Hallie, you win. For now, anyway." He caught his breath in ragged gasps and watched her warily.

Never taking her eyes off Pete, Hallie held the sickle before her like a sword and circled past him. When she reached the door, she turned and fled headlong toward the shelter of the house. Anguished sobs rose in her throat, but she fought to hold them back. She wouldn't give him the satisfaction of hearing her cry.

"I can be patient," he yelled from the barn. "Get it through your head, Hallie, you're mine. Next time there won't be a sickle around."

The air tore in and out of Hallie's lungs as she ran. *Oh, Lord, don't let there be a next time!*

The latch rattled under Hallie's fumbling fingers. She wrenched at it again and it finally shot home. Hallie sagged against the door, hardly daring to believe she had managed to escape. She bowed her head and clutched at her hair with both hands.

"I can't go through that again, Lord! I've got to make Pa understand."

But he wouldn't. The knowledge plunged a shaft of despair into her heart. In her father's eyes, Pete could do no wrong, and with his word against hers, today's encounter would be explained away as mere high-strung behavior.

If only the rustling situation hadn't claimed all Pa's attention! With him so wrought over the missing stock, his dependence on Pete outweighed his usual good sense. Hallie racked her brain. There had to be a way to get him to listen to her long enough to be convinced of Pete's true character.

And then what? A chill crept up her spine at the thought of what would happen next if he ever fully understood the extent of Pete's unwanted advances.

She knew it as sure as she knew the sun would rise over Mingus Mountain in the morning: He would go after Pete. And in his present agitated state of mind, he wouldn't hesitate to shoot him.

Hallie sank to her knees at the sobering thought of what she could set in motion with only a few words. If her father killed Pete, he would be tried for murder. He might not hang, but he would suffer the indignity of arrest and trial, a fate almost as bad as death for someone with her father's brand of pride.

Worse yet, from all accounts, Pete was fast on the draw. What if he killed her father? He could tell the law anything he wanted. Knowing Pete, he would be sure to make it look like a case of self-defense. And given Burke's outbursts of temper lately, most people would have no problem believing he had finally snapped and gone into a murderous rage.

And Hallie would be left alone, at Pete's mercy—a possibility too horrible to contemplate.

"I can't do it," she whispered to the empty room. Setting her father against Pete could ruin their lives, and the responsibility for that would lie at her own feet. She could not—would not—jeopardize her father's well-being, maybe even his very life.

She had no choice. She would keep her troubles to herself and do her best to stay away from Pete.

Chapter 10

Jacob tapped on Buckey's office door. "Do you have a few minutes, or are you busy?"

"Never too busy for a good round of talk." The mayor of Prescott set down his pen and slid the paper he'd been writing on to one side of his desk. "How goes the rustler hunt?"

"I hoped talking to you might give me some new insight. I'm fresh out of ideas."

Buckey's dark eyes held a gleam of sympathy. "It's that bad, eh?"

"Worse." Jacob slumped into the nearest chair. "I've covered more miles than I can count, looking for some clue to what's been happening. Every time I find a sign of someone moving stock, I lose it again. It seems like I can only get so far on a trail, then it just peters out."

He leaned his head against the back of the chair and stared at the map on the wall. "I've checked at the railheads in Ash Fork and Jerome, but neither place has any record of stock going out without the proper paperwork, duly signed by me."

"That would seem to eliminate that angle as a possibility."

Jacob jumped up and paced the office. "It beats me how they're moving these animals. Where are they taking them? How are they getting rid of them? They just seem to vanish into thin air."

Buckey leaned back and tented his fingers. "I heard a while back about a fellow up in Holbrook who was making a tidy profit butchering stolen cattle, then selling the beef. You might ask around and see if anything like that might be going on around here."

He pursed his lips. "If not, they almost have to be connecting with the railroad at some point in order to get that many head out of the area. Otherwise, somebody would have spotted them."

Jacob halted in midstep. "Unless. . ." He crossed to the map in three quick strides. "Have you heard of any new ranchers who have come into the area recently? Anyone who might have an interest in building up a herd without paying for it?"

Buckey nodded slowly. "We've had an influx of new people over the past year or so. There's a family near Walnut Creek, up past Williamson Valley. Then there are a couple of fellows over toward Clarkdale, on the other side of Mingus Mountain, who registered two or three new brands. And I heard about another outfit over at the base of the Bradshaws."

He stroked his mustache with the back of his forefinger. "I haven't heard anything to make me think any of those folks would be involved in something like that, but it wouldn't hurt to check them out."

"Thanks. I'll do that." Jacob resumed his seat with a lighter spirit. It felt good to have Buckey as a friend. At least one person didn't think of him as an incompetent loafer. He rolled his shoulders, easing away the tension that had been a part of him for so long. "I've been so busy running around like a headless chicken that I haven't kept up on the latest news. What's the word on Cuba?"

"Spain is trying to placate Washington, but it may be a case of too little, too late."

"You think we're looking at a war, then?"

Buckey's face took on a somber expression. "At this juncture, I'd say it's inevitable."

Jacob walked down the courthouse steps with a handful of scribbled notes. Acting on Buckey's tip, he had checked on new brand registrations. He stopped under a tree near the edge of the plaza and studied the sketches he'd made: the C Bar J, the Ladder M, the 2 Lazy 2.

Jacob chuckled at the last one. *Too lazy to what?* The clever ways some of the ranchers found to incorporate a sense of humor into their chosen brands had long proved a source of amusement.

His gaze shifted back to the Ladder M, and he bent to study it more closely. The Broken Box brand was made up of two facing brackets. Jacob stooped to pick up a fallen twig and used it to sketch the brand in the dust.

And the Ladder M... He connected the top and bottom lines of the brackets and extended them outward, then added another vertical line in the center. As a final touch, he wrote an M next to the figure, then rocked back on his heels to study the result.

His pulse throbbed in his temple. The Broken Box brand could be over-written into a Ladder M with very little effort. *This could be it.* He looked again at his notes. The Ladder M brand had recently been registered by one of the newcomers Buckey had mentioned over Clarkdale way.

Jacob tucked the paper into his shirt pocket and glanced at the sun's position. Too late to get all the way out there that afternoon. He walked to the hitching rail and loosened Cap's reins. He would go home to the T Bar for the night, then head over Mingus to visit the Ladder M at first light.

Jacob reined Cap in a southeasterly direction. "I know, boy," he said when the steel-dust tossed his head. "We're supposed to be heading for Clarkdale. But this is right on the way. Well, almost on the way," he amended.

Truth to tell, the detour took him a good bit out of his way, but he needed to check in on the latest state of affairs at the beleaguered Broken Box. It would remind Burke he was staying on top of the situation.

And if things went the way he hoped, he might get a glimpse of Hallie.

He felt a grin crease his cheeks at the thought of seeing her again. Cap whickered and flicked his ears back and forth.

"You're right," Jacob said. "Seeing Hallie is a powerful draw for going there, but I'm just as interested in focusing on my job."

Cap shook his head and snorted. Jacob tugged his hat brim down lower over his forehead. If he couldn't convince his horse, he sure wasn't going to convince Burke Evans.

He rode into the yard at a trot, anxious to put his best foot forward. Before he could swing his leg over the cantle, the front door burst open. Burke stormed outside and planted himself squarely in Jacob's path.

"I hope you've come to tell me you've got those thieves locked up and facing a trial."

"Not yet." Jacob pulled off his hat and rolled the brim in his hands, waiting for an invitation to go inside the house. After a second look at Burke's grim expression, he knew he might as well give up on that notion.

He sent a quick glance to the front windows, hoping to see Hallie peering out at him. The curtains hung neatly across the glass. It looked like this detour was going to turn out to be strictly business after all.

Jacob turned his attention back to Burke. "I just wanted to stop by and see if anything more had happened since the last time we talked."

Burked tipped his head back and spread his arms wide as if appealing to the heavens. When he looked back at Jacob, the expression on his face could have curdled milk. "Seems to me like you spend a powerful amount of time looking for answers in all the wrong places. For the life of me, I don't understand why you keep looking around here instead of trying to track down whoever's been stealing my stock."

He went on, his voice weighted with exaggerated patience. "If I had my cattle tucked safely away close to home, I wouldn't need your help. But they aren't here, are they?" He scooped up a pebble from the ground and threw it across the yard. "How hard is it to find some cowboy who's spending more money than he should? I could do it myself with one eye shut."

Be my guest, Jacob thought. *Let's see how far you get.* Aloud, he said, "If you have all the answers, maybe you don't need me on the case at all."

Burke fixed him with a glare. "I can't run a ranch and chase after thieves at the same time. Tracking these crooks down is what we're paying you for, and I say you're showing a pretty poor return on the wages you've been drawing."

Easy. Don't let him get to you. Jacob paused to draw a long breath and took his time forming a response. "Then instead of criticizing, why not help me do my job? Do you have any more ideas who may be behind this?" He watched Burke closely. "Anyone who might hold a grudge from the past? Someone who wants to get back at you, for whatever reason?" *The list must be a mile long.*

"I've never done anything to anybody, nothing that would be worth this, anyway." Burke set his lips in a thin line. "You seem to be mighty interested in what I may or may not have done. Suppose you tell me what you've been doing to earn your pay?"

Jacob drew himself up. "I'm on my way over to check out a new rancher in the Clarkdale area, see if he can account for all his stock."

"Don't waste your time harassing the other ranchers. They're a hard-working lot, all of them. If you're set on checking out newcomers, you ought to take a look at that batch of nesters back up in the foothills. All this started since they came here a few months back."

Burke spat on the ground and continued. "It wouldn't surprise me if the reason you can't find traces of any stock being moved is because they've been hiding them all back in the hills, trying to build a herd without having to buy foundation stock. Go see what you can find up their way, if you want to do something worthwhile. It's what I'd do. . .and what you'd be doing if you had a lick of sense."

Jacob felt his body go rigid. "I'll check into it. It would sure be hard for them to explain having cattle, though, if they didn't bring any with them when they came."

Burke scrubbed his hand through his wiry thatch of salt-and-pepper hair. "It's not your job to second-guess what will happen before you even go out there. You're supposed to get out and get to work and find these no-goods who are robbing me blind. Now get out there and do your job before I decide to find a rope and take care of things myself."

"Animals can be replaced," Jacob said. "You can't say the same for a man's life."

Burke tucked his head down between his shoulders, looking like a bull about to charge. "Someone has decided to help themselves to what I've worked for all my life. I wouldn't lose a bit of sleep over stringing up anyone who'd stoop that low. Those are my animals, my livelihood. I'm the one who worked night and day all these years. You have no right to tell me how I ought to feel."

"You may be right about that," Jacob admitted. "I won't try to tell you I know how you feel. But I do know what the Bible says about forgiveness. 'If ye forgive men their trespasses, your heavenly Father will also forgive you.' I know that if you harbor unforgiveness in your heart, it will do you more harm than the person you're holding a grudge against.

"Forgiveness is God's way," Jacob went on. "Maybe you ought to try it. You'll sleep better at night than you would if you went out and lynched a man."

Burke's face turned as red as a brick. "The Bible also says God owns the cattle on a thousand hills. I don't have nearly that many, and it's getting less all the time. That kind of talk is fine for someone who hasn't gone through what have, but I'm the one who's about to lose my livelihood. If you want to do something to spare a few miserable lives, you better get out there and catch those thieves before I do. Now I suggest you quit wagging your jaw and go get busy." With a low grunt, he turned and strode off toward the barn.

Jacob took his time tightening his cinch and scanned the front windows again. Still no sign of Hallie. He contemplated walking right up those porch steps and knocking on the front door like any normal suitor, but thought better of that plan. Burke's demeanor left Jacob in no doubt of the man's probable response to making a social call on his daughter.

He cast one last look at the house. His heart doubled its pace when he saw the edge of the curtain inch back.

Hallie peered out of the narrow opening and fluttered her fingers in a tiny wave. She mouthed something, but Jacob couldn't understand what she was trying to say.

He shot a glance toward the barn and saw Burke watching him from the doorway. As casually as he could, he made a show of checking his cinch and nudging Cap around so the horse blocked him from Burke's view.

He looked back at the window, where Hallie waved again, then pointed toward the southeast. Jacob dipped his head in a casual nod, then mounted Cap and rode off.

❈

Hallie ducked down into the wash that ran behind the house. Her moccasins sent tiny showers of sand up behind her with every step.

Had Jacob understood her signal? And if he had, what would his reaction be? Her bold action in setting up a clandestine meeting and slipping away from the house like this shocked her. She could just imagine what her father would say if he found out. The thought put wings to her feet. The farther away she got, the less likely he would be to spot her.

She rounded a bend in the wash and caught sight of Jacob, standing next to his horse twenty yards ahead. His presence both thrilled and terrified her. Bad enough to think about her father's reaction; what did Jacob think of her impetuous behavior?

His warm smile melted her fears. She slowed to a more decorous walk but was still panting for breath by the time she reached him.

"I was hoping I'd get to see you," he said, as though meeting her like this were the most natural thing in the world. "How's the calf?"

Hallie adopted a tone as casual as his. "He's fine. His leg is healing nice and straight. I even caught him trying to kick up his heels yesterday. He's going to be as good as new."

"That's good." Jacob shifted his weight from one foot to the other, looking suddenly ill at ease. "I guess you heard me talking to your father."

"Half the county probably heard him." Hallie grinned and tried to pull off a laugh, but her smile wobbled. "To be honest, I heard him bellowing, but couldn't make out what he said. I got the feeling he wasn't any too happy with you, though."

"You could say that." Jacob shot her a rueful grin. "He probably though I was way out of line when I quoted scripture to him. I told him he needed to forgive whoever is behind the rustling and let the law deal with them. He didn't take it too well."

"I can imagine." Hallie plucked a blue flax blossom from the edge of the wash and twirled the delicate stem between her fingers. "He's always had a temper, but it didn't used to be so close to the surface. Looking back, I think it's been getting worse ever since Mama died, but losing so much stock has pushed him right over the edge. It seems like he's angry all the time anymore. It's like a poison eating away at him." Unbidden tears stung her eyes. She dashed them away with the back of her hand, but more welled up and spilled over to trace slow trails down her cheeks.

Jacob closed the short distance between them. His eyes, normally sky blue took on the gray hue of a cloudy day. "I'm sorry. This can't be easy for you." He cupped her chin in his hand and wiped away her tears with his thumb.

Hallie leaned her cheek ever so slightly into the comforting warmth of his palm. "The Bible also says I ought to honor my father. How can I do that when the Bible itself doesn't condone his behavior or his attitude?" She blinked back another round of tears and stared up at Jacob.

His expression darkened. "He doesn't take his anger out on you, does he?"

"No." *Not unless you count being so preoccupied with his missing cows that he can't see his daughter's virtue is being threatened by his favorite hand.* She forced a laugh and tried to shrug away her concerns.

Though her tears had dried, Jacob still cradled her cheek in his hand. "That's a tough proposition when his actions run counter to God's Word. But I don't believe honoring your father means you necessarily agree with everything he does. Just remember that your highest responsibility is to the Lord. Love your father. . .but serve God first."

Hallie had a feeling that with her father being the one in question, that suggestion would be easier said than done.

Chapter 11

Lucas Rawlins and Morris Atwater smiled when Jacob approached them in the back room of the Palace.

"You have news for us?" A look of anticipation lit Rawlins's face.

"Only to give the two of you a report on my progress. . .or, rather, my lack of it." Jacob outlined his investigation and its resulting dead ends. "I feel like I'm at the end of my rope," he confessed. "I've tried everything I can think of, but I keep coming up dry. I'll go on as I've begun and keep looking if you want me to. But if you feel I'm just wasting my time and your money, I'll understand." He waited stoically for their response.

The ensuing silence was shattered by the sound of the outer door banging against the wall, followed by a voice Jacob knew all too well.

"Where's Rawlins and Atwater? This whole mess has gone on too long, and I want to know what they're going to do about it." Burke Evans stomped into the room. Crimson splotches mottled his face. He stopped abruptly when he spotted Jacob, and his mouth twisted in a sneer.

"I might have known I'd find you lollygagging around here instead of out doing your job. Did you ever get out to check on those nesters, or was that whole story a trumped-up excuse to stop by my ranch in the hopes of impressing my daughter?"

Lucas Rawlins stepped forward and gripped the angry man's shoulder. "Hold on, Burke. Jacob was just telling us about the steps he's taken to find out what's happened to those cattle."

Burke shook off Rawlins's restraining hand. "I'm not surprised. He's good with words, does a powerful lot of talking. He seems to have Hallie eating right out of his hand. But what's he done? That's what I want to know. Tell me what's happened beyond just talk."

"I went out to see those folks just after I left your place," Jacob said. "There were no signs of cattle, yours or anyone else's. They aren't rustlers, just decent, hard-working people trying to build up farms, not raise stock."

"Well, if it isn't them, who is it?" Burke thrust his chin forward. "You'd better get out there and find out instead of wasting your time loitering around town or hanging around my ranch trying to catch a glimpse of my daughter."

Burke narrowed his eyes to mere slits. "Or maybe I've been looking at it all backwards. Maybe you're just using Hallie as an excuse to snoop around my ranch. What do we know about you, anyway? Only that you showed up on our doorstep one day and waltzed right into this position without any experience to back you up. Maybe you know a whole lot more about this rustling business than you're letting on."

Muscles knotted in Jacob's jaw. "If you're implying—"

"That's enough, Evans." Rawlins stepped between them, holding his arms out like a referee in the boxing ring. "Go home and cool off before you say something you'll regret."

Burke stood as though wanting to say more, then swung around and made for the door. At the threshold, he turned and jabbed a stubby finger at each of the men in turn. "Just remember, someone out there deserves to swing at the end of a rope, and I don't much care who it turns out to be."

Hands clenched inside his pockets, Jacob finished his second lap around the perimeter of the plaza and began a third. The circular route wouldn't take him very far, but he had to do something to work off the head of steam that erupted inside him after Burke Evans's tirade.

He slowed to let a cluster of chattering women saunter past, chafing until he could pick up his pace again. It might be a mild April morning in Prescott, but his rising temper made him feel as blazing hot under the collar as a Tucson afternoon in July.

If it weren't for the fact he's Hallie's father. . .

He felt a hand grip his shoulder. Wheeling around, he spotted Buckey O'Neill's friendly grin. "What's eating you? You look like you're being chased by Coxey's army."

Jacob answered with a rueful smile. "Is it that obvious?"

Buckey hooked his thumbs behind his belt. "Let's just say I've been watching you from my office window for the past twenty minutes. By my count, this is the third time you've circled the plaza, looking like a man ready to throttle anyone who gets in his path. You want to talk about it?"

Jacob set off again, and Buckey fell in step beside him. His expression sobered when Jacob poured out the story of Burke's outburst.

"That description doesn't fit the person I met when I came here in '82," Buckey said. "Hallie was just a little thing, and her mother, Annabel, could light up a dark night with her smile. Burke struck me as one of the most contented men on the face of the earth back then. He had a temper, sure, but he knew how to keep it in check. Now it seems that temper rules him instead of the other way around."

Jacob considered his friend's words, then nodded. "That pretty well sums it up." The two men walked in silence, completing another lap around the courthouse square before Jacob spoke again.

"He has reason enough to be angry about what's happening now, but I get the feeling it goes back to more than just the loss of his stock. It's almost like he's mad at God for something. Whatever the case, he needs to turn it loose and move on instead of letting it consume him like this."

"You could be right. Bitterness can eat at a man like a canker." Buckey shook his head, then his face brightened. "Have you heard the news about Cuba? Major Brodie is ready to recruit a whole regiment from the West." His face lit up with an eager fire. "I say we can recruit a thousand from Arizona Territory alone. Why, we have the best of the West right here. These men have been tested by fire already. They can ride, they can shoot, and they won't run at the sound of a bullet."

He clapped his hands. "We'll put together the finest cavalry unit the world has ever seen. If that doesn't show the nation we're ready for statehood, I don't know what will."

His words stirred something deep inside Jacob. Buckey's passion was born of a love for a land he had come to as a young man. But Arizona Territory was Jacob's own birthplace, the place he planned to call his home for all the rest of his days. Why not take a leaf from Buckey's book and pour himself into helping to shape Arizona's future? "Statehood does have a sweet sound to it."

A spark of enthusiasm flickered and grew into a flame. "As for going to war to do it, I guess nothing good is achieved without some risk, is it?"

Buckey stopped abruptly and faced him. "Just think of what the results could be." His face lit up. "Who wouldn't gamble for a star on the flag?"

Jacob felt his excitement grow to match Buckey's. Giving of himself for his territory—his country—might be the finest thing he'd ever be called to do. Not everyone was handed the opportunity to invest themselves in such a noble cause.

A more prosaic thought insinuated itself into his mind: Going off to war would also serve as an honorable means to get him out of the tangle he'd become enmeshed in here. Unless God worked a miracle, this might be his only chance to prove to himself and everyone else that he wasn't an incompetent fool.

It's about time I show the folks around here I can do something right.

A broad smile spread across his face. "Let me know where to sign up. I'm going to Cuba with you."

Chapter 12

That's the best fried chicken I've had in a long time, Amy." Jacob leaned back and rubbed his full stomach. "I don't know why all these years of eating your Sunday dinners hasn't turned Dan into a round ball."

Amy blushed, and Jacob offered a silent apology to his mother. She would always be the finest cook he had ever known, but still, Amy's cooking came in at a close second.

Dan helped himself to a mound of mashed potatoes, then passed the serving bowl to Jacob. "Any more luck on finding those rustlers, or shouldn't I ask?"

"Nothing worth getting excited about," Jacob said. The change in subject dampened his contentment. Then he remembered his earlier conversation.

"I did hear something worthwhile, though. Buckey O'Neill told me they're getting ready to recruit troops for the war with Spain. I'm going to sign up the first chance I get."

Dan leaned forward eagerly. "It's getting that close, then?"

"It sure looks that way." Jacob took another bite of fried chicken and chewed with renewed enthusiasm. "At least that way I'll have something to show for my efforts. Not like—" A sharp clatter halted him in midsentence.

Amy stared at Dan, her face pale. "What does that look on your face mean? Do you have some notion of running off to join up, too?"

Dan shot an apologetic glance at Jacob before answering. "If I were a foot-loose young buck, I probably would. When I think about the way we tend to take our freedom for granted, then realize there's a country full of people not far away who have never tasted that kind of freedom. . .well, it makes me want to jump right on the bandwagon and go help drive the Spanish out.

"But then I remember that God has given me responsibilities right here at home. Who would take care of you and the children? Who would look after this place? I can't go haring off and leave all that in someone else's lap. It wouldn't be right." He reached across the table to take Amy's hand. "Don't worry, honey. I'm not planning to rush off anywhere."

He squeezed her fingers, then turned back to Jacob. "I almost forgot. I wanted to pass along something I heard yesterday. Tom Miller of the J Bar D said he saw George Dixon at the Prescott saddlery the other day. Tom figured he was taking an old saddle in for repairs, but it turns out Dixon was ordering a brand, spanking new one. Really fancy from the sounds of it—fully carved and with a passel of Mexican silver."

Jacob set his fork down and stared unwaveringly at Dan. "That had to cost pretty penny."

Dan nodded. "Nearly three months' wages, from what Tom figured. Dixon as never been known for being much good at hanging on to his pay. Tom wondered where he got hold of that kind of money."

Excitement throbbed in Jacob's veins. "This could be the break I've needed. Who does Dixon work for?"

"He's with the Flying V."

"The one a few miles down the valley from the Broken Box?" At Dan's nod, acob's mind whirled, considering the implications of this news. He picked up his vater tumbler and set it directly in front of his plate. "Let's say that's your place. This—" he positioned a spoon to the left "—is the Broken Box."

He lined up the salt cellar and a bowl of peas, completing the model. "That vould put the Flying V and the Rafter Five here. . .and here." He leaned forward over the layout he had created and studied the relationships of the places. "Look at this, Dan. The Flying V land butts right up against Broken Box range. It just might be the connection I've been looking for."

"And all those ranchers said they've been missing stock?" Dan eyed the diagram and pursed his lips.

"You figurin' out how to catch those rustlers, Uncle Jacob?" Ben spoke around a mouthful of mashed potatoes, earning him a reproving look from his mother.

Thoughts wheeled through Jacob's mind faster than he could keep up with them. "Do you remember hearing about what happened up in Wyoming when that bunch of cowboys decided they weren't getting paid enough and figured they ought to do something about it?"

Dan's brow puckered, then he nodded slowly. "Weren't they the ones who decided to pick up some extra money by rustling some of their employers' stock?"

"They're the ones. That was the beginning of all the trouble that led up to the Johnson County range war. Maybe we have something similar happening right here."

"You've already visited Owen Ladd at the Flying V, haven't you?" Dan leaned over the diagram, ignoring Amy's repeated throat clearing.

"He was one of the first ones I met." Jacob felt his newfound excitement flicker. "But he said he hadn't lost that much stock."

"But that could make sense if his own cowboys were a little hesitant to steal too much from their own boss."

Jacob stared at his friend, sickened by the thought of that kind of betrayal. 'I'd sure hate to be caught doing something like that. A man could get strung up mighty quick if—"

"Could we bring this conversation back to lighter topics?" Amy's honeyed tone softened the implied rebuke. "I'm afraid this kind of talk isn't good for ov digestion. . .or for little pitchers with big ears." She tilted her head in the direc tion of Catherine and Ben, both listening avidly.

"Sorry, Amy." Jacob ducked his head and scooped up a bite of potatoes. Am had every reason to be upset. Youngsters like Benjamin and Catherine shouldn have to listen to him expound on topics like lynching and the threat of war.

He'd been the one to steer the conversation in the wrong direction. It was u to him to find a new subject. A memory stirred, and he brightened.

"Hey, Catherine, I almost forgot. I have a message for you."

"For me?" The little girl looked up from gnawing a chicken leg, round-eye "From who?"

"Whom," Amy corrected.

"Whom from?"

Jacob grinned. "From Will Bradley's boy over at the Heart Cross. He said t tell you he has a new pet frog, and you can play with it anytime you want."

Catherine jerked upright so hard her red-gold curls quivered. "Tha Alexander Bradley! He'd better watch out."

Dan eyed his daughter. "What's all this about? Sounds to me like he's jus trying to be friendly."

"Not him." Catherine shook her head emphatically. "That wasn't what h meant at all. Last fall at the church picnic, he put a slimy ol' frog down the back c my dress, then he just hooted when I screamed and couldn't get it to drop out."

Ben snickered, and she rounded on him with a vengeance. "You hush! I wasn't a bit funny. I had to go down to the creek where there were some bushe to hide behind, then I had to peel clear down to my—"

"Catherine." Amy's voice held a warning note.

"Sorry, Mama." Catherine's lower jaw jutted out mutinously. "But it wasn funny. And now he thinks he's warning me he'll get me again. If he tries anythin else like that, he's really going to catch it."

"Catherine Elizabeth!" Amy's stern tone left no room for argument.

"Yes, ma'am." She dropped down to a whisper. "But he'd better watch hi own back, that's all I have to say."

Jacob caught the muttered threat and smothered a grin.

"Are you two finished?" Dan asked. "I think it's about time you wer excused."

The children scraped their chairs back with alacrity and scooted out th door.

Benjamin's voice floated in from the front porch. "They're just being nic because Uncle Jacob is here. I bet you're really going to get it later."

"Am not."

"Are, too."

"Am not."

Their bickering tones faded into the distance, and Amy sighed. "If it isn't ustlers, it's wild children." She rose and picked up a dish from the sideboard. "Apple pie, anyone?"

Jacob lay under his blankets that night, staring into the darkness and going over the information Dan had shared. Dixon had more money than anyone would expect him to. Dixon worked for the Flying V, which adjoined the Broken Box. . . and several other hard-hit ranches.

Could Dixon be responsible for the thefts plaguing the valley over the past few months?

The thought turned his stomach, but it had to be considered. What would make a man ignore his loyalty to his own brand?

Jacob punched the pillow into a wad and folded his arms under his head, pondering his next move. If Dixon was brazen enough to flaunt ill-gotten money around town like that, it would line up with the attitude he had observed recently in the rustlers' behavior. *That's one cowboy who's going to bear watching,* he decided just before he faded into sleep.

A sudden noise brought him bolt upright. Jacob sat motionless, every sense focused on the sound that had jolted him back to wakefulness. Had he imagined it or. . .

There it came again, a soft tap on the window glass. Jacob swung his feet over the edge of his bed, lifted his pistol from the holster slung over the bedpost, and padded across the plank floor. He had opened the window partway before retiring to let in the fresh spring breezes. Jacob caught one edge of the fluttering curtain and eased it back.

Only the darkness met his gaze, but he sensed the presence of someone just outside.

"Who's there?" he whispered.

A boot scraped against the dirt. "It don't matter," came the hoarse reply.

Jacob pushed the window open farther and started to lean out.

"Hold it," said the disembodied voice. "I've got some information to pass on, but I don't want to give myself away. Don't strike a match; don't try to see who I am. Agreed?"

"Okay." Jacob drew back inside. "I'm listening." He heard a whisper of sound, as though the other man shifted his position closer to the window.

"Those rustlers you've been after? They've got the makings of a herd bunched up in a box canyon back in the foothills at the north end of Broken Box range. They're getting ready to move them out soon. They're talking about calling it quits after selling this herd. They know they're pushing their luck, running the operation this long, and they're ready to move on."

Jacob clutched the windowsill with his free hand. "Where? When?"

"Late Friday night. There's going to be a full moon. They plan to push them over the mountain, then sell them to the mines and some of the army posts over in New Mexico. If you want to catch them, that's the time to do it."

"How do you know all this, and why should I believe you?"

"I've been a part of it almost from the beginning, but I can't do it anymore. Some good people are getting hurt, and it's been eating at me. I'm pulling out tonight."

"You know who they are. Give me some names."

"No." The emphatic tone told Jacob there would be no point in arguing. "I'm not that much of a traitor. You want to catch them, you get out there and do it. That's all I'm going to tell you."

Jacob fought back the urge to reach out through the window and choke the information out of the man. "Just one name then. Who's the leader?"

Gravel crunched and footsteps faded away into the night.

Jacob stuck his head outside and peered into the darkness. He saw the faint outline of a shadow melding into the deeper gloom, then nothing.

He stared up at the three-quarter moon. By Friday, it would be full, giving the rustlers plenty of light to move the stolen cattle.

And giving him plenty of light to put a crimp in their plans.

Jacob smiled and stretched out on his bed again, too wide-awake to think of sleep. He had plans of his own to make.

Chapter 13

Monday morning, Jacob rose with the sun, surprised he'd gone back to sleep at all after his midnight visitor. He made a quick breakfast of biscuits and coffee, then saddled his mount and rode south from the ' Bar in the direction of the Broken Box.

He took his time, studying the terrain with a new appreciation for the rus- ers' choice of location. It would be easy to drive stock from the other ranches 1 the area to this place. After a short push over Mingus Mountain, they would e able to hit well-traveled routes to the mines, army posts, or even Mexico. Vhoever was in charge of this outfit either laid his plans well or managed to tumble onto the perfect setup.

Cap seemed to pick up on his mounting excitement and moved into a risk trot. Jacob held him back to a more relaxed pace. No telling who might be vatching from behind rocks in these hills or from just inside the line of cedars. t wouldn't do to show undue interest in the area and take a chance on spooking is quarry.

Up ahead, a lone rider appeared over the top of a rise. An honest cowboy ust out doing his job or one of the rustlers? Jacob slouched back in his saddle nd adopted a bored expression, grateful the oncoming rider wouldn't be able to ee his heart hammering against his ribs. The rider waved, and Jacob returned he salute.

By the time they were thirty yards apart, Jacob recognized one of Edgar Vilson's riders. He pulled up and waited just west of a large rock formation.

"Morning," he greeted the lanky cowboy.

"Howdy. What are you doing over this way?"

"I'm supposed to see a fellow over in Camp Verde. Is there a quicker way ver Mingus than just following the road to Jerome?"

The cowboy shook his head. "Nah, this is probably your best bet. If you vanted a way that isn't as steep, you could cut over to Cherry and go around that vay, but that'll be farther and take longer to get there."

Jacob nodded his thanks, then touched his heels to Cap's flanks and set off again. At the rock formation, he twisted around to see if the other rider was vatching before moving to put the stack of broken boulders between himself nd the cowboy. To his relief, the other man seemed to be riding away with a otal lack of concern.

Jacob eased Cap toward the right side of the trail, then slipped in among some brush and faded into the tree line.

From his earlier studies of Buckey's map, he had a fair idea of where to loo for those box canyons, but he needed to determine their exact locations. He picke his way through the rough terrain until he found a rocky promontory. Tetherin Cap at its base, he climbed to the top and sat cross-legged at the summit.

Perfect. The higher elevation gave him a bird's-eye view of the whole are He took out his field glasses and proceeded to sweep the area. He took it in sma sections, examining a bit at a time, checking for movement of cattle or horseme When he headed back down and started investigating, he would need to kno just how to get to the box canyons. And he wanted to make sure he'd be alone.

He spent the better part of an hour checking things out and getting a fe for the lay of the land. From his vantage point, he spotted three likely lookin canyons. The hint of a trail appeared to lead toward the farthest one.

Jacob lowered the glasses and studied the approach to that area. If he wante to hide a bunch of cows, that spot would be a prime choice. He would check a three canyons, though, to be thorough. Anticipation at the thought of final getting the goods on his quarry made his pulse pound.

He clambered back down the steep slope and mounted Cap. He took hi time and chose what he thought would be the least visible route. He hadn spotted a soul out there apart from Wilson's rider but couldn't be positive n one sat watching him. "Come on, boy," he whispered. "Let's go see what we ca find."

Thirty minutes later, he had eliminated the first canyon as a possibility. / thorough examination showed only a few tracks heading into it. From the canyo rim, he spotted one lone cow grazing down in the bottom.

He made a mental note of her description: one horn pointed up and on pointed down. The tip of the upright horn had been broken off at some poin That cow would be easy to recognize if he ever saw her again. He pulled out hi glasses and looked for the brand. A Rafter Five. He'd have to remember that.

The second canyon yielded even less: no tracks, no sign, no livestock. With feeling of certainty welling up within him, Jacob pressed on toward the third.

Along the way, he spotted fresh tracks and cow flops. *This is it.* He guide Cap as close to the rim of the canyon as he dared to keep his own tracks fron being noticeable to anyone who might ride that way. And he felt sure there woul be someone. Every instinct told him this was the place.

Cap let out a soft whinny. "Easy, boy," he murmured. He stroked his hand along the steel-dust's neck. He hadn't seen signs of any other riders about, bu he didn't want to be surprised.

Spotting the glint of water on the canyon floor below, he pulled up and too a long look. A small pond shimmered in the sunlight. The earth around the poo had been churned into a patchwork of mud.

Beyond the pond, a brush fence stretched from one side of the canyon to he other. A trail led up to the line of brush, then reappeared on the other side. *Gotcha.* The tracks told the story. The cattle had been driven into the canyon, hen fenced in where they had abundant feed and water. And they were still own there, he knew it, just waiting to be moved on Friday night.

He dismounted and hunkered down in a clump of cliff rose so he could tudy the layout and determine his next move.

From deeper in the canyon, he heard lowing, and a line of cattle ambled into iew. Jacob swept the herd with his gaze and did a quick estimate. There must e upward of seventy-five head down there. If the rustlers got the going rate. . . Ie pursed his lips in a soundless whistle. That would add up to a nice chunk of noney. Depending on the number of people involved in this scheme, it could dd up to as much as several years' wages for each of them. Plenty of reason for ome men to ignore their scruples.

His sense of justice pushed for going down there right now and returning hose cattle to their rightful owners, but his better judgment held him back. Returning the stolen animals wouldn't bring the rustlers to justice. How often ad his father advised him to take his time and do things right? Waiting went gainst his grain, but he knew it was the right thing to do.

All right. He'd wait for Friday night and the full moon, then he would see t finished. He could have the whole matter resolved before he rode off for Cuba nd glory.

Jacob stood up and worked the stiffness out of his knees. He remounted and ode along the rim, seeking the entrance to the canyon and looking out for the est place to set up his ambush Friday night. More than likely, they'd bring in he last batch of cattle and slap on a road brand. That would cost them precious ime and give Jacob a chance to nab them.

Down there, he decided, where the canyon opened up to the valley beyond. The slope wasn't too steep and offered concealment in the form of scattered rush. He would lie in wait there and let them drive the cattle inside the canyon, hen stop the herd when they came back out.

He eased Cap through the trees to the edge of the meadow. Several likely lumps of manzanita and buckbrush caught his notice. Any one of them would make an excellent watching place.

Should he let anyone else in on his plans? Form a posse of trustworthy riders, perhaps? He considered the possibility but decided against it. The more people who knew about this, the greater risk of having someone give away information. Even if that were done unwittingly, it would still prove disastrous to his plan.

What about Dan? He discarded the idea almost as soon as it sprang into his mind. His lifelong knowledge of Dan's character left him in no doubt as to his friend's trustworthiness. But Dan had a wife and children, and cornering a group of desperate men could prove dangerous. Jacob had a feeling Amy wouldn't be any crazier about Dan taking on a bunch of rustlers than she was about the idea of him going off to war. No, he'd just have to do it alone.

He would arrive early and take up his position late Friday afternoon. Come full dark, he would be in a perfect spot to watch their every move.

In another four days, it would all be over. Jacob longed to get his hands on the miscreants who had been causing him such misery.

He glanced up at the sun's position. No point in continuing on the road to Jerome today. By the time he got to Camp Verde, it would be late.

But it didn't matter. A ripple of elation set his heart dancing. His sole purpose in talking to the rancher over there was to check with him about missing stock. With the lead his mysterious nighttime informant had given him, the trip over the mountain just might not be necessary after all.

Instead, he turned Cap in a wide loop and swung back by the Broken Box. It wouldn't hurt to put in an appearance and let Burke Evans know he'd been hard at work.

And there was always the chance he might see Hallie again—without having to sneak out to the wash this time.

⁂

The clang of a hammer on an anvil echoed throughout the yard when Jacob rode up. He spotted Burke shoeing a horse in the shade of the barn. The door of the house flew open at his approach, and Hallie trotted down the steps to greet him with a bright smile.

Burke started in their direction, still carrying the heavy hammer. Hallie pulled up and halted a few yards from Jacob. She settled a more demure expression on her face, but the light in her eyes didn't dim. Jacob felt his heart do flip-flops.

"Something you wanted to see me about?" Burke's lowered brows formed a hard, straight line over the bridge of his nose.

Jacob gave Hallie a quick smile and turned to Burke. "I wanted to let you know I've come up with some new information. There's a good chance I may be on their track at last."

The lines in Burke's face softened. "What have you found out?"

Jacob hesitated. Given Burke's hotheaded nature and tendency to shoot his mouth, did he want to trust him with the only decent lead that had come his way?

"I can't tell you anything definite right now," he hedged. "But I do have something pretty solid to go on this time." The answer sounded like a poor excuse, even to his ears.

Burke grunted and turned back toward the barn. "I've got to get back to that shoe while it's still hot. Not all of us can go lollygagging around, pretending we're working."

This isn't going well at all. If he ever wanted to make a connection with this man, he needed to start now. Jacob hesitated and glanced back and forth between Burke and Hallie. Tempting as it would be to stand visiting with Hallie, the better choice would be to start mending fences. He turned and followed Burke.

Hallie threw him a quizzical glance, then trailed after both of them. She dragged an empty crate over to the shade and sat on it not far from where her father worked.

Burke grabbed the red-hot horseshoe from the fire with a pair of tongs and held it on the anvil. He gave it a few more taps with the hammer, then held it up to check it against the old shoe.

After a minor adjustment or two, he dropped the shoe into a nearby bucket of water. Steam rose with a loud hiss. Burke slipped the tongs into a loop on the side of the anvil stand, then turned to Jacob and planted his meaty fists on his hips. "You got something else on your mind?"

"Not really." *This was really a stupid idea.* "I just thought we could visit a bit."

Burke snorted, then retrieved the tongs and fished in the bucket for the horseshoe. Water dripped off it to the ground, but no steam. Burke carried it to the tethered horse, where he checked the fit against the mare's hoof.

Still bent over beside the mare, he called over his shoulder, "So did you have anything to say, or were you just wanting to learn the right way to shoe a horse?"

Jacob felt his face grow warm. He'd come up with the bright idea of suggesting a visit; now he floundered for some topic of conversation. He glanced at Hallie, hoping for inspiration.

She shrugged, but gave him an encouraging nod and made hand gestures for him to continue.

"I guess you've heard the news about Cuba?" He flinched as soon as the words left his mouth. Of course Burke had heard the news. It was the topic on everyone's lips.

Burke picked up a rasp and leveled off the bottom of the horse's hoof. "Can't say I've paid much attention to it. I have enough problems of my own."

Jacob perked up. Finally, something he could sound knowledgeable about. "It looks like war is on the horizon. Mayor O'Neill is recruiting troops for a special Arizona regiment. I plan to sign up as soon as he's ready to accept volunteers."

Burke dropped the rasp and straightened slowly, his face growing redder by the second. He leveled a beefy forefinger at Jacob's chest and advanced toward him. "You mean to tell me you plan to take off and just leave this job hanging? Let me get this straight. You can tell me every last detail about what's going on, on some island nobody cares about, but you don't know the first thing about what's happening closer to home?"

He stepped nearer, so close that Jacob could smell the coal smoke that clung to him. "I want you to understand something, and understand it right now: I don't care about a bunch of foreign rebels three thousand miles away. I care about my cows!" A fresh wave of red crept up his face. "You don't seem to want to do your work, and I can't get mine done with you standing there jawing at me." He threw down the rasp and strode toward the house. "The mare can wait. I'll finish the job later."

Jacob stared after him, unable to look at Hallie. "I did a fine job of botching that, didn't I?"

Only silence met his question. He forced himself to meet her gaze.

She stared back at him, her face pale. "You're really planning to leave? Just like that?"

I'm doing a great job of breaking this news. "Riding gives a man plenty of time to think, and I've been doing a lot of that. We Americans have been blessed by God with the freedoms we have. It only seems right to help others who want to gain that same freedom. Don't you agree?"

Hallie looked down for a moment, then raised her head. Tears shimmered along her lower lashes. "In principle, yes. But I'm finding it's easy to agree with a principle when it doesn't cost you anything."

Jacob took her hands and drew her to her feet. Could her words mean what he hoped they did? She stared up at him, her eyes luminous pools of confusion. He pressed her hands against his chest. "This isn't a decision I've made lightly. I know we've barely had time to get to know each other, but leaving you is one of the hardest choices I've ever had to face. God brought us together, and I want to find out what He has in store for us."

Hallie's lips trembled. "I want that, too. But how is that going to happen if you go off to Cuba? You're willing to give your life for people you don't even know when there's so much here to live for."

He stared at the softness of her lips, longing to taste their sweetness. "Sometimes a man has to be willing to make a sacrifice."

"But it isn't just yours. You're asking your family. . .and me. . .to make that sacrifice, too. You want us to lay our happiness on the line, and we don't get to make that choice for ourselves."

Jacob lowered his head until he could feel the soft brush of her breath against his cheek. "Will you wait for me, Hallie? It shouldn't take long."

She pulled back slightly and stared at him as if fixing that moment in her mind for all eternity. "I feel like I've been waiting for you all my life. I'll still be waiting when you come back." Her voice quavered. "Just make sure you do come back."

Jacob pressed his lips against her eyelids, then crushed her against him in a tight embrace. "I'll come back to you, Hallie. I promise."

He felt her arms slide around his shoulders, and she pressed her face into the hollow of his neck. "I'll be praying," she whispered.

Chapter 14

The sun shone bright in a cloudless sky, and a light breeze filtered down through the cedars. A perfect spring afternoon, and all the more perfect because she could spend it outdoors. Hallie kicked Gypsy into a lope and reveled in the joy of being out on her own. She had plenty of time to herself at the house, but it wasn't the same as being outside where she could look across the rolling hills.

Somehow, prayer didn't come as easily at home when she found chores waiting for her everywhere she turned. Prayer was what she needed just now, and lots of it. In the four days since Jacob told her of his intention to march off to Cuba, she'd needed nothing more than time like this to pour out the cry of her heart to the Almighty.

"He's the one I've prayed for all my life, Lord. Am I going to lose him before we ever get the chance to discover this love You've given us?"

Her breath caught in her throat. *Did I say "love"?* "I do love him," she whispered. Then she threw her head back and said it right out loud. "I love Jacob Garrett!"

Her joy dimmed when she thought of their last conversation. "Please, God, isn't there any way You can keep him from going to war? I do want the Cuban people to have freedom. I think that's what You want, too. But I don't want to risk Jacob for them to have it."

She pulled Gypsy down to a walk and asked the question that had tormented her for the past four days: "Is it fair for me to ask You to keep him home when so many other women will be sending their loved ones off?"

Desire for Jacob warred with the desire to honor her Lord. "But I don't have any 'right' to him, do I? Jacob belongs to You and You alone."

A sigh of surrender escaped her. "All right. You win. I'll try to accept Your will in this, whatever it may be. And I leave Jacob. . .and our love. . .in Your hands."

She swept her fingers across her cheeks to brush the tears away and tried to regain her joy in being out on her own. At one time, her afternoon rides had been her delight. How long had it been since she'd enjoyed the freedom to come up into the foothills alone like this?

Since Pete Edwards started trying to push himself on me? The words flashed through her mind like a bolt of lightning. She rolled her shoulders as if she could shrug off the sudden impulse to look behind her. Pete wasn't anywhere around today. He and the other hands had been checking the grass at the south end of the range since Wednesday.

What a contrast! On the one hand, there was Pete and his unwelcome overtures. On the other, Jacob, with his tender heart and caring ways. Two more opposite men would be hard to imagine.

Hallie closed her eyes and breathed in the cedar-scented air. The first moment she laid eyes on Jacob, she sensed someone special had entered her life. *I just didn't dream how special. Please, God, don't take him away just when I've found him.*

Gypsy slowed when she reached the bottom of the slope, as if waiting for direction. Hallie glanced over her shoulder at the house and barn in the distance and wondered whether she should turn back or proceed up through the trees.

Her sense of adventure won out. She hadn't been up in the hills in months. She nudged Gypsy into a trot and rode uphill.

She smelled it before she saw it—the acrid stench of smoke. Hallie straightened in her saddle and peered around, probing the woods with her gaze. Where was it coming from? A brush fire could get out of hand more rapidly than anyone could imagine; the blackened area near the top of the hill attested to that. Hallie remembered watching from the safety of the ranch yard three years before, praying her father and the cowboys would get it under control before it could sweep across the plain, consuming everything in its path. She couldn't let that happen again.

She pushed deeper into the trees. *Where is it?* And could she put it out alone once she found it? Hallie's stomach clenched, and a dozen thoughts spun through her mind. Her father was moving one of the bulls to a different section, two miles or more away. How long would it take to track him down and bring back help?

Too long. She had no choice; she would have to take care of it alone.

Hallie tilted her head back and scanned the sky. *There.* Not far ahead, a thin gray thread of smoke snaked up through the trees.

She started to spur her horse forward, then frowned. That seemed an odd place for a fire to start. Could some drifter have gone off and left a campfire unattended?

He'd have to be an idiot to do something like that, as dry as it gets around here. But not everyone understood the possibilities of wildfire—or cared. However the fire started, Hallie had to check it out. She guided Gypsy uphill, weaving her way through the cedars.

The thick trees opened up onto a flat grassy area. Hallie heard a calf bawl somewhere ahead of her. Then she spotted it: slate-colored smoke seeming to rise from the ground. She looked again and realized it was coming up over the edge of a small canyon.

Prickles of unease danced along her arms. She could think of only one reason a fire and bellowing cows would go together: branding. But all their cowboys were busy on the south range.

Fear squeezed her throat. She slid off Gypsy and dropped the reins to the ground. "Wait here," she whispered, sliding her hand along the mare's glossy neck.

Hallie crouched and crept across the ground, careful not to make a sound that would give away her presence. Ten feet from the lip of the canyon, she dropped down and covered the rest of the distance on all fours.

She approached the edge gingerly. Even before she reached it, the telltale smell of singed hair assailed her nostrils, and she knew her suspicions had been correct. Someone was branding cows in the canyon, and none of the Broken Box hands were in the area. It could mean only one thing: She had found the rustlers.

Now what? It would be absurd to even contemplate trying to capture them on her own. But she had to do something. *What?* She flattened out, pressing her chest against the dirt, and inched nearer to the edge. If she could actually witness them at work, get descriptions of them or their horses, she could pass that information to Jacob. Finally, he would have something solid to work with. Elated at the thought, she raised her head high enough to peer over the dirt ledge.

A hiss of disappointment escaped her lips. A clump of cedars grew along the bottom of the shallow canyon. Their tops rose up directly in front of her, blocking her view. She would have to find a better vantage point. Drawing back slightly, Hallie pushed herself along a course parallel to the canyon rim.

Muffled voices floated upward. "Two more to go, then we'll run these on back with the others."

Hallie's stomach knotted. If she didn't hurry, they would leave before she could get a look at them.

A small clump of sagebrush stood near her. She reached out to grasp a branch and pulled herself up to the rim. The trees thinned out at that point. If she pushed herself forward just a bit, she ought to have an unobstructed view.

She inched forward. The ground crumbled away under her hands, sending a thin stream of dirt trickling down the twenty feet to the canyon floor below. Hallie scrambled back, heart pounding at her near escape. She pressed her knee into the dirt for better purchase and felt the ground beneath her shift, then give way.

Hallie clawed at the dirt frantically, desperate to find a handhold. Her fingers grasped the branch and she hung on. The stout bush held firm for a few moments, then she watched as the roots pulled free of the soil.

She slithered down the slope, her fingers digging into the loose soil. *Jesus, help me!* It took all her willpower not to scream the prayer aloud. Maybe by some miracle the rustlers wouldn't hear her bumpy descent.

Her body slammed against a rock, knocking the wind out of her and loosening her tenuous hold on the canyon wall. With nothing to slow her fall, she began to roll downhill with increasing speed. Branches tore at her clothing as she crashed through a tangle of bushes and landed in a heap on the canyon floor.

They know I'm here. No one could have missed the racket she had made on the way down. Hallie lay as she had landed, face down, hardly daring to breathe.

Heavy footsteps pounded across the dirt. Hallie lay motionless and prayed for God to intervene.

She glimpsed two pairs of denim-clad legs approaching. *Please, Lord, don't let them see me.* She squeezed her eyes shut.

Chapter 15

"Well, what do we have here?" A harsh voice spoke from a point in front of her, dashing her hopes.

"Looks like we've got us a visitor." The second speaker drew nearer, and his voice tightened. "Ain't that the Evans girl? What's she doing out this way?"

Hallie heard other footsteps behind her. A hand gripped the back of her head and shoved her face into the dirt. "Get a rope." She could barely make out the deep, gravelly voice over the thrum of blood pounding in her ears. "We'll hogtie her now and take care of her when we're finished here."

No! Hallie brought her hands up under her shoulders and pushed against the ground with all her might, but she couldn't raise herself an inch.

Her captor chuckled. "Won't do you a bit of good," he rasped. "Me and the boys are used to tying calves all day long, and calves are a lot bigger and stronger than a little thing like you."

As if to prove his point, the cowboy's rough hands seized her wrists from behind and bound them together with a few quick twists of rope. Hallie kicked and struggled, but she was no match for the men. She gasped for air and drew in a lungful of dust. She flailed wildly with her feet and felt her boot connect with something solid.

One of the men cursed. "That's enough. We'll see how much you can kick when I get through with you."

Hallie felt her ankles gripped and lashed together. Then her feet were yanked up toward her back and bound to the rope holding her wrists.

"There. That ought to take care of her."

"Just a minute." The deep-voiced man kept his hold on the back of her head. "It won't do a bit of good to tie her if she can still get a look at us." He pressed his knee into the middle of her back, holding her immobile while he wound a kerchief around her head and pulled it tight over her eyes.

"That's better." He stood, releasing the pressure on her back. "Let's get back to work."

Hallie rolled onto her side, spitting gobs of dust out of her mouth, fighting for air.

"Did you hear me?" the rough voice growled. "Get back to work!"

"Wait a minute." It was the first voice she had heard, now thin and tense. "What are we going to do with her?"

"We're going to finish what we've started, then you boys can get out of here. I'll see about letting her go. . .if she promises to behave herself."

The footsteps moved away, and Hallie heard a new set of noises: scuffles and thumps, the sound of something heavy being dragged across the earth, the sizzle of burned flesh, then a plaintive bawl.

They're altering brands. She heaved in great gulps of air, trying to calm herself. She had to think, to focus.

If they were going to kill her, they would have done it already. She was safe, at least for the moment.

But they can't just let me go. I know too much. Her chest tightened with the dull ache of fear.

"I knew things had gone too easy for us," the first speaker worried aloud. "Just when we're ready to wrap the operation up, look what happens. Maybe we oughta just pull out with what we've already got instead of waiting for tonight."

"Shut up! One more night means more money than any of us could make in three years of punching cows. I don't intend to quit before we've got all we can handle. Just leave it to me. I'll deal with her."

"You ain't going to kill her, are you?" Footsteps crunched on loose rock, and the voices grew softer.

Hallie strained to hear.

"And get the whole country out after us? Of course I ain't going to kill her." He chuckled. "Here's a thought: Maybe I'll take her along and send back word we've eloped."

His companions snickered.

A low moan escaped Hallie's throat. Maybe death wasn't the worst thing she had to fear.

She had to get away. If she could just reach one of the knots. . . No good. Her fingers had gone numb.

Hallie wriggled and strained against the knots. All she succeeded in doing was make the rope cut more deeply into her wrists. She rolled over to her other side, desperate for relief from the constant pull against her limbs. Her shoulders felt like they were being wrenched from their sockets.

"Let's get this bunch up the canyon with the rest. Then we'll call it good until tonight."

"What about the girl?"

Hallie froze.

"I told you, I'll take care of her when we get back. She ain't going nowhere." The creak of saddle leather was followed by horses snorting and the cowboys yipping as they moved the cows along.

Gritting her teeth against the raw pain in her shoulders, Hallie squirmed with all her might, but the knots held fast. Her desperation mounted. She had to get away. She *had* to!

Maybe she could find a sharp rock, something she could use to cut through the ropes. If she could only see! Hallie rubbed her face against the ground, trying to pull the blindfold loose.

She felt the vibration under her cheek before she heard the patter of feet running toward her. Determination gave way to despair, and the strength drained from her limbs. She had given it her best, but she had lost. She braced herself for what would come next.

Light fingers brushed against her hands and tugged at the ropes. "Hold still," a small voice ordered. "I had to make sure they were gone before I came down here. We've got to hurry before they come back."

"Wha— Who—"

"Oh, sorry." The knots on the kerchief loosened, and the blindfold fell free. Hallie blinked and squinted at the sun's glare. *"Catherine?"*

The young girl squatted beside Hallie, the tip of her tongue peeking out from between her lips as she concentrated on picking the knots apart. "Roll over a little farther. Maybe I can get at the rope better that way."

Hallie complied. "What are you—never mind, we'll sort that out later. Can you get the knots undone?"

"I'm trying. Almost done. . . There!" She sat back on her heels with a look of triumph. "Good thing Dad taught me something about knot tying, huh?"

Hallie brought her hands around in front of her and massaged her tender wrists, wincing at the pins-and-needles sensation when the blood flowed back into her hands. When she regained some command over her fingers, she forced herself to sit up and reached for the rope still holding her ankles. She picked at the knots and pulled the rope free, then flung it aside.

"Where's your horse?"

Catherine pointed toward the rim of the canyon. "Up on top, next to yours." She helped Hallie to her feet. "I was out looking for the calf Dad gave me last summer, and I came across a fresh trail. Looked like three or four head being driven this way."

Hallie attempted a couple of steps on her tottery legs. The pain from her abused muscles nearly drove her to her knees. Catherine put her arm around Hallie's waist, and she accepted the little girl's help gratefully. "How are we going to get out of here?"

Catherine pointed up ahead. "There's a trail over on the other side of those trees. We can climb up to the top that way and get our horses."

She led Hallie a few more steps and picked up the thread of her story. "Uncle Jacob is always complaining about not finding any fresh sign, so I thought I'd trail these a ways and maybe catch the rustlers. Then I saw you riding over this way and decided I'd catch up to you, instead."

She pulled at Hallie, urging her up the slope.

"But then I saw the smoke and saw you get down off your horse and start crawling on the ground." She giggled, then sobered. "I got worried when you rolled off the edge into the canyon, so I thought I'd better come see if you were all right." A grin flashed across her tanned cheeks. "Good thing I checked, isn't it?"

They reached the top with Hallie blowing like a winded horse.

"Catherine O'Roarke, I ought to tan your hide, but I'm too happy to see you." The feeling was starting to come back into her legs. She tried to ignore the sharp ache by reminding herself it would help her keep her balance in the saddle, assuming she could lift her leg high enough to reach the stirrup.

After two unsuccessful attempts, Catherine planted her shoulder against Hallie's backside and braced herself. "Ready? One, two, three. . .up!"

Hallie flopped into her saddle with all the grace of a sack of potatoes. She clung to the saddle horn for a long moment, trying to control the tremor in her limbs. "Where did you learn that little trick?"

Catherine shrugged. "It just seemed like the thing to do."

Hallie collected herself. She couldn't give in to weakness now, not when the rustlers could return at any moment. She gathered her reins. "Come on. We've got to get out of here."

They ran their horses for half a mile before Hallie felt safe enough to slow down a bit. She looked over at Catherine. "Did you see them?"

"Just their hats and the backs of their shirts. They pulled bandannas over their faces, remember?"

"Oh." She hadn't seen much of anything except clods of dirt, two pairs of legs, then blackness when the blindfold was tied around her face. Why had they bothered to cover her eyes if they were already masked?

She checked her surroundings to assess their location, then gave Catherine a sharp glance. "How did you get this far on your own? You must be a good three miles from home. Your parents are going to be frantic."

Catherine's face folded into a frown, then brightened. "You'd better come back home with me and tell everybody how I saved you. Then I won't be in trouble." She scrunched her forehead. "Well, not as much, anyway."

Chapter 16

Hallie dug her heels into Gypsy's flanks and cast a worried glance at the late afternoon sky. If she hoped to make it home before dusk, she would have to sprout wings and fly. Bending low over the gray mare's neck, she urged the horse on to a reckless pace. She didn't have a moment to lose.

Taking Catherine home had cost her precious time, but she couldn't in good conscience let the child go back alone. Not when there were ruffians about. Dan and Amy hadn't been home when they clattered up into the yard, much to Catherine's relief. Hallie's, too, if she were being honest. It saved her from having to explain her disheveled appearance and dust-coated clothing.

Hallie left the little girl with Benjamin, with strict instructions that neither of them was to leave the house until their parents returned.

Jacob hadn't been there, either, and hearing that sent a fresh wave of misery washing over her. With all her heart, she wanted to give him the information that would let him make an arrest and put an end to the matter.

Be honest, Hallie. You wanted him to take you in his arms and make what happened back in the canyon seem like a bad dream. Well, yes, there was that, she admitted. But right now her main focus was set on seeing the rustlers apprehended so they could pay for their crime. If she couldn't let Jacob know, she had to get word to her father.

The canyon where the stolen cattle were hidden lay southeast of the T Bar and northeast from the Broken Box. Hallie angled her horse behind a series of low hills on the west edge of the valley to keep from being seen. The wind rushed by her head, loosening her braid and setting her hair free to flow behind her like a dark ribbon.

Gypsy was laboring now, breathing hard with every step. "Hang on, girl," Hallie crooned. "It isn't much farther." The house and barn loomed up ahead.

Drawing nearer, she could see her father pulling the saddle from his favorite mount. "Pa!" she screamed.

Burke's mouth rounded in disbelief when Gypsy pounded up beside him. "What's gotten into you, girl? You know better than to lather a horse like that."

Hallie sagged over the mare's neck and struggled for breath. "The rustlers, Pa. I found them. They've got the cows penned up in the box canyon up near that old burn. They're going to move them out tonight."

Burke gaped as though staring at an apparition. "How do you know that?"

Here came the hard part. He'd be mad enough to shoot the rustlers on sight

313

anyway. If she told him how she'd been manhandled, she didn't want to think what he might do. "I heard them talking," she said simply. *Please don't let him ask me how.*

"Did you get a good look at them?"

Hallie shook her head. "I couldn't see them clearly." That was true enough.

Burke settled the saddle on his horse's back again and tightened the cinch.

"You're not going out after them alone, are you?" Worry stretched her voice reed thin.

"You see anyone around who's going to help me? I'm going to get my cows back and see some thievin' coyotes get their just desserts." He swung into the saddle and checked the rifle in its scabbard.

Sudden panic seized Hallie. *Of course he's going after them himself. What did you expect him to do?* "Please, Pa. Don't do anything foolish."

"They're the ones who've been the fools, not me." He kicked his horse into a gallop and rode off, grim determination written in every line of his bearing.

Hallie twisted her fingers through Gypsy's mane and watched him until the gathering dusk obscured him from view. "Keep him safe, Lord. Don't let him get hurt. . .or hurt anybody else."

The sun hung low in the western sky when Jacob arrived at the box canyon. He rode along the rim until he found the spot where the canyon opened out onto the range. Below him he could see the smoldering remains of a fire.

Worry tightened his throat. Was he too late after all?

Faint lowing from deep within the canyon reassured him. They hadn't left yet. He tied Cap in a thick clump of cedars some distance from the canyon mouth, pulled his rifle from its scabbard, and unhooked his lariat from his saddle horn.

Dragging a huge fallen limb to the canyon's brink, he stood it on end and propped it up against a tree trunk. He tied a secure knot around the middle and looked for a likely place from which to watch.

Over there, by that low-hanging cedar. He ducked under the drooping branches and braced his back against the rough trunk. With his Winchester propped across his knees and the free end of the rope in one hand, he settled in to wait.

His chosen position put him at the edge of the rim with an unobstructed view of this end of the canyon without putting him in harm's way. No point in giving them the opportunity to push those cows right over him. There wouldn't be enough left of him to scrape up and send home. He scooted around to make himself more comfortable, then focused his gaze on the point where they would drive the cattle out around the bend.

For the dozenth time, he hoped he hadn't made the mistake of the century by not taking anyone into his confidence. It seemed the right thing to do, back when he made the decision without the pressure of this moment on him. In the here and now, though, the odds of one man against a group of unknown size seemed painfully evident.

It would work out all right, he reassured himself. It had to. He went over his plans again. He'd known from the first that what he lacked in strength of numbers he would have to make up for in cleverness.

Knowing that, he'd taken a leaf from one of his favorite Old Testament stories. When the lead cows reached that scrawny cedar in the middle of the canyon, he would yank the rope to send the log crashing down below and create enough noise to convince them they faced an entire posse. If it worked for Gideon against the Midianites, it ought to work here.

If they didn't stop, he would place a bullet close enough to one of their horses to make it rear. If he could get just one rider on the ground, he could at least work on that one to get the names of the others.

The sun finished its descent behind Granite Mountain and the shadows lengthened. Silence settled over the canyon. Jacob shifted again and stretched his legs. He couldn't afford to be stiff when it came time to move.

A silver disk inched its way over the top of Mingus Mountain. Jacob watched the glowing circle slide upward until the whole valley lay washed in moonlight. He flexed his fingers and rolled his shoulders. Any time now. There was plenty of light for the rustlers' purpose. . .and for his.

He waited in the stillness, wanting them to come and dreading it at the same time. Numbness threatened his legs and had already defeated his backside. As he sat alone in the dark, doubts beset him again. Should he have asked for help, after all? Was his not doing so motivated by wisdom—or pride?

He heard the click of hoof on stone and felt his heart race. Too late now for second-guessing. A horse whickered. Low voices murmured. Jacob stiffened, all his senses on full alert. He gripped the rope, rose to his feet, and cocked his Winchester.

And waited some more. Jacob fidgeted with the rope end. The sound of many hooves echoed around the bend. Suddenly he saw the moonlight glint off dozens of horns.

This is it. Be with me, Lord. Against the silver-washed canyon floor, he could make out a sizable herd and three mounted riders pushing them forward.

Jacob held back a shout of exultation. He tightened his grip on the rope and waited until the lead cow neared the scraggly cedar.

Closer. . .closer. . .now! Jacob jerked the rope. The limb teetered on the brink of the canyon, then tipped over the edge and tumbled downward, picking up speed and pulling a shower of gravel down with it as it went.

Jacob stepped as close to the rim as he dared and shouldered the Winchester. "Hold it right there! We've got you covered. Throw down your guns."

He watched the three riders freeze, their doubt a palpable thing. Without warning, hooves pounded on the far side of the canyon.

One of the rustlers threw a shot up toward Jacob; another shot toward th opposite wall where the newcomer could be heard.

Who's over there? He couldn't take time to wonder. Jacob took aim, ready snap a shot in front of the nearest horse. He aimed at a point five feet ahead its front hooves and fired.

A gunshot cracked from the other side of the canyon. Jacob's leg went o from under him, and he teetered on the edge, then plummeted over the side.

Jacob lay still in the darkness, listening to the sounds of hooves pounding an riders yelling, and tried to get his bearings. The cattle were stampeding. He coul hear their frightened bellows and the mad scramble of hooves.

He lay on the canyon floor with a mouthful of dirt and enough bruises make him sore for a week. And he'd lost his rifle on the way down.

Hoofbeats drummed across the ground and faded into the distance. *They getting away!* Jacob jumped to his feet, but his leg gave way again, this time wit a stabbing pain that made him cry out. He grabbed at his thigh and felt a stick wetness under his palm.

A lone set of hoofbeats approached, making their way across the uneve ground. Jacob drew back against the canyon wall and scrabbled in the dirt fo his rifle.

"Come on out of there, you lowlife. I know I got you; I saw you fall."

Jacob shifted his weight and let out a groan. He heard a scatter of rocks an the sound of boots pounding across the ground. Moonlight shone on the barr of a Winchester much like his own, pointed straight at him. Jacob looked up int the triumphant face of Burke Evans.

Chapter 17

Clouds scudded across the leaden sky. Jacob pulled his coat tighter around his neck to ward off the blustery wind. He took two halting steps forward and looked down with distaste at the cane in his hand.

"It's only for a little while," Dr. Haskins had told him. "Just until those torn muscles heal." The doctor pulled at the ends of his white mustache. "It's a good thing that bullet didn't nick any bones, young man. You'd really be in bad shape then. You have a lot of deep bruising, and you won't be sitting a saddle anytime soon, but you're young and healthy. As long as infection doesn't set in, you'll be right as rain before long."

And what is the good doctor's definition of "before long"? Jacob tried to adopt a jaunty air, as though he carried the cane for show and not because he'd be sure to fall flat on his face without it. He swung his injured leg forward and staggered, putting an end to his attempt at nonchalance.

It had been nearly a week already. Jacob grimaced and forced himself to walk a few more steps. He'd never been laid up more than a day or two at a time before, certainly never faced the prospect of being out of commission for an extended period of time. The thought didn't set well with him, especially now.

Over on the plaza, people were beginning to gather. Jacob hobbled across the street to join them. He couldn't bear to miss this day; at the same time, he wished he could be almost anywhere else. The pressure of the bandage made the wound throb. He set his jaw and kept walking. If he could stand the jouncing wagon ride into town the night Burke shot him and the way Doc Haskins ran that rod through the wound to clean out any debris, he could endure this comparatively minor pain.

The doctor might be pleased about the location of the wound, away from any major blood vessels, but he didn't have to cope with the difficulty it caused Jacob. The bullet entered the side of his upper right thigh and exited just below his hip. Doc might be justified in his pleasure over it not nicking any bones, but Jacob could think of better places for it. Its placement made walking difficult and sitting in a saddle—or nearly anywhere else—impossible.

Jacob checked his pocket watch, then snapped it shut and replaced it in his vest. Three thirty. The crowd was growing larger by the minute. He wavered at the edge of the street. Maybe he should go to his room and forget the whole thing.

No. He had to see this through.

"Came to see us off, did you?"

Jacob used his cane to pivot around and saw Buckey O'Neill standing before him. The mayor's dark eyes shone with a sympathetic light.

"Wouldn't miss it." Jacob forced a smile, then dropped all pretense at pleasantries. "Go ahead and swear me in, Buckey. Let me go with you. This thing won't take long to heal. I'll be fit for duty before we get on the boat for Cuba."

Buckey's smile dimmed. "If I had my choice, I'd like nothing more than to take you with me, but I can't."

"But you know I intended to sign up the day after this happened." He gestured at his wounded leg. "I'm practically a part of the group already."

Buckey shook his head. "The requirements are that recruits be able-bodied and physically fit for duty, and right now. . ." He nodded at Jacob's cane. "Regulations. I'm sorry."

Jacob's shoulders sagged. "I know. I just had to try."

"You're right, though. You'll be back in the saddle in no time." Buckey's voice took on a more jovial tone. "I'll rest better in Cuba, knowing you're helping to take care of things here at home. You're a good man, Jacob. I'll be seeing you soon. It shouldn't take us more than three months to whip the Spaniards and be home again. One of these days, we'll be celebrating statehood together."

"Buckey!" shouted a man across the grounds. "We're ready to muster the troops. We need you with your men."

Buckey gave Jacob a quick wave and trotted across to where some men stood in a cluster along the north edge of the square.

Jacob watched the men try to form some semblance of order. All walks of life and manner of dress were represented in the group. They might not look like much of a military unit now, but he knew these men, knew their hearts. With a little training, they'd shape up to be as fine a company as ever served the country.

A lump swelled in Jacob's throat. Pride or longing? He couldn't tell which. He swallowed hard and pushed his way through the jubilant throng. Women stepped aside to let him pass, glancing at him, then his cane, then quickly away. Jacob gritted his teeth.

He took up a casual stance next to the bandstand, where the Fort Whipple band was in full swing. Might as well look like he was enjoying the music. Not a care in the world, not he. No one would have reason to think he attended the ceremony as anything but a well-wisher, nor suspect the fierce disappointment that burned within him.

The band music ceased, and the stirring tones of a cornet pierced the air. Jacob turned to look, along with everyone else. A young boy, no more than fourteen, held the instrument to his lips. The plaintive notes drifted over the plaza.

A man standing in front of Jacob turned to his companion. "Isn't that the band master's boy?"

His friend nodded. "LaGuardia's been a real boon to Fort Whipple. It's a shame he's leaving along with the rest. And this young fellow has his father's gift for music, that's for sure. If he keeps it up, he might make a real name for himself someday."

While the last notes still hung in the air, the young lad trotted down the bandstand steps. His father nodded at him with obvious pride. Jacob heard him whisper, "Good job, Fiorello," before taking up his baton and striking up the band again.

The boy's shoulders straightened proudly. Jacob watched him walk past, remembering when the prospects for his own future looked just as bright. His lips tightened. Not so long ago, he felt he was on the verge of capturing the rustlers and bringing them to justice; he had found the love of his life; and he planned to march off with the local troops and bring freedom to a captive people. *It just goes to show you how everything can change in a heartbeat.*

The men marched out of step to form ragged ranks across the plaza's north lawn. Jacob clenched his teeth together so hard he could hear them grate. *They're ready to go. And I should be with them.*

Bitterness choked him. They all stood on the same grounds on the same day, but he wasn't one of their number. And why? *Because some bullheaded rancher who didn't think I was man enough to do my job shot my leg out from under me.*

The crowd stirred and someone jostled his elbow. "Hello there."

Hallie Evans smiled up at him, her dark brown eyes shining with pleasure. The sight of her upturned face only added to his black mood. He tried to hold his feelings back. She had come, like the rest, to join in the patriotic fervor and send the able-bodied men on their way.

He gritted his teeth again. Not even to Hallie would he admit just how raw his feelings were. "So you came to see the troops off, did you?"

"No." She pressed closer to him. "I came to see you."

Came to see him, a cripple and a failure? Jacob stared at her intently. "Why?"

Her answer was drowned out by the swell of applause as the governor was introduced. Jacob worked his jaw and tried to focus his attention on the solemn proceedings going on just in front of them.

He had to settle for trying to look like his attention was focused there. Hallie's nearness drove all other thoughts from his mind. Jacob nodded and clapped along with the crowd during Governor McCord's address to the troops. He cheered when the governor presented Buckey with an American flag sewn by the ladies of the Women's Relief Corps of Phoenix.

He managed to applaud when Prescott's city attorney gave the departing mayor a tooled holster and engraved six-shooter and laughed along with the rest when the owner of the Palace Saloon presented the troops with a young mountain lion as a mascot.

And all the while, his whole being roiled in a tumult that rivaled the upheaval in Cuba. The speechmaking droned on. The crowd grew restless, but Jacob felt he could stand there all night, injured leg or no, as long as Hallie stood beside him.

And yet he stood there as one who could not serve his country or fight alongside comrades he admired. Desolation at being left behind threatened to consume him. He choked back the bitter taste of gall.

At last the ceremony ended. The band struck up a lively rendition of "Hot Time in the Old Town" and led the way north along Cortez Street to the depot, where a special Santa Fe, Prescott, and Phoenix Railway train awaited them. The new recruits straggled behind them in a ragtag version of a march. The cheering throng trailed along, shouting out exuberant words of encouragement.

Hallie moved as if to join the crowd, then hesitated. "Do you want to go or. . ."

He should have known. Jacob shook his head and bit back a hot retort. "Go ahead if you want to."

Hallie moved next to him and rested her hand on his arm. She seemed to be searching for words. "I know this is a big disappointment for you, having to see your friends go off together like that. But I look at them all." She took a deep breath and gestured in the direction the departing troops had taken. "I see how excited they are, but in my heart I know some of them won't be coming home."

She gave him a wobbly smile. "I guess God answers prayers in unusual ways sometimes."

In the distance, the band music faded away to be replaced by the sounds of the locomotive building up a head of steam. A chorus of voices took up the refrain "God Be with You Till We Meet Again." The solemn lyrics floated back to the plaza on the evening air.

Jacob stood without moving a muscle and stared at Hallie. Finally he lifted his cane and held it up between them. "You're saying you prayed for this to happen?"

A pink tinge flooded Hallie's face. "Having my father shoot you was hardly my idea of how to keep you here." She tilted her chin up in a gesture that reminded him of Catherine when she faced the consequences of some misdeed. "But I have to admit I'm grateful."

"Grateful." He felt an ominous calm settle over him. "Grateful that I've been turned into a useless cripple?"

"Better a cripple than a corpse," Hallie retorted.

Jacob stepped away from her. "What makes you so sure I would have gotten killed? I might have come back as an officer. At the very least, I'd know whether I could stand up to the sound of bullets whizzing past me without turning tail and running. I'd know that I'm a man." His tone grew rough. "And everyone else would know it, too."

Hallie spoke in a voice thick with emotion. "I said my prayers were answered, and I meant it, even though I never would have asked for you to be hurt. God really does know what's best, if you'll just let Him be in control instead of trying figure it all out on your own.

"Why do men have to be so bullheaded and determined to do things their ay?" She started to walk away, then looked back over her shoulder. "Don't you ow God cares about you, Jacob? He loves you even more than I do." She strode vay quickly, leaving Jacob standing alone in stunned silence.

~≈≈~

cob pushed open the door of the Ponderosa Café. "That's another fine meal," called to the proprietor. "I'll see you again this evening."

Stepping outside into the morning sunlight, he ran his finger along the side of his waistband. If he didn't get back to work pretty soon, he'd be looking ke some portly city slicker before he knew it.

He strolled along Cortez, still favoring his right leg. He'd seen significant provement, though. At least he could now walk unassisted. When he'd given the cane five days ago, he felt like dancing.

"Jacob? Jacob Garrett!" Lucas Rawlins waved from across the street.

Jacob limped across to greet him, and the two men exchanged a warm andshake.

"Good to see you!" Rawlins beamed. "How are you getting along? About ady to pick up where you left off?"

Jacob shook his head. "Doc says it'll be at least a few more days."

Rawlins's mustache drooped. "I'm sorry to hear that. It's been three weeks nce you got shot. We hoped you'd be back in the saddle by now."

Jacob gritted his teeth. Rawlins couldn't know how much he'd hoped the me thing. "So did I," he said mildly. "If that infection hadn't set in, I would ave been back at work a week or so ago. As it is, Doc says I'm lucky it wasn't iy worse."

"Mm." Rawlins chewed on his lower lip. "Things quieted down after that rush you had with the rustlers. We thought maybe you'd spooked them enough drive them out of the territory, but some of us have started losing stock again." Ie gave Jacob a long, measuring look. "I hope you're up and around again real oon."

Jacob watched him stride away. The breakfast he had so recently enjoyed ow lay in a congealed mass in his stomach. Did Rawlins think he'd considered is enforced time off some kind of vacation?

I'd like to tell him what it's like with nothing but time on your hands. To keep is legs from stiffening up on him, he walked the perimeter of the plaza several mes a day. By now, he'd become a familiar figure to the people whose businesses ced the town square. Familiar enough to receive smiles and nods every time he iade his circuit. But he hadn't missed the curious glances, the ones that asked hy he wasn't off with the troops.

Life had taken on an unfamiliar emptiness. In fact, the town itself felt empty ithout Buckey. The widely respected mayor's absence left a rent in the fabric

of community life, one that couldn't be filled by anyone else. Jacob sorely miss
being able to drop by Buckey's office to pass the time of day or exchange th
latest news.

And Buckey wasn't the only person he missed. Jacob hadn't seen Hall
since the day he growled at her over near the bandstand. The memory of h
ill-tempered behavior made him squirm. He'd lain awake every night since the
remembering her parting words, then wondering if he had imagined them. Wh
was she feeling now? Would she ever want to see him?

He couldn't blame her if she didn't. One brief moment on a moonlit nigl
had turned his world upside down. And all because of the impulsive, shoo
before-you-think actions of her father. If Burke's ill-conceived attempt to appre
hend the rustlers on his own led to the loss of Hallie's affection. . .

Jacob started another circuit around the plaza, more to work off his frustra
tion than for the exercise. Speculation was going to drive him round the ben
He had to get out to the Broken Box and find out for himself how Hallie fel
But how was he going to manage that?

He limped across the square to a sturdy bench and lowered himself carefull
wincing only slightly when his injured leg made contact with the wooden sea
That was an improvement. A week ago, he wouldn't have thought of sitting o
anything harder than a feather pillow, let alone considered trying a saddle.

A saddle? Where had that idea come from? The more he pondered it, th
more his resolve grew. He needed to see Hallie, regardless of the cost.

He could do it. He pushed himself up off the bench. Painful or not, he ha
to get out there. He headed toward the livery across the street from the sout
end of the plaza.

He would rent a horse and ride out to the Broken Box today. He'd mak
it, no matter what he had to endure. At the moment, any discomfort he migl
suffer paled in comparison with his concern over what he would say to Halli
and what her response might be.

He crossed the street lost in thought. A buggy wheel missed him by bar
inches, and a voice called, "Where do you think you're going?"

Jolted from his reverie, Jacob looked up to see Hallie perched on the bugg
seat. The sight of her brought a wave of pleasure so intense it shocked him
That joy was almost immediately replaced by profound embarrassment when h
remembered the churlish way he had behaved at their last meeting.

Hallie's lips parted in a wide smile, and light flooded back into Jacob's sou

He spoke before he could lose his nerve, watching for her reaction. "I wa
planning to rent a horse and come out to pay you a visit."

"Oh no, you don't." Hallie's dark braid swung from side to side when sh
shook her head. "I checked with Dr. Haskins. He told me any riding in a saddl
might tear that wound open again." Her mouth curved in an impish grin. "Bu
he said a buggy ride—on a nice, cushioned seat—might do you a world o

ood."

The light spread into every part of his being. A buggy ride with Hallie? Things were definitely looking up.

As though taking his hesitation for a refusal, she reached in the back of the buggy and held up a covered basket. "Fried chicken, biscuits, and dried apple pie," she announced. "We can go for a picnic. If you're interested, of course."

A buggy ride *and* a picnic? Only his game leg stopped Jacob from breaking into a jig. "I don't know," he teased. "I really ought to be trying to get some work done instead of going out for a pleasure ride."

Hallie grinned. "That's what my pa said. He offered to let you use our buggy while you're having trouble getting around."

"He *offered*?"

"Well, he did after I reminded him of the reason you couldn't be out riding." Hallie's lips twitched. "I thought maybe you'd want to drive around to some of the ranches after our picnic."

Jacob grinned and put his foot up on the buggy step. "Ma'am, you just made yourself a deal."

⚜

Jacob popped the last crumb of Hallie's flaky piecrust into his mouth and leaned back on one elbow. The edges of the checkered tablecloth she spread out to hold their repast rose, then lowered with every warm puff of breeze. Jacob sighed and stretched, feeling a sense of utter contentment he'd thought he might never experience again.

Hallie sat with her back resting against the broad trunk of one of the cottonwoods that dotted the banks of Granite Creek. Above them loomed the massive rock formations of the Granite Dells.

"I need to apologize for snapping at you the other day," Jacob said. "It wasn't easy to watch Buckey and the rest go off without me, but I had no call to take it out on you like that."

Hallie's lips stretched in the gentle smile that never failed to warm his heart. "That's already part of the past. I'd rather look ahead to the future, wouldn't you?"

"I'm not sure." The words came out without conscious thought on his part. He saw Hallie's startled look and tried to find a way to explain. "Just about the time I thought I had my future all mapped out, everything fell apart. I was going to put an end to that rustling operation; I was going to serve my country and help set a captive people free." *I was going to ask you to marry me.* He held that comment back. How could he even think about a future with Hallie when he'd made such a dismal failure of his present?

He cleared his throat and went on. "I had all these grand plans built up, and what happened to them? They've all turned to dust. I've failed at every one."

"Failed? Don't speak to me of failure, Jacob Garrett." Hallie reached out to

him and wrapped her fingers around his hand. "I know you've had some bitte
disappointments, but don't lose heart. It isn't over yet. You're going to com
through this all right, but you need to trust God."

Jacob drew his brows together. "Are you saying there's something wron
with the way I've been acting?"

"I'm saying you need to believe He has your best interests at heart, eve
if He doesn't have your life arranged the way you'd like it to be. He knows th
direction He wants your life to take. You need to ask Him to show you what i
is." She eyed him solemnly. "For both our sakes."

"All I want is to be able to finish the job I was hired to perform. Is that to
much to ask?" Bitterness edged his voice.

Hallie stood her ground. "Have you prayed and asked for an answer on hov
to deal with this, or are you just trying to figure it out all on your own?"

"We'd best get going if we plan to get any work done today. I'll help you pacl
this up." Jacob scooped up the plates and stacked them beside the basket, the
shook the crumbs out of the tablecloth.

Hallie loaded their dirty plates into the picnic basket without saying a word
But Jacob didn't miss the flash of disappointment that flitted across her face.

Chapter 18

I can't figure it." Tom Miller swept his hat from his head with his left hand and ran his right palm over his thinning hair. "They're disappearing without a trace, just like before. Some of my riders checked back around that canyon where you found them penned up the last time, but it looks like the thieves have already pulled out and moved that part of their operation somewhere else. That would be the sensible thing to do, at any rate, and it doesn't look like we're dealing with a pack of fools."

Jacob felt the familiar sinking sensation in his belly. "Do you have any thoughts on who might be behind this? Any at all?"

Miller pulled at his earlobe. "I keep wondering about those nesters holed up back away from everybody. There are plenty of blind canyons up that way, lots of room for them to keep a bunch of cattle on the quiet."

"I suppose it's possible," Jacob said. *Even if it isn't very likely.*

"They drift in and out," Miller continued. "They could leave here taking our stolen stock with them. The next place they light, they'll just be people who came in with some money in their pockets, and no one will be the wiser."

"I'll keep it in mind," Jacob promised. He picked up the reins and slapped them lightly on the horse's rump, turning the buggy back toward Prescott.

Hallie tapped her fingers together. "That's the third time today we've heard someone blame the nesters for this. What do you think?"

Jacob shook his head. "The ones I talked to didn't strike me as the type to do something like this." The sense of failure settled over him again like a pall. But maybe they're just pulling the wool over my eyes. It wouldn't surprise me a bit."

Hallie fell silent and stared off in the direction of Thumb Butte.

Jacob winced when the buggy wheel jolted in and out of a rut in the road. He shifted on the cushion, trying to find a more comfortable position. As tender as his backside felt, the pain in his heart felt worse. He would give anything to be able to take back that last remark, or at least remove the surly tone from his voice. Hallie didn't deserve that, didn't deserve the sour attitude he'd been showing ever since the night his dreams of success ended with the crack of a Winchester.

What Hallie deserved. . .his heart swelled. She deserved more than he, or any man, could ever hope to give her. What an amazing combination of attributes: that sweet nature with a core of steel hidden underneath. *And she's stood by me, even when her father—and probably every other rancher around these parts—doesn't think I'm the man for this job.*

What would it be like to have a woman like that stand beside him for the rest of his life? No. Not just any woman. Hallie. His imagination took wings and soared.

The wagon wheel bounced over another rut, bringing him out of his happy daydream. Probably just as well, he decided, easing his weight off his tender leg. Thoughts of romance would have to be set aside for the time being. He needed to redeem himself in his own eyes and prove himself to Burke first, and that wouldn't happen until the mystery was solved. That issue had to be settled once and for all before he could ever hope to ask for Hallie's hand.

Hallie set the last of the breakfast dishes back on the shelf and glanced around to see if anything else in the kitchen needed her attention. Satisfied she had finished her indoor chores for the morning, she donned her work gloves and walked out to her vegetable garden.

Her father cut a length from a roll of wire and stretched it over a gap in the garden fence. He looked up when she approached. "You've been fussing about the chickens scratching around your plants. I figured I'd patch that hole while I had the chance."

Hallie smiled her thanks and picked up her hoe. "That last rain did the vegetables a world of good, but it sure set the weeds to growing, too." She worked the hoe between the rows of carrots. Dirt rose in even heaps on either side of the blade as it cut through the soil.

Look at that. A few quick strokes with the hoe, and the weeds are rooted out. Hallie heaved a small sigh. If only the "weeds" in her life could be dealt with so easily.

She glanced over to where her father knelt beside a fence post. What had happened to them? Life seemed to have taken a ragged turn of late. It used to be that her days went along in a pleasant flow, with no problems more difficult than deciding what to fix for the next meal and staying out of Pete Edwards's way. Then Jacob came into her life, and the very thing that brought her joy became the cause of the greatest conflict she'd ever had with her father.

Why did it all have to be so complicated? She ran the hoe through another patch of weeds. Her father was a good man, despite his recent outbursts of temper. So was Jacob. She had adored her father all her life. She would always love him, but her heart had enough room for Jacob, too.

She loved them both, and yet that love didn't seem to be enough to bring the two men together and heal the hurts they had all suffered.

Something had to change. And neither Jacob nor her father seemed inclined to take the first step toward making that happen. That left it up to her. She finished the row of carrots and stopped to stretch the muscles in her back. Across the pathway that bordered the garden, her father hammered a fencing staple into the post.

Hallie leaned on her hoe and watched him work. His strength and unwavering devotion had sheltered her all during her growing-up years. She studied the face she had loved from her childhood. Throughout her early life, it had reflected that loving strength. Lately, its features were set in harsh, unyielding lines more often than not, and she felt a stranger lurked behind its stony exterior.

Today, though, her father looked more relaxed than she had seen him in months. He tapped another staple into the post, humming snatches of one of her mother's favorite hymns. Maybe this would be as good a time as any to speak to him of what lay on her heart. Hallie summoned up her courage and stepped across the path.

"It sure is good to see you looking happy again."

Her father looked up, his expression softening further when their gazes met. "It's good to lose myself in a routine job. Takes my mind off my troubles." He wiped his brow on his sleeve and fixed his gaze on a point across the valley. "I guess I haven't been too easy to live with ever since those cattle started going missing."

Hallie managed a small smile and gave him an encouraging nod. "I know it's been hard on you." She watched his shoulders relax and took heart. "At least we got most of them back when you and Jacob scared the rustlers off." She watched him out of the corner of her eye, trying to gauge his reaction.

Her father's jaw set, and he raised the hammer again. "But they got away. We still don't know who they are." He set the next staple in place and gave it a series of sharp whacks. "We had a chance to round them up and get rid of them for good. . .but it didn't work." He shook his head, suddenly looking years older. "After things went quiet, I thought they'd lit a shuck and left the country. Then we started losing steers again."

He straightened and flung the hammer to the ground. "We could have been rid of the whole mess by now if Garrett had shot right at them instead of spooking the herd and giving them the chance to get away."

"Or if you hadn't jumped into the middle of things without taking time to find out what was really going on?" Hallie kept her voice low, not wanting to provoke him. "He had a good idea; you know he did. It probably would have worked if things had gone the way he planned."

"If I hadn't shot him, you mean." Her father's face turned a dusky red. "How was I supposed to know it was him up there and not someone they'd posted as a lookout? Someone shot at me, and I fired at the only flash I saw. What was he doing up there, anyway?"

"His job," Hallie shot back, stung by the injustice of his attitude. "Just like you kept pushing him to do." She leaned the hoe against an undamaged section of the fence and stepped closer to her father. "You've acted all along like you thought he didn't care about our problems. But he does, Pa. He had it all worked out. He just doesn't do things the same way you do."

"So what you're saying is, it's all my fault? You're blaming me for letting those thieves ride away scot-free?" He drew himself to his full height and loomed over her. "Garrett's twisted your thinking so much you're willing to turn against your own father. I can't believe this is happening, Hallie. You can't see the truth when it stares you in the face."

"And you're so full of anger and hate, you can't give a good man credit for getting things done his own way or give him a chance to prove himself."

Her father's jaw worked. "Don't you talk to me like that. He's proven himself, all right. Proven he isn't half the man you think he is. Proven the only thing he's capable of doing is to stir up strife between the two of us. He managed to do that without even breaking a sweat."

Hallie saw the hurt in his eyes, and her own filled with tears. *Oh, Pa.* "Nothing is coming between you and me except that temper of yours." She rested her fingertips on his brawny forearm. "Can't you give Jacob another chance. . .for my sake?" She felt his muscles tense beneath her fingers.

"A chance for what? All I can see he's ever done is come sniffing around here trying to sweet-talk you. I just wish I'd shot straighter that night."

Hallie's knees buckled. She clutched at the fence post for support. "You don't mean that!"

"Don't I? Look at what he's done, trifling with your affections, getting you so stirred up you spend all your time mooning over a man who'll never amount to a hill of beans. Why, if I had my way—"

"But I love him, Pa." The whispered words stopped him cold.

Her father's face twisted and he raised his arm. Hallie ducked away, sure he was about to strike her. Instead, he hoisted the roll of wire above his head and pitched it halfway to the barn.

He turned back to face her, his chest heaving. "He'd better watch himself, or I will shoot straighter next time."

Hallie took a step back. "Pa, don't. You're frightening me."

"I mean it, Hallie. He's got your mind so full of pipe dreams you can't see straight, and I won't have it. You're not to go off the ranch again. Not as long as he's around."

"But, Pa—"

"Don't you sass me, girl! You stay up close, by the house and the barn. And if he ever shows his face around here again, you get inside the house and you stay there, you hear?"

Hallie clasped her hands under her chin. "You can't mean that!"

"Don't I?" His features contorted. "You just try to cross me and you'll find out."

Tears blurred Hallie's vision. She blinked them away, then wished she hadn't. In her father's face she saw no sign of the softness she had observed earlier; the hard-faced stranger had returned. With a low cry, she pressed her hands against her cheeks and ran for the house.

Chapter 19

Maybe I ought to just quit."

Dan O'Roarke looked up from where he sat braiding a lariat and stared at Jacob. "And do what?"

"Come back to work for you, if you'll have me."

Dan went back to weaving the strands of sisal together. "And what would you accomplish by that? I've never thought of you as a quitter."

"I'm no quitter, just realistic." Jacob strode across the barn floor and kicked at the center post. "I've never been this stymied before, Dan. They hired me because they thought I had what it took to stop the thieving. It looks like they were wrong. It's still going on, as strong as ever."

Dan set the lariat aside and leaned forward with his elbows on his knees. "It's a big territory for one man to cover. You came close that one time, real close."

Jacob shifted his weight to his left leg. "I'm just glad Evans didn't get any closer."

Dan raised his hand to his mouth, but it didn't quite muffle his snort of laughter. "They're bound to make a mistake sooner or later. When they do, you'll be there to nab them. . .assuming you don't walk off the job and settle for punching cows."

"It's honest work. There's nothing wrong with that."

"I didn't say there was, but there isn't a lot of money in it for a fellow who might be wanting to start a family one of these days."

Jacob felt his neck grow warm. "When did I ever say anything about that?"

"When did you need to? I've known you all your life, remember? Long enough to recognize the signs every time a certain young lady's name is mentioned." He walked over to Jacob and clapped him on the shoulder. "You picked yourself a good one, my friend. Hallie Evans is as true as they come."

Jacob looked away. "Yeah, and her father hates me. And I can't say as I blame him. Who'd want to trust their daughter's future to a man who can't do something as simple as track down a few rustlers?"

"It's not for lack of trying. You've spent many a night camped out there on the trails trying to spot some movement."

"And with absolutely nothing to show for it." Jacob sent a hissing breath out through his clenched teeth. "It's been weeks, Dan! How long is it supposed to take before everyone gives up on me, myself included? If I'd gone off with Buckey's troops, at least I'd feel like I was doing something worthwhile."

"Sweltering in the heat and coming down with fever? I hear they're losing more men to illness than to bullets over there." Dan stepped directly in front of Jacob and locked gazes with him. "You know as well as I do that God doesn't make mistakes. Getting shot in the leg wasn't in your plans, but He knew all along it would happen."

"Why didn't He stop it, then?"

Dan spread his hands wide. "His plans are bigger than ours. He had His reasons. And apparently having you here instead of in Cuba is part of them."

"But why, Dan? What good am I doing here? I can't find the rustlers; I can't even see Hallie. Her father's forbidden her to have anything to do with me, did you know that?" Jacob paced the width of the barn and raked his fingers through his hair. "I haven't talked to her for a month. I don't even know whether she's all right. The way her father acts, I wouldn't put it past him to—"

Dan put himself in Jacob's path, bringing him up short. "I don't know the answers any better than you do. I just know who I can trust."

A horse bolted into the yard at a dead run. Eb Landrum leaped down from the saddle and dashed to the barn.

Dan crossed over toward him, his face creased with worry. "What's wrong, Eb?"

The cowboy stood rigid in the doorway, his pale face twisted in a look of pain. Jacob could see traces of moisture around his eyes. "I just came from town." His voice was stretched as tight as piano wire. "A telegram arrived while I was there. Everyone was talking about it."

"What is it?" Dan demanded. "What's happened?"

Eb drew in a ragged breath. "It's Buckey. Some Spaniard shot him."

Jacob closed the distance between them and gripped the cowboy's arm. "He's dead?"

Eb nodded. Jacob saw the muscles bunch in his jaw. "Right away, from the sounds of it. He didn't even have time to say a word before. . ."

His voice trailed off, but Jacob had heard enough. He bolted out the door without listening for more. He strode across to the far side of the yard and stood with his hands balled into fists, looking up into the sky.

"Why, God? He was a good and decent man. He had so many plans for himself, for this territory. Why Buckey?"

And why wasn't I there with him? Anguish tore at him. Would it have happened if he'd gone along? Could he have seen something, done something to warn his friend and prevent this awful thing from happening?

Despair wrenched his heart. He would never know. The fact of the matter was, he hadn't been there. And all because of Burke Evans.

Hallie swished a dinner plate through the rinse water and set it on the drain board. She clenched her hands around the dishcloth and squeezed. Warm trail of water slid past her wrists and dripped off her elbows. She squeezed harder. Squeezed again, until her hands trembled with the effort and the cloth yielded its final drop.

She forced her fingers to open, one by one. The cloth fell back into the sink with a splash, but her hands continued to tremble. Hallie spread them flat against the counter to hold them steady.

There, that was better. Only a faint tremor remained. She hated the feeling of being out of control like that, loathed the inability to make her body obey the simplest commands.

And that happened a lot lately. The simplest tasks rose up before her like insurmountable obstacles. Even a routine chore like washing the dishes sapped every bit of her energy.

More than once during the weeks of her enforced separation from Jacob, she found herself walking into a room without remembering what she planned to do once she got there. And just last week, she spent hours searching for the eggs she'd just gathered from the chicken coop, only to find them tucked away in the flour bin.

Maybe I'm going crazy. That might explain why she jumped like a frightened deer at every sound and her recent tendency to burst into tears with only the slightest provocation.

Her father chalked it all up to feminine stubbornness. "Don't think you're going to change my mind by any of your theatrics," he warned. "I've always done what I thought was best for you, and keeping you away from Garrett is the best thing I've done in years."

No amount of tears or pleading could sway him from his resolve. Hallie now made it a point to retreat to her room when she felt tears threaten. There, she could bury her face in her pillow to muffle her sobs and save herself from being subjected to more of her father's scathing comments.

The loose fit of her clothes told her she had lost weight over the past few weeks. If she needed confirmation, she had only to stand in front of the mirror to see her sunken cheeks and the hollow circles under her eyes.

What was Jacob doing? The question pounded in her mind every moment of every day. Had he overcome his bitterness and reconciled his anger at God for allowing him to be injured? Was he any closer to ferreting out the band of rustlers?

And did she invade his thoughts as often as he did hers?

Hallie might be denied Jacob's physical presence, but he was with her in her dreams, her thoughts, in every fiber of her being. Without him, her familiar world felt out of kilter, as though she moved through it as a stranger. What used to be reality now seemed like a dream world, one from which she wished she could wake up and find herself in Jacob's arms.

She drained the water from the sink and used the dishcloth to wipe down the counter. Her hands moved in practiced strokes, mechanically following the same routine they had so many times before. But her mind wheeled freely, sifting through a myriad of thoughts in search of a way to escape her anguish.

If she could only find a way to send a message to him and to get word in return. More than once, she had considered sending a note along with one of the hands. But her father had made it clear that all contact between Hallie and Jacob was to be cut off, and the hands' first loyalty was to her father. Any message she tried to send through them would surely wind up in his hands.

She wet the cloth again and started on the dining table. Her hands began to quiver again, and she crossed her arms, clamping them tight against her sides. she never heard from Jacob again. . .

No. She pushed that grim thought out of her mind. There had to be a way. She just had to find it.

In her more daring moments, she made plans to sneak off the place without her father's knowledge and ride to the T Bar in the hope of finding Jacob there. The thought of what her father would do if he caught up with her was enough to put an end to those schemes before she worked up enough nerve to put them into practice.

Hallie pressed her fists against her temples. *There has to be a way. Think!*

The front door banged open. Hallie jumped and clutched the dishcloth to her chest, making a damp circle on the front of her dress. She heard the sound of several pairs of feet entering from the front porch. *Now what?*

She set the dishcloth down and pushed through the swinging door. "Pa?"

Her father stood near the fireplace, facing Edgar Wilson and Lee Moore. All three of the men turned stony faces toward her.

Despite the summer warmth, Hallie felt a chill run down her arms. She forced her dry throat to swallow. "Can I get you anything?"

"Just coffee, then leave us alone. We're talking business."

Stung by the curt reply, Hallie ducked back into the kitchen without another word. She grabbed the nearly full coffeepot from the stove and set it on a tray along with three mugs. A sob rose up in her throat, and she choked it back down.

It's a good thing he didn't ask for more in the way of refreshments. She hadn't bothered to bake a cake or roll out a piecrust in weeks. These days, she could barely manage just getting through the basic routine from day to day.

She lifted the tray and backed through the swinging door just in time to hear Edgar Wilson ask, "What do you plan to do if they turn out to be the ones behind it?"

Her father snorted. "I plan to take a short rope and find me a tall tree, that's what."

Hallie gasped. The mugs rattled against the tray.

All three ranchers wheeled and looked her way. Avoiding their glances she walked across the room with an air of calm she did not feel and set the tray down on a side table. She poured coffee into each mug, then walked back to the kitchen, schooling her features not to betray her.

As soon as the door swung shut behind her, she pushed it open again, just the barest crack. She pressed her ear against the tiny opening and listened.

"What about that so-called range detective?" Hallie recognized Edgar Wilson's irate tone. She clamped her lips together and held her breath, anxious not to miss a word they said about Jacob.

Her father made a sound of disgust. "You haven't seen him make any arrests, have you? The young fool wasn't any good before I shot him; he's worth even less now."

Grim chuckles followed his remark. Hallie had to restrain herself from bursting into the front room and flying to Jacob's defense. It would serve her purpose better to hear the rest of whatever the men had to say.

Lee Moore finally spoke, his nasal voice easy to distinguish from the others. "So we just ignore him? We don't let him know what we're doing?"

"It'll be easier that way," Hallie's father responded. "Easier and less likely to be botched up like the last time."

Hallie covered her mouth with both hands to hold back her cry of dismay. Tears welled up in her eyes. *What are they up to?* Whatever it might be, it boded ill for Jacob.

Edgar Wilson spoke again. "So what's the plan?" Hallie swiped the tears away with her fingertips and pressed closer to the door. She must not miss a syllable.

"You and Moore need to get back to your ranches and gather your riders," her father said. "Send the men you trust most to notify the other ranchers that we're going to settle this thing tonight."

A chair scraped on the wood floor, then her father's voice went on. "Wilson, your riders will cover the area to the north and east. Moore, yours will take in every place to the south and west. Tell them to round up as many men as they can and meet here this afternoon."

"What time?" Lee Moore asked.

"I say we make it four o'clock, no later than five. We'll catch those nesters napping and put an end to this foolishness."

A scream rose in Hallie's throat, and she clapped her hands over her mouth again. Ropes. Nesters. They couldn't be planning—

"That's a lot of territory to cover in just a few hours," Moore put in.

"He has a point," Edgar Wilson said. "Will we have time to reach everyone? What about O'Roarke? He's so tight with Garrett there doesn't seem to be much point in sending a man to his place. I can't see him agreeing to go with us, and he'd be more than likely to try to warn Garrett."

"Agreed. We don't want to give Garrett an inkling about what's going on and have him out there trying to save his precious nesters."

Hallie couldn't stand it another minute. She slammed the door open and rushed to stand before her father.

All three ranchers stared at her open-mouthed.

"What's the matter with you?" her father bellowed. "I told you we had to talk business."

"Is that what you call this? Business?" Hallie pivoted slowly to look at each of them in turn. "Are you all crazy? You're planning to murder innocent people."

"Innocent?" Wilson's lips drew back in a sneer. "Not very."

Hallie turned back to her father. He had a solid core of good sense, if only she could get through to him. "What proof do you have?"

"It's the only thing that makes sense," he said in a flat, emotionless tone that made the hairs on the back of her neck stand on end. "Look at them living up there the way they do, keeping out of sight of the rest of us. Pete thinks I'm right, too," he added with a note of triumph. "He said he's seen a couple of them in places they had no business being, and that happened right around the time some of our cattle went missing."

Hallie shook her head in disbelief. "You know that wouldn't stand up in court. If you have any real evidence, turn it over to the law. Sheriff Ruffner hates rustling as much as anyone. He'll see that justice is done." She didn't dare bring Jacob into it. No telling what the mere mention of his name might stir up, with the mood these men were in.

"What do you know about the law?" Her father waved his hand in a dismissive gesture. "Go back to the kitchen and quit wasting our time. We've got plans to make."

Hallie grabbed his arms. "Plans for murder, Pa? Mama always said she could hold her head up high, knowing you were a man who cared about the truth. Well, where is the truth in this? Do you think she would be proud of what you're doing today?"

Her father brought his hands up and seized her wrists in an iron grip. "Don't you question what I'm doing. I'm trying to save the living of every rancher in this valley. If you can't understand that. . ." He thrust her away from him. "Now go to your room and stay there."

A band of fear tightened around her chest. "But I can't let—"

"Enough!" Her father's roar echoed through the room. "I told you to go to your room. Now get!"

Chapter 20

Hallie lay across her bed, spent from the force of her crying. She stared dully at the sharp, ridged creases on her sheets where her hands had twisted them into knots.

Her pillow was a sodden lump beneath her cheek. Just when she thought she had used up all the tears left in her, a fresh wave of grief would wash over her to prove her wrong. But after an hour of weeping, the well had dried up. She pressed the tips of her fingers to her swollen eyelids and lay still, listening to the ragged sound of her breathing.

She had known grief when her mother died. But back then, she had her father to lean on. Now, the knowledge that he had turned away from her, bent on carrying out his heinous idea, plunged her into a depth of despair she couldn't have imagined before today.

Hallie rolled to her side and brushed her hand across her face. Damp strands of hair trailed across her cheek, glued to her skin by her own tears.

The meeting ended some time ago. She had heard the clomp of the men's boots on the front porch, then listened to the sound of hoofbeats fading into the distance. Wilson and Moore were gone, off to spread the word about a meeting that would stir up more trouble than this valley had ever seen—and ruin her father's life in the process.

"Hallie?" Her father's voice rumbled on the other side of her bedroom door.

She wrapped her arms around the tear-soaked pillow and held it against her chest. He could send her to her room; he couldn't force her to talk to him.

"Hallie?" he called again. "I'm going after Pete and the rest of the boys." He paused, then tapped uncertainly on the door.

Another pause, then: *"Hallie!"* His pounding shook the walls and set her hairbrush vibrating on the top of her dresser.

She bit her lip until she tasted blood. Not for anything would she give him the satisfaction of a reply.

"All right." His voice carried a note of barely suppressed fury. "Have it your way. If you want to keep your door closed, then it'll stay closed until I get back."

Hallie heard a *snick* in the lock, then her pa's heavy footsteps pounding across the floor.

The front door slammed. Hallie waited until she felt sure he wouldn't be coming back, then she slipped out of bed and crossed the room. She gripped the knob and jiggled it. *No. He wouldn't. . .*

She grabbed the knob with both hands and twisted it with all her might. When that had no effect, she shook it back and forth until the door rattled in its frame. It didn't give.

He did. Hallie stared at the locked door, feeling like she had received a final blow. The strength drained from her limbs, and she tottered back to sprawl across the bed. Realization settled over her like a heavy cloak. She was a prisoner in her own room.

The tears flowed afresh.

A hot, stuffy feeling replaced the morning coolness inside the house, reminding Hallie of how much time had passed. What was happening out there beyond the confines of her prison?

Had Edgar Wilson and Lee Moore had time to get back to their respective ranches? Hallie could picture them gathering their riders and sending them to bear their message of vengeance and death across the valley. And her own pa. . .

A shuddering moan rose from deep within when she thought of what he intended to do. What had happened to the father she had loved all her life? *Jacob was right, Pa. You need to forgive. Your anger and bitterness have turned you into a stranger, someone I don't want to know.*

Hallie pushed herself up to sit on the edge of her bed. What were the nesters doing at this moment? She could imagine them going about their usual routine, never dreaming that this day would be their last, that in a few hours death would descend on them in the form of grim-faced vigilantes.

Would they scatter and run or stand and fight? When would they realize there would be no escape, that the only future left to them involved a tree branch and a rope?

"Nooo!" The scream tore from Hallie's throat. She clutched at her hair with both hands. "Dear Lord, don't let my father's bitterness turn him into a murderer!"

Someone had to stop this madness, but there was no one.

Except her. Hallie stumbled to her feet and flung herself at the door. She pounded on it with both fists, but to no avail. Bracing herself, she raised her foot and kicked at the bottom panels.

Nothing happened.

Hallie shrieked in an agony of frustration. She clawed at the door, knowing it was futile, yet unable to stop herself. She had to get out. There had to be a way.

What about the window? Feeling foolish for not thinking of it before, she lifted her voice in a prayer of thanks and rushed across the room. She shoved the window wide open, then gathered her skirt and climbed onto the sill.

She teetered there for a moment, knowing she had reached the point of no return. Once she left the house in defiance of her father's orders, she would cross a line from which she could never turn back. "Be with me, Lord. I have to save those nesters."

I have to save my father. Hallie pushed herself out away from the sill and dropped to the ground.

She edged along the back of the house, then peered around the corner. She looked around the yard, halfway expecting her father to appear at any moment.

"He's gone." She said the words aloud, as if hearing the words spoken would provide added reassurance. "You've been given a gift of time. Make the most of it."

It took several attempts to saddle Gypsy. Hallie's fingers felt like wooden blocks as she fumbled to pull the cinch strap under the mare's belly, then buckle it in place. Finally the task was finished.

She led the horse outside the barn and swung up into the saddle. Which way should she go? Panic seized her. If she ran into her father, she didn't want to think about what would happen. Worse yet, what if she came across Pete, alone and unprotected?

Hallie forced herself to think. Her father had gone after Pete. Which way had he ridden? She squeezed her eyes shut tight to help her concentrate, then remembered her pa saying something about the hands all being up on the north range.

The decision had been made for her. She turned Gypsy toward the south and dug her heels in the mare's sides. She had to get to Jacob before it was too late.

Once out of sight of the house, she realized the utter impossibility of the task she had set for herself. The valley itself covered a large territory, and the boundaries of Jacob's jurisdiction extended many miles beyond that in all directions. He was out there somewhere in that vast land; that much she knew. But where? Covering the whole area would take days.

Maybe she ought to acknowledge it as a fool's errand and turn back now. She started to rein Gypsy around, then froze. What if she didn't make it back to the house before her father discovered she was missing? The thought was enough to change her mind. She had no choice now but to go on.

Hallie looked overhead and marked the sun's position, just past its zenith. She had less than four hours to locate Jacob and get back to the house in time to stop her father.

"Where is he, Lord? Please help me to find him." If she had been able to choose freely, she would have ridden to the T Bar. If Jacob wasn't there, Dan O'Roarke might have some idea as to his whereabouts. And even if not, she knew Dan would not hesitate to saddle up and help her look for Jacob—or ride down to the Broken Box and help stand off the vigilantes himself.

But Pete was somewhere up on the north range, between her and the T Bar. No telling which part of the range he might be on. He could well be several miles away from the route that would take her to the O'Roarkes' home, but she couldn't rely on that.

With that option eliminated, Hallie breathed a quick prayer and set off toward the southwest. She needed to avoid the nearest ranches as much as possible. Wilson's and Moore's messengers would have started stirring things up already. Even now, riders from the other ranches might be on their way to the Broken Box with bloodlust in their hearts. It wouldn't pay to put herself in their way.

Not only that. Hallie groaned when she realized the other side of her dilemma. The gossip level of some of the cowboys would put a contingent of little old ladies to shame. Some of them had surely heard of her isolation from Jacob by now. If they caught her out there on her own, they might well feel duty-bound to return her to her father. And that meant. . .

Hallie's lips tightened. It meant she would have to stay away from everyone. She had no way of knowing who would help or hinder her until it was too late. She kept to the washes and other low areas, as intent on hiding her tracks as she was on finding Jacob.

The sun continued its inexorable march across the sky. An hour passed. Then another. Hallie crisscrossed the area to the west and south of the Broken Box. She never saw a living soul, not even cowhands traveling to join her father in his deadly foray. Hallie stood in her stirrups and gazed from one side of the valley to the other. *Where, Lord?*

The T Bar. She had to risk it. It was the only place she could approach in safety. Surely by now Pete and her father would be back at the house, waiting for the others. She guided Gypsy north, keeping a line of low hills between herself and the open valley.

The distance seemed interminably long, but at last she clattered into the yard, barely able to stay in her saddle. "Help!" she cried. "Is anyone home?"

The commotion brought Amy rushing outside. She leaped down the steps, her face etched with worry. "Hallie! What on earth—"

Hallie cut her off. "Jacob. Is he here?"

"What's wrong, Hallie? Let me help you down. We've got to get you inside."

She reached up, but Hallie pulled away. "There's no time. Amy, tell me quickly, do you know where Jacob is? I must find him."

"I heard him talking to Dan earlier. He said something about scouting out an area about an hour east of here."

"You're sure?" Hallie pulled her weary body upright and braced herself for the next leg of her search.

Amy caught at the reins. "You're in no condition to ride. Let me send one of the men out after him, if it's that important."

"There's no time. I'll explain it to you later." Hallie urged Gypsy into as fast a pace as she dared, praying all the way. An hour would be too late.

Thirty minutes later, she spotted a rider outlined against a low hill. She pulled up, wondering whether she should head for cover. Something about him, though. . .

He turned his head, and she caught a clear view of his profile. "Oh, thank You, Jesus!" She spurred Gypsy on and raced toward him.

When she had closed half the distance, Jacob caught sight of her. He gave an exuberant wave and rode toward her at a gallop.

Chapter 21

At first Jacob thought his eyes were playing tricks on him. Growing up in Tucson, he'd seen mirages himself and heard plenty of stories of prospectors stranded in the desert heat, crawling toward shimmering pools of water that existed only in their imaginations. Had his own mind created an image of the woman he loved, an illusory vision that would disappear the moment he drew near?

The echo of galloping hoofbeats decided him. A mirage wouldn't affect his ears as well as his eyes. Joy welled up in him until he thought he would burst. This was no illusion. It was Hallie!

Cap didn't hesitate when Jacob dug his heels in. The steel-dust launched himself straight down the slope, closing the gap between them with amazing speed.

Jacob leaned over the gelding's neck, yearning for a closer view of that beloved face. How did she come to be out here? Had she persuaded her father to lift his ban on their being together?

It didn't matter. They could sort the details out later. All he cared about now was seeing Hallie, gazing into her sweet face, and taking her in his arms.

The gap narrowed to fifty yards. Twenty. Jacob felt a ripple of concern at the way Hallie slumped in the saddle. What happened to her usual easy grace?

At ten yards, worry built a knot in his throat. As he drew abreast of her, he took in her sharpened features, the way her clothes hung loose. *How much weight has she lost? Has she been sick, Lord, and I didn't know it?*

Hallie pulled Gypsy to a halt and braced her arms against the saddle horn as if it were the only way she could hold herself erect. Tear streaks stained her cheeks and strands of hair straggled along the sides of her face.

The knot in Jacob's throat threatened to choke him. *Hallie, sweetheart, what has he done to you?*

He opened his mouth to speak, but she cut him off before he could say a word. "You've got to stop them before they kill someone."

Whatever he had expected, it wasn't this. "Take a breath and slow down, Hallie. I don't understand."

"My father and some of the other ranchers. They're forming a vigilant group. They're riding out today, going after the nesters." Her mouth twisted and a sob erupted from her throat. "Jacob, they're going to hang them!"

His mouth went dry. "When? Where?"

"They're supposed to meet at our place, sometime between four and five o'clock." They glanced up toward the sun at the same moment, then Hallie turned toward him, her face set in a tragic expression. "It's almost four now. I don't know if we can get there in time."

"We can try." He looked at her doubtfully. "Are you up to it?"

Hallie gathered the reins in her trembling hands. "I'll make it. And if I don't, keep on going. You've got to stop them."

He didn't have time to argue her out of it. He ducked his head. "All right. Let's ride."

Hallie bent low over Gypsy's neck, feeling the mare's power as she raced to keep pace with Cap. The wind whipped against Hallie's face and tore at her hair. She ducked her head lower and urged Gypsy on.

"Come on, girl, you can make it. We have to get there." By her calculations, it must be just past four o'clock. If all the men her father called had shown up on time or even early, the vigilantes could be gone.

The miles Gypsy had run already that day began to take their toll, as Hallie felt the horse falter and heard her labor for breath. Jacob glanced over his shoulder. A frown crossed his face when he saw them falling behind. Hallie waved at him to go on. More important than their arrival together was Jacob getting there in time to keep her father from making the worst mistake of his life.

"Don't let it happen, Lord. Find a way to stop them, please." She couldn't let her father become a murderer. She *wouldn't*, as long as there was still breath left in her body.

The house and barn appeared as dots on the horizon, growing larger with every stride Gypsy made. Hallie squinted her eyes against the rushing wind and strained to see the yard. "Please let them be there. Please!"

Cap put on a burst of speed and increased the distance between them. Hallie felt Gypsy's pace slacken still more. She wanted to scream out her frustration, but bent all her concentration on staying in the saddle instead. She felt almost as exhausted as Gypsy. It wouldn't help matters for either one of them to become injured.

Ahead, she could see the dust rise as Jacob rode into the yard at a dead run. Hallie lost him from view when he passed around the far side of the barn. Was he even now confronting the band of vigilantes or waiting to break the news to her that they had been too late?

Hold on, hold on. You'll know in just a few moments. Uncertainty stretched her nerves to the breaking point.

It seemed like hours passed before Gypsy reached the barn. The mare stopped and stood with her head drooping between her front legs, her sides heaving in great gulps of air. Dreading what she might find, Hallie slipped from the saddle and rounded the corner on foot.

The sight she beheld stopped her in her tracks. Jacob stood facing a dozen mounted men. Every one of them stared back at him with stony contempt. Jacob's right hand rested on the grip of his pistol, but he spoke in a low, matter-of-fact tone.

"You have no proof, nothing more than mere speculation."

A hard-faced cowboy on a long-legged dun rode forward until his mount towered over Jacob. "We have all the proof we need. These nesters have been causing trouble all over the territory for years. It's time we were rid of this bunch. It might make others think twice before they try the same thing."

A rumble of assent came from the group, but Jacob didn't flinch. "What you're doing is wrong. Deep down in your hearts, I think you know that. You're all angry about losing your stock, and you have every right to be. Most of you are angry at me for not catching the men responsible, and I don't blame you for that, either."

He paused, and Hallie studied their faces intently. Jacob's last comment seemed to take some of the men by surprise. They watched him with guarded expressions.

"Now you've decided there's someone you can blame, and the idea of venting that anger sounds mighty appealing."

"You're right about that," Edgar Wilson called. "It's high time we took action. Some of us have felt all along that the nesters were responsible."

"Then why didn't you do anything about it before?" Jacob challenged him. "Why wait until now? Ask yourselves why it's easier to think about doing this as part of a group. Is it because it takes away the responsibility you'd feel if you acted alone? Because your consciences have been drowned out by the voices of a mob? That's what you are, gentlemen, if you'll just stop and think about it. Nothing but a mob."

"Enough!" Hallie's father rode forward, a look of loathing on his face. "We've been sitting on our backsides long enough. It's time to put an end to this, once and for all. If it takes more than one man to get rid of these thieves, then I say that's what is needed." He raised the coil of rope he held in his fist and shook it at Jacob. "I call it justice."

Jacob stood his ground. "The law calls it murder."

An uneasy silence settled over the group.

"If you go ahead with this fool scheme, you'll be breaking the law every bit as much as the men who have been rustling your stock. We still don't know who they are, but I can name every one of you."

The silence deepened. From the rear of the group, Lee Moore challenged, "Are you trying to say you'd go against the whole lot of us like that?"

The man beside Moore snorted. "I was there at the roundup, same as you and all the rest. If he felt that strong about a misbranded calf, what do you think he'll do about a thing like this?"

Moore drew back as if he'd been slapped. "Maybe you're right," he muttered. "This whole idea is starting to taste pretty sour to me. I'm going home." He signaled his men, and they rode off without further comment.

One by one, the other men followed suit until only the Broken Box riders were left. Finally, even they dismounted and began to unsaddle their horses. Pete Edwards paused in the act of loosening his cinch. Leaving his horse ground tied, he disappeared into the barn.

Hallie's father turned to Jacob. Fury smoldered in his eyes. "Well, you've driven off all my help. I guess you're mighty proud of yourself, aren't you?" He advanced a step and clenched his beefy fists. "Funny how you're so convincing as far as protecting these rustlers. How am I supposed to know you aren't in cahoots with them?"

"Pa!" Hallie spoke for the first time since her wild ride into the yard. "Stop and think what you're saying. He's saving you from going to prison, maybe worse."

Her father waved his arm through the air as though shooing away a troublesome fly and kept his gaze fixed on Jacob. "You've ruined this necktie party. But as soon as I know for sure who's doing it, as soon as I have that proof you keep talking about, they're going to pay. I don't care what you say."

Jacob's fingers curled into white-knuckled knots, then opened again. "You need to cool off," he stated in a flat tone. "So do I. So do our horses, for that matter." He walked back to where Cap and Gypsy stood, caught up their reins, and led them around toward the water trough.

With a muttered oath, Hallie's father stomped toward the house. He slammed the door so hard behind him, Hallie felt sure the wood would splinter. *Thank You, Lord. It's over.* Reaction set in, and she felt her whole body start to shake.

Pete strode out of the barn, carrying his saddlebags. *The last person I want to see,* Hallie thought. She gave him a wide berth as she circled around him to go join Jacob. Then something about his manner caught her attention.

She watched as Pete walked over to his horse and slung the saddlebags behind the cantle, then tightened the cinch.

All the others have put their horses up. Why would he be doing that, unless. . .

"You're leaving?" The words sprang out before she could stop them.

Pete glanced up, his features set in a surly expression. "You needn't sound so hopeful." He yanked the cinch. "Yes, I'm leaving. I've had all I can take. This whole business of turning vigilante is more than I signed on for."

Hallie wondered if he could sense her unbridled joy. "I'll wish you a good journey, then." *A long journey, as far from here as you can possibly go.* She turned to join Jacob around the side of the barn.

"Wait." Pete closed the distance between them with long strides. "I know we've had our differences, but all I ever wanted was for you to feel the same way about me as I do about you." He circled her upper arm with his fingers. "Why don't you come with me?"

Chapter 22

Let go of me." She wrenched her arm away and stepped back.

"I mean it, Hallie. You don't belong with Garrett. You belong to me; you always have." He lunged forward and gripped her shoulders with both hands. "Come away with me. We can make each other happy."

Hallie kicked out and caught him on the shin. He sucked in a quick breath and tightened his hold. "I told you this day would come. I thought I'd be around here long enough to make you see things my way. But it's time for me to leave, and you're coming with me." He shifted his hands to encircle her waist and dragged her toward his horse.

"Jacob!" she screamed. She dug in her heels and fought with all her might.

She heard hurried footsteps on the other side of the barn, and Jacob rounded the corner, his face dark with worry. He stopped abruptly. "Let her go," he ordered.

Pete swung Hallie around in front of him and clamped his arm across her throat. "Maybe she doesn't want me to. She's leaving with me, Garrett."

Jacob's eyes flicked back and forth from Pete to Hallie, then to Pete's holster. Hallie saw his jaw tighten and his hand settle on the pistol grip. Pete must have noticed it, too. He tightened his hold, pulling her closer to him.

"Don't!" she cried. The confusion in Jacob's eyes tore at her heart. "I've spent this day trying to stop bloodshed. I don't want to be the reason for any being spilled." *Especially if it's yours.*

Pete chuckled. "See? I told you. She wants to go with me." He dragged her back another step. "Come on, Hallie. It's time to mount up."

Jacob sprang forward, putting himself beside Pete in a single leap. "I said, let her go!" He grabbed Pete by the collar and swung him around. The whiplike action broke Pete's grip and sent Hallie flying. She landed on her hands and knees, with her palms skidding across the rough ground.

❧

Breathing heavily, Jacob turned Pete's shirt loose and stepped back. He had seen Hallie fall, but he didn't dare take his gaze off Pete to make sure she was all right. He moved forward a step, forcing Pete back closer to his horse.

"You said you were leaving. You'd better go now. Get on your horse and don't stop until you get to wherever it is you're headed."

Pete stood stock still for a moment, then he let out a string of curses and swung his fist.

344

The blow connected with Jacob's ribs. He caught his breath in a quick gasp and widened his stance. *I wasn't ready that time. I won't make the same mistake again.*

Pete threw another punch. This time, Jacob blocked it easily with his forearm. He pushed Pete away. "All right, we've settled things now. Let's call it quits."

"That's where you're wrong." Pete settled into a crouch. "This ain't over, not by a long shot." He rushed at Jacob, arms spread wide.

Jacob sidestepped and thumped Pete on the back of the head with his fist when he stumbled past. Maybe he could knock enough sense into the man to make him understand this fight was pointless.

Pete hit the ground on his knees, then staggered to his feet and turned to face Jacob. Pure hatred gleamed from his eyes. "When I get my hands on you, I'll beat you so bad nobody will want to look at your face, not even her." He jerked his head toward Hallie.

"There isn't any sense to this. You're ready to leave, so leave. Just pack up and go. But you're going alone."

Pete lowered his head and ran at Jacob, swinging his fists.

Enough. Jacob blocked the punches and responded with some of his own. *Sometimes there just doesn't seem to be any other answer.* They stood trading punches, then Jacob moved forward, gaining ground with every blow.

Pete stumbled backward and scrambled to regain his footing. The move brought him up next to his horse. The wide-eyed animal snorted and danced skittishly.

Pete glanced behind him, appearing to realize he was trapped. He feinted to the right, then the left, but Jacob blocked his escape. Pete turned as though to take his horse's reins. Then he whirled around, landing a savage kick on Jacob's right thigh, inches away from where he had been shot.

Jacob's vision turned dark and stars shot across the blackness. He had to end this now. He wouldn't be able to take another blow like that. Putting most of his weight on his left leg, he crouched slightly, then delivered a punch that started down at his knees.

His fist cracked against Pete's jaw, slamming him back against his horse. The gelding shied and whinnied. Pete slumped to the ground, out cold.

His saddlebags slid off the horse and flopped to the earth a few feet away, spilling their contents on the ground.

Jacob stood over the unconscious man, chest heaving and fists clenched, ready to deal with him again if he were playing possum. He watched Pete closely, waiting for him to move.

"Jacob?"

He shot a quick look over his shoulder. Hallie stood behind him, staring at a handful of papers.

"What is it?"

"These fell out of Pete's saddlebag. I think you'd better take a look."

"Later. I need to make sure he doesn't take a notion to start things up again when he comes around."

"I really don't think you want to wait." She moved closer and handed him the papers.

Jacob glanced at them quickly, then blinked and took a closer look. Bills of sale for small bunches of cattle, all dated within the past few months, and all listing Pete Edwards as the owner. Jacob looked up at Hallie and their gazes locked.

"Do you realize what this could mean?" he asked.

"Mm-hm. Look what else fell out." Hallie held out her other hand.

Jacob stared at a roll of bills big enough to choke a horse. "Where would a cowboy get that much money?"

"Not from working for my father, that's for sure."

As if on cue, Burke Evans threw open the front door and ran down the porch steps.

"What's all the commotion? What are you doing?" He stared at Pete's still figure and jerked his gaze back up to direct a menacing glare at Jacob. "You come here with all your talk about leaving people in peace, then you go and do something like this?"

Jacob held out the papers and nodded toward the money still in Hallie's hand. "Any idea where he'd come by that amount of cash?"

Burke gaped at the wad of money, then flipped through the bills of sale Jacob handed him. His features hardened. "No, but we're going to find out." He prodded Pete with his boot. "Wake up. We've got some talking to do."

Pete rolled his head to one side and moaned. Burke reached down and pulled him up by the front of his shirt. "Wake up," he repeated. He shook the groggy man and waved the papers in his face. "What do you have to say about this?"

Pete shook his head and blinked. His gaze lit on the papers in Burke's hand, and his eyes seemed to snap back into focus. He stiffened and shifted his gaze from side to side like a trapped coyote. Seeing no way of escape, he swung around and turned to Jacob.

"Don't let him hang me," he said.

❧

The sun hung low in the western sky. Hallie waited outside the barn door while Jacob and her father tied Pete securely in one of the stalls. Even though Jacob assured him he would be taken back to Prescott for trial, the sight of Burke Evans carrying a rope had been enough to frighten the cowboy into rattling off all the details of the rustling operation he had spearheaded.

Jacob had the names he needed now and enough physical evidence in the form of the bills of sale and ill-gotten money to bring the guilty men to justice.

In the morning, he could go after the rest of the lot and turn them over to Sheriff Ruffner along with their erstwhile leader.

Pete's sudden transformation from a blustering bully into a broken man shocked Hallie, but not as much as the plea he made while her father and Jacob dragged him into the barn. At the doorway he turned back toward her, his face pale and frightened. "You know I never would have hurt you, Hallie. I was going to let you go that day at the canyon, remember?" His voice cracked, and a sharp push from her father hurried him out of her sight.

So Pete had been one of the men she'd surprised in the canyon. The one who knelt in the small of her back and pushed her face into the dirt? Probably. It would fit with his enjoyment of bullying anyone smaller and weaker than himself.

And he had been the one who promised to carry her off with him, she felt sure of that. The bandanna over his face, coupled with the shock of finding her there, had distorted his voice enough to keep her from recognizing it. Besides, she had been so sure he was at the other end of the range that fateful day.

The creak of the barn door brought her out of her reverie. Jacob watched her father drop the heavy bar into place. "Thanks for your help. That should hold him until I'm ready to leave for town."

Her father nodded, then looked down at his feet. "I guess I owe you an apology. You kept me from doing something I would have regretted for the rest of my days."

Hallie could see the effort it cost him to reach his hand out toward Jacob, who took it in a firm grip.

"Apology accepted," he said. "We'll let this stay in the past, where it belongs. And I'm glad to think we're starting over fresh. There's something I want to talk to you about." He walked over to Hallie and stopped beside her.

Her father's mouth dropped open, then he pressed his lips together in a thin line. "If you're thinking about the kind of talk I suspect you are, you can just forget it." He looked straight at her. "Hallie, get in the house."

"Wait." Jacob stepped closer and put his arm around her shoulders. Hallie let his warmth flow through her and give her strength. "I love your daughter, Mr. Evans. I'd like your permission to ask her to marry me."

Please, Pa. Say yes. Hallie turned a hopeful gaze upon him.

He stared at them for a long moment, then gave his head a decisive shake. "No. You can put that notion right out of your mind. I'll lock her up again if I have to."

"How much good did it do you to lock me in my room today?" Hallie stepped forward, leaving the security of Jacob's touch. Her lips trembled so, she could barely speak.

She took a deep breath to keep her voice from shaking and plunged ahead. "My birthday is in August, remember? I'll be twenty-one in just a few weeks.

You can order me to obey you, and I will. . .for now. But you can't keep a hold on me forever, Pa. Once I reach majority, I'll do whatever needs to be done to be with Jacob."

She stepped back and put her arm around Jacob's waist. Lifting her chin, she said, "I love him, Pa. Nothing you can do is going to change that."

Jacob watched Burke and saw a flicker of uncertainty in his eyes. He decided to press their advantage. "Do you really want Hallie at your beck and call because you demand it? Or would you rather she gave her affection to you freely?" He wrapped his arm around her shoulders and drew her close.

Burke kept silent, studying the two of them. Finally he turned toward the house. "Hallie, you come inside." His mouth turned up in a wry smile. "Whenever you're of a mind to."

"Oh, Pa!" Hallie ran to her father and wrapped her arms around his waist. "Thank you. I'll never stop loving you, you know that, don't you?"

Burke stroked her hair with his work-hardened hand, and a tender expression lit his face. "I know that. I guess I always have." He dropped a kiss on her forehead, then looked up and leveled a stern gaze at Jacob.

"You take care of her, do you hear? I shot you once. I can do it again if you don't treat her right." With that, he turned on his heel and walked away.

Hallie pressed her lips together and drew in a shaky breath. "Coming from him, that's practically a blessing."

"I know." Jacob chuckled, then pulled her to him and tilted her head back so he could look straight into her eyes. "Hallie, I need to make it official. Will you do me the honor of becoming my wife?"

She cupped her hand around his face and traced the line of his jaw with her fingers. Her soft breath caressed his cheek. "God has answered all my prayers," she said simply.

"Even if it meant me getting shot?" Jacob tried to look stern, but he couldn't hold back a smile.

"Yes, Jacob." He stiffened, and Hallie looked puzzled. Then she laughed. "I mean, yes, I will be your wife."

Jacob's laughter mingled with hers. "God has brought us through heartbreak to joy." He slid his arms around her and cradled her head against his chest. "Who knows what He has in store for us along the road ahead?"

Hallie tilted her head to one side. Her breath came out in a soft sigh. "I have no idea what is going to come our way. But whatever it is, I know I can get through it as long as I have Him." She lifted her face and closed her eyes.

"And you," she whispered, just before his lips touched hers.

Epilogue

F or richer, for poorer, in sickness and in health, 'til death do us part." Hallie heard the quiver in her voice as she repeated the age-old vows that would make her Jacob Garrett's wife from this day forward.

Pastor Morris closed his Bible and smiled. "I now pronounce you man and wife. You may kiss the bride."

Hallie lifted her veil and raised her face to meet Jacob's kiss amid good-natured catcalls and shouts of congratulations.

Jacob clasped Hallie's hand and tucked it into the crook of his arm. Together they walked down the aisle toward the large, oak doors. Familiar faces beamed up at them as they passed: Jacob's parents and sister, so ready to welcome her into their family as one of their own; in the pew behind them, Dan and Amy, and sitting next to them, Dan's parents, Michael and Elizabeth O'Roarke.

"Don't forget to stay to wish the newlyweds well and enjoy some refreshments."

Hallie turned at the sound of the rough voice and locked gazes with her father. His look of approval nearly made her weep. Since the day he gave them his blessing, he had grown softer, more like the father she remembered from her girlhood.

A mist clouded her eyes, and she knew her smile must be bright enough to light the whole sanctuary. Truly, blessings showered down in abundance upon this, her wedding day.

The clamor of happy voices echoed through the church hall. Jacob looked around at the gathering of family and friends. He had found far more in Prescott than a job and a place to prove himself. He'd found a home and. . . Jacob looked at Hallie, her face alight with joy, and his heart swelled.

And a future.

"To the bride and groom," Dan O'Roarke called, raising a glass of apple cider high. "To a long life and much happiness." The crowd roared approval.

"And to statehood!" Will Bradley added with a grin. "May their children be born in the great state of Arizona."

Jacob's throat tightened at the reminder of Buckey O'Neill and his friend's ardent dream of Arizona joining the Union. He looked down into the shining eyes of his new bride and bent to rest his forehead against hers. "That sounds good to me. Our sons and daughters can grow up along with the state."

Hallie's smile deepened and laughter rippled from her throat. "Let's take things one step at a time, shall we? I'd like to have you all to myself for a while, if that's all right."

She laid her fingers against his cheek with a feather touch. "What would you say to making the toast one to us. . .and our future?"

Jacob looked into the sweet face of the woman he would love today, tomorrow, and through all the years ahead.

"To us," he echoed, and pulled her into his arms.

A Letter to Our Readers

Dear Readers:

In order that we might better contribute to your reading enjoyment, we would appreciate your taking a few minutes to respond to the following questions. When completed, please return to the following: Fiction Editor, Barbour Publishing, Inc., P.O. Box 719, Uhrichsville, OH 44683.

1. Did you enjoy reading *Arizona Brides* by Carol Cox?
   ❏ Very much—I would like to see more books like this.
   ❏ Moderately—I would have enjoyed it more if _____
   _____
   _____

2. What influenced your decision to purchase this book? (Check those that apply.)
   ❏ Cover   ❏ Back cover copy   ❏ Title   ❏ Price
   ❏ Friends   ❏ Publicity   ❏ Other

3. Which story was your favorite?
   ❏ *Land of Promise*   ❏ *Road to Forgiveness*
   ❏ *Refining Fire*

4. Please check your age range:
   ❏ Under 18   ❏ 18–24   ❏ 25–34
   ❏ 35–45   ❏ 46–55   ❏ Over 55

5. How many hours per week do you read? _____

Name _____

Occupation _____

Address _____

City_____ State _____ Zip_____

E-mail_____

♡

HEARTSONG
PRESENTS

If you love Christian
romance...

You'll love Heartsong Presents' inspiring and faith-filled romances by today's very best Christian authors. . .DiAnn Mills, Wanda E. Brunstetter, and Yvonne Lehman, to mention a few!

When you join Heartsong Presents, you'll enjoy four brand-new, mass market, 176-page books—two contemporary and two historical—that will build you up in your faith when you discover God's role in every relationship you read about!

Imagine. . .four new romances every four weeks—with men and women like you who long to meet the one God has chosen as the love of their lives. . .all for the low price of $11.99 postpaid.

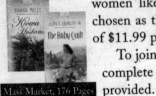

Mass Market, 176 Pages

To join, simply visit www.heartsongpresents.com or complete the coupon below and mail it to the address provided.

✂ -

YES! Sign me up for Heartsong!

NEW MEMBERSHIPS WILL BE SHIPPED IMMEDIATELY!
Send no money now. We'll bill you only $11.99 postpaid with your first shipment of four books. Or for faster action, call 1-740-922-7280.

NAME _____

ADDRESS _____

CITY _____ STATE _____ ZIP _____

MAIL TO: HEARTSONG PRESENTS, P.O. Box 721, Uhrichsville, OH 44683
or sign up at WWW.HEARTSONGPRESENTS.COM